Critical acclaim

The

'In this sixth Sam Turner novel Baker turns up the heat, producing an enjoyably pacy thriller that leaves its predecessors standing' *Time Out*

'Witty dialogue and sharp characterisation enliven this first-rate thriller' Susanna Yager, *Sunday Telegraph*

'The best entry yet in a unique series . . . Baker's increasingly well-realised characters communicate through an entertaining and convincing mixture of philosophy, banter and mutual incomprehension' Mat Coward, *Morning Star*

'John Baker brings altogether more heart, invention and wit to the business of adapting the tough-guy novel to the realities of contemporary Britain' *Independent on Sunday*

'Engagingly credible, off the wall, romantic without being sentimental, a sharp sense of humour . . . a great cast of characters I look forward to meeting again' Val McDermid

'Absorbing and well-written with an exciting finale' T.J. Binyon, *Evening Standard*

'Something quite unexpected . . . Entrancing and funny' *TLS*

'Strong, dark and discursive . . . there's no doubt that – with his York setting and up-from-the-gutter hero – Baker has added something new to the crime scene' Philip Oakes, *Literary Review*

John Baker is the author of five previous Sam Turner novels. He lives in York. Visit his website at www.johnbakeronline.co.uk.

By John Baker

THE MEANEST FLOOD

John Baker

ORION

An Orion paperback

First published in Great Britain in 2003
by Orion
This paperback edition published in 2004
by Orion Books Ltd,
Orion House, 5 Upper St Martin's Lane,
London WC2H 9EA

A CIP catalogue record for this book
is available from the British Library.

ISBN 0 75286 573 0

Typeset by Deltatype Ltd, Birkenhead, Merseyside

Printed in Great Britain by Clays Ltd, St Ives plc

For Anne

'The magician is quicker and his game
Is much thicker than blood and blacker than ink
And there's no time to think'

Bob Dylan

'Everything that deceives may be said to enchant'

Plato

'There is a tide in the affairs of men
Which, taken at the flood, leads on to fortune'

Shakespeare, Julius Caesar

'When the waves of death compassed me,
the floods of ungodly men made me afraid'

2 Samuel, 22:5

'It's gonna be the meanest flood
That anybody's seen'

Bob Dylan

1

As a professional he wore false cheeks and a wig together with a dark and shiny Van Dyck beard. Tan makeup to set off the sapphire blue of his eyes. The dinner jacket was compulsory, as were the patent-leather shoes, the top hat and cape, the white kid-gloves and his silk cane. Diamond Danny Mann sparkled in the footlights.

'I need another volunteer,' he said, eyeing the Nottingham audience, producing a fanned deck of cards from the ether. 'Perhaps a lady this time?' He walked to the edge of the proscenium, descended the steps and chose a short young woman from the second row of the stalls. Her warm damp hand in his, Diamond Danny returned to the boards and offered her a chair, using his considerable charm to ensure her breathing and heartbeat rapidly returned to normal. 'You're going to need both hands,' he told her. 'Please put your bag under the chair.' His concern for the lady's welfare was palpable and the audience warmed to it and to the magician himself.

Danny asked her to pick a card from the pack and when she drew the eight of spades he gave her a pen and asked her to sign her name on the face of it. Marilyn, for that was her name, used Danny's back as a desk and returned the card to the pack.

The magician shuffled the cards and handed them to his dimpled volunteer. 'Now find your card.' He passed his hand over the pack and threw back his head. '*Katha*,' he said, pulling out and extending the final vowel. 'A word to conjure with, given to me by a humble magician at Pak Nam Pho in Thailand. We did a little trade in spells and talismans.'

A murmur of soft laughter went around the audience but the magician didn't smile and neither did the woman with the pack of cards. Rings on every finger of one hand, Danny noticed.

Marilyn looked through the pack and shook her head. She looked through again. 'It isn't here,' she said. 'You didn't put it back.'

Diamond Danny smiled. A remarkable smile when it came, with all the clarity and innocence of a child. 'You're right,' he told her. 'I put it in your purse.'

Marilyn, flustered now, reached beneath the chair for her handbag, which had been in full view of the audience while she was on stage. She snapped open the clasp and looked inside. She shook her head. 'It's not here.'

'In the purse,' Danny said, 'next to your driving licence.'

The lady withdrew a wallet from the handbag. The wallet was black pigskin and fastened with a zipper. When she opened it, Marilyn's lower jaw dropped. 'Oh, no, I don't believe it,' she squealed.

She withdrew a card, folded twice. She straightened it and waved it towards the audience. 'It's the one I signed,' she said. 'How did you do that? It's impossible.'

The magician returned the lady to her seat while the applause resounded around him. He returned to the stage to take his bow before withdrawing into the wings. He had the unsettling feeling that he had not chosen the lady at all, that in some strange way she might have chosen him.

When the ASM delivered his cape and caddy to the green room she hesitated before leaving. 'How is it that the magician always knows which card you've chosen?' she asked.

'It's magic,' Diamond Danny told her with a twinkle in his eye. 'I could introduce you to the black art if you ask the right question. Or perhaps you will decide to leave well enough alone. Many an explanation turns out to be an illusion in itself.'

The wheel was running on wet tarmac illuminated by streetlights. It had a new radial-tread Bridgestone tyre, slightly warm from the journey. Rubber and carbon black designed to perform with low noise and to grip the road in all weathers. Some time ago, when the vehicle was new, he had fitted chrome wheel-well trim but this was peeling now, as was the black paint it had been designed to protect.

The wheel veered to the right and came slowly to a halt a couple of centimetres from a white stone kerb. An owl hooted softly in the distance. Apart from the contractions of the cooling engine there were no other sounds.

The magician sat in the driving seat. He was wearing his other face. He was still, composed, a sihouette. An observer might have noticed the regular rise and fall of his chest, the blink of an eyelid. But there was no observer present; only the moon and the stars.

Several minutes passed and the silence was broken by the mechanism of the driver's door opening and the slight but erect figure of the magician emerging.

It was late, well after midnight. He locked the vehicle and walked along the street, a thirty-five-year-old man wearing a neat black overcoat, a soft hat with a brim and polished shoes. He walked with his head erect and it was only when he passed those junctions with closed-circuit cameras in operation that he pulled the brim over his eyes and let his shoulders slump forward to hide his features.

He had taken this path several times before. He knew everything there was to know about it. Magic needs to be rehearsed. It involves manipulating and controlling the environment. When it is completely successful nothing has been left to chance.

This is how gods work. The magician was not a god but that didn't mean he couldn't emulate one. Magic is available to some people. Handed down through the centuries, through the long ages of man's journey. Before the Magus and beyond Houdini the brotherhood extends over the furthest stretches of the universe.

As he walked Diamond Danny pulled on two pairs of latex gloves.

God encourages the things that please Him, and those that He doesn't favour He destroys. This is how He is. Remember the flood? The magician had little time for people who believe that God is kindness and light. God is a planner and an engineer; He is an ambitious magician and He doesn't mind too much if some of His tricks go wrong. He can rest on His laurels for a while, on His reputation. He was in the right place at the right time and He managed to pull off a few stunning illusions. But you must have heard?

The house was nothing, a between-the-wars construction of red brick. Since it was built all the woodwork had been replaced at least once. It had single-glazed windows and no damp-course to ensure that it met the English standard of cold and draughts and a tendency to mould around the skirting boards.

The front door was painted red and the upper half was a single pane of glass. But at the rear of the house it was dark and whoever wanted to enter could do so undetected by one of the neighbourhood insomniacs.

The magician, of course, knew this already. He had been at the back door of this building twice before. Once during the day and once at the dead of night. There was a simple lever lock which the magician could open with a matchstick in a few seconds. There were bolts on the inside of the door, at top and bottom, but both of them were stiff from lack of use and a couple of attempts to paint them out of existence.

The occupant of this house had no worries. She didn't imagine that someone would wish to enter her home and harm her. She slept soundly. She slept as soundly at night as she did during the day. Her life was a dream.

We are all magicians now. Even the plodding policeman is a sorcerer these days. Recently Danny had seen on the news that a twelve-year-old rape case had been solved through the extraction of DNA from a speck of dandruff. Truly amazing. The perpetrator of the rape was now a fifty-year-old grandfather, but at the time of his crime he was only thirty-eight. For the years between he was a card hidden in the pack until – hey, presto – the conjurors of the forensic department found him curled up in a test tube.

The magician was not particularly interested in this woman. The female in the house, sleeping in the front bedroom. She was not the trick, only a component of it. He needed her but she was not an end in herself. She was neither the rabbit nor the top hat. She contributed to the illusion by the way she distracted the eye. She was a cipher who only took on the appearance of reality when she was removed from it.

The streetlights sent a pale glow through the windows of the house. The magician had a torch but he didn't need to use it. The kitchen was neat and tidy, all the surfaces had been wiped clean and there was a suggestion of pine disinfectant in the air. The living room had a fitted carpet and floral curtains that were closed against the night. There was still enough residual light to see the photographs on the mantelpiece: a studio portrait of an old couple, probably her parents, and one of the old woman alone, taken some time later with an Italian mountain in the background. There was another of a small girl with pigtails, something old-fashioned about it, perhaps the silver frame.

The magician removed his overcoat and laid it on the worn Chesterfield. He slid his weapon from the inside pocket and weighed it in his hand, took a moment to wonder at the balance and beauty of the polished hilt.

He removed his remaining clothes, folded them neatly and placed them on top of his overcoat.

When he was naked he ascended the stairs and waited for the instant when he would hear the woman's breath for the first time. She lived alone but all possibilities had to be taken into account. She could have a friend with her, a man or a woman. Either possibility would increase the night's workload but nothing would distract Danny from his main purpose. He had waited a long time for this. He was committed. Professional integrity was at stake. *Abracadabra. Katha.* Behold the woman; first you see her, then you don't.

Her bedroom door was ajar. On the landing there was a red dressing gown draped over the handrail of the banister. The magician stood in the open doorway and surveyed the scene. She was sleeping with the bedside lamp on, perhaps over-concerned with bogeymen and things that go bump, nyctophobic. Her dressing table was by the window. There was a chair on one side of the double bed and her clothes had been placed on it, neatly folded. Oh, symmetry.

On the other side of the bed there was a small cabinet with a couple of books on its polished surface. There was a picture on the wall, a reproduction of one of Hockney's swimming pools. Below it there was a small television on a black metal trolley.

This was not an impressive room. If you could choose, you would not choose to die here. But all the choices that this lady had ever had were finally tumbling down to zero.

She was lying on her side with her arms out of the quilt. Her hair was cut short and had been freshly washed, auburn with subtle highlights. Her shoulders were covered by a peach-coloured nightgown. There were freckles on her chest. She was breathing deeply and there was some activity going on beneath her eyelids. Over the area of the bed there was a canopy of confined bodily odours, something the woman unknowingly shared with the world. If she were awake she would open the window.

The magician brought her to life by pushing her on to her back and climbing on top of her. He straddled her chest, pinning her arms by her sides with his knees. There was a moment when they were face to face. An instant of awareness that she was not dreaming. Her eyes were the size of fists and her mouth opened wide to scream for help. The messages bombarding her brain and the rush of adrenalin combined to throw her system into chaos. What should have been a scream fluttered to a whimper. She begged for reason and to be spared pain. 'Who are you? What do you want? Please don't hurt me.'

The magician had bought the bayonet in an antique shop in Finchley years before. At the time he'd thought vaguely of incorporating it in his act. It had only been used once since the war, as far as he knew. It was forty centimetres long with a wooden handle which was engraved with the German eagle. The blade came to a sharp point and had a blood groove that spanned its entire length. It was a functional tool but it had a certain elegance and was originally used as an accessory to a dress uniform. If it had had the original scabbard it would have been worth serious money as the blade was mirror-bright.

The woman's initial wriggling and pleading gave way to more violent movements as she realized that her salvation was entirely in her own hands. The magician gripped her tighter. He took her spare pillow and covered her head and chest.

Diamond Danny held the bayonet aloft with both hands. Bringing it down forcefully he stabbed her once through the pillow, correctly estimating the point at which her heart lay pounding.

He ran the cold tap in the bath and rinsed the gore from the blade of the bayonet. He used her hand-towel to dry it, glancing at the bottles and containers of shampoo and conditioner, the nail varnish and lipsticks, powder and eye-shadow. The tricks of the feminine trade. Three different brands of perfume and an economy bottle of green makeup remover from the Body Shop. He looked in the mirror where her face appeared each morning and evening and the glass reflected his own image without a hint of sentimentality.

He washed away the blood that spattered his upper body and he put the plug in the bath and blocked the overflow with what was left of the woman's cotton-wool pleats. She wouldn't need them anymore and she'd possibly be pleased that someone had found a use for them. He turned on both taps and one by one emptied the bottles and containers of lotions into the bath.

He didn't return to the bedroom. All was quiet in there. He descended the stairs and dressed himself. He buttoned his overcoat against the night air. He placed his hat on his head and had a look around. There was the sound of water splashing into the tub, must be getting close to the top by now. And all those essential oils mixed together, filling the house with their aroma; they reminded him of his mother, not close to the end when she was old, but when she was younger, while Danny was still a boy. Lovely smell, delicious, made you picture tropical climates, soft fruits, birds of paradise and a life of magical ease and everlasting enchantment.

Two hours later Danny edged his car into the garage and went into his house. He took the bayonet from his pocket and placed it back in the cabinet with his other little-used accessories. He drank a glass of cold water while standing at the sink and walked upstairs to the bedroom.

Jody was sleeping on her side of the bed and the magician stripped off his clothes and crept in beside her, pulling her towards him. He wrapped his arms around her. 'Flawless,' he said. 'Went like a dream.' He nuzzled down and took her designer nipple between his teeth, letting his eyes close and the world fade away around him.

Diamond Danny Mann, whacked after a busy day.

2

That morning Ruben Parkins finished his milk-round at 7.50 and went back to his flat to clean up and change his clothes. Ruben was going to spend the whole day with his girlfriend and when he got in the shower he sang 'Everything I Do, I Do It For You', modulating his voice like Bryan Adams, crooning away in a deep bellow with the water from the sprinkler splashing around his head and shoulders.

Ruben was a good guy and he was feeling good about it. What made him feel so great, apart from the woman and the fact that he was in love, was that being a good guy was something he hadn't been before. Well, not for a long time.

He'd been cute as a kid. There were photographs his mother had kept and his auntie Sarah had a couple still, showing Ruben as a toddler, maybe a bit older, up to the time he started school. Dumb little kid with big eyes like a bush-baby, looking around wondering what the world was all about. When he saw those photographs Ruben could remember what it was like back then, when eye-level meant just above his mother's knees. There was an overhang to the Woolworth's counters in those days and little Ruben used to walk under it without banging his head. If he wanted to see what the grown-ups were looking at on the counter his mother'd have to lift him up.

The violence had started when he got to school. Ruben wasn't bigger than the other kids but one of the first

10

things he'd learned was that if he was going to hold his own he'd have to pack a hefty punch. He had a talented straight-right. The gym teacher said he could be a fighter if he wanted. He'd have to learn to block other people's punches, and do the little dances that pro boxers did, but he'd always have that killer punch. No one could teach him any more about that. It was a gift from God.

There'd been times after he'd left school when Ruben had wished he'd listened to the gym teacher and taken the fighting lessons. The main time he'd wished he'd listened was when he got himself banged away on a GBH count for breaking a nightclub bouncer's neck. What was unfair about that whole eighteen-month stint was that none of it was Ruben's fault. The guy had been a jerk-off. *Anybody* would have broken his neck if they'd been in Ruben's position that day. If they'd drunk the same amount of booze, if they'd lost half their wages on the last race at Kempton Park and if the slag they were supposed to be getting married to had run off with her own cousin. And then, to cap it all, they'd had to listen to a load of garbage coming out of the jerk-off's mouth, saying the place was full when he was ushering his own mates through the door on the QT. Fuckin' Italian into the bargain; nose like a parrot's perch.

So. Feeling good. Eighteen months banged away all done and finished with. The milk-round in the bag. Nicely showered and padding around his bedroom buck naked, freeing a new pair of leopard-skin skimpies from their cellophane bag.

Ruben nodded at his reflection in the full-length mirror on the back of the wardrobe door. Not an ounce of fat on him; all muscle and bone. Those black hairs on his chest and forearms and on his thighs and legs. He half-turned to see the same hair spread over his back, glistening across his shoulders. He adjusted his lunch-pack inside the skimpies, enough in there to keep a harem happy. Or a convent if they wanted a holiday from chastity.

What he'd planned was to get to Kitty's house around 9, 9.30, by which time she'd have dolled herself up and be waiting on the doorstep. They'd drive over to Harrogate and have breakfast in one of the posh cafés there. Then they'd shop, which was what Kitty liked to do more than anything else. They'd spend a couple of hours wandering round buying new clothes, whatever took the woman's eye. She'd see he wasn't a skinflint, which was the reason she'd got rid of her last boyfriend, and she'd see he had some earning power. That he could earn legitimate money from the milk-round, didn't need to go back to a criminal lifestyle.

She already knew he was a good lover, that he could get to the parts the other guys in her life couldn't reach. And she'd got to him, too. The only woman he'd ever met who had made him sit up and think. The one woman who had made him change his way of thinking about the world. Ruben had always said that he was number one, that no one else even came in close second. But now that he'd met Kitty Turner he no longer thought like that. She was number one and Ruben was prepared to do anything for her.

He put on his leather strides, sky-blue socks and new black slip-ons. He found his way through the packaging of a white polyester Double Two shirt, removed the pins and plastic clips and slipped it on. A silk tie the same colour as his socks and a brown suede jacket with his snake-skin wallet in the inside pocket made Ruben feel like the master of the universe.

He was out of the door when he had another thought and rushed back to the bathroom to hit the Brut for the second time since leaving the shower.

He left his flat on the Lenton Boulevard and nosed the Skoda into Derby Road, then south to Clifton, over the river and on to the quiet avenue where Kitty should have been waiting for him. He parked outside the house, watching the front door, expecting her to open it and step down the path to join him in the car.

Nothing.

Ruben looked at the upstairs curtains. Maybe she'd slept late and wasn't ready yet? Was that a wave from behind the nets or a trick of the light? His mind juggling with reality?

He drummed his fingers on the leather cover of the steering wheel, furrowed his brow and leant back in the seat.

Expectations fuck you up. You can look forward to something so much that you believe it's a reality before it has happened. That time he walked out of Long Lartin he expected to see a woman waiting for him with some wheels, but he ended up walking the six miles to Evesham station by himself, travelled back to Nottingham by train. The woman had left with a Londoner, guy still in his twenties. She was the gonest little girl in town.

But Kitty was different. She'd be out in a minute. This was a woman's privilege, that's what his mother used to tell him, way back, when he was still in shorts. Being late. They had this idea it set up anticipation in the guy, made them look better because he'd been waiting. Got his juices going so he couldn't see straight.

But what if Ruben had let expectation take over again and Kitty was out on the town with some other guy while he was sitting here outside her house? How would he handle that? Ruben shook his head. He knew he wouldn't handle it well. He wouldn't have the normal, expected reaction that society took for granted. He wouldn't shake his head and carry on as if nothing had happened. He wouldn't stomach it. There'd be violence involved. Some blood.

Christ, this was what happened if you let the inside of your head take over. Ruben had known it all along, not to entertain the thoughts. Get them out. Keep moving. He opened the car door and stepped on to the tarmac, walked up the path to her front door.

It was locked, but he had a key and she hadn't changed the lock. See? You blame the woman and she's done nothing. She'll be upstairs at the mirror. Ruben didn't shout her name. He knew she was there because of the smell of her. When you entered the house that scent that accompanied her everywhere she went, it pervaded the place.

Taps running in the bathroom upstairs.

He touched the kettle in the kitchen, see if she'd been down to make a drink. It was cold. He switched it on. Maybe she'd want coffee before they left. If she didn't that was OK. Whatever the lady desired.

He crept up the stairs breathing shallowly, a faint smile on his face. He imagined the shriek she'd come out with when he pushed open the bathroom door, the intake of her breath and the realization and relief as she came towards him, her arms outstretched.

The upper landing was sodden, water coming under the bathroom door and soaking into the fitted carpet. His feet squelched as he walked towards the bathroom with growing trepidation.

But she wasn't in there. The radiator was on and there was a pink bath towel hanging on it. A face-cloth lay on the lavatory seat. The taps were running and water was streaming over the side of the bath, flooding the floor. Ruben turned the taps off and fished for the plug. The water gurgled as it ran down the drain. In the mirror on the cabinet Ruben's face stared back at him like one of those Impressionist paintings. It was hot in the small room and a line of sweat ran off his forehead and into his eye. He brushed it away impatiently and turned for the bedroom.

And she was still in bed, asleep.

It was the silence that got to him. There were no sounds in the house. Nothing apart from the sounds he brought with him. There was tension in his chest, a tightening around his ribs and emptiness inside him. He took two steps into the bedroom, towards the figure obscured by the duvet, and there were flies as luscious as blackberries feeding at her gaping eyes.

For a moment the floor under his feet seemed insubstantial. He reached for something to steady him and touched the side of the bed. He took a breath and pulled the duvet away, watched it slip to the carpet. The pillow over her chest was soaked with blood.

When he'd broken the bouncer's neck Ruben had felt no twinge of conscience or remorse. And whatever they'd thrown at him in Long Lartin, the screws or the cons, he'd taken it all with a knowing nod. The sight of blood had never fazed him. He'd even shrugged his shoulders when his old lady had breathed her last. This was what happened in life; apart from the occasional shag there was only blood and violence and death, and if you knew that and you took it on board you survived, and if you denied it you were a two-time loser.

This woman, Kitty Turner, had taught him something else. She'd taken the whole of his life and his entire experience and turned it inside out and shown him something of the power of tenderness. He hadn't fully absorbed it, the world that she'd held out to him. He'd seen it in a dim image, shadowy, flickering, like a flame that could live or die. And as long as she was around there had been hope. His mind reeled. He picked up the pillow and watched as the thick blood oozed out between his fingers. This wasn't true, it couldn't be. It was senseless, meaningless. Ruben could find no image to tame it. It swarmed in his mind like an infestation of vermin.

It was worse, much worse than anything he could have imagined. Ruben collected Kitty's body in his arms and staggered out of the bedroom door. When he reached the head of the stairs he stumbled and recognized that the sounds filling his ears were his own cries for help. He was bawling and screaming at the top of his voice, her name and the name of God. 'Someone,' he yelled. 'Anyone. Look at this, what they've done.'

As he opened the front door and pushed his way through to the street, the beloved and bloody love of his life still cradled in his arms, the kettle in the kitchen behind him began to howl.

3

After breakfast the private detective got on a train in Nottingham. He had been there for two days, staying in the High Willows B&B, and was looking forward to returning to York and everyday life.

'Are you married, Mr Turner?' the owner of the High Willows had asked him. She was a woman who had been a beauty queen in extreme youth but had shed most of her petals and an errant husband after thirty-eight years of marriage. Sam Turner had guessed as much before she came out with the facts. He was, after all, a detective, and besides the proprietress of the High Willows B&B was precisely the kind of woman he seemed to attract. He had perfected the trick of folding himself into a small parcel when these ladies appeared on his horizon. Attempting, and to some extent succeeding in making himself invisible.

Sam wasn't averse to tasting the charms that such a lady can bestow, and on occasions, more than he cared to remember, had awoken to find himself enchanted by a surfeit of loneliness and rose-water. But Sam already had a girl-friend in York. Although they lived in separate houses, Angeles Falco and he had been lovers for almost a year. Angeles had been virtually blind since she was twenty-two, but that didn't mean she couldn't see what was going on. And in any case, Sam didn't want to jeopardize his relationship with her for the sake of a one-night stand. He'd done it before, too many times. Not with Angeles, but with many of the women who had passed through his life.

Sam wasn't young anymore, and he was beginning to learn.

On the other hand, Angeles had been distant lately, didn't always seem as pleased to see him as she had in the past. The waters were cooler. Not terminally as yet. Maybe there were ways to save it, turn it around. Sam was still keen. She was a treasure to him.

He wrote his report to the rhythm of the train's movement. The client's wife hadn't run off with a lover, as he'd suspected. Instead she'd organized a flat for herself close to the Lace Market and was hard at work in a new job at Trent University. She could walk to it on a fine day and in the winter it would be only a couple of stops on the tram. She liked the Arboretum where she spent time alone. She hadn't run *to* anything, which would have been some comfort to Sam's client. She had run away from the guy, preferring instead a strange and empty city, a single and lonely bed in which she could begin to identify the parameters of her own identity.

Sam looked through the rain-streaked windows of the train and tried to think of something upbeat to complete the report. A sentence or a phrase that would allow his client to go forward, to accept what had happened to him and not to regard his abandonment as a black hole. Sam the counsellor trying to elbow the detective aside. But in the end he settled for the ashes and dust of the truth.

He scored an excuse for coffee from the trolley and settled down to listen to the chatter of the two women sitting on the opposite side of the table. One of them had had a dream about buying a Mercedes. 'It was terrible,' she said. 'I suddenly realized that I'd done the most stupid thing. Landed myself with this huge car; it would need litres and litres of fuel and be impossible to park.

For the whole dream I was trying to reverse the process, get rid of this monster, swap it for a little Rover or a Renault, something manageable in traffic. It was a nightmare.'

Sam wanted to tell her that it was a middle-class nightmare. If he'd had a dream where he owned a Merc it would have been great. Even a second-hand one. He'd have spent the rest of the night smelling the leather upholstery, running his hands over the smooth lines of the bonnet. True, it would cost a heap to run, but status symbols don't come cheap.

The last nightmare Sam had had was when he'd bought a bottle of Scotch. He was halfway through it before he remembered it wasn't a dream and he'd fallen into the jug again. The future was a blur into which he would drag all his friends and his relationships, his health and his conscience and any sense of self-respect he had built up since the last binge.

But he didn't say anything. He sipped his coffee and gazed at the rain-soaked landscape. Two good women on their way to York for some shopping didn't want to hear about a drunk, have their dreams criticized by a guy who still wrote with a pen.

At York station there was a Chinese guy with a ponytail leaning against a wall and reading the *Guardian* and around the bookstall a young Yorkshire entrepreneur was busy taking Upskirt videos. There was the usual drone of tourists, most of them clutching three-colour maps of the city, all seeking ghosts of Vikings or ancient Romans, steam-trains or somewhere they could hire a bike.

Outside on the street the con artists were perfecting their pitch, the local traders polishing their wares, the restaurateurs thickening their sauces and the beggars sharpening their whistles. It was another day in the market place of civilization. You'd have to be blind not to see how far we'd come since the first Constantine was proclaimed the Great Emperor of the Western Roman Empire in this very town at the dawn of the fourth century.

The river was running high. From the Lendal Bridge the stream was fast and lively, an undercurrent forming eddies and swirling pools in the black water and various items of flotsam betraying the speed at which the waters fought their way towards the Humber estuary and the sea.

A young woman on the east side of the bridge gazed lovingly into the river. Sam imagined her climbing on to the parapet and taking a dive, bringing her few short years to a watery end. She was twenty years old, maybe a year or two older, with thin hair and a whole summer behind her in which she had not been touched by the sun. Not an ugly girl, but one who had not learned how to look pretty. Or maybe she had learned and simply couldn't be assed.

Sam wanted to go to her, find the words to tell her that nothing was hopeless, that there would come a point in the future when she'd feel better about the world, about herself. Tell her that we needed more people in the world like her, people who still felt things. But he didn't do it. Ours is not the kind of world in which you can tell a stranger not to jump. There are too many assumptions involved.

But as he turned the corner, heading towards the post office, Sam couldn't shake her out of his mind. He imagined the evening paper with her photograph, the tragic headlines and the knowledge that he might have been able to help. Sam had not experienced a moment when he wanted to take his own life. He had come to recognize that his years of alcohol addiction had been fuelled by a death-wish, but there had been no conscious decision to die in the relentless abuse of his health. He had wanted to blot out the world while still using its oxygen.

The girl on the bridge – and he turned now and headed back in her direction – had a countenance which retained no illusions. She didn't want herself and she didn't want the palliatives that the world had to offer. She had looked into the dark eyes of death and imagined some comfort there.

She was no longer on the bridge and Sam watched the tumbling stream, hallucinating a pale hand raised from the depths, a goodbye wave from a goodbye waif. When he turned away he saw her sitting on a bench with a bearded giant. The man wore a threadbare coat and huge trainers without laces and he had two plastic carriers overflowing with empty bottles. The girl had a cigarette between her lips and the man was leaning over her with the fag-end of another, passing on the light.

False alarm, Sam said to himself. He glanced again at the girl and her giant. The big man was accosting passers-by now, out of Sam's earshot but gesticulating histrionically. Looked like he was reciting poetry or passing on the achieved wisdom of his years.

I'm back, Sam said to himself. *This is the place. My home town.*

He took the steps up to the office two at a time. As he walked in Geordie, one of his assistants, got to his feet and held out his hand. 'Good to see you, boss,' he said. Geordie was in his early-twenties. Recently he'd let his hair grow and it turned up on his collar. He had a scraggy moustache seemingly painted on to the face of innocence. Geordie had been orphaned and had spent time on the streets before Sam had taken him on, but to look at him now you would think he had never left the maternal nest.

Sam took his hand and placed an arm around his shoulder. 'Everything all right? We still solvent?'

'You are,' Geordie told him. 'Me and the rest of the wage-slaves can't make ends meet, but that's not for you to worry about.'

'Yeah, it was great in Nottingham, Geordie. Like Amsterdam or Venice, really. No, I'll tell you what, it reminded me of the time I was in Florida. So hot you can't sleep. I spent every day on the beach.'

'I've been to Nottingham,' Geordie said. 'Never saw a beach when I was there.'

Sam cocked his head. 'There's this street with palm trees. All the guys there are Cuban exiles, they're selling girls, dope, aloha shirts, anything you want. Nottingham rock. Pie and chips. Anyway, you go to the end and take a right and there's the ocean. Bright blue. Everybody's stretched out half-naked, they have beach umbrellas to keep the sun off. Thongs, know what I mean?'

'Fuck off, Sam.'

'It's true. The hotel I stayed in had a swimming pool and I got propositioned every morning by a different rich widow.'

'You stayed in a guesthouse, Sam. Celia told me. You've been away for three days and you haven't talked to anybody. OK, you had a job to do, so you didn't actually go out of your skull, but you've had time to yourself and you've been digging up memories and worrying about the business and about Angeles. This is how you are, Sam. I know this because I've known you for years. Now you're back you'll be talking non-stop for a week, trying to catch up on all the talking you missed while you weren't here.'

'How's Angeles? She all right?'

'She's fine. But you know that because you've phoned her every night. And if you're so worried about her, how

22

come you get off the train and come to the office? If it'd been me away in tropical Nottingham the first thing I'd do is go and see Janet and Echo. I'd've left the office until tomorrow.'

Sam sighed. 'She's at work. If Angeles'd been at home I'd've skipped the office altogether. There's nothing to do here, apart from talk to you. You got any work on?'

'Nothing that I can't leave for a game of snooker.'

'On pay? I'll bet you can leave it. You wanna play snooker with me while I'm paying you to work?'

'Sounds good to me,' Geordie said. 'Of course, the final decision is yours.'

'Get your coat,' Sam said. 'I'm in the mood for you.'

After the game (two frames to Sam – highest break twenty-seven – one to Geordie), Sam Turner walked home. He'd got rid of the big house that his ex-wife Dora had left him and moved into a small house off Clarence Street. Bought it for cash, straight out, no mortgage. Had a guy come in and decorate it. Celia, his secretary, and Marie, another operative in Sam's business and an old friend, had helped him buy the furnishings, make sure the colours went together. They told him what he liked in the way of a table and chairs, a second-hand chaise-longue which had woodworm in the legs but which the woman who sold it had treated with chemicals. He brought some shelving out of Dora's old house to store his paperbacks and a new CD player; and he kept the double bed because he'd never been able to sleep in a single one. And because Angeles stayed over at least once a week. Except last week. And the week before.

He stopped at the shop and bought himself a frozen dinner – almost fat-free lasagne – and put it in the gas oven to cook while he mended the puncture in the front tyre of his bike. Took the wheel off and brought it into the kitchen. There was a thorn which had gone through to the inner tube and Sam covered the hole with a patch and sprinkled the area with French chalk. When he'd finished he took a fingerful of ecologically friendly heavy-duty hand cleaner and worked it into the muck and oil on his hands. Seemed to work fine, which was part surprise and part relief. He had tried the same brand of stain remover the previous week and ended up with haemoglobin patches on the front of his fake Paul Smith shirt.

Still had time for a shower and shave before the lasagne was ready. He played 'Baby Blue' while sitting at the coffee table in the living room and stuck his fork into the food, saw the police car pull up outside the house and the two plain-clothes goons get out and walk along his path. Sam couldn't help it: the sight of the fuzz coming to his front door made him want to run. It was a physiological response; like he'd downed a handful of French blues, his heart pounded and he looked around for the quick way out of there.

They gave that knock they teach them in training school, four hard thumps with the side of the fist. Designed to make you shit yourself and it worked every time.

And I'm an honest guy, Sam said to himself. He'd been fitted up with a dope cache a dozen years before and served some time for that; and when he was on the booze he'd steal anything from anywhere, but *usually* he was honest Sam. You would think twice about buying a second-hand car from the man, but that was down to appearances rather than reality. And it didn't often happen that he had a second-hand car to sell. The last three *he'*d paid the wreckers a tenner to take away.

There it was again: thump-thump, thump-thump, the hammering on the door synchronized with his heartbeat, as though the cops were demanding access to his soul as well as his house. But he didn't run. He put on a snake-skin exterior and opened the door. 'You just delivering something or you wanna come in?' he asked.

The first one looked along the street, both ways. 'Mr Turner?'

'You know who I am,' Sam told him.

'I wonder if we could come inside for a minute, sir. It's a little exposed here on the doorstep. I'm Chief Inspector Delaney and this is my Sergeant.'

Sam turned and led them into his sitting room. He picked up the carton of lasagne and took it towards the kitchen. 'This'll have to go back in the oven,' he said. 'I'm not prepared to share it.'

He couldn't see because he had his back to them, but Sam imagined their faces lighting up at his little joke. And if not now, then later, when the penny dropped.

He put the lasagne back in the oven and rejoined his visitors. He'd absent-mindedly brought the oven glove with him and kept it on his right hand as he sat on the chaise, his usual chair being occupied by Chief Inspector Delaney with an open notebook on his lap. Delaney had a long nose which complimented his thin cemetery tie.

The CD player turned itself off and Sam looked from Delaney to the Sergeant. He said, 'Somebody been breaking the law?'

'Do you know a Mrs Katherine Turner?' Delaney asked, glancing at his notebook to see if he'd got it right.

Before they got married she was called Katherine Crouch. Sam had wondered if she wanted to marry him for his name. She'd certainly hung on to it after their separation and divorce, not been at all keen on slipping back into the Crouch identity. Sam didn't mind. Hell, a woman is entitled to something out of a marriage.

Crouch might not have been such a bad name if

Katherine had been tall and willowy. But she was short and tended to walk with her chin tucked into her chest. This was a great pity as she had a nice face, a straight nose and large brown eyes that were completely lost to the world. When he first heard her name Sam had wanted to laugh at the irony.

But back in those days he hadn't been much of a catch either. The two of them met over a bottle and their whole liaison, including the marriage, was conducted in an alcoholic haze. Katherine had surfaced first, several years before Sam considered that he might be drinking too much. She'd gone on to another life, leaving him in much the same state .she'd found him – halfway down one bottle and plotting how to acquire the next. King of the drunks, only pausing between one swallow and the next. to throw up on the world.

It was so long ago it seemed like a different planet. Sam couldn't work out if his memories of the marriage were recollections or merely constructs of his mind. And he'd never been able to figure out what a memory was; if it related to something held dear, something unforgettable, or if it was a kind of shroud of something that was lost for ever.

'I wouldn't claim to know her,' he said. 'We were married. Long time ago.'

'Have you seen her recently?'

Sam shook his head.

'When did you last see her?'

'I dunno. Twenty years ago? We lost touch. I don't know what happened to her.'

Most of the women he'd known, Sam could track down if necessary. He'd have an address or a telephone number, or at least a general location. But Katherine had disappeared. She could be anywhere in the country, anywhere in the world. She'd spent as much time and energy on staying in contact with Sam Turner as he'd spent on staying in contact with her. No time at all. It wasn't Sam's shortest marriage but it was the most ill-matched. There must have been some attraction between them, but try as he might, Sam couldn't think what it was.

'Something happened to her?' he asked. 'What's with the questions?'

The cops exchanged a glance. Delaney, the talking one, said, 'Been to Nottingham recently, Mr Turner?'

There's a general rule when talking to the police. They're out to trap you so it's a good idea to stay as close to the truth as possible. If you were in Nottingham yesterday and they ask you if you've been to Nottingham recently the best thing is to say you were there yesterday. Explain what you were doing there. Let them see you've got nothing to hide. That way they'll go away and ask questions of someone else.

But rules are made to be broken. Sam said, 'Nottingham? Can't remember the last time I was there. Year or two back, I was on a case, took a day or two. I can't remember.'

'Where were you yesterday?' the Chief Inspector asked.

'My day off,' he said. 'I was here. One of my assistants, Geordie Black, came round late-afternoon. We took his dog for a walk.'

'Would there be anyone else who could verify your whereabouts yesterday?'

'Maybe,' Sam said. 'But I'm not sure I want to answer more questions unless you tell me what this is all about. Something happened to Katherine? What's the Nottingham connection?'

'Your ex-wife was found murdered in her bed this morning, Mr Turner.'

'In Nottingham? She was living in Nottingham?'

'Yes, that's right,' the policeman said. 'You don't seem particularly disturbed by the news.'

'I'm sorry for her,' Sam said. 'How did it happen?'

'She was stabbed through the heart with a long blade, maybe a sword.'

Sam shook his head, tried to recollect the woman he'd been married to all those years ago.

'Why would someone want to do that to her?' Delaney asked.

'I don't know. It was a long time ago I knew her. I barely remember what she looked like.'

'Do you own a sword, Mr Turner?'

'I want to ring my solicitor,' Sam said.

'You can do that from the station, sir. I take it you have no objection to helping with our enquiries?'

4

Celia Allison put the phone down and leaned forward on her elbows in front of the computer. She had been Sam Turner's secretary, bookkeeper and Girl Friday for seven years and she could read him like a book. She was wearing a black lace blouse with a high collar to hide the seventy-odd years' of wrinkles on her neck. Each wrist rattled with bangles and her ear lobes sported antique jet ear-rings. She wore an ankle-length black skirt and rather sensible chunky-heeled shoes.

She dialled a number and waited with the handset close to her ear. 'Janet, how are you?' Pause. 'Yes, I'm fine. I'm always fine. Is Geordie there?'

She waited, idly swirling the mouse around on its rubber pad, watching the pointer on the screen as it highlighted the icons on Word's standard toolbar. 'Geordie, have you shaved that terrible moustache off yet?' Pause. 'Well, you should. It looks awful. Did you see Sam today?' She tapped her finger. 'Oh, really, what a charmed life you lead. Who won?' She listened patiently as he described a game of snooker.

'Little problem,' she continued when Geordie had potted the last black. 'Sam rang me from the police station. Helping with a murder inquiry. He wants me to contact his solicitor, George Forester, and said to ask if you can think of anyone who saw you and him walking Barney along Gillygate yesterday afternoon?'

'He wasn't here yesterday,' Geordie said.

'Must've been if you and he took Barney for a walk along Gillygate.'

'No, he was in Nottingham, Celia. You know he was.'

Celia had been an English teacher all her previous working life. She assumed the tone of voice that had stood her in good stead throughout that career. 'Geordie, are you listening to what I'm saying?'

'Yes, but . . .'

'It's quite simple. There's no doubt that you and Sam went for a walk along Gillygate yesterday with your little dog. Reading between the lines, it seems our employer didn't go to that other town you mentioned. He was here all the time, especially yesterday. Now, we know that you saw him and we wonder if anyone else can corroborate that, OK?'

Pause.

Geordie said, 'Oh, yes. I see.'

Celia hung up and dialled another number. 'Mr Forester, please.' She waited, shifting the handset away from her ear when the 'Dam Busters' March' kicked in.

'George, it's Celia. Listen, Sam's down at the police station helping with enquiries into a murder. Can you get him out?'

'I'm on my way,' the solicitor said.

'Just a hint of relief in your voice there, George. Does it get you out of something else?'

'Jocelyn will be arriving in a minute to take me to our dance-class.'

'And?'

'I won't be here.'

Celia smiled. 'You don't like dancing?'

'What I'd like,' George Forester explained, 'is Flamenco or Tango, maybe some Salsa, something with passion. But Jocelyn's into ballroom. I hate it. It's like eating dry biscuits. Makes me feel as if I've got a number on my back.'

'You should consider rebellion,' she told him.

She looked at the phone. George Forester was one of those quiet, unassuming men who had become entangled with a woman who wanted to direct every aspect of his life. Freud or Darwin might have found an answer for men like him. Or perhaps the frequency with which the timid latch on to the bullies was a question too far for the founding fathers of modernism?

Celia got her coat and locked the office. She walked around the corner to the taxi stand on St Leonard's Place and directed the cabby to Angeles Falco's house. 'Wait for me, will you?' she said. 'I'll only be a few minutes.'

The cabby reached for the morning's edition of the *Sun*.

'Celia,' Angeles said as she opened the door wider to admit the older woman. 'How lovely, I haven't seen you for ages.' She closed the door behind her. 'There's nothing wrong is there? It isn't Sam, is it?'

'Nothing to worry about,' Celia said. 'No deaths or broken bones. You can relax.'

Angeles was almost totally blind now but if you didn't know you wouldn't have guessed. Not in her own house, anyway. She knew where everything was and she focused her eyes so you didn't feel as though she was gazing at empty space. She was in her early-thirties with a soft complexion and clear skin; the face of a model and the confidence of a successful businesswoman with a large bank-balance. When Sam had fallen for her he had landed on both feet.

'Have you seen him since he got back?' Celia asked.

'No, I've been working all day. He's coming round this evening.'

Celia shook her head. 'He might not make it,' she said.

31

'The police have picked him up. I'm not sure what it's about at the moment – George Forester is on his way round there now – but it seems he wasn't in Nottingham yesterday.'

Angeles looked surprised. 'He rang me last night, said he was in a B&B.'

'That's right,' Celia said. 'He was there for the last couple of days, but the official story is that he was here.'

Angeles smiled. 'You don't mind lying for him, do you?'

'I don't believe in lying, Angeles, and I don't like people who do. But if Sam Turner tells a lie it's because it's closer to the truth than the truth.'

'Do you want to stay for a drink?'

'No, thanks. I've still got one more job to do. Then I'm going to have an early night.'

The cab dropped her at Sam's house and she paid the driver. She let herself in with a key from her purse and stood listening in the hall for a few seconds. Nothing. Just the deep silence of a man gone away. In the kitchen she turned off the gas and opened the oven door. The top layer of lasagne was black and brittle. She used the oven glove to remove it from the shelf and placed it in the sink, where it hissed and crackled for a moment.

She shook her head. A grown man and he didn't even eat properly.

There it was again, that numb feeling on the left side of her head. She reached for the edge of the door to steady herself in case she was about to fall. She'd rarely been ill in her life and had always imagined that she'd die in bed, peacefully in her sleep. Never contemplated any kind of fatal illness or something that might take away her reason.

She'd been astonished when the doctor had suggested an appointment with a specialist. She'd submitted to the

X-rays, bitten her lip and grudgingly allowed the technicians to manipulate her, pretended not to understand when they'd avoided her questions. Ridiculous, she thought now, how she had felt impelled to allow them to feel good about themselves. That inexplicable willingness always to please doctors.

But there was that numb feeling and from time to time a shift in the visual plane. 'This is not something I want you to worry about,' the doctor had said, rubbing his hands together. 'There could be a completely reasonable explanation for it.'

Her appointment in Leeds, to get the results of the scan, was in a few days' time. Until then she'd keep it to herself. No point in starting a panic.

When her dizziness cleared she did a quick recce to make sure the house was secure. She was outside on the street within a few minutes, walking back towards Lord Mayor's Walk where her own house was. She'd have something to eat and a bath and then she'd get into bed with Gerard Manley Hopkins: 'Glory be to God for dappled things...' But she'd keep her mobile on the bedside cabinet, wait for George or Sam to ring and let her know that he was back on the street.

5

Marilyn was washing herself in the bathroom and taking her lithium, the first dose of the day, to correct the chemical imbalance in her brain cells when her mother, Ellen Eccles, crept into her daughter's bedroom and scanned the walls. Marilyn had straightened the crumpled playing card and placed it in a frame. She'd hung it on the wall between a promotional photograph of Diamond Danny Mann and a collage of his press cuttings.

The eight of spades, and written across it in red feltpen, *Marilyn Eccles.*

Ellen sighed. She hoped it wasn't going to be a repetition of the business with Jeremy Paxman: listening to *Start the Week* every Monday morning, watching *Newsnight* and *University Challenge*, and waiting for the postman in the morning, expecting a letter from the man.

When she looked at Marilyn's wall and the photograph of Danny Mann and his press cuttings she wondered why there wasn't a photograph of her dead granddaughter there. She was confused for a moment because it was wrong of Marilyn not to have a photograph of her baby.

But it was simple, the answer, because there *were* no photographs of the baby. It had been born dead and you don't take photographs of dead babies. In a way, Ellen thought now, the playing card was a kind of code for her granddaughter. And she wondered exactly what it meant to her daughter, this playing card, the one item in the whole universe that had been handled by both Danny Mann and Marilyn.

The absence of a photograph of the baby was problematic in other respects. Without a photograph people didn't realize that Marilyn had been a mother. Because she was so small, exactly one hundred and fifty centimetres, people regarded her as still a child herself. To compensate for her size Marilyn wore a belt with a steel buckle in the shape of a pentagram. Ellen could see the buckle now, dangling from the back of the chair by Marilyn's dressing table.

She wore anything that had a metallic colour or feel to it. Shoes with buckles, jingling bangles and necklaces, a hair-band in beaten copper and a silver chain on each ankle. Somehow, in her mind, Marilyn associated metal with height. The more metal she could carry around on her person, the taller she seemed to feel.

The pentagram buckle on her belt was something else as well. It was a magical sign, something that might catch the eye of Danny Mann. Marilyn had explained that it was a five-pointed star, the number of destiny. Ellen had shaken her head, it sounded like mumbo-jumbo to her. What Marilyn meant was that Danny Mann was her destiny, just as Jeremy Paxman had been and those other unreachable celebrities and actors she'd attached herself to. The difference with Danny Mann was that he lived in York, only a couple of streets away. The poor man's life was destined to become a misery if Ellen failed to keep her daughter Marilyn under control.

The lavatory flushed and Marilyn padded along the landing to her bedroom singing, '*Danny Boy. The hills, the hills are caw-aw-ling . . .*'

'I don't want you getting fixated on him,' Ellen said when her daughter came into the room.

'And I don't want you snooping in my bedroom,' Marilyn said. She threw off her dressing gown and stood in front of the wardrobe. She was pear-shaped with surplus flesh on her thighs, bottom and stomach, but surprisingly pert and firm breasts. Her skin was milky-white, dappled and becoming varicose on the back of her legs.

Ellen looked away. She wondered what had become of the small girl she had dragged around for all those years, the pretty teenager with the wide eyes. There was something gross and feral and unknown about this woman's nakedness that seemed to defy any relationship to her.

'All the signs are there, Marilyn.'

'What? What signs? What are you talking about?'

'Jeremy Paxman.'

'That was different. He was married, with kids.'

'And how do you know this magician isn't married?'

'I know.'

'But you don't, Marilyn. It's the same thing. You talk yourself into it. You convince yourself. This is going to lead to more trouble, I just know it.'

Marilyn slammed the wardrobe shut, turning to face her mother. Her naked back was reflected in the mirror on the door. 'He chose me,' she said. 'You were there, you saw it. He chose me last night. How many women were in that theatre? Come on, tell me, how many?'

'I don't know, love.'

'How many?' She stamped her foot, a residue of red nail varnish clinging to the nail on her big toe.

'A hundred ... five hundred? But it doesn't mean ...'

'A thousand more like, maybe more than that. And out of all of them Danny picked me. He took me on the stage with him. I was a star.'

'Not a star, Marilyn. You see what I mean, how you exaggerate? You have an idea in your head and it gets out of proportion. He needed someone to help with that trick. It doesn't mean he loves you. It was a card trick.'

'Fuck you, Mother,' Marilyn said. 'I know what this is about, you want him for yourself. You're jealous that he picked me instead of you.'

'I'm going downstairs now,' Ellen said. 'We can talk about this later, when you've got yourself dressed and when you've stopped using profane language.'

'Thank you,' Marilyn shouted after her. 'That means I've won.'

Ellen went outside to the back garden and lit up a Benson & Hedges, drawing the smoke and nicotine deep into her lungs. She watched the water from the river creeping over the field towards their house. Every day it drew a little closer. If it didn't stop raining up in the hills they would find themselves marooned one morning. Life had been a battle for as long as she could remember and looked set on remaining so for as far as she could see into the future.

There had been a period of calm when Marilyn married a soldier boy and went to live in a house near Fulford Barracks. Soldier boy helped to train dogs in the art of sniffing out bombs. Ellen felt her life had entered a tranquil patch then and had taken herself off to Scotland to live in a cottage by the Dee, reading books and growing flowers and trying to write.

She would willingly have lived out her last years there, free from the cares of the world.

But some of the soldier boy's mates had plied a couple of working Alsatians with gin and the dogs had gone mad and attacked him, killing him and consuming most of his face and throat.

So Ellen had said goodbye to Scotland and come home to help her daughter back from the brink of madness. What else was she supposed to do? She was a mother first, a Scot second, a gardener third, and a writer . . . well, not at all.

But being a mother is not everything. That is one of the great lies that people have told for ages past, and which they still perpetuate. Being a mother can make you feel that you should be everything to your children, to your child, but as you grow older you have to realize that it isn't true. When they are tiny you might be able to supply their needs, but as they grow they want a wider world.

Marilyn needed sex, she needed an emotional entanglement with a man, a real, loving and mutually supportive relationship, and Ellen couldn't supply that.

Almost as soon as soldier boy was buried in the churchyard Marilyn was head over heels in love with a Leeds United striker. Irish lad, no more than twenty-two, twenty-three. He had no idea. Not at first.

Ellen blamed herself. She had accepted the seed of the man who was Marilyn's natural father, knowing that *his* father and mother had jumped together off the Valley Bridge in Scarborough. Her egg had been fertilized by the sperm of a card-carrying screwball. A man who had opened his veins in the bath to save making a mess in the kitchen.

That was why Marilyn was like she was. Part of her a true Scot with a fierce independence and a natural appreciation of beauty and truth; and another part, inherited from her father, which was forever diagonally parked in an unremittingly parallel universe.

When Ellen had finished her cigarette she returned to the kitchen and watched her daughter eating cornflakes from a bowl. Marilyn was wearing a long wrap-around skirt. She had put on a pair of black tights and a top that her mother had starched and ironed the previous day.

Ellen pulled a chair up to the table and said, 'Marilyn, I don't want us to get into another one of these fixes.'

'What fixes?' Marilyn asked through a mouthful of cereal.

'Like the footballer. You followed him around. In the end he got the police on to us.'

Marilyn stopped eating. 'No,' she said, thinking. 'I don't believe that is what happened. It was his manager got the police out. He was spending too much time thinking about me. He couldn't concentrate on his game.'

'I don't want you making a nuisance of yourself over this magician.'

'Danny?' She smiled. 'He wouldn't call me a nuisance. He didn't think I was a nuisance last night. Not when he was holding my hand.'

'We shouldn't have gone last night,' Ellen said. 'I should've known better when you said you'd got the tickets. All the way to Nottingham when we could have seen him here.'

'Oh, I'm going to see him here as well,' Marilyn said. 'You can count on that. Danny and me, we'll probably end up working together.'

'Look,' Ellen said, 'I don't ask for much, Marilyn. But I want you to leave this man alone. I can see it's going to get you into trouble, and if you're in trouble I'm in trouble as well. What happened last night – it didn't mean anything.'

'It didn't mean anything to you, Mother. But it meant a lot to me and it meant a lot to Danny. You're an old woman, you've had your life. But Danny and me, we're still young. We're in love and our whole future is waiting.'

'He doesn't know you,' Ellen said. 'This is just like the others. You're going to hound the life out of that poor man, drive him to distraction. I'm asking you, please, Marilyn, leave him alone. Let him go.'

Marilyn continued eating her cornflakes. She added more milk and sugar. She said, 'Do you want to put some bread in the toaster and bring the strawberry jam over to the table? Danny likes a girl with some meat on her. He can't stand those anorexic types, bloody stick insects.'

6

'You think I killed her?' Sam said.

Delaney shook his head, a snide grin on his face. 'No one said you killed her. We're trying to establish why someone wanted her dead.'

'These things are usually domestic,' Sam said. 'What about the guy who found her? The boyfriend?'

The Chief Inspector touched his nose. 'The local police say he's not bright enough. He took her body into the street, laid it out on the road. There's no sign of the murder weapon.'

'He could have dropped it down the drain.'

George Forester, the solicitor, touched Sam's arm. 'Just answer the questions,' he said.

'They say he's really cut up about it,' Delaney said. 'They don't think he could put on such a convincing act if he'd killed her. He loved her.'

'It's good to know somebody did.'

'Which means you didn't?'

Sam looked across the desk at the policeman. He didn't mask his hostility. There were times when he believed he simply hated the uniform, the institution, but in clearer moments he realized that he hated the individuals, the people who were drawn to the profession. 'I didn't know her any more,' Sam said quietly. He looked at his solicitor and shook his head. 'I'm sorry she's dead. I'm sorry she died like that. But I haven't seen her, haven't thought about her, for years.'

'What about the boyfriend? Did you know him?'

Sam raised his palms. 'No.'

'Ruben Parkins? Mean anything?'

'Never heard of him.'

'He did a stretch in Long Lartin. GBH.'

'Your guys in Nottingham'll get a confession. Pull his finger-nails out; that usually does the trick.'

The solicitor held up his hand. 'OK, Sam.' He turned to Chief Inspector Delaney. 'Are you going to charge Mr Turner?' he asked. 'If not, I think we should take a break. My client is doing his best to help but your line of questioning is somewhat provocative.'

Delaney said, 'We're breaking for five minutes.' He switched off the tape recorder and got to his feet.

They finally stepped out of the station at 10.15. The moon was up and a light drizzle colluded with the store signs and the car headlights to give Fulford Road the Monet treatment.

'Home? Or shall I drop you somewhere else?' George Forester asked.

'Angeles' house,' Sam told him. 'I need to talk my way through this one.'

He phoned Celia and Geordie on his mobile, spoke to each of them for a few seconds. 'I'm out,' he said. 'Going to see Angeles. I'll tell you about it tomorrow.'

Angeles answered his knock and stood back to allow him into the house. She closed the door and stood still while he put his arms around her. 'There's an institutional scent to you,' she said. 'If I didn't know you'd been to the police station I'd guess the tax office or an army barracks. You smell of fixed ideas and intimidation. Good dollop of fear mixed in as well.'

She was a couple of inches shorter than him, slim and straight. She was wearing a pair of blue jeans and a sleeveless white blouse. Her feet were bare and her hair was mussed on one side, as though she'd been lying on it. There was Scotch on her breath, one of the Island malts. Laphroaig? When they'd first met Sam had thought she might be a soak but, unlike him, she was one of those people who can walk the line without falling into the vat.

Angeles had a hereditary eye condition, Retinitis Pigmentosa (RP), which was degenerative and incurable and which had now consumed most of her visual experience. During daylight hours she was aware of shadowy outlines, misty silhouettes, and at night she was utterly blind.

He took her by the hand and led her to the couch. 'That Coltrane?' he asked, nodding towards the speakers. Angeles didn't reply, waiting for him to answer his own question. He smiled as he recognized Bill Evans' fingers dancing over the piano keys. '"Kind of Blue". That how you're feeling?'

'I thought they'd locked you up.'

'Not this time. It was close, though.'

'Why didn't you tell them you were in Nottingham?'

He shook his head. 'Cops don't believe in coincidence. *I* don't believe in coincidence. I didn't want to give them an excuse to fit me up. If I'd come clean I'd be spending the night in a cell. When the cops haven't got a main suspect they get desperate.'

'Do they have anything? A motive?'

'Not a thing,' Sam said. 'She was knifed in her bed. As far as they can tell nothing was taken from the house. She was living a quiet life. She had a boyfriend with a shady past, but they reckon he's reformed. He's not in the frame.'

Angeles shuddered. 'So a complete stranger comes in the middle of the night, kills her and then fades away? Is that credible?'

'No. The police don't believe that either. They're

looking for someone with an old grudge. Someone out of her past.'

'Like you?'

'Yes, exactly like me.'

'But you didn't know she was in Nottingham. You were there to do a job.'

'Tell it to the judge,' Sam said. 'I already know it wasn't me.'

Angeles moved closer to him. She drew her legs up under her on the couch and placed her head on Sam's shoulder. 'What was she like?'

He squinted down at her, stroked her cheek with two fingers. 'We were both wild. I'd do anything for a drink in those days – steal, cheat, lie. Katherine was the same, or I thought she was for a while. But she was stronger than me. She wanted conventional things; a family, some kind of regular income. We mauled each other, we were each of us someone the other could blame.'

'There must have been more at the beginning,' Angeles said. 'When you met, when you decided to get married? A bond of some sort? Love?'

Sam shook his head. 'Maybe. There's a period of several years when I wasn't available. I would drink myself into a coma and when I came round go looking for another drink. Katherine was one of the things that happened during that time. She was there, we lived together, but I can't remember who she was. I don't have a memory of tenderness, or even of us being on the same wavelength. We were always daggers drawn. Then one day she got up and left, stopped drinking and started rebuilding a life. Not long after that we lost touch.' He smiled ironically. 'Language is strange,' he said. 'We never had any touch to lose.'

They were quiet for a while. He listened to her

heartbeat. Angeles said, 'What did you think when they told you she was dead?'

'Strange,' he said. 'You go through life and you think you know who you are and all the time there's parts of you come into view that you never saw before. Katherine was someone I lived with and never knew, and I'm the same. I live with myself but there's huge areas of me I've never managed to negotiate with, never managed to meet or come to terms with.

'I thought, when they told me, and later in the car when they took me to the police station, I thought it was like discovering that a part of me had been murdered, part of me that I'd never known had been killed and wouldn't be available to me any more. Felt like a waste. An opportunity squandered. One of those moments when all your good intentions have come to nothing and you can't do anything about it.'

Sam had intended to stay at Angeles' house for an hour or so and then go to a midnight AA meeting. A dry alcoholic can get through the everyday but stress leads to an overbearing thirst.

He didn't get to the meeting, though. Around 11.30 Angeles got to her feet and took him to her bedroom. He felt her cool fingers on his flesh and the warmth of her body next to his and the idea of his meeting evaporated into the night.

Sam wondered if in some strange, metaphoric way he had murdered every woman he had ever known. If he had managed through his own sense of ego to distance, alienate and eventually smother the essence of his relationships. He couldn't remember how many years he'd been telling himself he was getting better at it, that he was learning from past mistakes and failures. But the women still kept coming and going. When they came they were keen and excited, and invariably, when they went, they were a little greyer, not quite as perky in the life-force department.

Was he in the process of doing the same thing with Angeles? He hoped not. She filled his waking and often his sleeping thoughts. He couldn't remember who it was but someone had once told him that we can't exist unless the heart is full – we become dry and crumble away. Sayings, lines from songs, snippets of received wisdom, they lodge somewhere in your brain, never seem to leave.

In the small hours of the morning he came awake with a vision of his ex-wife, Katherine, a knife in her chest and dead staring eyes. He closed his eyes and fitted his body into the curve of Angeles' back and within a minute or two he was sleeping again, like a man without a conscience.

7

'How many times has he been married?' Janet asked.

Geordie looked up and closed his eyes. 'You don't wanna know,' he said. He scooped a teaspoonful of green mush out of the bowl and fed it into the open mouth of Echo, their daughter.

'Come on, Geordie. How many? Seems like I've finally got a grasp of his emotional history and now another wife crops up.'

'Dunno if you can say she's cropped up when she's freshly dead.'

Janet turned her mouth down. 'That's bad taste.'

'Taste *is* bad, the last I heard. It's part of one-upmanship. One of the ways the middle classes keep ahead of the competition.'

'OK,' Janet said. 'Don't change the subject. How many wives?'

'Depends what you mean by wife, how you define marriage.' Echo had had enough of the green mush and was sitting with her mouth firmly closed. 'Just two more spoonfuls,' Geordie said. 'Then you can have custard.'

'It's spoonsful, not spoonfuls.'

'I don't think so,' Geordie said. 'Strictly, it'll be spoonful. But I'm talking baby-talk.'

'Let's say we define marriage as in people who've been through a wedding ceremony.'

'If I asked Sam he probably wouldn't know. I think he's had more than four wives and a lot of girlfriends.'

Janet shook her head. 'Bluebeard.'

'He doesn't kill them. He chooses badly. He can't discriminate. First he goes for women who're too young for him, then he's bored because they don't understand what he's talking about.'

'They've got different cultural references,' Janet said.

'Yeah. That's what I said.' Echo opened her mouth and Geordie slipped another load of mush in there. 'Also he likes wild women, you know what I mean, over the top?'

'Indulge me,' Janet said.

'You know what I mean, Janet. Too much makeup, skirt up around her ass, deep cleavage, a mouth like a foghorn.'

'Oh, tarts,' she said. 'You mean he likes tarts?'

'Yeah, I guess. The guy's damaged. This is one of the ways he shows it.'

Janet smiled, showing her teeth.

'What?' Geordie asked.

She shook her head. She leaned over the table and mopped Echo's face with her bib. 'D'you want me to feed her the rest?'

'No, I'm doing it,' Geordie said, irritated. 'What're you laughing at?'

'Too much makeup,' she said. 'Mouth like a foghorn. You're not questioning your boss's taste, Geordie? Using bourgeois concepts to keep the working classes in their place?'

'You led me into that,' he said. 'You took me by the hand and walked me into a trap.'

'Would I?'

'Yes, you would. You just did it. Echo's a witness. This is the kind of woman you've got for a mother, Echo. Just remember that. How do you expect the child to grow into a rounded human being with you as a role-model?'

'She can always fall back on her perfect daddy,' Janet said.

Geordie went to the hob and brought a pan with crushed apple and custard to the table. He spooned the mixture into Echo's bowl and tested the temperature with his knuckles. Echo made a grab for the bowl but he moved it out of reach.

'Anyway, I don't think you're right,' Janet said. 'Dora wasn't a tart, and look at Angeles, she's got real class.'

Geordie was glad that Sam had settled down with Angeles Falco even though they didn't live together. In the past Sam hadn't been able to keep a woman. Some of the women he'd picked, Geordie wouldn't have wanted him to keep. Seemed to be particularly strong on baby-faced smiles and cleavage, gold-diggers and women who were long on legs and hair and short on nous.

'You should see some of the earlier ones,' Geordie said. 'He's getting better but he's still off kilter. Dora was old enough to be his mother and Angeles is at least twenty years younger than him.'

'And then some. But when I see them together I don't think about their ages. They seem like a good fit.'

'That's because you're a moral relativist,' Geordie told her.

Janet laughed. 'Big words.'

'I was talking to Celia about it. In the old days, before Einstein, everybody believed in good and evil. There were rules about what you could do, like the Ten Commandments. But now we think everything's relative. We look at the context of things and judge them from that. There're no absolutes anymore.'

'I feel an example coming on,' Janet said.

'There were a couple of Iraqi families in Bradford, one with two sons and the other with two daughters. They went through all the routines they would've gone through in Iraq and the two daughters were married to the two sons. They didn't have a registrar or anything like that but they had their own religious ceremony. A few weeks later Social Services moved in and took the girls into care. The boys were charged with sexual abuse.'

'How old were these girls?'

'I don't remember,' Geordie said. 'Thirteen, something like that, which is fine in Iraq, nobody thinks anything about it. That's how they do it. But here it's regarded as immoral and we make a law about it.'

'It's too young,' Janet said.

'Sure. I think so, too. I wouldn't like to see Echo getting married in ten, eleven years' time. But are you gonna say the Iraqi families are immoral for going through with it? Stone them to death?'

'That'd be an over-reaction, I think.'

'See what I mean? You're a moral relativist.'

'So this is what we're going to teach Echo, is it? That there's no such thing as right or wrong. That everything's relative?'

'We'll have to, Janet. That's what she's got to learn if she's gonna live in this society. If we lived in a different society we'd teach her different things.'

'What about these fundamentalists, Geordie? Seems like there's more of them all the time. People who see good on one side and evil on the other and nothing in between.'

'They're part of a backlash. But they're a minority. These're people who can't cope without certainty in their lives. They want a strong leader or a dominant church, and they want all their Ts crossed and all their Is dotted.'

Janet sighed. 'Sometimes that sounds attractive.'

'Yeah,' Geordie said. 'But it's a dream. If we don't take responsibility for ourselves then somebody else'll do it for us, and we'll be slaves again.'

Janet sniffed and looked at Echo.

'She's filled her nappy,' Geordie said. 'I shovel it in one

end and she pushes it out the other. *C'est la vie.*' He went to the bathroom and came back with a fresh Pamper and a jar of cold cream.

'I'll do it,' Janet said. 'Aren't you supposed to be at work?'

'Yeah. Same as you.'

Janet took the cold cream from his hand. 'You get off,' she said. 'I'll do this and drop her at the nursery.'

'What're we having for supper? You want me to pick anything up?'

'No, I'll find something. You fancy fish?'

'Sure. Whatever. Or bread and wine, we could have that if you like. The Last Supper.'

'I'll give you that one night, bet you wouldn't like it.'

'For just one night I could do anything, Janet. Even fast food.'

'I don't think . . .'

'What if they'd had, the disciples, instead of bread and wine double cheeseburgers and fries, chilled Coke on the side? The reason they had bread and wine was because that's what people had in those days. In that place, in that time, you wanted to have supper with your mates, you got some bread and wine and split it around a table. But if Jesus had been born the same time as us, what they'd've done, they'd've gone to some fast food place and had whatever was on the menu. I dunno, might've been pizza, curried king prawns and chips.

'Then in church on Sundays you'd get a few more people turning up for Communion. "*This is my body*", and the parson sticks a piece of Cumberland sausage in your face, "*and this is my blood*", and you suck up a Vodka Alcopop through a straw.'

Janet laughed. 'Are you going to work?'

'Maybe I should. Sam'll be briefing us on why he lied to the police.'

'Perhaps he killed her,' Janet said. 'That'd be a good reason to lie.'

'Sam? He'd never do that. What're you saying?'

Janet raised her eyebrows, put a grin on her face. 'Never say never, Geordie. Remember, there are no absolutes anymore. In the right circumstances, in context, it could all make perfect sense. This ex-wife of his – what was she called, Katherine? – she could've been the reason he was in Nottingham in the first place.'

'This's my friend you're talking about,' Geordie told her.

'Oh, I know,' Janet said as she lifted Echo out of her highchair. 'And he's a thoroughly nice bloke. It was probably a mercy killing.'

8

Mid-morning and Jody was lying on the couch half-naked. Diamond Danny Mann came in from the kitchen with a mug of tea. He wore shiny black trousers with braces and no shirt.

'I've moved the thermostat up,' he said. He sat on the edge of the couch and used the remote to flick through the TV channels. After a couple of minutes he hit the standby button and gazed over the rim of his mug at a picture on velvet hanging on the wall. In the centre of the picture was a wizard with a tall pointed hat, a black cape and a wand that looked like a sparkler. On the ground by the wizard's feet was a black cat and above his head a crescent moon.

'I've got this thing with my eye,' Danny said. 'The last couple of weeks. Maybe I'm rundown?' He turned his head to the left and then to the right. Focused above the velvet picture and then below it. 'Some kind of visual fault. It starts to twitch and a small kaleidoscope takes off on the edge of my vision, spinning away in a corner of the retina.'

Jody didn't reply. He imagined he heard her sigh quietly but he couldn't be sure. She wasn't easy to communicate with outside their double bed.

'Might be a brain tumour,' he said. He put his hand over his right eye and looked around the room. 'Right eye, left side of the brain. There's a rune you can use for tumours. Give them to somebody else or get rid of your own.' He put his mug on the carpet and walked over to a shelf of books. He selected a large tome with broken boards and ragged end-papers and took it over to a circular table in the pink-curtained bay window.

He thumbed backwards and forwards through the book for the better part of an hour. Eventually he closed it and sat back in the chair. 'A *Tiki*,' he said. 'That's what I need. Greenstone figure, something like jade. Might have to import it.' He glanced at Jody. 'Lot to do,' he said. 'Three shows this week, another woman to disappear, brain tumour to cure.' He left his chair and reached down to take her by the hand. 'And then there's the question of getting you sorted, my darling.'

'Do you remember,' Danny had said to the inert body of Katherine Turner, 'do you remember a time when the world was full of noises, sounds and sweet airs, that gave delight and no pain? When you thought the clouds would open and show riches ready to drop upon you? And did you cry to dream again?'

He spoke the lines to the still-warm corpse on the bed because there had been such a time in Danny's life, a time when he hadn't needed to make his own magic at all. When the whole of his known world had been filled with constant melody.

At the University of Durham all those years ago Danny's degree had been in Drama. He had not enjoyed the separation from his mother but there had been aspects of the course that had given him joy. He had learned how to present himself, how to project outwards from his centre, almost anything at all. He could make himself appear tall or short with a mere shift of his internal focus. In a group or in front of an audience he could be regarded as aggressive or passive or any of the nuances in between simply by an adjustment to his posture or a shift in the position of his shoulders.

And as part of the course he had had to attend lectures in the English department, where the gift of words had absorbed him and would continue to fascinate him for the rest of his life. The richness of his native tongue had been a revelation, a blessed relief for a mind which never dreamed on aught but butcheries.

9

Marilyn wanted to know everything about this man. The colour of the carpet in his bedroom, what he ate for breakfast, his favourite television show and the book that he'd always remember because it changed his life.

She knew already what his hand felt like, the tone of his voice and the sweet smell of menthol on his breath. She knew that his front door was painted red and his back door an olive shade of green. Marilyn knew that Danny had oyster-coloured net curtains and pink drapes at his double-glazed windows.

There was always something new to learn about a new man but already she had his telephone number and his car registration. From his dustbin she'd culled more information; that he was a member of the AA and that he used a MasterCard which expired next month. Danny's membership of the Magic Circle had lapsed. He paid his bills on time, gas, electric, telephone, garage, credit card, and he didn't have a mortgage. He used Wilkinson Sword razor blades and Gillette shaving gel in a pressurized container. But none of this was sufficient. There was still a sizeable part of the man that she hadn't quite grasped.

Marilyn was good at lying. She could convince anyone of anything. The key to a good lie was to tell it as if you believed it yourself, and that came easily to Marilyn because as soon as she started to tell a story she began living it as well.

'You love drama,' Ellen had said to her a thousand

times. 'It would be better if you didn't love it so much. Or maybe you should have been an actress, got it out of your system by playing it on the stage.'

But Marilyn wasn't so sure about that. She wasn't interested in the stage. It was real life that fascinated her. It was love and hatred, pain and romance, the ways that destiny threw lovers into each other's arms and wrenched them apart. It was separation, death, guilt and an overflowing heart.

'Who were you ringing?' Ellen asked.

'Mind your own business.'

'Where've you been?'

'That's for me to know.'

'Have you taken your lithium?'

'Christ, will you leave me alone? It's up to me whether I've taken my lithium or not.'

'Oh, no, it isn't, my girl. I live in this house as well as you. And I know what happens when you stop taking it. The next thing you'll be chasing this magician around, accosting him in the street. If you don't take it now, and if I don't see you taking it with my own eyes, I'll be on the phone to the doctor.'

'You want me tanked up with chemicals,' Marilyn said. 'You and the doctor both. It's as if I'm a child. I have to do what you say. I don't have my own freedom. I'm not allowed to decide if I need the lithium or not. If it was up to you you'd keep me on it for ever. For my whole life.'

'You'll stay on it for as long as it's being prescribed for you, Marilyn. Doctor knows best. You get out of yourself when you're not taking it. Fixating on people, going into a fantasy world, speaking to me as if I'm a piece of dirt.'

They stared at each other. Marilyn narrowed her eyes but Ellen didn't give way.

'You don't know what it's like to be lonely,' Marilyn told her, a perceptible crack in her voice.

'I do,' said Ellen. 'I'm lonely as well, Marilyn. But the answer isn't to fixate on the first man who comes along.'

'Danny isn't the first man to come along. He's the answer to all my prayers.'

'Go and get the lithium,' Ellen said.

Marilyn tramped up the stairs and came down with a single tablet in the palm of her hand. She walked to the kitchen sink and splashed water into a mug. She stood in front of her mother and placed the lithium tablet on her tongue. Then she took a gulp of the water, emptied the mug.

'Satisfied?' she said.

'Yes, I am,' Ellen said. She reached out and stroked her daughter's cheek. 'You know I love you, Marilyn. That's why I'm here. That's why I'm here and not in Scotland. And it's because I love you that I want you to take your medicine and not get out of yourself. We don't want another episode like, you know, the footballer or . . . You don't want that, either, do you?'

Marilyn shook her head. 'No. I don't want that.'

'So, who were you talking to on the telephone?'

'The hairdresser. I want a trim, something to make me feel better.'

'And where were you this morning? You took the car.'

'It's a surprise. I don't want to tell you.'

'I don't want a surprise, Marilyn. I've had enough surprises in my life.'

'I went to look at some earrings. They were supposed to be for your birthday. A present for you.'

Ellen shook her head and smiled. She held out her arms and Marilyn let herself be enfolded in her mother's bosom. While there, snuggled up between arm and breast, she removed what remained of the lithium tablet from her mouth and tucked it into the back pocket of her

58

jeans. Outside the window the river water on the field was creeping closer to the house, every day a little closer.

'It's not that you're bad,' Ellen was saying. 'I know that. You're a good girl at heart, always were. You just go off the rails from time to time, when you're left to your own devices. But if we stick together we can beat it, Marilyn. The two of us together are bigger than this thing.'

'I know,' Marilyn said, making her body shudder like it would at the onset of tears. 'And I'm so glad you're here. Without you there'd be nothing to live for.'

10

Sam watched the weather from his office window and wondered where he was with Angeles. Had the best of their relationship already happened? Was the future another slow decline into separate paths? Was there anything he could do to influence the situation one way or another? Grey city was almost deserted. There were a few damp tourists in Betty's tea shop but the usual queue to get into the place had been absent since the rains came. 'What do you think?' he asked Marie. 'We gonna have a flood?'

'The river's high,' she said. 'Another couple of inches and it'll be over the towpath. I might have to move out of my house.'

'Come and stay with me,' he said. 'Be it ever so humble it'll be nice and dry.'

Marie smiled. 'Celia's already offered me a room at her place. Thanks.' She joined him at the window, looked down on scurrying figures with umbrellas, a middle-aged woman in a tartan plastic raincoat and a street person standing outside the Mansion House with a tin whistle and a dripping nose. The sky was padded with black cloud. It was as if the divinity had gone into clinical depression and His system had developed an immunity to all the usual drugs. He wasn't interested any more.

Marie was wearing a loosely knitted jumper from French Connection with a pair of trousers in shiny black cotton and new laced boots of Spanish leather. She was a large-boned woman, above average weight but well capable of carrying it. She wore her hair short and was conscious of an overbite which gave her face an interest that eclipsed mere prettiness.

'Do we have any work?' she asked.

Sam shook his head. 'Not a lot. There's routine stuff that keeps Geordie busy. And there was the Nottingham job last week, but the telephone doesn't ring. I keep thinking they've disconnected us.'

'I suppose it gives me more time to work at the Centre, but if I don't earn money the bills don't get paid.'

The Centre was a women's refuge where Marie helped out whenever the detective business was in the doldrums. She'd been a nurse and had the ability to listen as well as a well-honed social conscience, and there were times when she was utterly convinced that she could live without men.

'If you need money . . .' Sam said.

'Thanks.' She smiled. 'I'd just ask. You'd be the first person I thought of, you being so rich. But I'm not broke, there's money in the bank. And tomorrow or the next day or next week, whenever, some time soon you'll be telling me we've got so much work we can't manage. Celia'll be going out on surveillance and you'll be bringing in the part-timers like JD and Janet.'

'This is true,' Sam said. 'Whatever goes around comes around. We've got a million customers, it's just a marketing problem. You busy at the Centre?'

'Always. Why is it that a young mother with a baby attracts a guy with shit for brains and fists the size of lump hammers?'

'Sometimes seems like understanding or tenderness are too much to hope for,' he said. 'The culture these guys move in regards reason as unacceptably intelligent.'

'You blame the culture?'

'The government if you like, the way we've let

ourselves be organized. I don't have those kinds of answers, Marie. I'm a PI not a medic. My job's to blow the bad guys away.'

'You don't believe that.'

'Belief isn't any kind of answer.'

'Neither is violence.'

'Not in the long run,' he said.

'Have you ever hit a woman, Sam?'

He didn't answer.

'Does that mean you have?'

He pursed his lips. 'Could mean I have but I've opted to forget it.'

'Yes or no?'

'Only in self-defence, m'lawd.'

'What happened?'

'I shot her,' Sam said. 'You know that. It's not my best memory but I'd do it again in the same circumstances, it kept me alive to fight another day.'

'What about Katherine?'

'Did I hit her? Or did I kill her?'

'I know you didn't kill her.'

'What's the question, Marie?'

'Who was she? Did I meet her?'

'No, she was before your time. We were both drinkers. She got out. In a way her getting out was an encouragement to me. I found a way around it myself later, a few years later, but if someone else gets free it gives you strength. You don't resent them, you appreciate the lesson. It's good to know that something's possible.'

Marie nodded encouragement.

'We were young,' he said. 'I met her in a bar. It was opening time and she was more or less as pissed as I was. We were the only people in the place, six o'clock in the evening and drinking doubles. I was at the stage I could focus better if I kept one eye shut. The barman was a soak

62

as well and he told us the old joke about the drunk who couldn't work out what his limit was because he always passed out before he reached it. And Katherine said she'd been in a bar earlier in the day and asked for the usual so the landlord carried her outside. And we were laughing together, all three of us, and I was supposed to tell a drunk joke but I couldn't remember one and they both thought that was funnier than if I'd told a good one so we laughed some more.

'I dunno how long we kept going that night. At some point I ended up at her place. It was one room somewhere and we slept together with the light on because she was frightened of the dark. Sometimes we'd go to bed during the day and we still had to sleep with the light on because Katherine would say we might wake up in the dark.

'We were swimming in booze. We'd laugh a lot and we'd always come up with some kind of scam to get the money together for another bottle, or we'd fight like cat and dog and still come up with a solution. We convinced each other we were a good couple, we couldn't live without each other. So we got married.'

'Sounds like you were in full flight,' Marie said.

'No doubt about it. I was half-crazy. When Donna and Bronte were killed I stopped sleeping. I used to stand at the corner of that street with a pad and a pen and jot down the number of every car that was over the speed limit. When I got a full sheet I'd take it round the police station and then go back to the corner and fill up another one. I did that for a year, never missed a day. Must've started taking a bottle with me about nine months in and soon the bottle became more important than watching the cars.

'I'd wake up screaming in the street, sitting on the pavement, or the cops would put me in a cell. Bronte was two when she died. I'd play the impact over and over again in my head. The head-on collision with iron and steel at ninety miles an hour, her body sailing through the air like a missile. And I'd know it was a dream, although I wasn't really asleep, it was a vision, a nightmare. The whole thing would take place in silence, like a film when the sound has been lost. And then I'd be awake, wide awake again and back in the world, and Bronte and Donna had both gone in the same fell swoop and it wasn't a dream at all.'

Marie touched his hand and stood beside him while they looked out at the rain. He'd still been a drunk when she first met him. The police had brought him into the hospital where she was in the final year of her SRN training. He'd got into a fight with a gang of squaddies; he had a fractured arm, two broken ribs, and his head and face had been used like a football. Before they left him one of them stabbed him in the neck with a sheath knife. By that time his drunk had lasted too many years. After they'd nursed him back to health he'd carried on drinking for another five.

Sam laughed.

'Something funny?'

'When I came round,' he said, 'at the hospital, the police came to see me. Check if they should launch a murder hunt for the squaddies or give them a medal each. I was half-asleep and you came to the side of the bed with the Chief Superintendent – what was his name? – and he said, "What's the prognosis?"

'You told him, "Oh, his condition is very satisfactory." And then the two of you wandered away towards the nurses' station.

'Very satisfactory? I thought. Must mean I'm going to die.'

Marie smiled. 'Didn't stop you drinking though, did it?'

Sam shook his head. 'It made me think,' he said. 'Made me realize I wasn't the man I'd set out to be.'

'And now you are?'

'Still need to develop some humility.'

'Shall I tell you something, Sam? About you?'

'Don't be bashful.'

'You don't talk about them much, but when you get around to telling about past relationships, how they failed, it's always you who was at fault.'

'It's because I'm the centre of my own universe,' he said. 'I look at the world from my point of view and I report what I see. If I could see it from Katherine's point of view it'd look different.'

'But which is right?'

Sam laughed. 'And where is reality?' he said. 'Maybe it's somewhere in between or it could be in another place entirely, somewhere we haven't looked yet.'

The telephone rang and he turned to his desk and picked up the handset. 'Sam Turner,' he said.

'The detective?' asked the voice in his ear. Sounded like a mobile connection. A voice which was croaky and at the same time slightly nasal. An uncertain individual; not a voice to trust.

'That's me. Can I help?'

'I need someone to investigate my staff,' the man said. 'Things are going missing.'

'And you are?' Sam asked.

'The name's Bonner,' the man said. 'But I don't want to speak over the phone. Could you come to my home?'

'Address?' Sam reached for his pad.

'I'm in Leeds. Do you know Headingley?'

'The cricket ground?'

'No,' the voice said. 'North Lane. There's a pub at the top called the Taps.'

'Yeah,' Sam said. 'I know the place.'

He scribbled the house number and street on his pad. 'Today?' he asked.

'I'm away today,' the guy said with the speed of a young Mozart. 'But tomorrow morning would be good. Nine o'clock?'

'I'll be there, Mr Bonner.'

Sam replaced the handset in its cradle and looked at it.

'Something wrong?' Marie asked.

'No, it's work,' he said. 'Exactly what we need. Something odd about the guy is all. He seemed to be winging it, making it up as he went along.'

Marie made a face. 'That's the main drawback to this business,' she said. 'The customers. Some of them are fine but we get a higher percentage of slimeballs than North Yorkshire Water.'

11

After he was released from the police station Ruben Parkins went back to his flat on the Lenton Boulevard and thought it through. The police had believed him. When he'd found himself in the interview room he'd expected to be fitted up. In the past, whenever he'd found himself facing a couple of them in that room or another room identical to it in other police stations, they'd always been absolutely sure he'd done the deed. Sometimes they'd been right and sometimes they'd been wrong, but either way they'd do their damnedest to pin the crime on Ruben. Every other time but this. They didn't suspect that he'd killed Kitty, even though he was on the spot and covered in her blood.

The difference was Kitty herself. She had brought something intangible to his life. She would have laughed if he'd said that to her. 'No, I haven't,' she'd have said. 'Everything you are was already in place when we met. All I did was help you find something that was part of you.'

She had natural modesty. Ruben had never met that before. Not like Kitty's. Most people you met, they were falling over themselves to prove how great they were. Among guys it was direct competition, the strut or the curled lip, the way they'd show off their women or their biceps or the length of their schlongs. Women were subtle sometimes but even the quiet ones with no equipment weren't modest, not really. They just drew attention to themselves without all the hullabaloo. They shouted as loud as the leggy blondes but they used a different language.

Kitty was different because she was *interested* in Ruben Parkins. She caught a glimpse of something in him that, from time to time, he'd suspected might be there but had never found the courage to believe in. 'You complete me,' she'd said. 'All the other men I've known were aliens. Some of them were nice and some of them were shite but either way you could take them or leave them. They were wallpaper, didn't really touch me. But with you it's like finding a key. You open me up; you make me grow.'

'It's the same for me,' he'd told her. 'I'm a different man, someone I didn't know I could be. Weird.'

She'd smiled. 'It's not weird, it's love. That's what it does to people. I love you.'

And it was like a jolt going through his body. Because women had said that to him before but it had been an act, one of the things you said when you were into a heavy sweat. And he'd said it back a couple of times and it hadn't meant a thing. It was convention, manners, like saying thank you to your aunties when they gave you a present for your birthday. Even when the present was something naff like a colouring book.

But when Kitty said it to him and he said it back to her, that was something else. That was closer to religion or 'Bohemian Rhapsody' or a fuckin' space rocket. Ruben didn't know what exactly.

It was like discovering that an obvious and blatant lie was the only truth in the world. That everything you'd given credence to in the past was false, full of holes, designed to lead you into corruption and despair. The truth was what the world said it was and all your fighting and opposition to it hadn't made one jot of difference. There was a rock there, beneath all the chaos and confusion. There was nothing to worry about or to kick against. There was certainty.

Kitty.

Kitty and Ruben.

Together they could conquer the world.

He went down to the Skoda but it wasn't in its usual parking space. It would still be outside Kitty's house. He could picture it there, up against the kerb, after they'd put her body in the ambulance and hustled him into the patrol car.

He walked, letting the re-runs play over inside his head. The water splashing down the side of the bath, the sodden carpet, the blood-soaked bedclothes. He'd clasped her to his chest and refused to part with her when the two cops arrived. They'd held his arms while the paramedics prised her from his grasp.

The neighbours had come out of their houses and formed a circle around him. Ruben and his dead lover pacing the tarmac; she a rag doll in his arms, he howling at the bright day which had promised so much. And Kitty was weightless in his arms, as if her physical substance had departed together with her life. That fracture of her spine in the crook of his arm. Her body telling him how the murderer's knife had plunged through her chest and pierced her heart, but as if that wasn't enough he had thrust deeper still, smashing through the fibrous cartilage of the discs and vertebrae and rupturing the spinal cord.

Why?

Why would anyone do that to Kitty? There were fifty other houses in the street and they had all been left untouched. This killing seemed so personal: the overflowing bath, the intimacy of the bedroom setting. This was no random killing, not a lone psychopath on the night-time streets of Nottingham. This was a planned crime,

Kitty had been targeted. But by whom? And what had she done to bring out such wanton violence in the murderer?

The Skoda was where he had left it. The front of Kitty's house had been sealed off from the road and the constable on duty refused to let Ruben through.

'But I know the house,' he explained. 'I might see something you would miss. A clue?'

'You'll have to talk to the governor,' the cop said. 'I can't let you go inside. I'm not allowed in myself. SOCOs only allowed in there.'

Ruben eyeballed the guy but he was never going to shift. He looked straight ahead as if he was part of the Queen's guard; should've had a busby on his head.

They kept him waiting for an hour in the police station. Even then he didn't get to see the Detective Chief Inspector who had interviewed him the previous day. A Detective Sergeant with a permanent smirk on his face took Ruben into a small interview room behind the front desk. 'We don't have any news,' he said.

'Who's the chief suspect?'

'Earlier we thought there might be a connection with her ex-husband. But we can't prove he was in Nottingham. He has witnesses who place him in York.'

'But you think he did it?'

'We're following several leads at the moment, sir.'

They had nothing. If they were following several leads that meant they didn't have a clue. Ruben would have to find the killer himself. He'd talk to everyone who knew Kitty and somehow he'd track the murderer down. He pushed his chair away from the table and got to his feet.

'You should have some counselling, son,' the Detective Sergeant said. 'See your doctor and set something up. Or ring these people, they're there to help you.' He handed over a card with the telephone number of Victim

Support. Logo in the top corner of a dark cloud and a yellow sun rising over it.

'Thanks for seeing me,' Ruben said. He turned and left the room and walked into the city. Something had changed in him. He felt no sense of urgency but in that tiny room in the police station he had committed himself to avenging Kitty's death. His own life held no joy for him now. With splendid clarity he knew that there was only one thing left for him to accomplish. Everything else was dross.

Back in his flat he wrote down the name of every person he could think of who had known Kitty. He racked his brain to recall everyone she had ever mentioned, however distant. When he'd finished he sat back in the chair and looked at the wall. He was like Superman, as if he had X-ray eyes and could pierce through bricks and mortar with his vision. But beyond the walls there was only Kitty mothballed in his memory. Kitty as she had been in life. Her hair and fair skin, her bright eyes and the brilliant promises she could no longer deliver.

He put his mobile and camera on the passenger seat and filled the Skoda's tank with petrol, headed out towards the M1 and took the slip-road to join the north carriageway. Kitty hadn't talked much about her ex, Sam Turner, and she'd never said anything to indicate she was frightened of the man. In fact, there had been a wistfulness about her when she'd remembered her marriage, not enough to make Ruben actively jealous because Kitty always let him know that he was number one, but there had been times late at night when Ruben had definitely seen the ex-husband as a threat.

Could be him. Ruben remembered someone in the joint telling him that most murders were domestic. Either the guy tops his missis with an axe or a broken bottle or she finally gets it together and feeds him Warfarin for breakfast – the point being that the statistics about murders are misleading. There's all these little old ladies scared to go out of the house because the murder rate's going up every year. They sit at home and watch killings on the box instead. But they've got nothing to worry about really; they could walk around all night and nobody'd bother them because the guy most likely to blow them away is the one they go visit in the cemetery on a Sunday morning.

This life, Ruben thought, it hasn't got anything going for it. You start with demons on all sides and they chip away at you until you're on your knees. Then you're given Kitty and you fall on your feet again. Least, you think you've fallen on your feet. That's what it feels like, you're so up you'd have to be psychic to remember that there's no substance under you. The devil's got you by the tail and he's shifting the parts of the universe around all the time so you can't see where anything fits. You think you're set up with a woman by your side and the woman is telling you there's nothing to worry about and she's the one you were looking for and you're the one she's been looking for and now you've found each other. It's like the whole world is a fairy story and you two've got the starring parts.

So you arrive where she lives to take her out for the day and she's drained of blood and there's a hole in her chest where someone tried to cut her heart out. The fairy story is a nightmare, the demons never went away, you're back on your knees and nothing fits. It was all illusion.

Some prick in a Jaguar honked his horn, telling Ruben to get out of the fast lane, pulled up to within a metre of the Skoda's rear end. Ruben stayed in the lane, slowed his speed a little, gave the guy the finger. The driver of the Jag waited for a gap in the traffic and overtook him on the inside. Ruben gritted his teeth and took off after him, pumping the Skoda for everything it could give. No contest. The Jag pulled ahead with ease and when they came to the junction with the M18 Ruben turned off and let it go. He wasn't here to play around with guys in fast cars.

On the A1 he pulled into a Little Chef and got himself a cup of coffee and a full breakfast with extra bacon. For a moment there he couldn't remember the last time he'd eaten. There'd been a tuna sandwich in the police station the previous day, a couple of biscuits in the saucer every time they gave him a cup of tea.

He sat back for a time when he'd finished eating, thought about his world. He should keep the milk-round going. It got him out of bed in the mornings and provided readies. He didn't want to go back on benefits, the hassle of all that. And after he'd finished work there was still a good chunk of the day left for him to track down the bastard who'd wasted Kitty.

He'd have lost some of his customers already. You can't leave people for two days without milk before they start looking for another supplier. But there were plenty of them who'd sign up again if he delivered tomorrow. There were a lot of them owed him money anyway, women who couldn't afford to go anywhere else. That was economics. It wasn't so much to do with supply and demand like they taught you on the small business start-up course. The real key to economics was market share, getting rid of the competition, buying them out or making it so difficult for them that they threw in the towel. When Ruben had started the milk-round he was going to take over the world, corner the market, become king of milk distribution, maybe expand horizontally into production. Corner that market as well.

Kitty never understood that. She was a woman. For her the world was about sharing and fair-play, even arguing that he should give milk away if his customers had children and couldn't afford to pay. That was another reason Ruben liked her so much, because she had compassion and thought that everyone should have humanitarian principles, even the government. Ruben had never given milk away but he could see it as a possibility. Something to work towards. Once he got the market share, he argued, then he'd be in a position to be generous.

Something else nagging away at the back of his brain. If he didn't have a job at all he'd start brooding and before he knew what was happening he'd be knocking back too much drink, end up taking it all out on some schmuck down the boozer. On one level that would work for him, like it always had in the past. You ignore the real crap that is fucking up your life and find someone you can slap around, maybe break a few bones. Therapy. You end up back in the can and blame the system for being unfair, blame your folks for not giving you a good start in life.

But if he did that now, whoever had killed Kitty would go free. Ruben had never come across justice. When the word came up in conversation there was a part of him that wanted to laugh. Justice? What's that?

Only now there was a chance for justice, because it wasn't going to be meted out by the cops or the courts, it was going to be administered by Ruben Parkins. In fact Ruben *was* justice. He was the thing itself, the concept, and he was also its executor.

Justice should be about justness. Making sure that everyone got what they deserved. The world didn't understand that. They only understood the statue, that goddess with her scales and her sword. But the scales and the sword weren't reality, or they hadn't been up to now.

With Ruben in charge the scales would weigh out how much Kitty's life was worth and the sword would chop mercilessly into the flesh of the man who'd sent her to her maker. Ruben would be just, impartial, he would ensure that everyone received their due.

He paid for his breakfast and got back behind the wheel of the Skoda. At junction 45 he left the motorway and followed the signs to York, watching his speed on the A64. He pulled into the park-and-ride centre on the outskirts of town and took a bus into the city. Had a seat behind a couple of German tourists wrapped in water-proof clothing. In the seat opposite was a woman who looked like Kitty might have looked when she was twenty, only she couldn't smile, not even with her eyes.

The bus put him down in the centre of York and he stopped to watch the swollen river breaking free from its banks. Ruben was one of a gaggle of tourists and sightseers looking down from the Ouse bridge. The river had flooded King's Staith and swamped a pub and a restaurant and cut off the houses along the waterfront. In the pale sunlight the rising waters didn't seem to pose a threat and parents lifted their children so they could look over the parapet of the bridge and watch the unthinking power of natural forces unfolding and invading the preserves of human beings.

Ruben wondered if it would go on for ever. If the waters would continue to rise until there was no trace of the pub and restaurant. If the bridge would be swept away and all the people with it. If this was God's revenge on humanity for allowing Kitty to be taken from the world. From now on there would be nothing but rain, the towns and villages and cities would be obliterated. York Minster, which had towered above the city for eight hundred years, would be reduced to rubble under the swirling waters. The priests and the choirboys would become food for fishes, their bloated corpses useful only as landing stages for exhausted birds.

And at some point in the distant future a latterday Noah in a hastily converted river boat would release a pigeon, and when the bird did not return there would appear a vision of Kitty's face and the sailor would deduce that the waters were receding. It'd be a new start for the world and all the children would learn about the murder and the floods and how a huge vision of Kitty's face had filled the sky on a new dawn.

But that would only happen if there was a God. And if there had been a God He would never have let Kitty be killed in the first place.

Ruben enquired his way to the Central Library and found a copy of the York telephone directory. The Sam Turner Detective Agency was situated in St Helen's Square, only five minutes' walk away. The woman at the desk drew a map with a ballpoint pen, showing him how to find the place. An L for the library and a large misshapen H for St Helen's Square.

Ruben sat on the bench outside the library and dialled the number on his mobile.

A female voice said: 'Sam Turner Detective Agency.'

'Sam Turner, please,' Ruben said into the mouthpiece.

'Just a moment, I'll get him. Who's calling?'

Ruben closed the keyboard cover on the phone and cut off the call. He tucked the mobile into his pocket and let a smile spread over his face. So the guy was there, available.

In St Helen's Square he found the office by a wooden plaque on its wall. He took up position on the other side of the square ensuring that he'd see the guy as soon as he came to the door. He made sure that his camera was switched on, that the zoom function was working. He knew what Sam Turner looked like because he could remember the guy's face from the photographs in Kitty's albums.

There was a middle-aged woman waiting for someone in the square. Little blue suit and an expensive-looking floral stole. Tinted glasses to filter out the grey of the day. Strappy shoes and a pair of legs could've belonged to a teenager or a film star. Legs built for high summer and blue swimming pools. What was fascinating about her was the way she held her head; straight, tilted backwards as if she was balancing something on it. Maybe it was her bank account?

The rains came suddenly and people ran for cover. Betty's tea shop was packed within a couple of minutes. Ruben pushed his back against the wall and stood his ground. The downpour lasted three, four minutes and it was over. Sam Turner came out of the office door and hesitated for a moment at the top of the stone steps. He was trim, wearing a short black jacket with a mandarin collar, black jeans and shoes. He was older than in the pictures Kitty had had of him. There was nothing boyish about his face which had become an amalgam of angles and jowls. There were touches of grey in his hair but his body was still erect and quick. What betrayed him was his bearing, a kind of natural arrogance, a stubborn certainty of his place in the world. There was power there – not necessarily physical power although the guy could obviously look after himself. Charisma, maybe that was it. The ability to look as though he had God on his side.

Turner moved to his left and made for the entrance to Stonegate. Ruben took a couple of shots with his zoom but could only get the man's profile. Breaking cover he ran across the square, cutting the detective off, clicking away with his camera as he moved. By the entrance to Stonegate he stood his ground and took a couple of full-face shots of the guy.

Sam Turner was a couple of metres away and stopped in his tracks as if he might be considering posing for the camera. He looked behind him to check that the guy with the camera wasn't focusing on someone else. Then he turned back and said, 'What the . . . ? What you doing, man?' Real confusion on his face.

Ruben took another photograph, made sure he had what he'd come for. Then he turned away and walked quickly along Davygate.

He heard Sam Turner call after him but took no notice, kept on walking.

When he heard Turner's footsteps and felt the guy's hand on his arm, Ruben turned quickly and brought up his knee.

As he increased his pace and distanced himself from the man crumpled on the wet pavement, Ruben reflected that the detective still had some balls. If slightly crushed at the moment. The thing about having balls was, you had to be able to look after them.

12

Sam was sprawled in the chair with his legs spread in front of him. His right foot was balanced on a wooden stool and his left on a low table. He held a cushion over his groin and to avert the pain held himself still and tried to concentrate on Springsteen's lyrics to 'Hungry Heart' which Geordie had put on the CD player. Geordie had his dog Barney and daughter Echo with him, and he was explaining to both of them what had happened to his boss.

'Most people,' he said, 'guys like me and Barney, we've got a couple of grapes hanging down between our legs. But Echo doesn't because she's not a guy, she's a girl like her mum and girls have fannies, which are different, right? Now, Sam here, he used to have a couple of grapes hanging down like the other blokes but somebody came up to him in the street and turned his grapes into melons.' Barney cocked his head to one side and glanced at Sam with something like sympathy in his brown eyes. Echo didn't seem to take in her father's words and was more concerned with trying to remove one of his eyes.

Sam shifted his weight from one buttock to the other. 'Very droll,' he said. 'Not too far off the mark, though. They've shrunk back down now, more or less normal size. Except they ache, feel like somebody's been playing snooker with them.'

'Cue-ball syndrome,' Geordie said. 'I've had it myself. Got it on my honeymoon. What it does, it keeps you on the straight and narrow. That old argument about sex being for pleasure or for reproduction loses all significance. You don't have to concern yourself with safe sex, wearing a condom or doing the rhythm method of birth control. All that stuff is for the rest of the world. The Pope, AIDS, all these great questions of our time, they go out the window. It's a chance for you to concentrate on morality and on improving yourself as a person. You could take up meditation or write poetry. Nothing is entirely negative.'

'You come to visit me or just to piss me off?' Sam said. 'I've been attacked here, Geordie. Sustained a physical injury. Apart from that there's the trauma of the thing, the shame of curling up in the middle of the street clutching your balls, a million tourists taking snaps. I'm supposed to be the tough-guy detective. I've got a reputation to protect.'

'You should've just let the guy take his photographs. You could've offered to pose for him. He was probably a fan taking photographs for his scrapbook. Why'd you have to chase after him?'

Sam shook his head. 'I didn't think. There was something wrong about it. I followed my instinct.'

'You try to take the guy's camera off him, what d'you think he's gonna do?'

'I wanted an explanation,' Sam said.

'And you got a knee in the balls.'

'And I got you,' Sam said. 'So I don't have to worry about beating myself up. I can rely on you to come round at the first opportunity and make me feel good about it.'

'What did he look like?' Geordie asked.

'Big guy.'

'Of course.'

'He was dark, swarthy, lean, sharp clothes, bright socks, six foot two.'

'Fashion freak. You ever see him before?'

Sam shook his head. 'And I don't wanna see him again.'

'You want my opinion, you never will,' Geordie said. 'The guy wouldn't've attacked you if you hadn't gone after his camera. For some reason he wanted a photograph of you. Once he'd got that he was happy. Maybe thought you was a film-star.'

'Gene Hackman,' Sam said, 'when he was younger. People always say I look like him. The Popeye Doyle period.'

Geordie shifted Echo on his knee and gave her a slow wink. Sam had a sense of humour about most things but not his looks. He still believed he looked like that guy. Times in the past Geordie had tried to show him that Gene Hackman had a different-shaped face, that Gene Hackman was kinda good-looking in a sweet old-fashioned way. But Sam wouldn't have it. According to him Providence had sorted it that he and Gene shared the same DNA.

And this was a guy who had a face like a broken bag. OK, he had the kind eyes and he could make them twinkle, but in a face with so much old leather in it, what wouldn't twinkle? And he had a good voice, kind of mellow with some of the blues in it, and when you heard it it made you feel safer, closer to a world that only seemed possible when you were young. Come to think of it there was a whole load of things you could say about Sam Turner: he was a good friend, he could be brave, and was often the only guy around who had the right idea.

'JD thinks it's karma,' he said. 'The universe's way of telling you to slow down and take time off.'

'Me and the universe,' Sam said, 'we've been together a long time. Neither of us works like that. I think the universe needs something, I write a letter to the papers or I get Celia to write it and sign my name at the bottom.

The universe thinks I need a lift it'll send me a ticket to ride, Barcelona or a new Dylan CD. In cases of extreme deprivation I'll get both. This is how we work together. In our long association the universe has never found it necessary to send a photographer to knee me in the balls. The times I've been kneed in the balls it always turned out that the knee that did it belonged to a guy who was out of sync, someone with a universe of his own.'

'So what are you telling me?' Geordie asked. Echo was wriggling so he put her on the floor and she toddled over to the bathroom. Barney followed her like a minder.

'It feels like there's a connection with Katherine getting herself killed in Nottingham while I was there. I still can't believe that was a coincidence.'

'You heard about Plato's cave?'

'Is this more of JD's wisdom?'

'He mentioned it but I've talked to Marie about it, Janet, and I've got the book. It's an allegory so you have to imagine it.'

'This is just what I need,' Sam said. 'Better than Lucozade.'

'There's these people in a cave. They're chained up so they can only kneel down and face one way, towards one of the walls. Way back in the cave there's a fire burning and between the people in the chains and the fire there's a walkway, like a stage. You getting this?'

'I guess. Up to now.'

'OK. The next thing is that there are figures on this walkway and some of them are carrying things, like animals or different figures, and some of them are talking but not all of them. And because of the fire behind them the wall is lit up and the shadows of these people on the walkway are thrown on to the wall.'

'It's like a marionette show, right?'

'Right,' Geordie said. 'Except that the people who're

chained up have been there all their lives so they think it's reality. It's the only thing they've ever seen. They've seen shadows but because they can speak to each other they give the shadows names and don't think that they're naming shadows, they think they're giving names to reality. Also there's an echo in the cave and when one of the people behind them speaks they hear the echo and think it comes from one of the shadows.'

'Echo,' said Echo from the bathroom door.

'Not you, darlin',' Geordie said, laughing. 'I'm telling Sam a story.'

'Where we going with this?' he asked.

'Imagine what'll happen if some of these people are unchained. First of all they're gonna be stiff, right? Disoriented. They're looking into the light for one thing, so their eyes are gonna hurt. They've got stiff necks. They can walk around in the cave and everything is a new experience to them. They see these characters walking on the stage and they see the things they are carrying. But if we go up to them and tell them that everything they saw before was an illusion, and that now they've been unchained they can see things clearer, what d'you think they'll say?'

'It's your story, Geordie.'

'When they look at the people on the stage and the things they're carrying and we ask for their names, what'd happen would be they'd look back at the shadows and for a while they'd still think that the shadows were the reality. They'd believe that the shadows were more true than the objects.'

Sam took his foot off the table and placed it tentatively on the floor. 'This is the power of myth and allegory,' he said. 'It forces you to get up out of your chair.'

'I haven't finished yet,' Geordie told him. 'Hold your horses. Next thing is we take this guy, the one who has been chained up, and we drag him out of the cave into the sunlight.'

'There's only one of them now,' Sam said. 'When we started, there were six or seven of them. We didn't think they were all guys, we thought maybe some of them were women. Suddenly we've only got one guy. What happened to the rest?'

'This guy is a representative. He stands for all the rest.'

'The women as well. He stands for the women?'

'Yeah. Just listen, Sam. I'm gonna finish the story. If you keep interrupting it's gonna take longer than long. We could be here all night.'

'All right, get on with it. The representative guy's been dragged up into the sunlight.'

'OK, so what'll he see?'

'He won't see anything. He'll be blinded by the light. He'll think he's in Hell, he won't understand why we're torturing him like this.'

'Yeah. But after a while his eyes'll get accustomed to the light, he'll see outlines and then he'll see reality. This is what we have to do to escape from the shadow world of appearances.'

'Shrug off our chains?' Sam said. 'And strive for the sun? Sounds like a pop song, Moody Blues, someone like that.'

'This's Plato,' Geordie told him. 'Real philosophy.'

'Yeah, what do I know?' Sam said. 'Long time since I came out of the cave but I still see shadows everywhere. Some of the realities you meet in the sunlight aren't as convincing as the shadows back in the cave.'

Geordie scratched his head. 'It's got to be better, though, Sam. The more you see, the clearer it all becomes.'

Sam rested his chin on his hand. 'Trouble with Plato, guys like that, they give us the impression we can see for miles. The truth is that everything starts to get hazy after a few centimetres, and by the time we've seen half a metre we need a white stick or a guide dog.'

'This guy kicking you in the nuts,' Geordie said, 'it's changed the direction of your life. You're entering a deeply philosophical stage, could end up writing books like Wittgenstein, Bertrand Russell, one of those.'

Sam watched as Echo came toddling back to her father; Barney, as ever, bringing up the rear. 'He was wearing leather trousers,' Sam said.

'The guy who put you down?'

'Yeah. I ask you, what kind of guy wears leather trousers?'

'I've seen Britney Spears wear 'em. Geri Halliwell, Elizabeth Hurley. But you see what I mean?' Geordie said. 'Questions, questions. Your mind's working differently. You're a thinker. You've become pensive.'

13

He was a beautiful man, there was no doubt about it. Even at midnight, after sitting outside his house for four hours, Marilyn could see him as nothing less than beautiful. He stopped at a traffic light on the outskirts of York and Marilyn, in her mother's car, drew up alongside and glanced over at him.

Bathed in red from the stop light he had a long face with a prominent chin, deep brown eyes, and hair that was turning silver around his temples. On the passenger seat next to him was a brimmed hat in felt, possibly a trilby or a Borsalino. Marilyn didn't know the difference, maybe something to do with the width of the brim?

He pretended not to notice her but Marilyn smiled. She wasn't going to fall for that old trick. This was a man who had gazed down on a capacity audience in the theatre and picked her face from all the other hopefuls sitting there with their fingers crossed. A magician who had cast a spell on her, enchanted her so that she was his to command. He was a woman's man. A man who attracted women. She'd have to watch him.

After her ill-fated affair with Jeremy Paxman, Marilyn had tried to read a book by a feminist. Got more than halfway through before she gave up. All that freedom and independence had turned her limbs to stone. She liked the anecdotes, the way the writer pinpointed the wooden ways of men, how they refused to open their hearts in case there was nothing inside and how they were afraid of pain because they didn't understand how liberating it was.

She liked the way that the feminist writer talked about her childhood, her relationship with her mother and father and brothers. The way that everyone had loved her, wrapped her in a protective shroud of concern to keep life's dragons at bay, and how she had finally realized that without dragons life wasn't worth living.

But after that the book had dried up; the writer had urged her to rely on her own resources and spurn every outside attempt to control her behaviour. If you read that book all the way through and listened to what the woman was saying and tried to put it into practice you'd end up being like a man.

Ellen, Marilyn's mother, had read the book right through and, it was true what she said, she wasn't at all like a man. But Ellen's problem was different. First of all she was shallow. She didn't think things through. And secondly she had turned off her emotions some time in the past and was no longer capable of divorcing herself from reason.

If Ellen had love in her life, if another wizard would swoop down out of the ether and take her under his magic wings, she would see the world differently.

Marilyn had a silly and secret dream. It would never happen because she had found Danny Mann and they loved each other and the future was a star-studded sky. But before she found Danny, or rather before he chose her from all the other women, Marilyn had built herself a dreamland in which both Ellen and she had been courted by a father and son. The father had chosen Ellen to be his bride and the son had chosen Marilyn. The father and son were wealthy and they lived together in a large bungalow on the outskirts of York, close to the river. Neither of them needed to work but they had talented hands and made furniture and musical instruments from Brazilian hardwoods.

Before the double wedding the men worked hard building extensions to the bungalow while Marilyn and Ellen shopped for their dresses and added names to the guest-list. Many of the guests were well-known television celebrities, though they both agreed that Jeremy would not get an invite. Better to be safe than sorry, Ellen said, and Marilyn nodded her head silently. They had a tiff about Ruby Wax's invitation. Marilyn thought she'd be fun and ensure that the celebrations weren't too serious but Ellen said that Ruby was common and she didn't want her dominating the photographs.

There'd been a whole lot more to the dream ... the day that the children were born and the unending happiness they enjoyed together under a rainbow-coloured sky. But Marilyn let it fade as she pulled in behind her magician's car and followed him along the A64 to Leeds. Danny Mann was reality, not a dream. He had happened like reality happens, in a flash of light, a thunderbolt out of a clear sky which had sent the dream-world of the double wedding back where it belonged into the realm of fantasy.

The father and son would never have happened, Marilyn could see that now. She would have spent the rest of her days waiting for them to appear. Amazing how one could let oneself be convinced by a piece of whimsy, blot out the breathing, shimmering world of reality with an imaginary movie playing inside the cinema of the mind. A bungalow by the river, for goodness' sake. The way the weather was these last days, they'd have been flooded out. What would they have done then?

The magician followed the Leeds ring road and Marilyn followed the magician. Some lines from 'The Pied Piper' came into her head and for a moment she wondered what it was that had brought him to Leeds at the dead of night. An errand of mercy? Some clandestine meeting of Northern wizards? It really didn't matter. What was important was that she knew everything about him, his habits, his friends, the kind of food he liked and the ways in which he relaxed. A wife has to know these things because it is in these little ways that love is nurtured and grows to become an all-embracing passion.

Danny's car left the ring road and followed a tree-lined avenue, eventually coming to a halt outside a block of recently erected flats. The magician took the only available parking space and Marilyn sailed by and pulled into a side street where she wedged Ellen's car between a VW camper and a motorbike and sidecar.

Pulling her coat around her, she walked briskly back to the corner and was in time to see that Danny had crossed the road and was making his way up the hill, keeping close to the houses. He was carrying a holdall, long but not bulky, and wearing his trilby. At the midpoint, between streetlights, it was as if he became transparent. Marilyn had to blink her eyes to keep him in focus. The magician, transmuting his physical body into spirit and back again to the corporeality of the flesh. There had been men in Marilyn's life before but they had been more or less equals. The footballer had been better at his sport than she was and Jeremy Paxman was arguably a better journalist. In both cases Marilyn's personal qualities had more than compensated for whatever talent the man had possessed. Her dress-sense, for example, and her ability to plunge herself into the emotional depths of a problem.

But Danny Mann was something else. There was a superhuman quality to him which was beyond her experience. Just as he disappeared and reappeared between the streetlights, he was probably behind her as well as in front of her. Marilyn could be sure of nothing about this man, whether she was following him or he was following her. So inextricably was her destiny entwined with his that her intentions lost form and meaning without reference to the will of the magician.

And Danny's life force, his ability to sustain a relationship with the world, was likewise compromised without reference to Marilyn's intuitive nature. Their undying love for each other created a third being which was not Danny and was not Marilyn and was far more than the sum of their parts.

At the top of the hill he crossed the road in front of the Taps and headed down North Lane.

After a hundred metres he turned into a narrow alley which took him to the back of the houses. Marilyn hesitated. She stood at the entrance to the alley and dithered for a few seconds. She didn't know why. If she had been a man she would have plunged into the darkness after him without thinking. But something about her socialization as a woman held her back. This was Leeds, a big and alien city, and it was already well after midnight. As a woman alone she was vulnerable. And since Danny had disappeared into the dark passage she had felt alone. She would go into the alley after him when she had conquered her fear, but he would not be there.

Marilyn didn't know who would be in the passage. It was as if she was being tested. In a relationship with a man like Danny there would be many tests. Was she worthy? That was a question that only a god would ask. Marilyn had a woman's heart and questions of worthiness didn't enter into the equation. She was a woman in love and there was nothing else to say. She would live for him or she would die for him, whatever was required.

She felt her way forward. The glow from the street lamps was consumed within a few steps of the entrance.

When she glanced behind, before turning the corner into a black soup, it was like looking into the warm but commanding eyes of a lover. Go on, Marilyn, the eyes said. I'm right behind you. There is nothing to fear. Danny again, Danny's eyes behind her when she had seen him go on before. Danny all around her, Danny inside her.

There was a high brick wall which she could explore with her fingers. She could feel the groove between each brick where the cement and mortar had eroded. Beneath her feet were damp leaves, the odd twig and stone, and the enclosed space was permeated by an overpowering smell of cats. Up above was the huge bowl of the night sky, the Milky Way and a pale moon obscured by billowing clouds. The city's hum was low and constant but there were no other sounds, no footfalls from Danny, no humorous chuckle from his throat as he watched her cling to the wall, carefully placing one foot after another.

Marilyn thought that the passage would be filled with light. She thought that it would be transformed. She'd seen an advert on the television where an old man climbs the steps of a dark tenement, inserts his key into the lock and pushes open a heavy door into the dark interior of his apartment. He sighs, his lungs wheezing with the effort of the stairs, and then suddenly someone throws a switch and the lights come on. All of the old man's relatives and friends are there. There is a table heaving with food and drink and the children have balloons, the women are dressed in their finest clothes and the men are holding up glasses and smiling.

Marilyn was in two minds. Part of her thought that something like the TV advert would happen, that the magician would work his magic and obliterate the darkness with spiritual light. And another part of her knew that he was no longer there. That he had abandoned her to the darkness. The only light available was the light she could bring to the situation from within herself.

Danny had left her here so that she could grow. In a way it was an initiation, a rite of passage in a dark and dingy passage in the heart of Leeds in the middle of the night. If she could come through this she would be nearer to her love. There were certain steps to be taken before they could be together. This alley was one of those steps. It was a threshold, but one at which she would not flinch.

At the end of the passage she followed the wall. There were high, wooden garden gates separated by a few feet of continuing brick wall. She increased her pace now, sensing that she was returning the way she had come. A cat spat and scattered a pile of wet leaves and Marilyn barely flinched at the sound. The magician had given her something easy as a starter. He was leading her gently into his world of transformations. Damp leaves and darkness, a crumbling wall and a spitting cat. You'll have to do better than this, Danny, she said to herself as she turned the corner which led back to the lights of the street. I've been into your darkness and I wasn't afraid. Not much, anyway.

There was a man on the street, watching her emerge from the alley. He had his legs apart and he was swaying. Big man with a long, open raincoat with epaulettes, blue jeans and long greasy hair in a widow's peak.

'Y'lost' darlin'?' he said, moving his lips as if they were part of an engineering experiment.

Marilyn shook her head. She looked up and down North Lane, wondering where Danny was. She wasn't lost but she was confused. Could it be that this drunk was part of the test? Was the presence of this man with his flapping raincoat and slurred words an extension of the darkness of the passage? Or was the test over and this real life, real danger?

The man lurched over the road towards her. 'C'm'ere and give us a kiss,' he said, attempting to mask his desperation with levity. '"Only the lonely, dum, dum, dum, dummy do waa". Sing you a fucking song, girl.'

He fell forward, pinning her against a garden fence, his huge hands on her shoulders, his breath like the waste pipe from a brewery. Close up his eyes were bloodshot, the veins in the white desert around his pupils overflowing their ruptured banks and spewing tiny falls of crimson plasma.

Marilyn watched the man's foul mouth come down on hers, his wet lips and thick tongue. At the same time he wormed his hand inside her coat and kneaded her breast while his crotch was pushed up against her. He was so tall that Marilyn's head only reached halfway up his chest. She found his balls and squeezed and twisted with all her strength, feeling the man reel away from her, head snapped back in a gesture of pain and bewilderment.

He drew back his hand and clenched it into a fist, aiming at her head. In the fraction of a second that remained to her, Marilyn realized that if she allowed him to hit her she would be unable to stop him from raping her. She gave a final twist to his balls, pulling down and to the right while ducking away under his left arm.

And she ran. Within seconds she had put enough distance between her attacker and herself to take a look over her shoulder. He was slumped on the pavement, supported by his head and knees, and showed no intention of giving chase.

Marilyn kept running, up to the top of North Lane and past the Taps, back to the side street where she had parked the car. She flashed the remote to open the doors and locked them behind her, sitting trembling behind the steering wheel, her eyes nailed to the street corner in case the man had decided to come after her.

The clock on the dashboard ticked away for half an hour. Marilyn's breathing returned to normal. She rationalized what had happened. She'd had a close run-in with a drunk but she'd handled the situation well. If he hadn't had so much to drink she wouldn't have managed and he'd have dragged her back into the alley and raped her, maybe beaten or killed her. But that was speculation. What had happened was that the man had tried it on and she'd escaped and she was safe.

She no longer knew if she'd lost Danny Mann or if Danny had lost her. There had been the idea of some kind of initiation while she was in the passage, but surely that didn't include attempted rape?

Marilyn was confused. She reasoned that she was in shock. In which case she should have a cup of strong tea with sugar. Leeds, half-past one in the morning. Strong tea with sugar wasn't going to be easy.

She started the engine and drove along the main road, heading towards the centre of town. She stopped at a hot-dog stand and bought a plastic cup of boiling water with a tea-bag in it and four sugar lumps. She asked the vendor for a spoon and stirred until the water was black.

Back behind the wheel of Ellen's car she sipped the liquid without removing the tea-bag. When it was gone and she was no longer in shock Marilyn drove back to the block of flats where Danny had parked his car. It was still there, standing alone now, so that she could pull in behind it and wait for him.

She took a sprig of privet leaves from a hedge and wedged it under his windscreen wiper so that he'd know she was there. Then she settled down in the driver's seat of her mother's car and closed her eyes.

She dreamed about the attempted rapist twice, and

woke each time she failed to escape him. But she finally settled into a kinder dream, with the magician, Danny Mann, and a long blue room the colour of a clear sky. They didn't speak. They didn't need to. They loved each other more than words. Sometimes, more than once in the dream, Marilyn wasn't sure if they had or needed physical bodies.

When she awoke she was calm, composed. It was as if the blueness and the spiritual feelings that had accompanied the dream had permeated through to the very essence of her.

She didn't mind that she had slept through the night and it was now bright daylight, or that there were pedestrians at the entrance to the flats looking in at her. She didn't mind that Danny's car had gone and that he had abandoned her once more. This was one of the things she would have to learn to live with, at least in the short term. A small price to pay for the love of a good man, a special man, a man with extraordinary talents and abilities.

14

If he leaned forward into the bay and looked along North Lane he could see the Taps at the top of the street. Still closed, of course, no customers at this time of the morning. The early mist was giving way to thin sunshine and if he half-closed his eyes he could see undines and sylphs and salamanders, a host of elementals in the magical air dying into and out of each other, allowing themselves to be divvied up into kaleidoscopic patterns before the life-force rushed in to resurrect them.

He hadn't eaten since leaving home the night before but he had a small plastic bottle of sparkling spring water from which he took sips at hourly intervals. 'Chew your liquids and drink your food,' his mother used to tell him when he was small. Funny, the things you remembered. 'Beef tea,' she'd say at other times. 'Beef tea, Danny, will cure anything.'

When he thought back on his life the magician couldn't remember anyone who had been as constant as her. Not his father. Not uncles or aunts or cousins or school-friends. Not grandparents or agents or other performers. Not audiences. Not women. Most of the people he'd known were fickle, many of them competitors or actual traitors. There'd been illusions of warmth like small oases in memory; a Christmas Eve with his father, a football match with one of her boyfriends, a conjuror with a spotted hat and six doves and a brolly up his sleeve. But the final outcome was always rejection in one form or another. Only she was faithful until the end. Only she was magic.

The second phase of the trick had brought him to this house in Leeds. The couple who lived here were not important, the man was purely incidental, a nuisance. But the woman, the lady of the house, was an essential component in the presentation of the illusion. Her death would be a deception, it would create a false impression.

In the simplest of cheats a magician misleads his audience by showing them an apparently empty container. He goes to great lengths to convince his onlookers that there are no secret chambers or drawers or compartments within the container. And then, hey presto, he withdraws from within it a dove or a rabbit or a rag of silk. The trick is in the presentation of the container and this woman, like the last one, is part of that process. Her death creates an impression, it draws the eyes of those involved in a certain direction. It distracts them from the truth.

But Danny smiled to himself. Only a certain audience would see it that way. Another crowd would be transfixed by the power of the metaphor. They would witness transformation. They would feel themselves to be in the presence of magic. And as every magician knows, no audience is an accident. An audience is created, coaxed into being, moulded by the man with the secrets; the virtuoso on the stage.

The man, the husband, was already dead. The magician had had to dispose of him in the early hours of the morning. He had carried the body to a spare bedroom and dumped it on a bare mattress. He didn't want that smell in the same room as the woman, in their bedroom where Danny would have to go to work on her at the appointed time. The man was gone but that didn't stop Danny from checking on him throughout the night. He had been a small man in life and now he was a small cadaver. There was that distinctive mark on the bridge of his nose that indicated his use of spectacles. His hair was thinning and he had delicate wrists like a woman. He was a specialist in phenomenology at the University of Leeds and his profession and Danny's were not so distant in essence. They were both privy to the secrets of intuition.

Before rigor mortis occurred the magician had gone to the spare bedroom and laid the corpse out, placing its hands on its chest, closing its eyes and wiping away the clotted blood from its forehead. There was a sense of distant kinship about it, as though in life they had shared a slice of the same reality. If it had been possible to keep the man alive the magician thought they might have become friends or fellow researchers.

Black silk pyjamas, he was wearing. A red hand-embroidered motif over the breast pocket identified one of the man's heroes: *Heidegger*. Danny had tried to read philosophy, feeling that it might have bearing on his life, and from time to time he would try again. But the terminology and the way that philosophical writers tended to be trapped in the jargon of their subject always defeated him. He didn't understand them but he was glad that they were there. One didn't have to understand everything. Secrets were important.

Danny, like many other boys of his age, had discovered magic during the period of adolescence. While the child's physical body was being transformed into maturity and when the mind and soul was confined in doubt and insecurity there took place an unconscious search for power. Ultimate power is control and dominance over others and it is achieved by those who know the secret of transformation. As a twelve-year-old boy if you can change the Queen of Hearts into the Ace of Spades while all around look on amazed, it doesn't matter if your

History teacher thinks you are lumpen and the Science teacher refers to you as pond-life. What do they know, these people? They don't know secrets, they can't see the processes of alchemy taking hold of your being.

It would be possible to bring the man back to life.

Diamond Danny was under no illusions. He didn't have the kind of magic that could accomplish such a feat. He didn't know anyone who could do it, had never in his life met anyone who could do it. But what did that mean? It only meant that he hadn't come across that person. It didn't mean that that person didn't exist. Jesus of Nazareth had brought people back from the dead. He had even resurrected himself.

What happens once can happen again.

A secret learned can never be lost. Not completely.

Only a few ingredients were missing from the corpse on the mattress. His heart was not beating, his lungs were not expanding and contracting, floating their filigree wings in the oxygenated cave of his chest, and the gushing streams of dusky red and blue blood were sticky and congealed against their venous banks.

But a word can start or stop a heart. If the right word at the right time is known and uttered.

All magicians know these things.

Danny took a high-backed chair to the bay window and watched the waking day through the net curtains. He thought about the Indian Rope Trick. During British rule in India there were many reports of this trick. A fakir throws a rope into the air. Before the rope can fall to the ground it inexplicably becomes solid. An assistant to the fakir, a small boy, climbs the rope and when he gets to the top he disappears. The fakir then ascends the rope with a knife. When he gets to the top he also disappears. From up above, though they can see nothing, the crowd then hears the cries of the boy as he screams in pain.

Moments later the ground around the rope is littered with the amputated and bleeding limbs of the young boy. The fakir descends his rope, collects the parts of human anatomy and puts them into a basket. When he lifts the lid of the basket a second or two later the boy is in there, intact, smiling and ready to receive the pennies of the crowd.

Over the years there had been various explanations of how the trick was done. Some people had suggested that the fakir was a hypnotist and that the entire crowd in the dusty square were put into a trance. One elaborate explanation had suggested that the rope was thrown up into strands of woven hair dyed the same colour as the sky. That the bloody limbs were shaven monkey-limbs. Another that there were two boys, twins, and for the trick to succeed one of them had to be murdered.

Danny didn't know the answer. It wasn't one of his tricks, though he was connected with it through centuries of association with magic and the practices of magic. Well before the advent of Christ magicians like Diamond Danny Mann were confounding audiences with cones and balls in exactly the same way they do to this day. There was a red thread, a line connecting all those practitioners through the ages. It was like a family tree.

He watched the milkman float into the street on his electric cart. Delivering bottles of milk and cartons of cream and collecting empties and pursing his lips together like he was whistling but there was no audible sound. There were several rhythms to the man's physical work; the pulse and throb of his footsteps up and along the paths to the houses, the pace and tempo of his arms and shoulders as he sorted the empties into their various crates. In the back of his mind the magician could almost make out the lyrics of a work song, something to do with black people and slavery, though the milkman was white and the name on the side of his float was Dai Evans.

When he came up the path to the house the magician froze. Dai Evans was on the other side of the glass and the net curtain, perhaps a metre away. Danny could pick out the stray hairs in his eyebrows and a couple of tiny strands sticking out of his nostrils and ears. He placed one red-topped bottle on the step, semi-skimmed for health-conscious people. The couple who lived in the house and who didn't want to take too many chances with their cholesterol levels.

The milkman waited a moment, adopting the listening position, as if he could hear the steady rise and fall of the magician's respiratory system or the stillness of death on the mattress in the spare room. But there was nothing tangible or audible for the man to connect with, just an uneasy feeling, the sense that all was not right with the world. Too much for a milkman to handle in the early morning. He shrugged his shoulders and continued with his round.

The magician didn't move. He sat like a Buddha, naked behind the window, and watched his own body and his own reactions to everything that happened in his immediate environment. The milk reminded him of his mother and how she hadn't been able to eat at the end. It had begun with her avoiding olives or anything spicy. She'd stopped eating meat, saying that it was indigestible, then fish and beans. For the last couple of months she'd eat only a couple of spoons of cauliflower cheese, a glass of milk, a poached egg and pasta alphabet shapes. Her body had gradually lost the power to transmute food to flesh and bone, to transform protein and vitamins and minerals into consciousness. This would happen to Danny as well; one day, like everyone else, he would lose his individual magic and become part of the wider magic of the cosmos. He would become food for worms, contribute selflessly to the regeneration of the earth.

But not yet. In the present there was work to be done. Ego work. There were runes to be rhymed and charms to be chanted. There were thunderbolts to be fashioned and hurled at the sun and there was a dreadful noise of water in his ears and sights of ugly death within his eyes.

Danny felt a smile crease his face. Outside the window the rain was coming down again. In Nottingham there had been a group of creationists outside the theatre, their placards predicting the end of the world. Well, anything was possible. But Danny believed that the flood in Genesis was a homily, a local flood like any other, and the 'world' that was flooded merely the world that was known to Noah.

When the metallic-coloured Montego entered the street the magician got to his feet. He watched as Sam Turner left the car and walked tentatively up the path of the house opposite, number thirty-seven, where Danny Mann, alias Mr Bonner (his mother's maiden name), had arranged to meet him. A good-looking man in a tracksuit and trainers answered the door and stood with his hands on his hips. He listened to Turner then shook his head.

Turner fished in his pocket and brought out a scrap of paper. He said something to the owner of the house and the other man shook his head again. Danny could almost hear his words. *There's no Bonner lives here. No, I don't know anyone of that name. Not in this street.*

The good-looking man closed the door and Sam Turner returned to his car. He stood by the side of it in the rain and looked up and down the street, unable or unwilling to admit that his journey had been in vain.

He unlocked the driver's door of the Montego and then locked it again. He walked along the street, tentatively, as though his trousers were too tight for him, though they looked like a perfect fit. He crossed over, rang the bell of house number seventy-three to make sure he hadn't become aphasic. No one answered his ring. Back at his car he stopped a young black woman with an umbrella and must have asked her if she knew of anyone called Bonner. He showed her his scrap of paper with the name and address scribbled on it. But it wasn't his lucky day.

When Sam Turner got back into his car and drove away Danny went upstairs and entered the woman's bedroom. She was tied to the bed as he had left her. The gag, which consisted of her own face-flannel and two-inch-wide masking tape, gave her an eastern appearance, as if she was wearing a yashmak, just the eyes staring out at the world.

Black silk pyjamas like the man, but without the *Heidegger* crest. In place of it she had embroidered the words *Hi, Guys*. Her hair was cut short and brushed forward, one or two strands of grey in there, but her face was unlined apart from the crow's feet around her eyes. Danny might have ended up with a woman like her if he'd managed to maintain any of his relationships. If everything hadn't gone wrong in his life at such an early age. It didn't matter now, of course, it was just something to think about.

There had been a student of Bakhtin in his group at university; she was fascinated by dialogical and monological language, the former characterized by a person speaking towards at least one other person in response or anticipation with living language. Dead language was monological like that of the medieval church or any religious state that admits of the existence of no other voice. They had been an item for a while and Danny had discussed Bakhtin's theories with her, agreeing that poetry was monologic and the novel dialogic. But eventually she had walked off hand in hand with a poststructuralist critic who couldn't tell the difference between a novel and the Highway Code.

Nicole Day was no longer terrified. She was frightened of the man but that initial terror had been partially replaced by rage. When he'd taken Rolf away she'd listened to the sounds coming from the spare bedroom and had expected the man to come back and rape her. But that had been hours ago. Her hands and feet had long since gone numb from the tight rope that bound them. For a while she had thought she would choke to death, that she would swallow the flannel that the man had stuffed into her mouth. But she was still alive, alive and resolved.

At the first opportunity she would tear at his eyes. If he gave her one moment of freedom she would hurl all of her strength at him. Claw her way to his obscene balls, hanging there like a sack of old coins. His silence, the way he came to the door of her room from time to time and hovered there in the shadows, was calculated to undermine her. He knew that if he did nothing, said nothing, but kept her tied and confined and in ignorance of what had happened to Rolf she would go to pieces. He thought that if he wore her down like this then she'd be pliable when the time came for him to assault her.

When the time came! My God, the time had been here all night. Nicole had been assaulted over and over again simply by having this naked maniac in her house. Rolf was assaulted when the man slapped him across the head with that huge dagger.

But she also knew that if she was going to survive this intrusion into her house she would have to be clever. The man was clearly mad. She would need to talk to him, to win him over, to show him understanding. She would have to pretend to be his friend, even his lover.

104

She spoke to him through the flannel and the masking tape. She said, 'Hello, I wondered when you would come back.'

The words didn't get through the obstructions in and around her mouth. She heard the sounds that resulted, what amounted to a long modulated moan. 'I'm sorry,' she said. 'Please take this thing out of my mouth so we can talk properly.'

He shook his head, an arrogant smile around his lips. He couldn't understand what she was saying. 'Don't worry,' he said. 'I'm not going to hurt you.' He had the heavy dagger with him, hanging from his right hand. So long that the tip of it brushed the floor.

He took another step towards her. 'Remember Sam Turner?' he asked. 'The detective? He was here a moment ago. Over the street.'

Nicole wanted to cry. 'Sam? Here?' Why would Sam be here? What had this man got to do with Sam Turner? She hadn't seen Sam in years, hadn't thought about him for months. She couldn't imagine any way in which Sam Turner could be mixed up with this madman.

Sam had been a mess and he'd treated her badly towards the end of their relationship. His drinking and his lack of self-esteem had led him to an attitude of contempt for almost everyone else in the world, and being his woman had meant that she was in the front line of his derision and loathing.

But he'd let her go. When the crunch had come and he'd eventually transformed her love to a cynical despair, he hadn't gone into battle. He'd fought against it for an instant and then shaken his head, walked away. Left her with her freedom. Surely he hadn't come back after all these years to torture her like this, to leave her in the hands of a deranged nutcase with an antique bayonet?

Nicole felt a whispering breeze pass over her forehead.

She was calm. The man with the weapon was outside of her. Perhaps he was close, in the same room, or perhaps he was a figment of her imagination, a dream figure. Either way it didn't matter. Sam Turner may be in the street or not, he might have been here to save her or to destroy her. He was in the past. Something, someone, she had known. Another of those relationships that had held eternal promise but had resulted only in tears.

Even her husband, Rolf, with his phenomenological theories, seemed part of another and distant universe. What seemed real was an image from her childhood, a long and empty beach, her mother huddled in a deckchair and her father downwind arcing a Frisbee across the painted sky towards her.

The picture was like an early video. The colours were not quite true but every detail was known and recorded for posterity. It was something that had already happened and could not be undone. Her mother was reading a medical dictionary, trying to discover if heliotherapy would cure her dermatitis. She was wearing a short flowered skirt with a bikini top and dark glasses.

Her father was wearing long shorts and open sandals with knee-length brown socks. He'd grown a paunch and accentuated it by wearing his short-sleeved shirt tucked into the elastic top of the shorts. He was still handsome, though. Dashing with his green eyes and dark moustache.

The Frisbee curved around the sun. It rose and disappeared from sight for a moment before falling, looking for all the world as if it would not reach her. Nicole took a step towards it and at the last moment saw that its trajectory would bring it down in front of her. She dived with her arms outstretched, saw the missile come towards her and grasped it with both hands. Her father laughed and cheered and her mother looked up from her book of miracle cures.

The man with the weapon took Rolf's pillow and placed it over her face and chest. She tried to shake it off but he held it firm. Nicole didn't want to scuffle. He wasn't pushing down on it. She could still breathe perfectly well.

She fought for the memory. She got to her feet and brushed the sand from her knees. Replaced the plastic sandal that had come off when she caught the Frisbee and fell. She brushed the hair from her eyes. Her hair was long that year, so she was eleven because she had it cut short for her twelfth birthday. She took the Frisbee and flicked it towards her father, watched it rise away from her, somehow capturing the air and using it to propel itself in the perfect arc that would take it to his hands.

The sheer flawlessness of its flight took her breath. The beauty of it was like a pain in her heart.

Diamond Danny Mann stood back. He cleaned the bayonet on a corner of the sheet. A flash vision of a barber's pole. *Figaro, Figaro* . . . Rossini's control of the strings. The deep startled hush of the audience. His mother's voice, frail, distant: 'Danny? Danny, have you run my bath?'

He untied the woman's hands and feet and collected the rope. There would be odd fibres left behind and some overworked and ambitious genius in the forensic lab would eventually discover that the rope was purchased from a branch of Woolworth's sometime during the last five years. But they'd have nothing else. Nothing to connect him to the scene. And their eyes would be averted anyway; the circumstantial evidence and his appearance in the street at the exact time of the killing would focus their attention on Sam Turner.

In the bathroom he washed himself and replaced his clothes. He blocked the overflow on the bath and the hand-basin and left both taps running. In the kitchen downstairs he blocked the sink and watched for a moment as the water splashed into it.

Symmetry again. Life begins in a womb, the developing foetus swims in a bath of amniotic fluid, it knows only liquid and is swept along, unknowingly, towards the hard realities of life. How fitting, then, how indescribably beautiful, that these beginnings should find their echo in death. Symmetry had informed Danny's own life and it seemed natural to him to want to share its magic with others.

He left by the back door and after a short walk was safely sitting behind the steering wheel of his car clutching a twig of privet that someone had tucked under his windscreen wiper. He glanced at the seatbelt on the passenger side and remembered that he still had to get it fixed. He removed the two pairs of latex gloves from his hands and put them into a paper bag with the rope. He started the car and drove along the A64 to York.

Jody would be waiting for him in his empty house. Lying still and cold and naked in the double bed. His darling Jody, his life companion since the departure of his mother.

His compensation was the knowledge of a job well done. And that was how it should be. He was, after all, a professional magician. Danny wondered if he should worry about the twig of privet. But for some reason it didn't seem threatening.

15

Sam got to the office a little before ten in the morning. Geordie was talking to Janet on the telephone. Barney, Geordie's dog, got up from his sprawl on the floor and wagged around Sam's legs for a minute. Sam patted him, tickled his ears. He walked over to his desk and sat in the swivel chair. He thumbed through the morning post, putting most of the circulars and envelopes into his waste bin without opening them.

At the end of the office, in the dark section away from the windows, there was a sink and a draining board, the makings for tea and coffee and a single power point with a kettle attached. Sam filled the kettle and switched it on. He spooned four measures of ground Italian coffee into a small cafetière and fished a carton of milk from the smallest fridge in the world. While he waited for the water to boil he found the first Biograph CD and played 'Lay Down Your Weary Tune' so loud that the cups rattled.

'Just a minute,' Geordie said into the mouthpiece of the phone. He cupped his hand over it and shouted at Sam, 'It's too loud.'

Sam said, 'I need comfort.'

'I'll have to go,' Geordie shouted down the telephone to Janet. 'The boss's having a nervous breakdown. He thinks it's 1963.'

Sam watched the kettle. The man and his guitar somehow contrived to evoke bagpipes, a Highland silhouette of a mountain with a stag, though there was nothing in the lyric to suggest either. Geordie sat quietly for the whole four minutes of it and then came over to turn down the sound at the opening bars of 'Subterranean Homesick Blues'.

'What's up?' he asked.

'I was set up,' Sam told him. 'The guy in Leeds, the address he gave me nobody had heard of him. Some kind of practical joke. You want coffee?'

'Coffee'd be good. You could've written down the wrong number.'

'I don't do wrong numbers. He said it was thirty-seven, but the guy there'd never heard of a Bonner. And I tried seventy-three, make sure I hadn't written it backwards. No reply.'

'Could've been *twenty*-seven,' Geordie said.

'It wasn't, it was thirty-seven, I remember the guy saying it on the phone.'

'So why'd you try seventy-three?'

Sam eyeballed him. 'Just in case.'

'Could've been any house in the street when you think about it,' Geordie said. 'Might even've been the wrong street. Are you sure it was Leeds?'

'Fuck off, Geordie. I've just driven to Leeds and back, wasted half the day for nothing.' He waited until the kettle stopped singing and wetted the grains in the bottom of the cafetière. 'Where is everyone, anyway? I expect to come back to a busy office and there's just a dog here and you talking to your wife on the phone.'

'Celia's helping Marie move out of her house. They're putting everything upstairs and leaving sandbags round the doors. The river's flooding tonight.'

Sam filled the cafetière with hot water, fitted the plunger over the top.

'You know what a flood is?' Geordie asked.

'Yeah, it's when I get my canoe out.'

'Metaphorically,' Geordie said. 'What it means to us?'

'I don't know what I'd do without you, Geordie. Slack times, like we're in the middle of just now, I'd probably be out hustling for business, trying to make something of my life. Know what I mean? But with you around, I don't have to worry about stuff like that. I can talk philosophy instead.'

'It's not philosophy,' Geordie said. 'It's a question.'

'And the answer is?'

'A flood is chaos, that's what it means to us. When the water breaks its banks it's the same as if all the rules of society are suddenly breached.'

'Breached?'

'Yeah, broken. Or if you're flooded by someone's passions or emotions you want to leg it, get as far away as possible. Because they're out of control, like the river. Then there's all that stuff about Noah's Ark, God destroying the earth to punish us for our sins.'

'That's two different things,' Sam said.

'How come?'

'In the first place you're saying the flood is chaos or anarchy, everything out of control. But once you bring God into the equation there's no chaos involved. He's controlling the thing. He's decided to flood the earth and save Noah and all the animals and get rid of the rest of the fat cats who've fucked up, eaten all the apples, whatever. It's not chaos, it's divinely controlled genocide. If God's in control of the flood, He's worked it out to the last centimetre.' He poured the coffee into cups and handed one to Geordie.

Geordie took a sip. Sam watched the coating of milk form on the bottom of his moustache and reminded himself never to grow one. Geordie said, 'OK, they're different things. Whatever, Marie is really pissed about it. She thought it'd be wonderful living next to the river.

Now the river's moving in with her, taking over the ground floor. Looks really nice in the spring, the sun shining and all those little swirls and eddies going past the house, but it's not the same when it's covering your three-piece suite and slopping about in your cooker.'

'Eddies?'

'Yeah, something wrong with that? Eddy, it's a contrary motion in a stream.'

'Knew a bloke called Eddy once. He sold fish and chips in Manchester.'

'I'm not listening, Sam. If there's a sucker in this, it's you wearing the cap.'

Sam laughed. 'Maybe I should go give them a hand,' he said. 'Celia won't be a lot of help moving the big stuff upstairs.'

'Marie's got JD there as well.'

'I'll go then,' Sam said. 'JD lifting furniture, somebody could get killed. You OK to hold the fort here?'

Geordie looked around the office. 'Me and Barney'll cope. If it stays this busy we'll be doing laps in the pools of our own sweat.' He gave it teeth to prove he understood irony.

Sam walked to Marie's house. No rain, the sky was clear, but he could hear the river chafing and snarling as he got closer. It was raining up in the hills and on the moors and as the waters ran off into the main stream the ancient banks were too narrow to contain them. Lines of sightseers watched the broiling mass of black water as it hurtled past, tourists and voyeurs for the main part. Local householders were too busy packing their belongings to stand and watch the growing threat to their homes.

Sam stood close to the bank. The rushing water had risen ten feet in as many days and was only inches away from his feet. Broken branches and debris were whipping past at speed and some guys were posing their wives and girlfriends in front of the flow, taking photographs so they'd be able to show their kids and grandchildren. It was like life itself, going past so fast you couldn't take it all in. You focused on one segment of it, something there that looked like a bed, and you watched it ducking and diving as it came towards you and again as it came close and disappeared downstream and you were never sure exactly what it was or where it had come from.

Do people throw old beds into rivers? Or did the river reach out and pluck it from somebody's bedroom as it went past? But it was gone now, leaving no trace behind, and Sam couldn't be sure that it was a bed anyway. Could've been anything or nothing. Something he invented.

The river was rushing away. Trying its best not to get stuck in the town. Once it breached its banks it wouldn't be a river anymore. It would be an alien in the city, an agent of misery and destruction. Once it lost its form and its identity it would wreak havoc, turn the relatively civilized and settled lives of the local population into a whirlpool of misery.

Marie and JD were having a tea break, sitting in the bay window of Marie's house looking out at the raging river. Celia was having a tea break as well, but in her normal manner, pottering around, collecting small ornaments and books and taking them upstairs then coming back for another sip from her cup.

'Are you another pair of hands?' she asked Sam. 'Or a tourist?'

'I'll help with the heavy stuff,' he said.

JD took a notebook from his pocket and scribbled in it. 'Good line,' he said. 'I can use it in the current novel. Post-modern ring to it. A character who helps with the heavy stuff or sees himself as helping with the heavy stuff.

Someone who gets involved with other people's emotions or traumas. Inflated ego.'

'Tell you what,' Sam said, 'I'll go out and come back in a couple of minutes. Try to make a different entrance.'

'No, it's a good line,' JD insisted, looking down at his notebook. 'I mean it. It was worth coming out for.' JD wrote and published crime novels and from time to time worked with the Sam Turner Detective Agency, ostensibly for research purposes, though he also got a kick out of it if he could avoid violent confrontations. And he needed the money. When he wasn't doing either of those things he was a drummer in a country blues band called Fried (not Freud) and the Behaviourists and he was a voracious dope smoker. He was also ridiculously in love with Marie, probably more so since she had made it clear to him that he wasn't an item on her emotional agenda. They had once had a brief affair but in recent years Marie found her emotional and sexual fulfilment elsewhere. She used JD when she had to move furniture or if she needed a driver.

JD said if he couldn't have Marie, he didn't need emotional or sexual fulfilment because he was an artist and good at subjugating. But there were people who said he didn't remember what he got up to when he was strung out on loud country blues and electric feedback and the devil weed was pumping through his brain. Whatever it was it didn't deter the handful of painted and bejewelled groupies who turned out when the band were strutting their stuff.

Celia padded through from Marie's kitchen and put a mug of hot coffee in Sam's hand. She was a small woman. She wore a ring with a pearl on her middle finger, a gold band with two tiny diamonds on her index finger, and on her ring finger she had a signet ring on the second joint and a bed of assorted jewels in a heart on the third joint.

The little finger was bare, poor thing. Celia's hair had been thinning rapidly over the past months but she still used a bottle of red dye on it every few weeks. Her neck was festooned with a lightly billowing silk scarf to hide the wrinkles and she wore tight velvet trousers. Didn't look the type to give up without a fight.

'So, what's to do?' Sam asked.

'Finish your coffee first,' Marie told him. 'Maybe you and JD could get the fridge upstairs? The cooker? And the kitchen table if it'll go. Me and Celia'll carry on shifting the silver and the Modiglianis.' She drew the back of her hand over her forehead. 'Then there's the antique Spode and my collection of Degas bronzes.'

Sam grinned and JD laughed as though Billy Connolly had done a fart impression. Nearly fell off his chair.

They humped the fridge up the stairs, one step at a time. Looked incongruous sitting there next to Marie's bed, like a fish in the desert. JD wiped his brow with a red handkerchief. 'What're you writing?' Sam asked.

'Another novel. About halfway through. I'm past the part where I decide whether to go on or give up.'

'About cops and robbers?'

'On the surface, yes. At the heart it's about exile. About being separated from the thing that feeds you, gives meaning to your life.'

'You've talked about that before, in other books.'

'I've skirted round it once or twice. In this book it's the main theme.' He laughed. 'Don't know who it was, some writer or other, said we all rewrite the same book over and over again. A writer usually only has one or two things to say and he or she goes on saying it until somebody stops them. The best writers find a new way of saying it with every book.'

'There's nothing new in the world,' Sam said. 'Only new ways of seeing the same old things.'

JD nodded agreement. 'Yeah,' he said. 'Something like that. Shall we get the cooker?'

One step at a time again, JD above the cooker and Sam lifting from below, remembering all the rules about taking the weight on his legs rather than his back. They left it standing next to the fridge.

'Exile is when you're away from home,' Sam said. 'When you're not allowed to go back. Used to be a kind of punishment.'

'Still is in different countries,' JD said. 'To be banished. That's how America got started, Australia. People the state didn't want around, shipped them overseas.'

'This an historical novel you're writing?'

'No. I'm using exile as a metaphor. It's about the places we're not allowed to go or the places we don't allow ourselves to visit.'

'Physical places? Geographic places?'

'Sometimes. Places can be in the mind too. We're often exiled from ourselves, from our own experiences, our own memories.'

Sam took a couple of steps over to the window and looked out at the river. 'I've been thinking about that,' he said. 'When I heard about Katherine the other day. Seems unreal, somehow, that we were married, spent all that time together, intimate time. It's as if I wasn't there, or I dreamed it or read about it in a book. Like it was somebody else's experience.'

'You were a drunk, Sam. You were exiled by definition. The alcohol kept you away from everything, yourself, your pain.'

Sam shook his head. 'It didn't, though. Not really. I always thought it would help, that the next drink would solve something, some longing, that it would insulate me from life. But it never did. It made every day harder to cope with, harder to bear. I can honestly say that I never had a drink that solved a problem.'

'You're an outsider anyway,' JD told him. 'A natural exile. That's why you're a private eye and not a cop. You never opt to accept the defaults. It's a custom installation every time for you, even if you don't understand the jargon. It's almost as if you're frightened of convention.'

'Yeah,' Sam said in a low voice. 'Convention makes me shiver. I've seen what it does to people.'

'I read about an old Pawnee warrior,' JD said. 'Guy called Small Ankles. Somewhere around the end of the nineteenth century he was already an old man and it was near the time of the tribe's creation ceremony. Small Ankles told his son the ceremony would be hard to perform because there weren't many wolves around any more. The wolf was a central character in their creation myth. In this ceremony the Indians got together and practised "historic breathing", they inhaled the past and tried to show how it was contained in the present, in the now. And Small Ankles and the other old men of the village were worried that if they lost the ceremony they'd also lose the past. They'd be undefined, broken. If they didn't have a past or access to their past they wouldn't be able to continue. Later, when Small Ankles had gone to his ancestors and the tribe had been moved to a reservation, his son would tell this story, about how his father had seen the demise of the Indian as it became more and more impossible for him to inhale his past.'

Sam looked at JD. 'Are you trying to tell me something?'

'I tell stories,' JD said. 'That's what I do.'

The kitchen table wouldn't go up the stairs. Marie scratched her head but that didn't make any difference. 'It's going to get ruined,' she said.

'What we could do,' JD said, 'is plastic bags around the

legs. Tie them at the top to keep the water out.' Sam looked at him for nearly a minute, realized why the guy couldn't be anything else but a writer.

'Give me a hand,' he said. JD followed him out into Marie's yard and together they brought in about forty concrete paving slabs. They made four columns with the slabs and lifted the table into position, one leg on each column. The top of the table was only a couple of inches short of the ceiling. Looked like an abortive attempt to reconstruct a Greek temple.

'Clever boy,' Celia said to Sam.

'I carried most of the slabs,' JD told her.

Angeles was managing director and majority shareholder in the soft drinks business which had been founded by her father. It was a demanding job, not made easier by her blindness, but one for which she had been groomed since her earliest childhood. It took her out of the house every day of the week and committed her to a couple of evenings as well.

Sam arrived at her front door shortly after dark. Her lips were tight and the skin of her face was pale, almost transparent around her cheekbones and under her eyes.

'Something wrong?' he asked.

She flashed him a smile. 'Do I look that bad?'

'No, I just thought . . .'

'It's OK. A hard day. Trying to get everything ready for the Christmas rush. Planning with a couple of line managers who don't believe in planning. Sometimes I wonder if it's worth it.'

She splashed a dollop of Talisker into a cut-glass tumbler and added a measure of Highland spring water. She took a sip and closed her eyes, swivelled her head around to ease the tension in her neck. She took another glass from the sideboard, splashed a dollop of Highland spring water into it and topped it up with more Highland spring water, handed it to Sam who poured it down his throat. He reached for the bottle and poured himself another one. He was a hard-drinking man.

Angeles had slipped down into a cocoon of a chair, lying back on the base of her spine, her legs spread in front of her. One of her shoes had come off but she didn't bother to retrieve it. Sam knelt and removed the other shoe. He put her feet on his lap and massaged them alternately, kneading the soles, wondering at the tiny perfection of them.

'You and me,' he said. 'It's gone quiet.'

She sipped from her drink and looked over the rim of the glass. 'Yes, I know. Why is that?'

'You're not here. Most of the time we're together you're somewhere inside your head. Feels like you've met someone else.'

Angeles sat up. 'No,' she said. She didn't shout but her voice went into a higher octave. 'I wouldn't do that, Sam.'

'You wouldn't meet someone else?'

'Not without telling you. You'd be the first to know.' She sounded hurt, misunderstood. Sam recognized the territory. An intimate moment metamorphosed into injury and reproach in less time than it takes to sing a love song.

He gave her her feet back. 'I'm sorry,' he said. But given the same circumstances he'd play it exactly the same again. If there was any chance, and in Sam's experience there was always a chance, that she was seeing someone else, he wanted it out in the open. What made it harder was the double-bind: that if she wasn't seeing someone already, his lack of trust and his general insecurity about relationships could easily push her to look for someone with more sensitivity and understanding.

'Why do you think that?' she asked.

He shrugged. 'The distance,' he said. 'The spaces between us.'

'You're often distant yourself, Sam. Preoccupied. But I don't think you've found somebody else. I try to work out what's dragging at you, see how the job is making demands on you. A person can only be spread so thin. When you're not there for me I hold my breath and tell myself to be patient. Tell myself you'll be back when you can make the space.'

'I was out of order,' he told her. 'If you're not seeing some other guy I'm the happiest man alive. I'll take you dancing, whatever you want. I'll try to like Robbie Williams.'

She pushed him and he fell over backwards, spilling water on his shirt.

'Shit.'

'Are you all right?' she asked.

Sam got back on his knees. 'No. I'm wet.'

'As in drip?' she asked. 'Or d'you mean like feeble?'

Angeles had gone upstairs and he could hear her running the bath water. He loaded used cups and glasses on a tray and carried it through to the kitchen. He put the crockery in the dishwasher and wondered for a moment if he should take it out again and wash it in the sink. He could see why she needed one, being blind. It must save some angst if you couldn't see, knowing that things weren't piling up on the draining board.

But Sam believed in washing up. It was one of those things; he didn't even know that he believed in washing up until he discovered dishwashers everywhere. Seemed like everybody had one these days. Old-age pensioners living by themselves, with only a bowl and a spoon and a cup with *Mother* on it, had dishwashers. Families had them. Couples.

That's what you did these days. Everybody was too busy to wash up. Unless you were poor; then you had plenty of time.

He flicked the remote towards the TV, caught the late news. But his mind was not focused. It had been a long day and he was coasting in neutral, letting his brain wander among images that touched his life. His useless journey that morning, Katherine being found murdered in Nottingham, Angeles upstairs getting into the bath, a crazy guy kicking him in the balls, the river rising. The voice on the television was talking about the economy, how the government needed to cut the interest rate.

Sam switched the lights out, left one lamp lit in the sitting room. He slumped on the couch and watched the flickering images on the box, waiting until Angeles had finished in the bathroom. A coach carrying a party of school children had run off the road in northern Spain, tumbled into a ravine. A rescue party were bringing small broken bodies back up to the road and covering them with blankets. The driver had thrown himself clear and was sitting in the back of an ambulance with his head in his hands.

Sam frowned. He flexed his shoulders and sat up, leaning forward to inspect the new image on the screen. It was the public house, the Taps. Top of North Lane in Headingley, the very place he'd been that morning.

The voice-over was saying: 'Police were called to a house in the Headingley district of Leeds tonight where the bodies of a man and a woman are believed to have been discovered. Neighbours were alerted when they noticed water flooding out of the house.' The image cut to a close-up of the face of a middle-aged man with a bald head. He looked into the camera and said, 'There was water seeping under the front door. It was as if the house was full of water and it was coming down the step and running into the road.'

Another shot of the Taps and then the camera swung into North Lane. Sam saw the house he had been to that morning and across the road, almost directly opposite, there was the familiar yellow scene-of-crime tape that the police used to isolate the area they wanted to keep uncontaminated for forensic investigation.

Sam was on his feet. The reporter on the spot was signing off. He said, 'The police are treating the deaths as suspicious and just a few minutes ago a spokesman said that it was obvious as soon as the bodies were discovered that a horrific crime had been committed. The names of the deceased will not be released until the next of kin has been notified.'

He looked at the screen again, blinked as the image shifted back to the studio. The newscaster was smiling and announcing that a celebrity couple – cut to a photograph of the woman in a scanty dress; a man with blond hair, his arm protectively around her waist – had decided to separate in order to devote more time to their respective careers.

Sam picked up the remote and hit the kill button. He went to the phone and keyed the number pad.

'Yeah?' Geordie's voice said in his ear.

'Did you see the news?'

'I'm still watching. Trying to. I mean, I was watching it and then the phone rang. Now I'm on the phone. The news is history.'

'The house in Leeds. The bodies, you catch that?'

'Yeah. Sounds nasty.'

'Geordie, that's where I was this morning. The same street.'

Silence.

'You still there?'

'Yeah, I'm still here. The house? You mean you went to the same house?'

'No. The address I had was across the road, opposite the house with the bodies.'

'It could be a coincidence, Sam. No need to panic.'

'OK, let's look at it. Last week I was in Nottingham and Katherine was killed. The cops pulled me in and I had to lie to get out of it. Now this Bonner guy rings and asks me to meet him in Leeds. I go to the house and the same day a couple of bodies turn up over the road. People know I was there. The guy in the house. I went to another house, to make sure I hadn't got the wrong address. My car was parked in the street.'

'But why would they think of you, Sam? We don't even know who these people are, the dead guy and the woman.'

'That's why I'm ringing. Can you find out?'

'How do I do that? It's the middle of the night.'

'Drive out there. Walk along the street. Ask the neighbours.'

'At midnight?'

'Nobody'll be sleeping, Geordie. The place will be buzzing with reporters. Just hang around and listen to what they're saying. When you find out ring me at home.'

'You sound worried, Sam.'

'I need to know the score. If the bodies belong to people I know, how long will it be before the cops come knocking on my door again?'

'You think it's a set-up?'

'I think I need to be careful. I'll wait for your call.'

'OK, I'm on my way. But here's a thought for you.'

'I've got enough thoughts, Geordie.'

'Who do you know who lives in Headingley?'

There was a gentle click as Geordie put the phone down at the other end of the line.

Sam went upstairs and walked into the bathroom. Angeles was lying in the bath, her skin glistening in the rising steam from the water.

'You looking for me?' she asked.

'Listen, something's come up. I have to go out.'

'Oh, Sam, I thought you were staying. What is it? Can't it wait?'

'I'll explain later,' he told her. 'Got to get moving.'

He kissed her on the lips and she ran a damp hand over his head. He closed the bathroom door behind him and shook his head. 'Who're you gonna miss the most?' he asked himself as he ran down the stairs.

Back at his own house, Sam thought about Geordie's question. He didn't know anyone in Headingley. He knew a couple of pubs there, or he used to know them in the old days. Places he'd gone looking for a good time but only scored a length of oblivion. He'd once woken up on the floor of a flat in Headingley. No one around but there was a three-legged cat, student posters on the walls and some naïve artist had painted stars on the ceiling.

And way back in the mists of time, when Elvis was still alive, there'd been a house in Headingley with a guy who did embroidery.

There was such a thing as coincidence, of course, everyone knew that. It was statistically possible that Mr Bonner had given him the wrong address in North Lane and asked him to go there at the same time as a murder was committed. The two things could be unrelated. But Sam didn't believe that. When you'd worked the streets for as long as he had worked them you were suspicious of coincidence. It could get you into trouble. Better to dispense with it as a theory altogether. Concentrate instead on the near certainty that if two things happened simultaneously it was more than likely that someone was orchestrating them.

Maybe the guy at number thirty-seven was Bonner after all? Or he was a guy who called himself Bonner when he was setting someone up on the phone? Sam tried to recall him, think if he'd seen the guy before. He'd worn a track-suit and trainers. And he was good-looking in that modern way; his head and face like a successful product of Hitler's experiments in genetic engineering while his mind proved that the concept was a fallacy. Couldn't have been him, he'd have had to read from a script. When he'd opened the door and Sam had enquired, 'Mr Bonner?' the guy had had to think about it.

It was interesting to speculate, a possible area in which to dig, but it didn't fill Sam with enthusiasm. Better than the student squat and the embroidery guy but he could think about it all night, it wasn't going to light any bulbs either.

You sit alone in an empty house waiting for the call from Geordie, waiting for something to happen. You go into those spaces inside your head that the AA handbook tells you to steer clear of. Scary places where the voices tell you you'll be fine if you have a drink. You don't want to get drunk, this isn't the point at all, you just fancy a nip in the middle of the night, something to keep the demons at bay. Medicine. One single shot.

Sam shook his head, a smile on his lips. The voices had tried it on before, they came back from time to time. They were opportunist voices, insinuated themselves whether he was ready to hear them or not. And sometimes they were lucky. They'd have him going down the road to that all-night club on Bootham where you could score anything if you had the cash.

But tonight wasn't their night. Sam didn't keep booze

in the house and he wasn't going to move an inch until he got the phone call. He might see the world differently after that, he didn't know, couldn't tell from here. But he didn't think that Geordie's news, whatever it was, would alter his focus. He was feeling strong, alert. There was something going on that he didn't understand but he knew that it was going to require all of his strength and all of his attention to keep pace with it.

Sam Turner knew about the illusions that are stored up in bottles of alcohol and he knew better than anybody else that his own physical and emotional constitution couldn't cope with them. For whatever reason he was an alcoholic and he always would be. And the lesson meant that he couldn't drink without getting drunk. Not ever. He could bluff it with a bottle of wine and some candles, make it look like he was a social drinker for a while. But once his system tasted the real thing he'd put his head down and charge at the red rag of reason.

He listened to the night. The expansion and contraction of the house, the gently falling rain, panicking wind trapped in the howling cul-de-sac of the guttering. He heard the occasional footfall as a neighbour or a prowler sought some private meaning of their own. And he started from time to time as the local tomcats fought off the competition, then returned to their soliciting of Miss Debbie and Lala, the neighbourhood's resident feline beauty queens.

Sam made a pot of coffee and brought it over to the table and the phone rang before he could pour it into a cup.

'Yeah?'

Geordie said, 'OK, I've got it. The couple were called Day. Rolf and Nicole. They moved in last year so the neighbours don't know much about them. He was a lecturer at the university.'

'Small guy,' said Sam. 'Glasses. An existentialist. He thought he'd discovered how reality is constituted by consciousness.'

'You knew him?' Geordie asked.

'Never met the guy,' Sam said. 'But Nicole and I were an item before she ran off with him. She talked about him all the time. I got the impression he was a genius.'

'Jesus, Sam, somebody wants you nailed to a cross.'

'Seems that way. I'd better make myself scarce before the knock on the door comes.'

'Where will you go?'

'Dunno yet, Geordie. I'll be in touch. Look after yourself.'

'You too, Sam. And let me know what to do next, get you out of this one.'

Sam put the phone down. He scratched his head and reached for his rucksack. No time to waste. With all these clues about and modern policing methods, the boys in blue might put two and two together and be here before Christmas.

He was ready to leave when the phone rang again. Something Geordie had forgotten to tell him. But as soon as he picked up the handset he knew it wasn't Geordie. A discernible silence for a moment, then the voice of Bonner. 'Am I talking to Sam Turner?'

Sam kept shtoom. Waited.

A thin laugh came down the wire. No humour to it. Bonner said, 'I know it's you, Mr Turner. I've an observation for you. It's the middle of the night now but this morning, when your ex-partner was transformed – could have been you.'

'Who are you?' Sam said. 'What do you want?'

'Think of me as a man with a list, Mr Turner. You might recognize some of the names on it. Katherine

Turner, Nicole Day, Holly Andersen, Alice Richardson, and I think you can add the last name yourself.'

'Indulge me,' Sam said, knowing whose name would complete the list, but wanting to keep the guy on the phone, hoping he would give himself away, or at least leave a tiny clue to his identity.

'Miss Angeles Falco,' the voice said.

The line went dead and Sam headed for the door. 'File that away,' he said to himself. 'That single word, transformed. "When your ex-partner was *transformed*".'

16

Ruben dropped the empties off and parked his van. Since he'd crushed the detective's balls there'd been the nagging suspicion that the police would pick him up, lay another assault charge on him. But he hadn't heard anything. The detective didn't know who he was anyway, and he'd brought it on himself, chasing Ruben down the street like that. For what? For taking the guy's photograph? Like that was an offence?

The detective, Sam Turner, Kitty's ex . . . he should be happy that he came out of it with only a knee in the balls. Any other time Ruben would've landed a straight right on the guy's honker, his killer punch. Could've been broken bone, blood and smashed cartilage instead of a couple of bruised pills.

Ruben had noticed this before with other people. They tended to escalate situations. What Ruben did, his instinct was to *contain* any situation which arose. Violence can flare up in a moment, sometimes it only takes a word or an accidental shove, anything can start the thing off. Ruben would respond by downing the other guy as simply and as quickly as possible. Finished. The situation's over and contained and everybody can go about their business. But what happened if Ruben didn't get in there first, sort the thing, was that the other guy would start shouting or shoving, maybe put his fists up and come for you. Other people'd join in, especially if it was in a pub, Saturday night, say, or a football match and everyone'd had a few. You could end up in a brawl. Then before you know where you are the local bottles are round and pushing you into the back of a Black Maria. *They*'re escalating the situation as well. Next day they'll have you in front of a beak and there'll be a fine at least, something you can't afford. Somebody's old lady will have to fork it out of the housekeeping or get another loan and so she's dragged into it now. The kids aren't getting enough grub. The guy feels guilty because he's let his family down so the kids and the missis all get a slap or two and the thing's escalated out of all proportion. And for why? Because somebody like Ruben wasn't there in the first place to contain it, that's why. You didn't have to be a politician or a copper or a soldier to keep law and order. You just needed to have your head screwed on the right way.

After he showered, Ruben put on a pair of black jeans and a leather belt with a Cherokee buckle and a T-shirt that showed off his biceps. He wore white socks with black trainers and round his neck he hung his gold ingot on its gold chain. Bit of class there to prove he wasn't a common thicky.

Kitty's last boyfriend lived near Anstey and Ruben headed down the A46 imagining what would happen when he came face to face with the guy. All he had was his name – Pete Lewis – and the fact that Kitty had dumped him because he was a skinflint. Ruben couldn't understand why she'd gone out with a skinflint in the first place. The word conjured up a picture of a Scrooge-like character, somebody who wouldn't buy himself a razor blade and wore those fingerless gloves and in the winter he'd sit around a candle to keep warm.

Maybe the guy had gone to the house to rob her? He'd seen she was living OK and thought he could add a few quid to his hoard. Only the robbery had gone wrong. Kitty had found him in the house and he'd killed her to keep her quiet, cover his tracks. Ruben decided to ask him straight out. He'd know if the guy was lying, squeeze the truth out of him.

He enquired in the village from some tiny gentleman type with a pooch who looked as though he'd be more at home in the city. Straight people like that, Ruben always thought they'd run off if he spoke to them, but some of them, like this one, didn't even blink. He knew the area, pointed Ruben back down the road to a building that looked like it had been converted from a ruin.

He glanced back, got the pooch guy in his mirror and idled the engine while he took in who the man was, what made him tick. But there were no clues. Everything about him was small. He had short legs and a round little body. Made his head look big but Ruben reckoned if he measured it it'd be the same size as other people's, maybe even smaller. He wore a dark grey suit made for a midget, a checked waistcoat and tiny, highly polished shoes, one on each foot. Gloves with itsy-bitsy fingers. The guy was a doll, and his dog was a doll as well, like a couple out of Toytown.

What kind of life can somebody like that have? Ruben wondered. If he was any shorter he'd be underground. No woman is gonna look at him twice unless she's running her own circus. Nothing ever changes for someone like that, it's the same day rehashed time and time again. No guys would wanna be out with him; like imagine taking him down the boozer on a Friday night. What's everyone gonna say? *Hey, Rube's brought his uncle out; can you make him walk the walk?*

This's why euthanasia is such a good idea. Especially for little guys like him. Save all that suffering, all that pain and humiliation. Kitty'd say you couldn't measure somebody else's pain and humiliation. You could never say for certain how someone else experienced existence.

And the things that Kitty said, Ruben listened to them, he gave them serious consideration because she was a woman who was usually right. More right than wrong. He could hear her voice from somewhere beyond the grave, sticking up for the little guy, little people all over the world. Anything to do with prisons or with corporal or capital punishment, torture, anything like that Kitty would say it was wrong. You could guarantee it. If it was gonna hurt or someone was gonna end up dead, she'd have an argument against it. It was like a principle with her. Only Kitty had never actually seen the guy with the pooch. Maybe he would have changed her mind?

Ruben drove up to the old mill building. From a distance it looked like it'd been restored but when you got close up you couldn't see where any work had taken place for a long time. At least a hundred years. The place was still a ruin. There was a part of it towards the west end that had fallen down and was a heap of bricks and broken window frame. But the end nearest the road was more promising; if you were an optimist you might think people could live there.

He knocked on the door and listened to the hollow sound that echoed back. He waited a few moments and knocked again, louder. There was a scuffling sound from inside and then that distinctive pad of bare feet on wooden boards. The door opened and the pale face of a girl, couldn't have been more than sixteen, peered up at him from the dark interior. She had a silver stud above her right eye and a red stone in her nose. She had a blanket around her shoulders and was clasping both ends of it together under her chin. Abnormally long finger-nails, could take your eyes out in a flash. Ruben could see she was naked under the blanket and her pupils were large in the light as if she had just been wrenched from sleep.

'Pete Lewis,' Ruben said.

'He's still in bed. What time is it?'

'Half-eight, nine.'

'Jesus. D'you wanna come back later?' Her tongue was pierced and the silver stud clattered against her teeth.

Ruben leaned on the door and pushed her to one side. He went inside and closed the door behind him. 'Tell him he's got a visitor,' he said. He followed her along a dark corridor, the property smelling more like a barn than a place inhabited by humans. Rank body odours, stale cigarettes, sex and home-brewed wine. Ruben wouldn't have been surprised to see a couple of chickens in there, a flock of sheep.

At the end of the corridor she pushed open a large oak door and scurried over to a double mattress in the centre of the floor. Her clothes and shoes were scattered on the floor on one side of the bed and the guy's clothes were on the other side, next to the bulge under the blanket.

'Peter,' she said, her hand on the bulge, 'there's a chap here. Someone to see you.'

'Uh. Yeah.'

But the guy's breathing returned to normal and he remained under the blanket. The girl turned to Ruben and shrugged her shoulders. Tried a smile on him, the kind of facial expression which suggested complicity. We're never gonna wake him, it said. Might as well let him sleep.

Ruben took a couple of steps to the side of the bed. He grabbed the blanket and pulled it off the bed.

'Aaaagh,' said the guy, lying there naked with his eyes screwed shut. His hands patted around the bed for the missing blanket. 'Oh, aaaagh.'

Not at all like Scrooge, Ruben thought. He was skinny, it was true, but he was young, still in his twenties, and he had long blond hair and a choker of coloured glass beads around his neck. He was unconscious, his morning hard-on the only thing about him that wasn't sleeping.

'What are you doing?' the girl said, raising her voice as Ruben took hold of the guy's foot and walked towards the door. The guy came awake but not quick enough to stop his head cracking against the floorboards. Ruben walked around the room. The guy's free leg was crumpled under him and his bare back was scraping along the floor. He was spitting profanities, trying his best to wriggle free, but Ruben kept a tight grip of him. The girl was hysterical. She'd done a couple of ear-splitting screams and jumped up and down for a minute. Now she'd abandoned her blanket, which was the only thing that covered her, and was throwing herself at Ruben in a valiant and fearless attempt to rescue her man. Ruben brushed her aside but he was conscious of her talons which were intent on raking the flesh from his face.

Her final attack was so ferocious he had to let go of the guy's foot. He grabbed both of her wrists and held them behind her, pushed her face-down on the bed. 'OK, it's over,' he said.

The girl didn't hear or didn't want to hear. She carried on flailing her legs, twisting her neck and showing her teeth as if she'd been attacked by termites. 'OK,' Ruben roared close to her ear. 'It's over. Shut the fuck up.'

That got through. She quietened down, looked around the room and saw that Pete Lewis was sitting on his hands in the corner by the door, his knees drawn up under his chin. Ruben released her wrists and she rolled herself up in a sheet, still muttering under her breath. She said something about muscle-bound tossers, didn't sound like a compliment. Then there was a reference to testosterone and macho posturing. Kind of things that Kitty might have said, only not about Ruben because he didn't do macho posturing around Kitty. Or when he did do it he dipped it in a bath of irony first, which seemed to make it acceptable.

They were both sobbing, the girl on the bed and the guy in the corner by the door. Ruben looked around for someone to blame but he was the only one there. 'Christ,' he said. 'I only wanted to ask you some questions. I drove out from Nottingham and you don't even get out of bed.'

'It's the middle of the night,' the girl shouted at him through her tears. 'I thought you was gonna kill us.'

'My head's bleeding,' Pete Lewis said.

The girl scrambled off the bed and crawled over to him. The sheet didn't cover her ass but no one seemed to mind. Ruben didn't think it was erotic. It could have been if there hadn't been all that tension in the air or if he didn't feel guilty or if he was the kind of guy got turned on by a bony ass.

The girl was ministering to her man's wounds, whispering sympathetically and dabbing away at the back of his head with a corner of the sheet. His face was white.

'Listen, I wanna apologize for my behaviour,' Ruben said. 'I was out of order back there.' Pete Lewis and his girlfriend looked at him with big eyes. Ruben couldn't tell if his apology had the effect of calming them or putting them on red-alert. The guy was shaking, his mouth was open and he was wringing his hands like a bereaved mother. He said, 'I think I'm going to be sick.'

Ruben took a step towards them but the guy shrank away, tried to push himself through the wall. 'He's in shock,' Ruben said.

'What do you expect?' the girl asked.

'It's my fault,' Ruben acknowledged. 'I already apologized. I shouldn't've lost it.' He watched them together for a moment, remembering what you did about shock. 'I'm gonna make tea,' he said. 'You see if you can get him into bed. Keep him warm.'

He went through to the kitchen and found a kettle and filled it with water. Lit the flame on an ancient gas stove. He emptied the teapot of a mash of cold leaves and flushed them down the sink. 'Where do you keep the tea?' he shouted. Then he saw it on the shelf. 'It's all right, I've got it.'

What it was, shock, it was to do with the lack of blood supply. The vital functions of the body couldn't get working properly. 'How's he doing?' Ruben shouted through to the bedroom.

There was no reply.

'What's his skin like? Is it clammy?'

'Yeah,' she shouted back. 'He's cold and he's sweating.'

Ruben made the tea and poured it into a mug. He added a couple of spoons of sugar and a good dollop of milk. He carried it through to the bedroom and sat on the edge of the bed. Pete Lewis was lying on his back, the eiderdown close up against his chin. His eyes followed Ruben's every move. His breathing was shallow and rapid.

'Make him sip this,' Ruben said, handing the mug to the girl. He looked at the guy long and hard. There was no way he could have killed Kitty. It wasn't even worth asking. 'Maybe you should ring the doctor,' he said.

'No.' Pete Lewis shook his head.

'There's no phone here,' the girl said.

'I've got a mobile in the car,' Ruben told them.

'No, I'll be all right,' Lewis said. He reached for the mug and took a sip. 'What's this all about?'

'Kitty Turner,' Ruben told him.

His already large eyes almost popped out of his head. 'Kitty Turner? You mean Katherine? She was murdered.'

'The woman who was knifed in Nottingham?' said the girlfriend. 'In her own bed. What about her?'

'It was me who found her,' Ruben said. 'We were . . .

We had a relationship.' He gritted his teeth for a moment, nearly lost it for some reason. The thought of Kitty and what they'd had going. The image of her broken body and the sound of her name on his lips. The police had offered him counselling and he'd turned it down. But maybe he shouldn't have done. There might be some comfort there.

Grief counselling. How to live out the rest of your life without betraying your devastation.

'But why come here?' Lewis said. 'Why the violence?'

'I already apologized for that,' Ruben told him. 'That wasn't in the plan. I know she went out with you a while back. I wanted to check if you were the one.'

'If I was the one what? If I killed her? Jesus.'

'And I can see you didn't do it. You haven't got that, whatever it takes. But I didn't know that before I met you.'

'Met him?' the girlfriend said. 'You call this meeting people?'

'It's not how I planned it. When I thought about coming here, even driving over this morning, in my head it was all calmer. I just had some questions.'

'Well, ask away,' Lewis said. 'But I didn't kill Katherine and I don't know who did. I couldn't believe it when I read it in the paper. That she was dead.'

'You might know someone who was around, someone who could have done it.'

Lewis shook his head. 'I met one of her neighbours,' he said. 'An old guy who brought cuttings over from his garden. But there was nobody else.'

'She didn't talk about anyone else?'

'Not that I remember. I can't think of anyone.'

'Shouldn't you leave this to the police?' the girlfriend asked.

'I wanna make sure the guy doesn't get away with it,' Ruben told her.

But Pete Lewis didn't know anything. Ruben would have to call it quits for now, look up some of the other people on his list. Explore different avenues, like they said in the movies.

'Keep him in bed a few hours,' he told the girl. 'He'll be OK tomorrow.'

'If I was you,' Lewis said as Ruben was stepping out of the door, 'I'd look up the guy she was married to. Sam Turner. He runs some outfit in York, security, private detection, that kind of thing. He might have some ideas. In fact, come to think of it, he could be the one.'

Back in Nottingham Ruben collected his snaps from Prontaprint. He sat in a newly opened coffee house and looked at the images. Liverpool in late-summer. Kitty with the Catholic Cathedral behind her, laughing at the joke he'd told her. *'Doctor, when my broken arm is better will I be able to play the piano?' 'Of course you will.' 'How strange, I could never play it before.'*

Not even funny. But to see and to remember how she'd laughed, Ruben would have gone on telling Kitty jokes for the rest of his life. He'd never have run out. He would have bought joke books.

To live with that laugh.

There was another one, the two of them together outside The Beatles Story on Albert Dock, a yellow submarine over to the right of the entrance. Ruben had given his camera to a woman from Munich, asked her to point and click, but she couldn't do it. Then he'd found a Frenchman who took the photograph sweet as you like, no problems. He had his arm around Kitty's waist and she was looking up at him and about to plant her lips on his cheek when the guy pressed the shutter. He closed his eyes and tried to remember the kiss.

It came back easily. There was nothing about Kitty he could forget. He imagined a time in the future, a hundred years from now, when he would still be alive and still remembering. He'd be a mass of leathery wrinkles and memories. When he looked back at the photograph in his hand his knuckles were white.

The next photograph showed Sam Turner in York. There were four or five of them where the guy was too far away, side on so you could see his profile, get some idea of his bearing but not close enough to see what he looked like. Then there was another, much closer, but he was looking surprised, not clear if he was having his photograph taken or if he was accidentally being caught in a photograph of somebody else. It wasn't a perfect photograph but it was the best of the bunch. The last two were close-ups and you could see his features clearly but he had realized what was happening by then and was pissed off. If the pictures had been able to talk you would have heard the guy yelling.

Ruben swilled the remains of his coffee in the bottom of the cup and drank it down. He went back to Prontaprint and ordered six photocopies of the Sam Turner print and asked them to enlarge the ones of Kitty.

'When do you want them, sir?'

'I want them now. I'll wait.'

The assistant did the thing where they stop writing on the form and let the pen hover for a moment, deciding if they'll do you a favour or turn themselves into an obstacle. Ruben kept his cool. He'd already put two people into shock this morning and split open the head of one of them. He didn't want to go through that again. He hoped this broad with the big hair and the pen would make the right decision.

She looked at him and smiled. 'The technician's busy at the moment but if you come back in half an hour, I'll have them ready for you.'

Ruben said, 'Thanks.' He said, 'You've got a nice smile, you know that. You should use it more.'

He tucked the ticket she gave him into his top pocket and made his way back to the coffee house. He took a copy of the *Sun* out of the rack and read it while he waited for his double espresso. There was an article about a priest with a mistress, and a soldier somewhere had borrowed a gun from the army to shoot a teenager. An obituary for some surgeon who had performed more than three thousand mastectomies. Strange, the different jobs in the world. Ruben always thought delivering milk was an odd way to make a living, but there were weirder jobs. Pleading with an imaginary God to care for someone's soul. Shooting rubber bullets at Ulstermen. Sticking knives into the breasts of women with cancer.

But there had been something about the girl behind the counter at Prontaprint. The typeface of the *Sun* swam before his eyes when he thought about her. It was the smile, it reminded him of Kitty. Not that they had the same smile, or the smile of the counter assistant resurrected any smile that Kitty had ever given him, the connection was more distant and proved something that Ruben had suspected for the last couple of days. That anything could remind him of Kitty. Anything in the world. 'I love you until it comes out of my eyes,' he had told her. He didn't know where the words came from. They weren't part of a song or a poem and he'd never heard anyone else say them, not even in a film. He'd invented them in order to tell her how he felt. 'I love you until it comes out of my eyes.' He hadn't needed to sit down to think up the words in that particular order. He'd just opened his mouth one night when they were sitting on opposite sides of the table in Kitty's house and the words had come out like that, as a complete sentence.

A couple of times he'd tried to do it again but the words never fell out of him so naturally when he forced them. He wasn't a poet. They'd worked that once, though, and that was enough. They'd shown her something about him that he wasn't sure of himself. Something that had been born in him when he met Kitty Turner.

There'd be another time, Ruben thought. He'd have Sam Turner at his mercy again. Maybe today, maybe tomorrow, they'd find themselves in the same position. The detective would be on the tarmac and Ruben would be standing above him. But that time Ruben wouldn't walk away. He'd stomp the life out of the bastard.

By early afternoon Ruben was on the south side of the river a couple of streets from Kitty's house. He rang the bell on the door of the Greenwood Guesthouse and waited until the lady of the house answered. She was one of those women who had a smile that was a wince in disguise. If he'd been looking for somewhere to stay Ruben would have had serious misgivings. But that wasn't why he was here.

He showed her the photograph of Sam Turner. 'I'm trying to trace this man,' he said. 'He might have stayed here in the last week or so.'

The woman looked at Ruben for a long time without glancing at the photograph. Her face betrayed nothing of her thoughts.

'It's a serious matter,' he told her. 'Do you recognize him?'

The woman looked at the photograph. She shook her head. 'Never seen him before.'

'Are you sure?'

'If he'd stayed here, I'd remember. I don't forget faces.'

'Thanks,' Ruben said. 'Sorry to bother you.'

He left the house and closed the gate. If necessary he'd visit every guesthouse and hotel in the city. If he could find someone who recognized Sam Turner, someone who could prove that he was in Nottingham when Kitty was killed, then he'd have the bastard.

Simple proof, that's all he needed. And the way to get it was down to leg-work. That's how the police solved crimes, they didn't follow up clues and solve puzzles except in books and films. They used leg-work.

And that's what Ruben would do. And when he found the place where the detective stayed, he'd go back to York and kill him, hang him out to dry.

17

It was raining when he left Newcastle but by the time his plane circled Gardermoen, Oslo's airport, the sky was pastel blue and the landscape shimmered in an extraordinary early-evening light. It made Geordie think about those filters that photographers use to bathe everything in red or blue. It was as if someone had invented a filter that simply made everything clearer, undermined the blurring effects of distance and pasted them into the windows of the plane.

He'd got himself a book called *Welcome to Norway* and had read it from cover to cover during the flight, probably knew more now about the country than the people who lived there. He knew they'd been occupied by the Nazis during the war and that they liked to think of themselves as progressive even though they had a king. This airport, if they ever got to stop circling round it and land, levied a surcharge on all flights operating between midnight and six in the morning. This was so people who lived close by could get a better night's sleep. Keep the decibel count down. Cool. Government for the people by the people. Nearly like communism.

Geordie knew about Ibsen and another one of their writers but he couldn't remember his name. Would come later, on the tip of his tongue. Guy who didn't write plays like Ibsen but novels like JD. He knew about the painter, Munch, madman who had people screaming and merging into each other, except that one called *The Kiss* which reminded Geordie of him and Janet. There was the composer as well, Grieg, who'd written the *Peer Gynt* tune which Celia had played for him. Made you think of fairies.

That was history, all those people. There were probably people writing and painting and composing now in Norway who were just as good as those old guys, maybe even better. But countries liked to have a history so they remembered the old guys for as long as they could. Governments would do anything to keep you from living in the present. Geordie had seen a play by Ibsen at the Leeds Playhouse, *A Doll's House*, something like that. He'd thought it would be old-fashioned and full of 'thee' and 'thou' but it wasn't. Really exciting, kept you on the edge of your seat for two hours. Made you think all the way home. Made you question your attitudes.

The woman at passport control looked more like a waitress than a government official. She barely glanced at Geordie's passport. The customs guy eyed him suspiciously and Geordie was expecting a strip search when the man nodded him through.

Geordie was lost in a foreign country. He stopped a tall fair man dressed in a new lightweight suit with matching shirt and practised the words from his Norwegian phrasebook. '*Kan de fortelle Meg hvor tog stasjonen er?*'

'The railway station?' the Norwegian said. 'Yeah. Take the escalator down and keep walking. You can't miss it.'

Geordie had brought a novel to read but hadn't got very far with it. Le Carré's *The Constant Gardener*, about the murder of a woman in northern Kenya. Janet had given him it at York station when he'd got on the train to Newcastle. He'd kissed Echo and then he'd held Janet and kissed her for a long time. She'd whispered love to him and the old words started an echo that lasted more than a thousand kilometres.

He watched Norway go by through the windows of the

train. Red barns and wooden houses. Seemed like whichever way you framed the view through the window you'd end up with something like a postcard. Geordie would have liked to watch the view, see how this new landscape was different from England or Holland, the only other country he'd visited. Either that or he'd have liked to read more of the le Carré, try to understand how Lake Turkana, where the woman in the story was killed, was the birthplace of mankind. Far as Geordie could remember, the birthplace of mankind was somewhere in India. But who was he to argue with le Carré?

But he couldn't do either of those things because he didn't know why he was here and he didn't understand the events that had led him here. Geordie was disoriented. Not only that, he was probably alienated as well because events in the outer world were spinning in directions he had never envisaged. One, Sam's ex-wife Katherine had been killed in Nottingham when Sam just happened to be visiting the city. Two, another woman, one of Sam's old girlfriends, Nicole Day, and her husband Rolf, had been killed in Leeds when Sam was knocking on the doors of houses in the same street. Three, Sam had split. He had packed a bag well quick and disappeared without trace. Four, the police were after him. There was a manhunt on, with pictures in the newspapers and captions telling people not to approach this man because he was dangerous. And the man was Sam Turner.

No word for three days, then last night the telephone rang. Geordie was sitting by the window looking out at the dark and he could hear Janet singing upstairs, trying to settle Echo for the night. Barney was curled in front of the wood-burning stove, sleeping as usual. Geordie was worried that Barney was getting near the end of his life. Well, worried wasn't the right word. Barney and Geordie had been together since the dog was a pup. They'd been on the street together, looked after each other when there was nobody else to care, before Sam came along and offered them a job. And if Barney gave up the ghost some day soon it would be the end of a friendship. More than that, it would mark the end of a whole stage in Geordie's life.

Yeah, worrying about Barney and the phone rang. Geordie moved quickly, not wanting the ringing to disturb Echo who was descending into that whimpering stage which would soon be deep breathing and sleep. And as he picked up the handset he knew it was Sam.

'Where are you?' he asked.

'Oslo. Can you come over?'

'Oslo? That's in Finland, right?'

'Norway,' Sam said.

'Right, Norway. Just testing. When?'

'Tomorrow.'

'Why?'

'You know those puzzles psychologists use, where there's a sequence and you have to find what comes next?'

'There's a two and a four,' Geordie said, 'and you have to decide if the next number is six or eight.'

'Yeah,' Sam said. 'When the marriage to Katherine hit the dust I got myself mixed up with Nicole. And they've both been killed in that order.'

'That's not much of a link, Sam.'

'It's all I've got.'

'So how does that lead to Oslo?'

'After Nicole dumped me I fell into the arms of Holly.'

'Holly? What kind of name's that?'

'If my bet's right it's the third name in the sequence.'

'But why Oslo, Sam?'

'Because that's where Holly lives.'

'Jesus. Then that's the place you shouldn't be. If she's

killed in Oslo while you're there you're never gonna be able to explain it.'

'Geordie, I'm here to make sure she doesn't get killed.'

'You're the kiss of death to these women, Sam. Why do you want me there?'

'To help, of course. And . . .'

'And? And what?'

'If it goes wrong and we can't save Holly, you'll be my witness.'

'Why would it go wrong, Sam? If there's two of us on the job we should be able to keep her safe.'

Sam sighed down the line. 'Holly doesn't always do what I tell her,' he said. 'In fact, when I speak she turns off, doesn't listen.'

Sam hadn't asked what was happening in York. Maybe he knew the police and the press had painted him as a demented wife-killer. You read the news or you listened to the local radio station and Sam Turner, the neighbourhood good guy, had been transformed into a cynical murderer who stalked the environs of his ex-wives and girlfriends, waiting for the moment when they were most vulnerable. You believed the media and Sam was back on the bottle with a vengeance, often so drunk he couldn't stand. He sprawled on the threadbare carpet of his flat wearing a string-vest with his flies forever open. He didn't shave for days and his body was emaciated from lack of food and vitamins, his skin slack and pale as he plotted the evil end of the women whose lives he had already ruined.

Everybody in the business had been hauled down to the police station. Celia, Marie, they'd called in JD and George Forester. Even Fred Taylor had been questioned, and his only connection to Sam was that he failed to sell him an insurance policy from time to time.

Geordie had spent seven hours in the Fulford Road

nick, helping them with their enquiries. They'd come for him at eight o'clock the evening after Sam disappeared and he'd walked back home again at three o'clock in the morning. Chief Inspector Delaney had all the questions, beginning with: 'I don't like Sam Turner, son, and I don't like the people who do like him.'

Geordie had told the truth, more or less. Yes, he worked for Sam Turner. No, he didn't know of any crimes the man had committed. Yes, he had heard that one of Sam's ex-wives and one of his girlfriends had been murdered recently. No, he didn't think Sam could have committed the murders. Yes, he was married with a small child. No, he didn't know where Sam Turner was at the present time. He'd given the same answers the second time he was asked and again the third and fourth time.

The parting shot had been, 'Do you want the perpetrator of these crimes to be brought to justice?' Delaney had said it just like that. He wasn't the kind of cop to say, 'Do you want us to catch the murderer?' He was like a cop out of a fifties movie. He had a confused moral agenda based on his own prejudices and the lessons he remembered from cop school way back in the mists of time, and some Sunday school lessons even before that.

Chief Inspector Delaney wasn't a good guy to have as an enemy because he'd find a way of getting you even if it wasn't legal. On the other hand if he was on your side you'd have to wonder why it was you attracted people with shit for brains.

'Is Sam your only suspect?' Geordie had asked.

'You think we should be looking for someone else?'

Geordie had smiled. 'Yes, I don't think Sam did it. In fact, I know he didn't. He couldn't do something like that.'

'You got any ideas who we should be looking for? I'm

not making any promises here, son, but if you can come up with a name maybe we'll forget that the dead bodies were both connected to your boss and we'll forget that said boss is on the run and go after your guy instead.'

'I don't know who did it,' Geordie had told him. 'I only know that as long as you chase Sam, the real murderer is getting away with it.'

Delaney shook his head. 'You know it's an offence to harbour a fugitive from the law?'

'Yeah.'

'Or to withhold information that might lead to said fugitive's apprehension?'

The language was worse than the interrogation. Geordie thought if the guy carried on talking like that he'd have to confess to the killings himself. *OK, OK, I did it. But please, no more jaw.*

The train pulled into the Sentral Stasjon in Oslo and Geordie got his bag and stepped down to the platform. He followed the crowd. Sam was leaning up against the kiosk outside the barrier with a plastic cup of coffee in his hand, but Geordie walked past him. He clocked the guy with the coffee but didn't give him a second look, thought he was a Norwegian version of a down-and-out, the kind of guy you looked at him too long, he'd come over and give you some grief.

It must have been the third time he glanced at the guy propping up the kiosk that something clicked in his consciousness. First off the guy hadn't shaved for days. It was way past designer stubble, the beginnings of a beard, except if you were growing a beard you had to trim it, shape it, or it looked like shit. The guy hadn't shaped it at all so you had to think he didn't care, that he didn't have a razor or he was ate up on Alice or Aunt Nora.

Second, he was wearing glasses. Thick plastic frames,

looked too heavy for his head, as if they'd forced his chin into his chest. Sam didn't wear glasses. Hell, he was a past master at refusing to see the things that were staring him in the face, but he didn't need specs.

And third, the body language was wrong. This guy had let the world get to him, you could see there'd been a significant moment in his life when he'd thrown in the towel and he was replaying it every moment that followed. He was a man in a constant act of surrender. That didn't tally with Sam Turner. Sam was the guy who never gave up. Capitulation wasn't part of his act. You could chop his arms and legs off and he'd come at you with his head.

So everything was wrong. But Geordie smiled and went over to him. Sam kept his eyes down, didn't crack his face for a second. The closer he got, the more Geordie could see there was Sam Turner, or at least a shadow of him, hidden deep in the folds of this derelict propping up the kiosk in Oslo's Sentral Stasjon.

'How you doing?' Geordie asked.

Sam adjusted his spectacles. He shook his head.

'What's with watching me trying to find you?' Geordie said. 'How long was I supposed to wait before you would've let on?'

'I wanted to make sure you weren't being followed,' Sam said. 'I don't want Interpol scooping me up before I've sorted out what's going on.'

'OK, that I can accept. I thought you was testing me. Trying to improve my powers of observation.'

'That, too,' Sam said. 'I wondered how many times you'd look at me before you saw who I was.'

'That's a crap thing to do, Sam. I wouldn't do that to you.'

'I didn't plan on doing it, either. But once it started I got into the mood. It was like a game.'

'Yeah, a game where you're the only one knows the rules. I'm a stranger in a strange land and wondering if I've been dumped or landed in the wrong country and you're playing silly buggers.'

Sam took a step towards the exit and Geordie followed. Sam said, 'I knew you'd see the funny side of it, accept it in the right spirit. Somebody else, a guy with no sense of humour, might have taken it completely wrong. I could have ended up with you giving me a row for it.'

Geordie followed him out of the station to the side of the road. Everything was moving too fast. There was a huge bronze tiger prowling the cobblestone square outside the station. Size of a small elephant. And cold. You could feel the temperature; as you breathed in the air chilled your chest. Traffic zooming around, every last one of the cars and trucks on the wrong side of the road. He touched Sam's shoulder. 'We could go back in the station,' he said. 'I'll get on the train and get off, try to do the whole thing over again but get it right.'

'You mean, me get it right?'

'No, both of us get it right.'

'OK,' Sam said. 'I'm sorry. I'm under pressure.'

Geordie offered his hand. 'I'm sorry, too,' he said. 'I'm under pressure as well.'

Sam took his hand and shook it. He opened the door of the taxi that had stopped for them and whispered to Geordie before he got in, 'Watch what you say while we're driving. Norwegians understand English better than we do.'

Sam asked the driver to take them to Storgata and Geordie kept mum and watched the city. New buildings, old buildings, some attempt at symmetry by successive generations of architects. The area around the station was the same as in any big city: cosmopolitan, busy with the usual sprinkling of dropouts and dopers, street-girls with hollow eyes wearing short skirts and lipstick among the shoppers and office-workers. Indians and Pakistanis and black Africans with stalls on the pavements and blue-haired ladies with kid-gloves, seemingly oblivious to change, laden with parcels from GlasMagasinet and Steen & Strom.

Every other street there was a glance of the harbour with Stena, Fjord and Colour line ships tied at the quay waiting for their passengers to Copenhagen, Kiel and Gothenburg. Geordie had never been here before but it wasn't as strange as he'd feared. He saw two different McDonald's within five minutes. Much of Oslo was instantly recognizable. It was like one of the bigger English cities after a clean-up but with more wealth and style thrown in.

Trams and tramlines ran along the major arteries and every once in a while the taxi shuddered as it crossed them or hit a cobbled area of the street.

The car left them in a street off Torgata with three- and four-storey flats on each side. Geordie read the street name aloud: 'Osterhaus gate.'

'The *e* isn't silent,' Sam said.

'Osterhaus gat*e*?'

'Yeah. Pretty close.'

Geordie mouthed it again to himself. He looked around him. 'Like Russia,' he said.

'You been to Russia?'

'Never.'

Sam gave him the long sad-bastard look which he'd been practising most of his life. Used to do it with a shake of the head for emphasis but these days he'd pared it down to a minimalist incarnation. No shake of the head, no movement of facial muscles; it was all in the eyes. Less is more.

'But it's the twenty-first century, Sam. We've invented

picture books, you know, cameras? There's this new invention called TV, still being developed at the moment, under-funded and the technology's primitive but if it takes off, well, we'll be able to sit at home and watch people in other countries doing all their foreign stuff right in front of us. Janet reckons we could have a big TV set in our sitting room and me and her and Echo, we'll be sitting in front of it with Chinese take-aways and there'll be satellites up in the sky so we can beam down to any country in the world. Watch the Olympic games or the latest war in the Middle East.'

'You finished?' Sam asked.

''Course, you being so advanced in years, you might not be around when they've finished tweaking the technology. But it's coming. It's on the way.

'Her grandma, Janet's mother, she bought a picture book for Echo and it's got a couple of photographs of St Petersburg in there. Something about the style of architecture, the feel of it, and then when we got out of the taxi and we're in this street I wouldn't be surprised to see a *Droshki* come along or a young Cossack in high boots.

'So what's happening is I'm making associations. I've just arrived in a foreign country and my identity, the guy who I think I am, is out of his depth. I'm looking around and trying to make sense of what's around me. I'm comparing these new things with the old things that are part of my experience. I'm not fully in control of the situation yet. I might never be. But as long as I'm drawing breath there'll be a part of me which is weighing and calculating and judging my relationship to the world.'

Sam opened a door and stepped into the vestibule of a block of flats. He took the stairs two at a time. Geordie followed.

'You finished now?' Sam asked.

'If you've finished giving me the sad-bastard stare.'

'I got it wrong again.'

'At least you're admitting it,' Geordie said. 'Usually takes you a month or two to see where you went wrong. Sometimes a year.'

Sam stopped on the third landing and inserted a key in the lock of flat number 34. The door opened inwards and he stepped inside. Geordie followed and closed the door behind him. They stood facing each other in a tiny entrance passage. 'Give me some leeway here,' Sam said. 'I've been living inside my head the last few days.' He avoided eye-contact. 'Angeles?' he said. 'She all right? You seen her?'

There was the crack in his voice, the hint of vulnerability that came to the surface so infrequently it was always a surprise.

Geordie dropped his bag and threw his arms around Sam. He held him close. Sam tried to return the hug but his arms were trapped by his sides. Geordie could feel Sam's new beard tickling the side of his neck. 'She's fine,' he said. 'You don't have to worry. Everyone's looking after her.'

They let each other go and stood back. The eye-contact was there now. 'We'll get the bastard,' Geordie said. 'It looks bleak at the moment but we'll come through the other end. Whoever's setting this up, he's not gonna get away with it.'

Sam served up something called *Fiske Boller*. Seemed to be white fish and flour pulped and tossed around in a frying pan. Frozen fries with that which he'd cooked in the oven until they were almost warm. No pudding. Geordie reflected on the stark reality of his situation. No Janet or Echo, no decent cooking unless he did it himself and got lucky. Sam the man still fighting but looking low and verging on something not many miles from depression.

Geordie could understand that. The guy had lost an ex-wife and an old girlfriend and was hoping he wouldn't lose anyone else. What must that be like? Geordie didn't have ex-wives of his own to compare it with, only one ex-girlfriend. He could only imagine what it would be like if he and Janet got divorced and then some years later he discovered that somebody had murdered her and made it look like he, Geordie, had done the deed.

But his thoughts didn't lead to empathy with Sam. First he couldn't imagine Janet and him being divorced. Sure, lots of people got divorced but still, they weren't the same as him and Janet. Him and Janet, they were serious. What they had together was so much better than what either of them had had before, better than they could have dreamed. Geordie had thought he'd always be an orphan. He didn't imagine himself living in a house until Sam came along, much less meeting Janet and getting a house and a garden and having cats and a dog which didn't fight and neighbours and then Echo being born.

How could he get divorced from all that? Go right back to Go? He'd never get to the bit where Janet was murdered and the murderer tried to make it look like Geordie'd done it. He'd be out of it, mad or dead or both. He wouldn't still be around like Sam, the ultimate survivor, rocking around in the debris of his past lives.

'What does it feel like?' he asked when he'd finished pushing the cold fries about his plate.

Sam shook his head. Stared at the black space of the triple-glazed window. 'There's guilt mixed up in there,' he said. 'Which is never helpful. There's all the shit about gender as well, being the male, the protector.'

'Come on, Sam.'

'I know.' He held his hands up. 'I know the score with

all that stuff. I'm not inviting it in but it's part of the cultural bag. It's like nationalism, military music ... I don't believe in it but I took it in with my mother's milk. Whatever I do with it, however much I rationalize it, it's still there. I think it's gone, I tell myself I've overcome it, but there's traces of it in my blood and sometimes they all flow together. It's like a shadow that starts to take on substance.'

Geordie had talked to Celia about that. About how the past sometimes came together like a great weight and dragged you down and Celia had said it wasn't just the past, it could take any form because it was the devil. And the devil always came for you when you were weak.

'I can't believe Nicole is dead,' Sam continued. 'It was different with her. I'd still not let go. I don't mean there was anything between us. She was married and I'm sure she never thought of me. I only thought of her a couple of times a year. But she was still there, in my memory. There were things we'd never reconciled.'

Sam had stopped drinking for Nicole so many times he'd lost count. He'd watched her thrown against the gnarled reef of his inadequacy and deception until her being couldn't take any more. That afternoon she'd left to live with Rolf Day, the phenomenologist, Sam had been drinking since before dawn. She came into his den and turned the sound of Dylan's 'St Augustine' down one notch. Sam turned it up two. He sprawled at the table, a bottle in each hand. His eyes were like separate shrieks, blind and dwarfing his already shrivelled face. 'I'm going,' she said. Must've been summer because she was wearing a silk blouse with no sleeves. Plum-coloured. Her arms were thin, just bones covered with skin. Her face was hollow, high cheekbones protruding. Her freshly washed hair and the palpable relief in her statement were barely enough to dispel the association with a skeleton.

'It's not just you being punished here, Sam,' she told him. 'You're trying to bring the whole world down with you.'

For an instant he'd seen her as a cadaver and then he'd remembered her as she was when they first met. He saw what had happened to her in that house with him. There must have been a choice in that moment, he told himself later. He could have wept or he could have held out a hand to her or told her goodbye with a shake of his head. He could have made more promises.

What he did was to take another swig from one of his bottles and sit back in the chair with fiery breath. He laughed at her, a deep throaty roar of male pride and complacency. And as she backed out of the room and turned to stumble along the hall to freedom and independence he dug his finger-nails into the wood of the table and hooted and honked and shook long after the house had fallen silent and consciousness had drifted beyond his grasp.

It was midnight in Oslo and Sam didn't want to leave the flat because he still had some thinking to do so Geordie walked outside by himself. There was graffiti everywhere in Osterhaus gate, graffiti in English and Norwegian and Arabic, other languages that Geordie could only guess at. Tamil, maybe, if that was a language? Urdu? Russian? On the corner of the street was Hornaas Musikk, windows crammed with guitars and banjos, piano accordions and mandolins. In Storgata he peered through the windows of the Mai Vietnamesisk restaurant, looking in at the faces around the tables and wondering at the dishes of food and the glasses of alcohol. Maybe Sam was right again, it wasn't at all like Russia.

Geordie wandered in Grønland, the city's Little Pakistan, and wove through Grensen and Karl Johans Gata.

All the shops were closed but there were people spinning wax in the cafés and restaurants and the insistent beat of reggae and hip-hop, soul and rhythm and blues drifted together in the night air. He veered off to Aker Brygge and passed lovers talking and dancing by the side of the water, all of them swathed in woollens and skins, scarves and hats and warm leather boots. He got on the blower to Janet and told her he was safe and asked about Echo and Barney and the cats.

'Don't worry about us,' she said. 'We're fine. I'm more worried about you.'

'Listen,' he said, 'I hardly recognized the man, he's grown a beard.'

Janet laughed. 'Can't imagine it. You sure it isn't false?'

'If it's false,' Geordie told her, 'the guy who made it is gonna starve to death. OK, you got the picture of him with a beard? Now add a pair of specs.'

'He's in disguise,' Janet said. 'He doesn't want to be recognized and repatriated.'

'But who does it remind you of?'

'Beard and specs? The only person I know like that is JD.'

'Right on. He went to JD's place, borrowed an old pair of specs and the guy's passport and birth certificate. And he's travelled halfway round Europe under a false identity.'

'Yeah, it's easy to do something like that now,' Janet said. 'European Union.'

'If I travelled on someone else's passport, Janet, they wouldn't let me on the boat. This's one of the things that's infuriating about Sam. He can get away with stuff like that. He thinks, Oh, I'll be JD, and next time you turn around he's disappeared and a kind of cheap imitation of JD has taken his place.'

'How is he?'

'He's cool on the outside, like always. You know what he's like. You look at the guy, you listen to him and you wouldn't know he was *feeling* anything. But this thing is getting to him. He can't understand what's happening. He doesn't have any more of a clue than you or me. I'm worried he might crack.'

'He's under a lot of pressure, Geordie.'

'I've seen him under pressure before. Usually pressure gets him going, makes him sharp. But what's happening to him now's the opposite of that. Seems like it's putting him to sleep.'

Janet was quiet at the other end. She said, 'You take care, you hear?'

'Don't worry,' he said. 'You can worry about Sam but I'm OK.'

'Where are you staying?'

'Sam's got this flat. Belongs to a friend of a friend. Somebody he knows. Nice place. The guy who owns it is in Helsinki.'

Janet was quiet at the other end of the line.

'You still there?'

'Yes,' she said. 'Are you watching your back?'

'All the time. This's a foreign country. How're you managing without me?'

'We'll get by,' she said coyly. 'But don't take too long.'

'Don't worry 'bout that,' he told her. 'There's nothing here I believe in. Except you.'

18

The magician was pleased. 'He's gone,' he told Jody. 'First you saw him, then you didn't. Disappeared.' Sam Turner, private eye, alive and well, living in York until Diamond Danny waved his magic wand.

The world was astonished. The police and the newspapers, the television people and the man's neighbours, they were spinning round in disbelief. Where could he have gone? Where could he be?

Sam Turner was like a rag doll. Diamond Danny's magical powers had lifted him up in a flash and deposited him in the capital city of another country. The spectators, even the subject himself, were only aware of the movement of the wand and the accompanying flash. They didn't realize that everything was in the preparation, that everything had been arranged weeks in advance.

Danny finished moving his bowels and collected the breakfast tray. Jody was lying on the rug in front of the couch, one of her legs behind her neck in a parody of some yoga position. As he washed his bowl and cup at the kitchen sink he smiled to himself. It was the best trick he'd ever devised, no doubt about it. Elegant. But at the same time it carried enormous risks. The research had been rigorous and that was certainly one of the factors that had led to its success. Turner had a logical way of thinking and he rarely panicked. Danny had always known that the man would follow the sequence and take himself off to Oslo. He had to be there, after all, in order to be implicated in the crime.

If Turner wasn't by her side the woman couldn't die. The dominoes were carefully placed. If one of them remained standing the illusion would fail.

'The symmetry is captivating,' he told Jody. 'Beguiling.'

As a teenager, Danny had gone to the National Gallery of Art in Washington with his mother and stood before Picasso's *Tragedy*. The painting had brought the young Danny Mann to tears. Perhaps that was symmetry, too? Danny didn't know what it was. The painting was blue. There were three figures on a beach, thin, emaciated, a man, a woman and a boy. They appeared to be a group but they didn't communicate; there was no eye-contact. The man and woman looked down at their bare feet and the young boy weighed imponderables in the palms of his hands. Danny thought they were poor but that didn't explain the title of the painting. It felt as though a death had taken place, that they had lost someone and the loss had fractured their existence as a family. But there was no real story. Only a conclusion.

Danny had stood before the large wooden panel and let the tears stream down his face. His mother had returned and put her arms around him but he was inconsolable. She had led him from the gallery into the sunshine and eventually he'd stopped crying and agreed to go back for another look. Danny believed that in the whole of his life nothing had touched him more deeply than that painting.

The attendant had told them that Picasso had painted two other pictures underneath *Tragedy*. There was a thickly painted action scene from the bullring, and another bullfight painting, showing a dead horse being dragged from the ring. Danny thought that that might be a clue to the tragedy, but he wasn't sure what the clue meant.

After his mother died, Danny would wake in the night

or in the early morning enfeebled and debilitated, weak in spirit and his physical body. And he would recall the picture of the three blue figures and think of the young Picasso labouring away in Barcelona in 1903.

Symmetry, perfection. It made you weep because the parts fitted so neatly together. It was a rare thing in the world when that could be conjured up. That moment of harmony when the spinning and exploding atoms of chaos fall into a trance of blueness.

To the south of York, on the outskirts of Selby, Diamond Danny parked outside an old gabled house set back from the road and surrounded by a line of conifers and waterlogged fields. There was a white canvas kitbag on the passenger seat of the car, held in place by the seatbelt. Danny struggled with the release mechanism of the seatbelt but it was faulty and would not open for some time. He swore quietly under his breath as he tried to locate the exact angle at which he had to press the release button. A ridiculous situation for a magician. He could open any door, make solid objects pass through brick walls, and here he was struggling with a seatbelt. Tomorrow, no, today he would get it fixed. The mechanism finally gave way and Danny tucked the kitbag under his arm. Leaving the car unlocked, he approached the front door of the house and gave three thumps with the heavy brass knocker. A small plaque on the wall declared the occupier to be J. C. Nott.

The young man who answered the door was slight, bespectacled and balding prematurely. He wore a striped shirt which looked like it had been a pyjama top in a previous incarnation. The sleeves were rolled to the elbows. He raised his eyebrows when he saw Danny Mann. 'Hello,' he said. 'What brings you here?'

'Problem,' Danny said. 'Can I come in?'

'Yes. I'm in the workshop.' He led the way through the rambling house to a room at the back which had a single high window. There were workbenches on two walls, racks for tools above them, and several angle-poised halogen lamps.

A headless female figure was stretched out on one bench, knees drawn up and hands clenched together over her lower chest. Under the bench was a wicker basket which contained two arms, one with a hand and the other without. Next to the basket was a large glass jar with long tresses of auburn hair.

'Is it Jody?' the young man asked, indicating the kitbag under the magician's arm.

'Yes, afraid so.' Danny laid the bag on the floor and pulled Jody out. She was covered by one of his shirts and he unfastened the buttons to reveal her left breast. The young man winced as he came forward to inspect the damage. Jody's nipple was almost severed from the breast, hanging on by four or five millimetres of flesh-like plastic.

J. C. Nott adjusted his spectacles and brought his face close to the injury. He ran his index finger around the torn area, gently pushing upwards to reunite the papilla with the surrounding aureole. 'Nasty,' he said. 'Teeth?'

The magician nodded, tight-lipped. 'What do you think?'

'It's bad,' the young man said. 'I can fix it but it's going to happen again. Better if I replace the whole breast, reinforce it somehow. Or both breasts? It's not going to be cheap.'

'You're the artist,' Danny told him. 'I don't want to know the details, and I don't care about the money. How long before I get her back?'

'I'll need a week,' the artist said. 'Give her a complete going over. She got any other problems?'

Danny shook his head. 'A week's a long time.'

'Give me a ring on Thursday,' the young man said. 'I'll try to get her done for the weekend.'

'I don't want anything changing,' Danny told him. 'I mean size. They're just right as they are. I'm used to them now.' He'd wondered, shortly after taking delivery of her for the first time. He'd imagined something bigger, something he could bury his head in, but he'd made adjustments in his thinking, accepting the reality of the situation. Now he liked her exactly as she was. If she came back with a different cup size it'd be like committing adultery.

He glanced back at her on the bench as he left the workshop. The bottom corner of the shirt had fallen away over her hip and her blonde pubic hair was visible. The magician took a couple of steps back into the room and covered her. Jody didn't mind who looked at her or what kind of state she was in. But Danny minded.

On the dashboard of his car was a white petalled flower, its heart deep crimson, as if stained with blood. Danny reached for it and brought it to his nose. He peered through the windscreen and the side windows of the car, but there was no one in sight. He smiled to himself. Could be magic.

Women did this to him. He released something in them so that they gave him presents. But their ardour didn't last. They were fickle. The only constant in his life these days, apart from his work, was Jody.

Driving home without her, he felt bereft, as though some cord had been cut. He was stoical about it, all of these things were sent to try us. And it wasn't as if she was a lot of help about the house. He smiled, glad that he had a sense of humour. It had been his salvation on many occasions, the ability to see the funny side of a situation. Some men let life get them down, fell into depression and negativity. But Danny didn't do that; he didn't need to, he had magic on his side.

Before Jody he had been lonely. There had always been women, but their presence only added to the loneliness. After his mother died it'd got worse. He'd gone to Bangkok to meet girls who wanted a western husband. Had a fortnight there, interviewing one girl after another, so many of them it was difficult to choose. Their quiet obedience was impressive, their flowing dresses and bright black eyes. He'd learned some magic there as well, on the banks of the Chao Phraya River. The magic of the void. The importance of Zero.

Back in England he almost got around to ordering one of those girls.

If it hadn't been for the man in the Adult Shop suggesting he have a look at the work of J. C. Nott, Diamond Danny would have got himself a Thai wife and he'd never have met Jody at all.

On reflection Danny was confident that he'd made the right choice. In a way a Thai girl would have been an attempt to replace his mother, and you can't do that. You can't replace your mother, not ever. Jody wasn't anything like a mother.

She was a work of art.

Marilyn waited in the street and when the magician drove out of his garage she followed at a discreet distance in her mother's car.

He followed a route out of York, through the flooded main street of Fulford and along the A19 in the direction of Selby. When he pulled into the left, behind a plantation of conifers, she drove past and parked by the side of the road. She left Ellen's car and walked back. She could see Danny's car in the driveway of a large gabled house but Danny was no longer behind the wheel.

She avoided the pebbled drive and pushed her way through the trees. The house was quiet, the windows showing only empty rooms. There was no movement and no sound of voices.

In a small garden around the side of the house she found *Hibiscus sinosyriacus* 'Autumn Surprise', brilliant and cheerful against the dark soil. She plucked the flower from the stem and carried it back to Danny's car, thinking she would tuck it beneath his wiper-blades. But as she approached the car she could see that the locks were standing proud. With a glance towards the house she pulled open the driver's door and kissed the flower before placing it on his dashboard.

From the shelter of the conifers she watched as the door of the house opened and Danny was framed there with a bald young man in a pyjama top. They shook hands and the young man went back into the house, closing the door behind him. Danny got into his car and Marilyn watched as he reached for the 'Autumn Surprise' and brought it to his lips. He looked for her, but she kept still and quiet and waited for him to start the car and steer it down the drive, turning back towards York when he reached the main road.

When he'd gone Marilyn walked over to the door of the house and read the plaque on the wall: J. C. Nott. Nothing else. Just the name. It didn't say J. C. Nott, Magician, or J. C. Nott, Magicians' Supplier. From reading the name on the plaque Marilyn couldn't decipher what it was that J. C. Nott did and what it was that Danny had been to see him about. Danny hadn't come out of the house with anything, but it was possible that he had taken something inside. She couldn't say for sure.

She thought of knocking on the door with the brass knocker. She could pretend that she was lost or she could say Ellen's car had broken down and ask to use the telephone. But she didn't knock. There was something about the young man in the pyjama top. She didn't want to find herself trapped in that house with him. Maybe it was his baldness or the way the light had reflected off his glasses? Marilyn didn't know what it was but there was something when she thought of being alone with him that made her want to shudder.

Back at home she looked up the number in the telephone directory.

'J. C. Nott,' the voice said.

'Do you make magic tricks?' Marilyn said into the mouthpiece.

There was silence. 'Are you sure you've got the right number?' he said finally.

'Yes, I think so,' Marilyn said. 'What do you do?'

'My name is James Nott. I'm an artist.'

'Oh, I see,' Marilyn said. 'I've got the wrong number.' She put the phone down.

An artist. That explained it. Danny was going to have his portrait painted. Maybe it was to be a surprise? For her? That was one of the problems of snooping, especially on a lover. You discovered things you'd rather not know. Spoiled a nice surprise.

But Danny wouldn't know what she'd done. So long as she didn't let it slip during one of their long conversations. So long as he continued to sit for the artist. So long as she could act surprised when he eventually presented her with the portrait.

The doorbell rang and Danny collected his suitcase and checked that he'd switched off the gas-ring and the grill. He locked the door behind him and climbed into the back of the taxi.

'Where we going, guv?'

'The railway station, please. No need to rush. We've got plenty of time.'

'The river's still rising,' the cabby said. 'They're talking about evacuating people from their houses.'

'I don't think it'll come to that,' Danny said.

The taxi-driver shrugged his shoulders. 'It's looking bad, worst I've seen, and I've been driving over it for the past twenty year.'

On the train to Newcastle Danny looked out at the waterlogged landscape. Everywhere rivers had crept over their banks and taken to the fields. There was no rain that day and pale sunlight illuminated scenes of reflective stillness. White clouds in glistening lakes surrounded the railway tracks. All wildlife except a smattering of birds had been drowned or moved to higher ground. Here and there the tops of hedgerows were stubbornly visible and magnificent oaks and beeches affected a lofty disregard for the rising tides.

'Beautiful.' The speaker was a young man sitting opposite Danny. Blond hair, blue eyes, slight shoulders and a hard-backed book. The word left his lips like a sigh, a whisper.

'And deadly,' said his companion, a bespectacled, squat youth who looked around the table for a sympathetic response from Danny and the tall, stately black woman who sat beside him. Danny avoided eye-contact.

'Climate change, this is happening all over the world. The result of western nations opting for economies which entail pumping greenhouse gases into the atmosphere. As the climate warms the polar caps begin to melt and sea levels rise. Result is more rainfall and flooding. Blame the oil companies and the American Senate.'

'Beautiful, though,' the original speaker said. 'Breathtaking.'

The squat one looked around the table shaking his head and smiling, proud of his friend's sensitivity.

Danny wondered if they were homosexuals and closed his eyes to imagine them together. He pictured them naked by the sea under a blistering sun, the scene suffused with an air of tragedy. The beautiful one would die and his companion would be left alone to wander the earth. He'd never worry about climate change again.

People didn't know about magic even though they were surrounded by it. All that water standing on the fields, they just accepted it, called it rainfall as though that explained something. These days everyone had a school-boy grasp of science and they believed in it implicitly. But they were hypnotized. Seduced and beguiled by the power of advertising or the fashion business or the dumbed-down norms that society and the political parties paraded as virtue. Everyone, almost everyone, had forgotten that human life is a miracle and that we are all conjurors and wizards. They have been denied so often that the prophecy has become self-fulfilling.

The history of the world has been a war between wizards. Slowly, insidiously, those with the greater magic have stripped the rest of mankind of their powers. And the final act of the victors, the twist in the tail, has been the vanishing trick to end all vanishing tricks. By a neat sleight of hand the wizards and warlocks of the earth, the necromancers and sorcerers and enchanters who make up the vast bulk of mankind, have had the knowledge of their own magic whisked away from them. Now, instead of mixing potions or guaranteeing a food supply or guiding the destiny of their communities, they sit in front of TV screens and store junk information in databases and fervently defend the infantile thesis that two and two make four.

'Danny, Danny! There he is. He's got the tickets.'

A small mousy-haired woman, vaguely familiar, was speaking his name, pointing towards him. She was talking to the ticket inspector, a tall and gawky Asian with bad teeth. The heads of fellow passengers appeared in the aisle as they tried to see what the commotion was about.

'Tickets, please,' the guard said, standing over Danny. The magician reached into his inside pocket, a little miffed at being asked for his ticket for the second time.

'I'm terribly sorry,' the mousy-haired woman said. She had a copper hair-band on her head and at least five necklaces around her neck, silver, gold, something else that looked like brass, and a pewter choker. She was wearing silver hooped ear-rings that stopped an inch above her shoulders. On her wrist there was a thick steel or chromium slave bracelet.

'This ticket is only for you, sir,' the guard said.

'That's right. I'm travelling alone.'

The guard turned to the woman with the necklaces. She didn't speak but looked directly at Danny, pursing her lips and slowly shaking her head from side to side. 'It doesn't matter,' she said. She turned and walked back along the aisle.

'I'm sorry to bother you,' the guard told the magician as he turned to follow the woman.

Danny made light of it with the travellers seated around him. 'I don't know what that was about,' he said.

But the blond young man avoided his eyes, looked out of the window, and the black woman picked up a magazine. After a moment she asked to be excused and he let her get out of her seat. He thought she was going to the lavatory and would be back in a minute or two but she didn't return. Unkind, the magician thought. The stature of the woman had been pleasing and her smooth black skin had given her the quality of a trophy sitting beside him. The only white hunter on the train to have bagged one that beautiful.

The incident was disturbing. It preyed on his mind. The mousy-haired woman shaking her head and walking away was the kind of gesture his mother used to make when she was disappointed in him.

Danny took the Metro to the airport and the mousy-haired woman from the train came and sat opposite him. 'I'm sorry about what happened,' she said. 'Please forgive me.'

'It's fine,' he told her. 'No one got hurt. Mistaken identity. Happens all the time.'

'I shouldn't have put you in the spotlight like that,' she said.

Perhaps she was deranged? A bangle around each of her ankles seemed to confirm it. And all the metal on her person. A large brooch on her lapel which he hadn't noticed on the train. A white bird perched on the edge of a cliff, caught on the point of lurching into space.

'I didn't have enough cash for the fare and I couldn't think what else to do.'

'No, I can see your predicament,' he said, winging it, unwilling to disagree with her in case he triggered some violent reaction. But curiosity got the better of him. 'Have we met?' he said. 'What I mean is, do we know each other?'

'You chose me,' she told him. 'In the theatre. Nottingham?'

'Ah, yes.'

'And now we're lovers.'

Danny coughed. He looked around the carriage to check if anyone had heard her. She gazed at him with rapture, her eyes unblinking.

'Quite,' he said.

The woman was a nutcase. Out of it. Danny got ready

to defend himself if she attacked. There was no guard on the Metro but surely the other passengers would help him. She was a small woman but quite obviously raving mad. Without any civilizing restraints she could cause a lot of damage and as things stood at the moment Danny Mann was the likely target of her aggression. The magician wasn't a coward but he tried to avoid physical pain, especially the kind that involved unknown elements like sharp finger-nails and teeth and the pulling out of hair.

He smiled at her.

She returned his smile with one of her own. There was coyness in it, something approaching innocence. It was the kind of smile that believed in itself. A rare thing. If you didn't know that it was fuelled by insanity, you would be moved by such a smile.

'Where are you going?' he asked, keen to maintain the equilibrium.

The smile again. 'You are funny,' she said.

Danny felt confused, as if he'd been caught out in something. But he couldn't imagine what it was.

'I'd go anywhere with you,' she told him. 'Obey any command.'

'Yes, but . . .'

She was racing ahead of him. A moment ago he'd been in touch. He'd felt equal to whatever it was she was going to throw at him. But already he was stuttering. What on earth was she talking about? 'Obey any command?' he asked, his voice low and coming from way back in his throat.

'Try me,' she said. She parted her legs and ran the middle finger of her right hand around her knee and along her thigh.

'Oh my God,' Danny said. He glanced around as though he might find his God in the carriage. 'Sweet

Jesus,' he said. 'Sweet Jesus Christ.' His hands were fluttering like a couple of birds. He clasped them together and placed them consciously on his knees, watched them sternly until they were still. But as soon as his consciousness lapsed they were off again, fluttering away as if a cat had raided their nest.

'You like me, don't you?' the woman said. She had injected a throaty sound into her voice, like a jazz or blues singer, someone who has smoked a lot of marijuana and has sore and inflamed vocal cords.

'I do, yes,' he said decisively. 'I like you. I find you a pleasant and interesting person to be with.'

'And what's my name?' she asked.

God, there it was again. One minute he was taking control and less than a minute later she was running rings around him. 'Name?'

'My name, yes. A magician like you should know my name.'

She'd been in Nottingham. He would have asked her her name then. But that was hopeless. He'd never remember. 'Josephine,' he said, hoping for a miracle.

She studied his face. After a time she said, 'My name is Marilyn Eccles and you know it very well. You can call me Josephine if you like because Josephine was an erotic woman and a disciple of passionate sexuality.'

'No,' he said. 'I'll call you Marilyn ... Marilyn, very nice name.'

The Metro train pulled into the airport and Danny grabbed his bag. Marilyn ran after him. 'Where are you going?' she said. 'Take me with you?'

'I can't do that,' he said, running up the steps to the airport concourse. 'I'm working away for a few days. We'll have to sort things out when I get back.'

She slowed down, let him get away. Good riddance, he thought. Go bother someone else. But as he looked back she seemed to be shrinking away. He couldn't understand how she could have frightened him on the train. She was all vulnerability and loneliness and reminded him of himself as a child.

He checked in for his flight to Oslo. Yes, only hand luggage he told the receptionist at the Braathens ASA desk, a plump girl with a permanent smile and sparkling eyes. He was only going for a couple of days, quick business trip.

'Enjoy your flight, sir.'

The magician smiled and nodded. Of course he would enjoy it. He had never been on a flight that he didn't enjoy. Soaring above the earth like that, it reminded him of the contest between Simon Magus and Peter, how they had conducted their magic battles in the air above Rome.

Danny would have liked to be alive then, when the profession of magic was held in high esteem. The time when his own knowledge would have led to respect and acceptance. He had never reconciled himself to the fact that his destiny had borne him into a time when respect and adulation were only awarded to pop stars and footballers and computer geeks.

When he thought about it he would rather have been alive at any time in the past. Not only because magic and the profession of magic were better understood and appreciated but because it seemed to Danny that earlier incarnations of society were better regulated. The Ten Commandments were an absolute code which left no room for error or misinterpretation. They were a yardstick by which people could measure their contribution to the community. Well into the Middle Ages the Church continued to offer a stern but just moral landscape in which the battle between good and evil was clearly delineated.

But wherever one looked now there was only a

confusing array of data. Everything of value in the world had been deconstructed. There was no narrative any more, only a series of meaningless snap-shots. Marilyn Eccles was everywhere you looked.

The in-flight magazine had a photograph of a one-legged black toddler and explained that the amputation had been inflicted as a punishment by a teenage commander in one of Sierra Leone's rebel armies. The crippled child stared at the camera with huge round eyes and it was as if the curtain of Maya was lifted at the exact instant that the photojournalist depressed the shutter on his camera. The child becomes an actor in his own drama. Another crippled and starving African child who will do nothing except harden the hearts of his Western audience. To reach them he has to offer more and in that instant he is filled with the consciousness to provide what is needed.

A magic moment occurs.

It is not enough that the child is maimed and hungry. He also has to be pretty and brave. And the child not only knows this but he knows how to accomplish it.

Magic.

He turns his head slightly while keeping his eyes on the camera, and although he doesn't smile he contrives to suggest with his lips and the set of his jaw that a smile is not beyond him. I am not only a helpless amputee, he says. I am also attractive, quaint, fascinating, clever and keen-witted.

He's three years old and he's a master of public relations.

He's three years old and he reaches out of his poverty to enchant millions of people in the richest nations of the earth.

The woman sitting next to Danny on the plane looked

across at the photograph on his lap and shook her head. 'Terrible,' she said.

'Wonderful,' he told her. He didn't bother to explain.

He booked into a non-smoking room in the Scandinavian Hotel in Kongensgate, a couple of minutes from the centre of Oslo. There was a satellite TV and a direct-dial telephone in his room. He could press his trousers while watching an in-house movie, iron his shirt while listening to the radio and drink an old malt from the mini-bar. He was provided with a full-size mirror, an alarm clock, a hairdryer, a bathrobe and an assortment of soaps and shampoos. A corner of the room was given over to a kitchenette and on closer inspection he found he had fax and voicemail facilities and access to in-house shops with newspapers, tobacco, souvenirs and books. In addition to all of this he would be welcome at the hotel swimming pool and fitness centre and there were facilities to ensure that he enjoyed himself riding horseback, cross-country or downhill skiing, biking and ice-skating.

For his valuables the Scandinavian Hotel had a safety deposit box and could offer him a dry cleaning and laundry service as well as the usual room service between 7 a.m. and 11 p.m. After that the heartless management of the place would throw him on to his own resources.

With the aid of an Oslo shopping-map which he had picked up at the station, Danny found his way to Calmeyers gate. He took up a position from which he could see the entrance to the block of upmarket flats which were home to Holly Andersen, another ex-girlfriend of Sam Turner, another whore.

Not that the magician had anything against whores. On the contrary, he had one of his own in Jody who had become his life companion since his mother passed away. Danny's mother had not been a whore, she had been a lady. He remembered her with her hair parted in the centre and arranged smoothly on either side of her face in a Madonna braid. He remembered the bow of her lightly painted lips and her starched apron and the great sadness she bore in silence for the last years of her life. She was an Anglican who had no secret longings for Catholicism. Her relatives and some of Danny's school-friends thought she was stern and dry and austere but they didn't understand. She was a good woman. She was pure.

Jody was a slut and a harlot. He shouldn't have left her with J. C. Nott while he was out of the country. They'd be rutting day and night, the artist and the tart.

And there was Marilyn Eccles, a woman who could prove to be a great nuisance. Danny was aware of his charisma, that it attracted women to him. And he was aware also that he couldn't control it. This woman, for example, he could live without. But it wasn't an immediate problem. Marilyn Eccles was back in England. She couldn't get under his feet for the time being. In Oslo he was safe from her.

Two women passed the magician and went into an exotic seafood shop with crayfish and lobsters in the window. When they left the shop they entered the flats. They were wearing gloves and holding hands. One of them was Holly Andersen. She had aged since the photograph that Danny had of her. The time-span between the photograph and now was twenty years but the lines on her face spoke of at least thirty. Blue jeans and boots and a quilted jacket. She wore a woollen hat with ear-flaps and traditional Lapp patterning. Her hair was shorter than in the photograph but still blonde.

Danny waited until his toes turned numb. He walked the length of Calmeyers gate and back again. A large Norwegian man went into the flats. Later two teenagers arrived on bicycles. An old couple came down the street, she walking with the aid of a stick, and they entered the building. But there was no sign of Sam Turner.

For long after it got dark Danny watched the flats. It might be that Turner wasn't as bright as the magician had anticipated. That Sam Turner hadn't come to Oslo at all. It was possible. The man may not have believed that Holly Andersen was next on the list. Or he may have seen that she was next and simply not cared. He could have run in the opposite direction or even holed up in York in the house of one of his friends.

The magician had not contemplated failure. He had divined that the man would react according to his character, that he would walk into the jaws of the lion because that was what he always did and because that was the only way to save the woman's life.

But if he'd miscalculated and Turner wasn't here at all, not even in the country, then the woman was reprieved, at least for the time being.

Back at the Scandinavian Hotel, Danny sat on his bed and calmed himself with a cognac from the mini-bar. Sam Turner would be here, or he would be on his way. Just because he hadn't shown today didn't mean he wasn't around. Danny hated Sam Turner more than any other man in the world, and you can't hate someone that much and not know what their next move will be. Tomorrow was another day.

19

When Marie Dickens saw that she had an e-mail from someone calling themselves Alcopop her impulse was to delete it. But the first sentence of the message caught her attention.

> Marie, Geordie arrived today. No problems. Will you check marriage records, Katherine and Nicole, Nottingham and Leeds, enquire if anyone else has done the same? Also ask their relatives, friends, if anyone making enquiries. The guy must have done some research. Need to know who he is. *Alcopop*.

Sam in cloak-and-dagger mode. Marie scanned the rest of her Inbox and grabbed a coat. No point wasting time. She'd become a good investigator and she knew it. She had the knack, which was the best starting point. But over and above that she'd learned quickly from Sam, and from Gus, her long-dead husband. She'd been taught to read clues when she was a nurse. No one in the medical business knew how to speak plainly, you had to guess what was expected of you at every twist and turn. Doctors spoke in riddles and consultants often didn't speak at all. The hospital hierarchy and administration didn't know what they wanted themselves and were incapable of giving simple guidelines.

In her work at the women's refuge in town she likewise required an ability to read between the lines. Abused women often had difficulty expressing their emotions and their needs. They lived in fear of their men, but often the fear of loneliness and abandonment was greater. A woman might say that it was over, she never wanted to see him again, but if you looked deep into her eyes you could see she'd be on her way back to him within a few days.

Not always, though. There were women who came to the refuge who were capable of putting their own interests and the interests of their children first. Women who had found a grain of strength and who were keen to build on it.

So why are you working for a serial philanderer? she asked herself as she headed across town towards the library. Checking the marriage records of a couple of his conquests, both freshly departed?

Marie had known Sam Turner for as long as she could remember. She reckoned that she and Celia were the only women Sam had ever known he hadn't considered sleeping with. Maybe Janet as well, Geordie's wife. Yeah, Janet was in the clear. And his mother.

But everything else in a skirt he'd either had a go at it or thought about it. And the women were nearly all of a type. Usually younger than him and vulnerable in some way. Dependent. They'd been pushed around too much and couldn't see straight. They thought Sam was someone to lean on even during those long alcoholic years when he couldn't stand on his own feet.

There were exceptions, of course. You go through so many women and the law of averages is going to ensure that one or two of them are different. So there were independent women on the list, as there were freeloaders and opportunists. There was a smattering of intelligent women, the odd one or two who were older, but these were outnumbered by the majority who were plain unsuitable.

The other thing about Sam's partners was that they didn't stay. Angeles, his current flame, had already lasted longer than most. She was blind, of course, which must be part of the answer as to why she was still around. She was another one who was far too young for him and yet they seemed happy together. She was vulnerable because of her lack of sight but she was also strong. And she was emotionally and financially independent. So all in all there were more pluses than minuses.

Marie liked Angeles. You could talk to her and it didn't have to be about drinking or TV soaps or about how men were from Mars.

She asked for St Catherine's Index in the Central Library and when the librarian found it Marie asked her if it was popular.

'It's used a couple of times a week. Sometimes more.'

'All the marriage records are in here, right?'

'It's fairly comprehensive.'

'So if I wanted to find a marriage record and I didn't know how to do it, would you do it for me?'

'Of course, but it's easy to use.'

'I'm a private detective,' Marie told her. 'I'm trying to find out if anyone has been making enquiries about Sam Turner.'

'Is he the one who's gone missing? The one who killed those women?'

'Yes, he's a suspect. The police want to talk to him.'

The librarian took a deep breath. 'How exciting,' she said. 'What's your question?'

'Has anyone asked about marriage records for Sam Turner in the last few weeks? Or do you recall the name or description of anyone who has recently used the St Catherine's Index?'

'Is this what you call a long-shot?' the librarian asked.

Marie smiled. 'Yeah. We're scraping the barrel.'

'I don't recall anyone asking about that particular name but I'm not the only one who works here. I'll ask my colleagues and get back to you. Do you want to leave a phone number?'

Marie gave her her card. 'You can get me at either of those numbers.'

'We know most of the people who use St Catherine's,' the librarian said. 'Many of them use it frequently. They're interested in family history, ancestry, genealogy. People are fascinated by it.'

'So if someone new came in you'd probably remember?'

'It's not out of the question. If it's been a busy day I can't remember anything that happened when I get back home. But if it's slower I remember the interesting ones. I'll remember you.'

Marie let her have a faint smile, but she didn't say anything.

'All right,' the woman said. 'I'll ask around and come back to you.' She waved Marie's visiting card in the air like a miniature fan.

Back at the office Marie got the keys for the Montego and asked Celia for some cash.

'As in wages?' Celia asked. She was wearing an ancient black dress with slits at both sides. Tango shoes with a chain around her ankle. She'd been quieter than usual since the death of Nicole Day in Leeds and Sam's disappearance. Although she was over seventy, Marie usually thought of her as much younger. But today Celia looked her age. The extravagant clothes and jewellery that she normally carried with aplomb seemed excessive and overindulgent. She could have been an ageing transvestite.

'No, expenses. I'm going to Nottingham. Might have to stay overnight.'

'I've got about a hundred. If you need more than that I'll have to go to the bank.'

'A hundred'll do. I've got a credit card.'

'Be careful, Marie. Whoever's behind these killings won't let anyone stand in their way.'

'Don't worry. I'll be back tomorrow, maybe tonight if I run out of people to talk to. I don't expect to go head to head with a psychotic butcher. Besides I was never married to Sam Turner, which seems to be a guarantee of immunity in this case.'

Celia shook her head. 'I don't know if anyone's immune.' As an afterthought she added: 'Have you had something to eat?'

Marie laughed. 'I'll get a sandwich on the way.'

'Pity. I got us a couple of pork chops for tonight.'

'They'll keep,' Marie said. 'Put them in the fridge.'

As she was ready to leave she looked back at Celia who gave her a quick smile and looked away.

'There's something wrong, isn't there?' Marie said.

'Yes, there is,' Celia said. 'I'm still not sure how wrong.'

'Tell me?'

'I've been having these headaches. The side of my head goes numb, inside, as if part of my brain has frozen. Sometimes my sight goes wonky, I see things in twos and threes.'

'How long has this been going on?'

'A few weeks, couple of months. I've been to see a specialist, had a scan.'

'And?'

'Inconclusive. There's some kind of growth. They think it's still growing.'

Marie wrapped her arms around Celia and hugged her.

'I've tried to get a prognosis out of the medics but they

won't commit themselves. I'm so old, my whole metabolism is so slow that it could take for ever. If it accelerates they're worried I might develop epilepsy.'

'So what happens next?'

'Another scan in a few months. See if the growth has got any bigger.'

'A few months? That's a good sign in itself,' Marie said.

Celia smiled. 'Yes, I suppose it is. They don't seem to think that death is imminent. But they don't always tell the truth.'

'I won't go to Nottingham today,' Marie said. 'I'd be worrying about you all the time.'

'You certainly will go,' Celia told her. 'If I'd thought you'd be so fussy, I wouldn't have told you. And don't say anything to the others. I can't cope with baleful looks.'

The late Katherine Turner's house in Nottingham was boarded up. The police and forensic people had obviously finished with it because there was no one on sentry duty. The terrace was one of several that had been put up in the late-forties or early-fifties and the houses had been well maintained and refurbished over the years. The terrible act that had taken place in one of them and the subsequent nailing of chipboard panels over its windows and doors seemed to reflect on the whole terrace. The seemingly senseless and particularly brutal death of Katherine Turner had reverberated throughout the fabric of bricks and mortar, seeping like a stain through party walls and running along shared joists and roof-beams. The perpetrator of the crime had been in one house but he had left his mark on all of them. None of the curtains were fully drawn back and there was a silence about this part of the street that was tangible. It was like walking through the entrance of a great cathedral, the feeling of being in the presence of something unseen. But the cathedral feeling was usually benign, benevolent. Whereas Katherine Turner's house and the others adjoining it seemed to embrace the aura of something much older and darker. Something, Marie thought, that you wouldn't want to disturb from its slumbers.

The woman next door was happy to talk. She introduced herself as Jade Chandler and at twenty-five years old was already a faded beauty. She had a light brown baby, the same colour as herself, in a sling on her stomach. In Jade's sitting room Marie had to step over half-completed jigsaw-puzzles and wooden trucks and action-man figures. They sat opposite each other at a table piled high with dirty washing, lemonade bottles, an ash-tray and the remains of several tabloid newspapers which had been used for Origami and confetti-making.

'You knew Katherine?'

Jade Chandler smiled. 'She was my neighbour. We didn't live in each other's pocket but we talked from time to time. She'd baby-sit occasionally and she'd bring me things from the shops if I couldn't get there.'

'Did she have a job?'

'Yes, she worked for a letting agency. Flats and houses. She made sure people were paying the rent and that the houses were maintained properly. Fought landlords to get fire certificates. She liked to talk about it. I reckon she was good at it.'

'Boyfriends?'

'From time to time. Nobody special until the last one.'

'The guy who found her?'

'Yes, Ruben, she liked him. The others were ships passing in the night. She could take or leave them. But she had no kids and she'd get lonely sometimes. You know what it's like.'

Marie nodded. She knew exactly what it was like. Sometimes the desire to be held by a man, to be up close against someone else's skin or inhale their scent, was so urgent it was like a pain. You lost a certain amount of judgement when loneliness echoed around your being, your standards and values tended to slip.

'Some of the guys she'd bring home, they were just wrong.'

'Any of them wrong enough to kill her?' Marie asked.

Jade thought about it. She ran her hand over the sleeping baby on her stomach. 'The police asked the same question,' she said. 'But who can say? Katherine would hook up with a guy from time to time. He'd be a loner or a married man who was looking for something extra. All of them were inadequate in one way or another. Weasels or opportunists, people who had failed in a hundred other relationships. There was one man who was subnormal, a speech defect and he'd never learned to shave properly, Dennis. Another who was thirty years older than her, an old-age-pensioner.

'Most of them were a waste of time but I couldn't see them as murderers. Not like that, anyway. So cold-blooded. I think any of us could kill in a rage, on the spur of the moment. But whoever killed Katherine planned it. The guys she knew, most of them were incapable of planning. They were like leaves in the wind.'

'So you don't think it was a boyfriend?'

'No. They didn't hang around, anyway. She wouldn't play them off against each other. Since she'd been going with Ruben Parkins she hadn't seen anyone else.'

'And Ruben, what was he like?'

'At first I thought he was the same. He'd been in prison and he had that machismo thing. Flashy type. He'd wear shades at night, know what I mean? Tattoos, big shoulders, ear-ring, chemical blue suits, chewing gum, hair-gel. It was like he didn't want to be left out of anything. I've seen him wearing Day-Glo socks and decorative chains on his shoes.' She laughed. 'Imagine! He was a fashion nightmare. There was so much going on with him you couldn't focus on who he was.'

'But Katherine liked him?'

'Yes. She saw through all that stuff immediately. She saw his vulnerability. Sounds corny, but she saw the good in him. And he responded to her, listened to her. He modified his opinions, dropped some of his masks. He took her shopping with him when he wanted a new sweater. He was turning into Mr Nice Guy.'

'He sounds a bit flaky, though,' Marie said. 'A man who would let a woman take over his personality like that.'

Jade shook her head. 'He wasn't flaky. It happened slowly. Ruben had never learned how to live. When he met Katherine he realized she could teach him. For her part she'd never met a man who loved her for herself. They were good for each other. Each of them allowed the other one to grow. It was something to see. Something special.'

'So Ruben's not a suspect?'

'No, he never was. He brought her body out of the house and round to my door. He was making noises like an animal. No one could have acted that. He was a man who had had his heart ripped out. She was everything to him.'

Marie kept quiet. She didn't know if she believed that a woman could be everything to a man. No man had ever been everything to her. Oh, way back when she was sixteen it might have seemed like that. When her hormones were leaping and dancing around like a chorus from *Swan Lake*. Or even later, when she and Gus were planning a family and it seemed like they'd be together for the rest of their lives. But she hadn't been in touch with reality on either of those occasions.

'Did you like Katherine Turner?'

Jade Chandler looked at her and smiled. 'Yes, I liked her. She was a good neighbour.'

'Not a friend?'

Jade shook her head. 'She was older than me. We weren't friends. But we could have been if we'd spent more time together.'

Marie gave her a few seconds to digest her own words. 'So who do you think killed her? You must have a theory.'

'I can't tell you,' Jade said, 'because I don't know. But I'll tell you what we told the police.'

'We?'

'My partner Ben and I. He's at work at the moment. It was a few months ago. I'd lost my ring. We'd been up late with the children and it must have been one-thirty, two o'clock in the morning.' She looked down at the sleeping child. 'This one had just gone off to sleep and the other two were finally settled. I said I'd put the kettle on, make us a nightcap, and Ben went outside with a torch to see if he could find the ring.'

'In the middle of the night? In the dark?'

'You lose your marbles when you've got three kids under five. Now you mention it, it was a weird thing to do, but at the time I didn't give it a second thought. And he didn't find the ring because it wasn't out there. It turned up a couple of days later in the bathroom. But that's another story. Anyway there was a man outside – Ben didn't see his face. He got an impression of his size, about average height and weight, and the man was wearing a black overcoat and a trilby. It was something to see anyone down the street at that time in the morning but the funny thing was Ben said he'd looked up and down the street a couple of seconds before and there'd been no one there then.

'He hadn't heard anyone either. But when he turned the torch on at the gate the beam fell on the man's feet. Highly polished shoes, that's what Ben remembered, and the man was wearing those trousers with braid down the outside seam. You could see them as he walked off down the street.'

'Braid?' Marie said. 'As in a uniform?'

'No, not like that. More like the trousers you see when someone is in full evening dress.'

'Last time I saw someone wearing them he was waiter.'

'Or ballroom dancers, they wear them sometimes. But the shoes weren't dancing shoes.'

'And you think this was the murderer?' Marie asked. 'Why?'

'He wasn't in the street when Ben went outside. The only place he could have been was in Katherine's garden.'

'Another boyfriend?'

'No. She would have mentioned it. She was with Pete Lewis at the time and she didn't two-time. Katherine had morals.'

'But did you ask her about it?'

'Yes, I asked the next day. She didn't know anyone who wore a trilby. And it wasn't that important, we let it drop, forgot about it. It only came up again when Katherine was killed.'

Marie liked Jade Chandler. A strangely old-fashioned girl, open and straightforward. She reminded her of an era when falling in love wasn't complicated by the spectre of children on alternate weekends. The other neighbours were not so helpful. When Katherine was alive they'd distrusted and envied her, especially the string of assorted men she'd brought back to her house, and obviously equated her death with some unthinking and ancient code of just deserts. Neighbours from Hell, the kind of people who thought you got AIDS from homosexuality.

Braid. A killer with braid down the seam of his trousers. This was the first indicator they had had. Before they had been looking at everyone in the world. Now the field had narrowed down.

Marie parked the Montego in the NCP car park on Mount Street and walked to the offices of Shaw & Shaw – Let Us Let It – Estate Agents and Letting Agency, which was situated on a corner position in a dark street behind the Playhouse. There was a receptionist with bright red lipstick who answered the phone and an office boy with one of those mouths that won't close.

'Can I speak to either of the partners?' Marie asked.

The receptionist pursed her painted lips and said, 'No. Not without an appointment, I'm afraid.' She wore a floral-pattern dress with a grey cardigan draped around her shoulders. She had just missed being attractive and dressed to accentuate the fact.

'I'm only here for the day. I wanted to talk to someone about Katherine Turner.'

'You can talk to me, if you like. And Saul. You don't mind talking about Katherine, do you, Saul?'

The boy was a contortionist. He managed to shake his head in such a way that his bottom jaw remained stationary. A minor Vesuvius was erupting on his forehead.

'It's up to you,' the receptionist continued. 'Mrs Shaw's been up to here since Katherine, well . . . you know. Katherine dealt with the rented properties and now Mrs S has to do it all herself.'

'And Mr Shaw?' Marie asked.

'Well, he's out of it, isn't he? Hasn't been to the office for years. If he walked in today I don't know if I'd recognize him. He's got that disease . . . turns you into an old codger. Mrs S has someone come in at home to see to him while she's running the business.'

'Did you know Katherine Turner well?'

'Well as anyone, I should think. We saw more of her before the accident than we did of Mrs S.'

'Why do you call it an accident?'

'It sounds nicer, don't you think? The other word's more violent.'

'Murder. She *was* murdered.'

'I don't like saying it. Neither does Saul, do you, Saul?'

He swallowed some air but the fly-trap remained open. Marie saw him ten years down the line, a captain of industry, a magnate in the tradition of Robert Maxwell, Nick Leeson, Jonathan Aitken and Lord Archer. Perhaps he was Mrs S's nephew or the son of a friend? Another instance of the old school tie and nepotism saving British industry from any form of change or innovation. Vesuvius threw out a fine spray of lava when he shook his head.

'Did she talk about boyfriends?' Marie asked.

'She talked about Ruben all the time. Ruben this, Ruben that. You would've thought he was Prince Charming to hear her go on about him. But he came to collect her from the office a couple of times and he was, well, you know.'

'No,' Marie told her. 'I don't know. What was he?'

'Common,' said the receptionist. 'You wouldn't've given him a job. He looked like a criminal.'

Dear God, Marie said to herself. What kind of work is this, where you have to talk to morons all day long?

'I was thinking about other boyfriends,' she said. 'Did she ever mention a dancer or a waiter?'

'Tell you the truth,' the receptionist said, 'she liked them rougher than that. I don't usually talk ill of the dead, Saul will bear me out about that, but Katherine was the type who wouldn't look twice at a decent man. Always went for the *exotic*.'

'A dancer?'

She shook her head. 'No, Katherine had two left feet. She liked films and she bought CDs. Rock 'n' roll. But she didn't go dancing.'

'What about a waiter?'

'I don't remember her talking about any waiter. She might have . . . someone who worked in a café, some kind of greasy spoon place. But if you're thinking of a posh waiter in a proper restaurant, she probably wouldn't.'

'What I'm thinking of,' Marie said, 'is someone who wears trousers with braid down the seam of the leg.'

'Oh, no, not Katherine. She'd never look twice at someone like that. What do you say, Saul?'

Saul performed something approximating to a smile followed by a grunt which moved a body of viscous fluid from his lungs to his tonsils.

Back at the car Marie tried to put a list together. Who wears braid on his trousers? If we dismiss the military there are people who wear it as part of the uniform for their job, like waiters or professional dancers. There are a whole group of other men who might have been to some kind of formal function, a wedding or a posh dinner party. And after that there are entertainers, singers perhaps, a compère at a cabaret, or someone in the theatre.

Then there was the question of the trilby. Who wears a trilby? Sam Turner did sometimes, but not a lot of men, not these days. It was a kind of affectation.

In itself a trilby would be something to think about, but in combination with dress trousers it was decidedly odd. With dress trousers you would expect a top hat, white gloves and a cane. And the overcoat was odd as well. With trousers like that it would be more fitting to wear a cape.

Did the man who was in Katherine Turner's garden that night have these other clothes? If so, what had he done with them? In the full rig he would have looked like a professional gambler or a vampire. A roué. Where had he been before checking out Katherine's house?

The other explanation, of course, was that he didn't have the rest of the clothes. He'd bought the trousers at a second-hand or charity shop at the same time as he bought the trilby and the black overcoat. They were a working disguise, something to throw would-be pursuers off the scent. And to throw away once the deed was done.

But Marie was not here to make guesses. Not in the age of the CCTV camera.

The Riverside Student House was not on the side of the river. It was a quarter of a mile away from Katherine Turner's house and constructed of redbrick with a black pantiled roof. A small plaque under the name of the house informed Marie that it was built in the year 1815, but some modernization had occurred since then, the double-glazing for example and the high-mounted camera that scanned the street outside.

The manager of the house, Jurgen Grimes, was a technophile and only too happy to show off his system. 'Do you know about digital imaging?' he asked Marie.

'Not a lot,' she said. 'I know the quality's good.'

He sat her in front of a bank of screens in one of the upper rooms. 'I've got eight cameras at this house,' he said. 'Another eight at Warwick House further along the street. There's eight at Windermere, which is closer to the main campus, and there's still room on the system for more when I need them.'

Most of the screens, some of which were split, showed

internal scenes, halls and stairways, but others showed front and rear views from the various houses and tracked images of people and vehicles approaching from either direction.

'Do you keep archived material?' she asked.

'How far back?'

Marie mentioned the date of Katherine Turner's death.

'That's not archived,' Jurgen said. 'That's still current. The system is set to compress stretches of time when nothing happens but any movement in the camera area is saved to the hard disk.' He used the keyboard to enter the date. 'What time of day?'

'Night,' Marie told him. 'Try between midnight and around two in the morning.'

Jurgen pointed to the monitor to her right and Marie watched it change from a four-part split screen to a full-screen view of the street outside the house. The digital clock in the lower right-hand corner of the screen showed 12.01 a.m. but quickly changed to 12.17 when the camera locked on to a couple of girls swaying along the street with their arms around each other. They were around twenty years old and had been drinking. One of them was crying. The camera followed them until they drew level with the house and then switched and followed them along the street until they turned the corner and disappeared.

The digital clock leapt forward again, 12.51 a.m.

At the far end of the street was a figure with a hat. As he drew closer to the house it was apparent that the hat was a trilby and that the man was wearing a neat black overcoat. 'Can you zoom in?' Marie asked.

'We'll lose quality.'

'That's OK.'

Jurgen operated a mouse and the camera zoomed in on the area of the man's face. But there was nothing recognizable there, only a mass of pixels. The camera pulled back fractionally but the man kept his head down, his eyes on the pavement, so that his features were hidden in shadows.

'Damn!' Marie said.

'He's avoiding the camera,' Jurgen said. 'But he's white, we can see that.' He entered something on the keyboard and the man's height and weight flashed up on the screen. 'He's one metre seventy-eight and around sixty-eight kilos.'

'That's neat,' Marie said. 'Will it give us his name and address?'

Jurgen laughed. 'The way the technology's progressing it might be able to do that one day.'

'Can you go down to his feet?' Marie said. 'His shoes.'

Jurgen moved the mouse down the length of the man's body.

'A little higher,' Marie said. 'I want to see the bottom of his trousers.'

The man was wearing grey trousers with a sharp crease. There was no braid on them.

'Highly polished shoes, though,' Jurgen said. 'Shows someone who's fastidious.'

'Or he lives with someone who is,' Marie said. 'Maybe his mother?'

Jurgen let the image run and they watched the man pass the house and the camera switch to his rear view until he turned out of the street in the direction of the quiet avenue where Katherine Turner, unknowingly, waited for him.

'Can you give me a copy of that?' Marie asked.

'If you give me an e-mail address I'll send it as an attachment,' he said. 'You might lose quality but you can always come back here for a better view.'

Marie left the house and followed in the footsteps of

the man in the trilby hat. She could feel Jurgen tracking her from his terminal as she walked the length of the street.

20

Sam watched an Oslo dawn through the windows of the flat in Osterhaus gate. He'd turned in around half-midnight and gone deep for a couple of hours. Dreamed of the Christmas Eve that Holly walked out on him. It was all there in his mind, the tinsel and the whisky on his breath. Kind of dream if it was a play you'd say, *Great set, but I couldn't believe the characters, especially the guy.*

He'd gone out and bought a turkey and eight bottles of Scotch in the morning. Brought them back home safely. He'd noticed the van outside the house but didn't think it was anything to do with him. Blue transit with the rear doors open, straw inside, looked like it'd been used to transport animal feed.

Holly had the wardrobe door open and was piling her clothes on the bed. 'I've met someone,' she told him. 'I'm moving out. We want to spend Christmas together.'

Sam went downstairs, opened one of the bottles and filled a glass. He was truculent but buried it under an avuncular mask. Thought civilized thoughts. He brought the drink upstairs and said. 'I'm in reasonable mode. I'm not gonna be violent. Who is it? Anyone I know?'

He didn't know anyone who would have handled it better under the circumstances.

Holly was wary, but she answered. 'No one you know. A doctor. Norwegian.'

'Going up-market,' he said. She gave him a look that might've been imported from the Arctic.

He told her, 'I'm trying to be calm but there's a residue of bitterness in me. And I just bought a turkey.'

'I hope you'll be happy together,' Holly said.

'I can't believe you said that.'

'Sam, most of the things I've said these last months, you haven't heard.' She collected the clothes in both arms and picked her way down the stairs. She got a cardboard box and flicked her way through the CDs, taking the ones she thought belonged to her. Sam looked over her shoulder, to make sure she didn't take anything important. And there was something strange: they'd definitely been CDs in the dream when in reality they were vinyl, albums, maybe a few audio-tapes in there.

When she went outside to the van he poured himself a refill. Cheap and nasty, he could feel it going to work on his liver.

He sat on a chair in the kitchen and put his head in his hands. He caught glimpses of the world fragmenting around him. 'It's fucking Christmas,' he said when she came back into the house.

'I know the date, Sam.'

'Christmas Eve.' He was going to tell her he'd bought a turkey again but she hadn't been too impressed the first time.

She looked good, as though she was on the verge of something. Sam hadn't looked at her for a long time, or if he had he hadn't seen her. She looked as though she had a life and she looked fired-up, as though she couldn't wait for it to get going. Didn't really matter what came, she'd make something of it.

'You can take half the turkey,' he said. 'If there's room in the van. I'll get a saw.'

'Look,' Holly said, 'it hasn't worked, that's all. We both tried and it didn't come to anything. You haven't been happy.'

It was true, he hadn't been. Not for years, long before Holly came into his life. He didn't understand what happiness had to do with it. While they were together there was hope, that's how he'd seen it. He'd known it wasn't enough, but as long as they had each other . . .

'You'll be all right?' she asked him. 'You won't do anything silly?'

He wanted to laugh at that but why torture the woman? No, he wouldn't do anything silly, he'd carry on making sensible and rational decisions. Soon as he'd finished these eight bottles he'd stop drinking and get a job. Become respectable, rich, maybe famous.

There was a moment, in real time and in the dream, when he thought of going down on his knees, begging her to stay, at least over Christmas. But he didn't do it because it might have worked. He saw them stuffing the turkey together and sitting down at the table with it between them. And he knew that what he thought was hope was no hope at all. If he begged long and loud enough it would prolong the nightmare. Perhaps indefinitely. But he saw himself with the possibility of alternative nightmares. A man with the luxury of choice.

It was best that she ran off with her Norwegian doctor. And it was best that Sam stayed behind in the empty house. There was so much of him he didn't know, so much of himself he had avoided. Sam Turner didn't need a relationship, he needed time and space.

'I hope you find what you're looking for,' he told her. While he was forming the words he tried to make himself believe them. She didn't reply and he didn't have anything to add.

When she'd loaded up the van she came back into the house with a small blonde woman. 'This is Sam,' she said. 'And, Sam, this is my friend, Inge Berit Andersen.'

He tried to get to his feet but it was too far to go. He held his glass in a salute and swigged the whisky down.

They left together, hand in hand like a couple of kids.

Sam lived with the turkey and the blowflies for ten days before he propped the carcass against the dustbin by the back gate.

He looked out at Osterhaus gate, found his clothes and got dressed. For a while he sat against the floor-to-ceiling stove which heated the flat and listened to Geordie talking to Janet in his sleep. He listened to Geordie talking to Echo in his sleep, and to Barney, and to his long-lost mother and his dead brother. This was the longest period that Geordie and Janet had been apart since they got hitched. Not surprising the kid was having withdrawal symptoms.

Sam thought about Angeles and wondered how she was doing. He shrugged his shoulders. She'd be all right. She was a strong woman. She'd managed without Sam Turner before they met and she'd manage OK now while he was away, on the run, trying to defend an old girlfriend against a madman.

He couldn't phone Angeles. The police would trace the call. He could communicate with her through e-mail, using the Hotmail or Yahoo addresses, but he'd need an Internet café to do that and it was too early. The news told him that back in York the river level had risen by over four metres and was expected to rise again over the weekend. It was still raining up in the hills and the rivulets and tributaries were collecting every last drop of the stuff and channelling it towards the town.

In theory it didn't have to stop. York could turn into another Venice and eventually a small Atlantis, buried and lost for ever in a watery grave. He imagined himself and Geordie arriving home and finding a bottomless lake where the town was. No trace of the lives they had known before. A vast expanse of water with a solitary bird soaring high in the sky.

He pulled on his boots and wrapped up warm to brave the night. He'd always made excuses about the women in his life – why he couldn't get home one night, why he didn't bother to phone another. Sam was a past master at letting it roll on past, feeling somehow that if the world was really interested it would come knock on his door. They'd all been worth fighting for, the women in his life, but Sam had usually been looking the other way, chasing multi-coloured impossibilities. By the time he got home she'd left and taken the home with her.

He found a tiny Internet café by the station, three terminals, all Apple Macs. The proprietor was a teenage entrepreneur who looked like he never slept. Huge young man, cholesterol on the hoof. Sam settled himself down and logged on to his Hotmail account. He told Angeles about the flat and about how well Geordie was sleeping. He told her about his fears for Holly's safety and how he hoped he wasn't losing Angeles as well. *I'm in a cool room*, he said, *a room made for long talks.* He wrote words that don't come easily and sent them unencrypted over the world-wide web, imagining them being reinterpreted by her Braille writer at the other end.

He told her about the 50–50–90 rule: *Anytime you have a 50–50 chance of getting something right, there's a 90% probability you'll get it wrong.* And he told her he was working on the statistics, trying to get them into a different order. *I hope my train hasn't been and gone*, he wrote.

He didn't know how to finish the e-mail. He sat with his head in his hands for a long time, hoping for words that would make a difference. Then he told her he loved her and signed off.

*

Sam was back by the window when Geordie padded through from his bedroom. 'You didn't sleep?' he said. 'Is there something to eat?'

'Cupboard over the sink,' Sam told him. 'Bran flakes. Milk in the fridge.'

'Bran? I can't eat that, Sam. Janet bought bran once and we were both shitting through the eye of a needle for a week. I'm not gonna put myself in that situation in a foreign country. You got anything else?'

'There's bread,' Sam said. 'No butter, though. There might be some cheese left. Continental breakfast.'

'What about muesli? We have muesli at home. Janet buys the oats and sunflower seeds, dried banana ... I can't remember everything she puts in. There's apple and granola, pineapple. She mixes it together and we have it in a big jar with a lid, keep it fresh. Barley flakes, that's another thing in there.'

'There's bran or bread,' Sam said.

'Even Weetabix would've done,' Geordie said. 'Just once, for a change. It's not what I like to eat every day. If I thought there was gonna be Weetabix every morning I wouldn't get out of bed. Bran or bread and cheese, I'd end up like you, not being able to sleep.'

'You can go to the shop,' Sam told him. 'Buy some muesli.'

'What do I ask for?'

Sam looked at him.

Geordie said, 'I don't know if they know what muesli is. I could go all the way down there and ask for muesli and the guy could look at me like I'm a legend in my own lunchtime.'

'It's called muesli. People here understand English. Not all of them speak it, but most of them understand what you're saying.'

'OK. D'you want anything?'

'Get some eggs,' Sam said. 'Pack of bacon. Thin-cut. I'm in need of comfort.'

'Good idea,' Geordie said. 'How about a couple of sausages and some mushrooms?'

'You've gone off the muesli idea, then?'

'No point being fussy, Sam. I'll have the same as you.'

Sam got the coffee makings together and found a frying pan. When Geordie came back with the food he said, 'There's faces from every corner of the globe out there. There's black and Asian and Russian and Chinese. Every way you look there's mothers with children in prams. In the shop there was this Ethiopian woman with her kids, real tall woman, elegant. You seen her?'

'Maybe. Did she mention me?'

'I went in a Vietnamese shop, a Thai shop, couldn't find sausages in either of them. Most of the stuff in there doesn't look edible. There's vegetables you never heard of.'

Sam was ready to cook. He drizzled olive oil into the pan.

'What's that?' Geordie asked.

'Read the label.'

'I read the label. It's olive oil.'

Sam turned up the heat and tipped the pan to move the oil around its base. 'Why'd you ask me what it is when you already know what it is?'

'I wanted to be sure. Just because it says olive oil on the label, doesn't necessarily mean there's olive oil in the bottle.'

'Nitro-glycerine,' Sam said. 'I can't cook bacon without something highly explosive in the pan. But it's illegal so I keep it in an olive oil bottle. Saves me going to jail.'

'Y'know what I think?' Geordie said. 'I think you must've had a real fucked-up childhood. That's why you're so defensive all the time. I asked you a simple question, like what's that in the olive oil bottle, and you have to give me a hard time. You should see a therapist, Sam, I mean it. A good therapist would turn you around in no time. Jungian, somebody like that, he'd find out where the blockage was and set you free. There's this childhood trauma backed up in your psyche, could be you were jealous of your father because he slept with your mother or you were frightened of his dick.

'What these Jungians do, they're trained to see what type of trauma it is and they get you to say it and once you've said it, admitted it to yourself, you're cured.'

Sam put the sausages in the pan and peeled the mushrooms. 'Sounds like an AA meeting,' he said. 'My name is Sam Turner and I'm an alcoholic. Doesn't cure you, though. What it does, it helps you stay in touch with reality.'

'That's important,' Geordie said. 'If you lose touch with reality, where are you?'

Sam continued peeling the mushrooms. After he'd peeled one he chopped it in half and went on to the next one.

'Is that a real question?' he asked. 'If you lose touch with reality, where are you?'

'It's a real question,' Geordie told him. 'Why would you think it wasn't a real question?'

'It's like the olive oil question over again, that's why. "What's that?" when I'm pouring olive oil out of an olive oil bottle. "If you lose touch with reality, where are you?" when it's obvious if you lose touch with reality you're lost, out of sync. I can't believe this is happening sometimes. I'm locked in a flat with you and you're asking me these questions that don't make any sense. I think it might be a dream or I've ended up on a mental ward. I keep looking round for big nurse.'

He turned the sausages and added the mushrooms and

the bacon. He reached for the olive oil and added a little more to the pan.

'This's exactly what I'm getting at,' Geordie told him. 'It's this defensiveness. What you should do, you should ask yourself why you get so worked up in response to a couple of questions.'

'I'm *not* worked up,' Sam said. He cracked the eggs on the side of the pan and dropped them into the hot oil. 'You got some plates ready?'

Geordie walked around the kitchen, opening cupboard doors, on the hunt. 'This is typical of suppressed schizophrenia,' he said. 'You think you aren't worked up because you've discovered the best way of handling it is to appear calm. Anytime you get worked up you worry that people'll think you're worked up so you slow yourself down and talk calmly to make them think you're not worked up. That's understandable, you want everyone to think you're normal.'

Sam watched the eggs. He said, 'You know this breakfast I'm cooking here? Your half of the sausages and the bacon and the mushrooms, one of the eggs, and the bread I'm gonna fry in the olive oil that's left over?'

'My half?'

'What I'm thinking at the moment is, I don't have to give it to you. Long as it's in the pan and I cooked it, it still belongs to me. I could eat it all, or I could pour half of it down the John and eat my half by myself at the table.'

'There you go again,' Geordie said. 'It starts off and you're defensive, like someone's attacking you when they're only asking questions. And now we're moving on to the next stage, which it always comes to, and that's where the defensiveness stops and you get outright aggressive.'

'Stop!' Sam told him, taking the frying pan off the cooker and holding it with two hands.

'Is that a threatening gesture?' Geordie said. 'Or is that a threatening gesture.'

'I'm taking it to the John,' Sam said.

'If you could see yourself objectively, Sam, really, this is ridiculous.'

Sam set off down the narrow corridor, taking the frying pan with him.

'OK, I've stopped,' Geordie called.

Sam turned. 'Am I worked up?'

'Not at all. No.'

'Do I need to see a Jungian therapist?'

'Would be a waste of time and money,' Geordie said. 'Therapists – what do they know?'

'Have you got the plates ready?' Sam said, arriving back in the kitchen with a grin on his face.

'Yeah,' Geordie said, sitting at the table. 'Oh, the smell. Can't remember when food smelled so good.'

After the food Sam poured the coffee and sat back in his chair. 'You know what he makes me feel, this guy?'

'The killer?'

'He makes me feel numb. I can't stand far enough back from it to get a handle. I want to be able to say, "OK, the guy is killing these women because of their involvement with me." But as soon as I start to think about it, I see their faces, I remember when we were young and together. All those memories come flooding in and then I can't see the wood for the trees.'

'Mixed metaphor,' Geordie said.

'What?'

'It's a mixed metaphor. You start off with a flood and end up with woods and trees.'

Sam's mouth fell open. 'Are you listening to what I'm saying?'

'Yeah, I hear you. I just pointed something out.'

'I'm trying to stay calm, here, Geordie. I don't want an English lesson right now.'

'OK, I'm listening. All those memories come flooding in and you're swamped. It's like you want to concentrate on the foundation of the crime, get to the guy's motivation. But the flood of memories rises so high you can't see the foundations any more.'

'Right. Which is one of the reasons I brought you here. I need somebody who can be objective, somebody who can keep me objective.'

'Thank you. I appreciate that,' Geordie said. 'I appreciate that you appreciate my objectivity. That's one thing. And the other thing is that it's Scandinavia. Which means I've really been abroad, not just to Amsterdam.'

'Tell me what you know about the killer.'

'It's probably a guy,' Geordie said. 'There are women serial killers but not many of them so almost certain to be a man. He's killing women who have been married to you or who you've lived with and he's arranging it to look as though you've done it. First he murdered Katherine Turner when you were in Nottingham, then he arranged for you to be in the same street as Nicole Day in Leeds at the exact time she was killed. What I get from that, the guy has got a real boner for you.

'You must've upset him big time, which you're good at, upsetting people. But this one, I can't imagine what you did to him. Maybe you should write down everybody you've ever got under their skin. Try to think of the guy in the world you've given the most grief to. You might've robbed him or screwed his wife and he's been nursing it for years. It's grown in his mind like a brain tumour, so now all he can think of is revenge.

'You can bet he's not getting on with his life, this guy. He's so obsessed about setting you up for a life sentence he's forgotten to have relationships. If he's married, his wife'll never see him. This's what I think we're looking for, Sam. I might be wrong about one or two of these things, but most of 'em will be right. Mainly it'll be somebody you've taken to the cleaners and now they're coming back, looking for a bite at the cherry of revenge.'

Sam laughed.

'What's funny?'

'Cherry of revenge,' he said. 'This from the guy who criticizes *my* English?'

'What's wrong with that?' Geordie said. 'Revenge is sweet. Cherries is sweet. Nothing to laugh about.'

'All right, let's not get waylaid here. Anything else about this guy?'

'Oh, yeah, there's the biggie. The knife he's using, sword, whatever it is. Some huge implement. In psychology terms it's a penis substitute, like a car, but it's not a car, therefore the guy'll probably have a crap car.'

'You been reading those books again.'

'Yeah, I've been reading those books again. This weapon, whatever it is he's using, it's about power. Cars, bullets, guns, rockets ... anything that's powerful and makes a lot of noise, something you can use to poke with or stick in somebody ... can be penis substitutes. Guys who use them or have obsessions about them, they're either impotent or might not be impotent but they certainly worry about it. So somebody who kills women with a sword, that's gotta be significant. This is a guy who doesn't understand women. Might be a misogynist. Has trouble getting a hard-on.'

'And there's one other thing,' Sam said. 'The guy's manipulative. Always moves me into position before he closes in for the kill. That could be one of his strengths, the way he manipulates people. Could be something to do with his job. What kind of job could that be, where you manipulate people? Is he a politician? Some kind of manager?'

'Yeah,' Geordie said. 'But he doesn't just manipulate people, he manages the whole scene. He manipulates events as well.'

'So think about jobs that involve all that,' Sam said.

'Could be in the Army or the Navy?'

'Another thing too,' Sam said. 'Because he's into manipulating the scene, he makes himself vulnerable.'

'How do you work that out?'

'He has to get me into place before he can kill the next victim.'

'Seems like he's managed that fairly easily up to now,' Geordie said. 'He got you here, to Norway.'

'That's right. He did. He told me Holly would be next. And he knows enough about my character to realize I'd come here to protect her.'

'Which means he's sussed you,' Geordie said. 'How does that make him vulnerable?'

'Because he can't be sure I'm here.'

'How do you mean?'

'He's guessing I'm here, *hoping* I'm here, but he doesn't know. Before he can kill Holly, he has to see me.'

'Right,' Geordie said. 'You might've gone to Scotland. He's given you the clues, and he knows you're a detective, hopes you get it, that there'll be enough to lure you here.'

'But he has to *see* me,' Sam said. 'If he doesn't see me here, then Holly's safe. He won't touch her.'

'Does that mean we're going home? I haven't seen the Munch Museum yet.'

'No, we're staying. We can play him at his own game. He'll be watching Holly's flat, hoping to see me going in there.'

'Which means we watch the street, Calmeyers gate,'

Geordie said, 'looking for the guy who's watching the flat.'

'You got it,' Sam said. 'That's exactly what we do.'

21

'You can sit there until you decide to give me some civilized answers,' Ellen said.

Marilyn was seated on a high stool at the end of the kitchen table. She'd stopped crying but her eyes were red and she was sniffing and blowing her nose into the remains of a man-size tissue.

'It's that Danny Mann character, isn't it?' Ellen said.

Marilyn nodded her head. 'Yes.'

'You've been following him? Stopping him in the street?'

'Not exactly.'

'Marilyn, I'm not going to beat about the bush here. The signs are all too clear. You're not taking your medication. You're clearly obsessed with this man – all that stuff on your bedroom wall. Two or three times lately you've stayed out all night, or most of the night. You're weepy and erratic in your behaviour.'

'Only when you go on at me.'

'Correction, not only when I go on at you. Usually you behave like this when the chosen man of your dreams doesn't know what is happening to him and tells you to get lost.'

'God!' Marilyn said, getting off the stool. 'I don't have to stand for this.'

'Oh, yes, you do, my girl. Sit on that stool now or I'll ring the doctor immediately.'

'And what'll that prove?'

'It'll prove that you're not taking your medication, that

you're highly emotional and unstable, and will probably lead to another spell on a locked ward. You know exactly what it means, Marilyn. We've been here before, remember?'

'I'm not listening to this,' she said. 'I've got things to do. I'm going out.' She flounced across the room and pulled at the door, which remained closed.

Marilyn turned on her mother.

'You can try the front door, too, if you like,' Ellen said. 'And the windows. You are locked in here with me, and that's the way it's going to stay until I know exactly what's going on. It's for your own good, Marilyn. If you think about it, I'm only doing what's best for you.'

'This's ridiculous, locking a person in her own house. There's laws, personal rights laws. You can't treat me like a criminal. Civil liberties are involved here, Mother. I could contact Amnesty International. I'm a prisoner of conscience.'

'No, you're not, Marilyn. You're a prisoner of your own making. I want to hear the whole story and I'm not prepared to compromise until I do. Sit on the stool and talk.'

'No. I don't have to.'

'OK, my girl, I'm going to ring the doctor.' Ellen walked to the kitchen door and opened it.

'Stop! What do you want to know?'

Ellen closed the kitchen door and stood with her back to it. 'Sit on the stool.'

Marilyn climbed back on the stool and dabbed at her eyes with the saturated tissue. 'This is unfair. It's not right.'

'Never mind that. Danny Mann, isn't it?'

'Yes.'

'You've been following him?'

'Sometimes.'

'I knew it. Stopping him in the street, going to his house?'

'Not in the street. I had to talk to him. I had to go to his house, Mother. I don't know where he is.'

'Start at the beginning.'

'We met in the theatre.'

'In Nottingham. I know that, I was there. And it wasn't a meeting, Marilyn. You helped with one of his tricks. There was another woman helped him the same night, and two gentlemen. You were already fixated on him before that night. You had his picture on your wall. We only went to Nottingham because you were obsessing about him, remember?'

'I remember what I remember,' Marilyn said. 'And you remember what you remember. The trouble is that you think what you remember is what happened.'

'No, Marilyn, the trouble is that as soon as you stop taking the tablets you make up an alternative reality inside your head. I take it that this man has not encouraged you in any way whatsoever, that he has probably asked you to stop bothering him. Therefore the tears. Am I right?'

'No, you're wrong. Danny loves me. He's been testing me.'

'What does that mean? Testing?'

'He sent me into the dark in Leeds, to see how I coped.'

'Goodness, Marilyn, was that where you stayed out all night? In Leeds?'

Marilyn nodded. 'It was magic. Danny was there all the time, on the edge of things. Invisible. He was watching over me.'

'I can hardly believe you're saying these things. You know what it's like in Leeds at night. A couple were killed there last week, in their own home.'

'Danny wouldn't let anything like that happen to me.'

'I'm going to see him, Marilyn, explain about your illness. We don't want him calling the police.'

'You can't see him, he's disappeared.'

'He'll be on tour or something like that. He's a theatrical. They go away all the time.'

'He's not on tour. He only had one bag. He flew to Norway.'

'How do you know that?'

'I followed him.'

'To Norway? You couldn't have.'

'Not to Norway, I followed him to the airport, Newcastle. Saw him checking in.'

'When was this?'

'Three days ago. He got a taxi to the station and I followed in the car. He got on the Newcastle train and I got on it too, at the last minute, and didn't have a ticket. That was the problem.'

'So when the guard came to inspect the tickets, you said?'

'I told him that my boyfriend had our tickets.'

'And he didn't believe you?'

'I took him to Danny, and Danny said he'd never seen me in his life before.'

'He didn't remember you from the theatre?'

'It was a test. I have to be worthy of him.'

'What happened about the ticket?'

'I had to show them some ID, and the guard gave me an invoice with the amount on. I have to pay it in thirty days.'

'Carry on. You're on the Newcastle train.'

'Danny got on the Metro and went to the airport. I went with him. I tried to explain about the ticket, said I was sorry to put him in the spotlight, asked him to forgive me. He said to wait until he got back from his trip, that he'd sort everything out then.'

'Are you sure he said that, about waiting until he got back? Seems to me in a situation like that he'd be wondering why a strange woman was attaching herself to him.'

'I'm not a strange woman, Mother.'

'I'm sorry, Marilyn, I'm your mother after all but this is one of those times we are going to have to agree to disagree. If you take your medication and get yourself together, though, you'll stop being such a strange woman and go back to your normal self. Then we can draw a line under all this. But if you don't I'm going to call in the doctor, and when this magician chap comes back from Norway, I'll have no option but to go and see him as well. Do you understand me?'

22

Weird things happened to Ruben the first Wednesday after Katherine was killed. He got up at the usual time in the morning – 4.30 a.m. – and went down the depot. He loaded his van with crates of milk and drove to the Marple Square Estate. Not many people around at that time in the morning. Some houses with lights showing, people trying to con the local burglars that they were wide awake.

The estate had a bad name and it was true there were a few wide boys about and some of the kids ran wild. You asked people who didn't live there and they'd tell you the place was riddled with crime, robberies and violence; you listened to the Nottingham intelligentsia and the media and you'd imagine Marple Square was terrorized by gangs of drug-crazed vandals ripping down trees and spray-painting their neighbours' houses and cars twenty-four/ seven.

But it wasn't so bad. Occasionally Ruben would put milk on a doorstep and when the woman came to collect it for breakfast it'd be gone. But that wasn't once a week, not even once a month. Two of his customers had been burgled while he was doing the round. One of them lost a video and a wide-screen TV and the other had the house stripped of everything, including a freezer full of pizzas and sausages and onion rings. An old black guy had been mugged coming out of the post office with his pension, and a group of Asian teenagers had tried to set fire to a pub. There must've been other incidents that Ruben hadn't heard about but altogether he didn't think it was worse than other estates. If he compared it to Hyson Green, where he had been a kid in a high-rise, Ruben would've classed Marple Square as crime-free.

When they'd let him out of the joint Ruben had gone back to have a look at Hyson Green and they'd torn all the high-rise flats down. Looked like a good place to be now. Lot of life on the street, made you feel like you were part of something. Only Ruben wasn't, because he didn't live there any longer. Ruben wasn't part of anything any more, not until he met Kitty Turner, and then he became part of the world.

He must've delivered about half the milk when it happened. He'd dropped two bottles of semi and collected nine empties from the same step. He'd stuffed the empties into crates and got back behind the wheel of the van. What he'd have done normally, he'd have turned the key in the ignition and pulled forward a hundred metres, parked outside number thirty-nine. But he didn't do anything. Instead he sat behind the wheel and looked out through the windscreen. Didn't see anything particularly, didn't feel anything, and nothing was going on in his mind.

It was like he'd wound down. When he was a kid he'd had a truck did that. Ran off a battery and it'd suddenly stop. The battery'd die and the truck was no good until you got the old battery out and put a new one in.

Ruben sat behind the steering wheel for nearly two hours. He wasn't unconscious, he could see people walking along the street. Sometimes someone would look in at him through the side window and Ruben would see them out of the corner of his eye. But he didn't turn his head. He didn't move. He played with the idea that if he moved his head it would fall off, that if he lifted his arm his hand would disintegrate. But it wasn't playing. There was no fun in it. It was serious. He closed his eyes a couple of times and then he daren't open them in case he'd gone blind.

Weird things. Your battery goes dead and your mind fills up with fantasies of disintegration. Perhaps he was dying or already dead? Once or twice since Kitty got hers he'd thought of topping himself. So maybe he'd done it to himself, gassed himself with exhaust fumes from the van, or he could've taken an overdose of Paracetamol. Didn't remember doing it, but if he was dead he wouldn't remember anything.

There was this place, he seemed to remember, place called Limbo where you went after you died. Somewhere off the shores of Hell. It was like a huge waiting room, white walls fading into blue. But Ruben didn't know where he'd heard about it. He knew there was something Jamokes did, arching their backs and going under a stick. And that was Limbo as well.

The woman from thirty-five knocked on the side window of the van and stuck her big face up against the window. 'D'you know what time it is?' she shouted.

Ruben didn't move.

She knocked again. 'What's wrong with you? I want my milk.'

Ruben moved. Slowly. He got out of the van and went around the back. He got a pint of each and handed them to the woman.

'Don't bother apologizing,' she said. 'He's only been waiting for his breakfast half an hour.'

It was 7.30. Ruben was usually back at the depot by this time, unloading empties. He got into the van and parked outside number thirty-nine. He went through the actions. He delivered milk, collected empty bottles. But his limbs were heavy, his body slow and his mind numb. He stopped again in the next street, spent another hour sitting behind the steering wheel.

It was 2.20 in the afternoon when he pulled into the last street on the estate. Two women were standing together, their arms folded. They watched him roll the van up to the kerb. Ruben got out of the driving seat and went around the back to load up his hand carrier, and he froze there. He dropped a bottle of skimmed and watched it land on the floor of the van and roll out of reach. Didn't break.

Some time later the two women came and got him. Ruben didn't know how long he'd been standing there with the door of the van open.

'He's crying, Shaz,' one of them said.

'Jesus. Whatever next? Help me get him in the house.'

'Big bloke like this, crying.'

They took him by the hands, one hand for each of them, and led him away from the van, through the gate and along the cracked concrete path to the front door. There was a rectangular lawn with a kid's bike on it. A blue plastic dumper truck with three wheels.

These women were the smallest things in the world. Tiny hands, faces like fairies.

'Mind the step,' the one called Shaz said. 'Jesus, look at the curtains going. They think we've got a feller. Give 'em a wave, Stell.'

They ushered him into the house and sat him on a red leatherette sofa with imitation zebra-skin cushions. There was a TV with the sound turned up to maximum less than a metre away from his face and a log-effect gas fire blazing in a pale-blue tiled fireplace.

'I'll put the kettle on,' Shaz said. 'Watch him.'

'Are you all right, darlin'?' Stell said. 'D'you want some tissues?'

Her shins were scorched and mottled by long hours of

sitting too close to the fire. Ruben took the tissues she offered and held them in his hand while the tears rolled down his face and dripped from his chin.

'What happened to you?' Stell said. 'You're six hours late. I went round the shop and bought a carton. Thought you weren't coming, or you forgot us.'

There was a war on the TV. A Pacific paradise was littered with the dead and broken bodies of Japanese soldiers. Guns were shooting off-screen. A helicopter flew over. A dumb American hero larded with olive oil was staring into space while he listened to it-shouldn't-have-been-like-this music coming from stereo speakers.

He was the kind of man Ruben had dreamed of becoming when he was young. A man with nothing except an extraordinary punch who would find himself in a position to save the world. When he was a teenager Ruben didn't know if he would use his punch or let the world go to Hell and it was the same with the figure on the screen. You could see it in his body language. He had done his duty and the world was safe but it might have been better if he hadn't bothered. The man was still alone. His government would give him a few gongs to mask the bloodstains but even if they gouged out his eyes he'd see the horror every day of his life.

'Kitty,' he said.

'What's he say?' Shaz said, coming back into the room with three mugs of tea on a tray.

'Kiddie, something like that.'

'Sounded like titty to me,' Shaz said, and they both shook for a moment.

'Might be your lucky day,' Stell told him.

'Kitty,' Ruben said, getting an edge into his voice. The tears stopped falling and he wiped his face with the tissues. He looked from one woman to the other. Shaz had blonde hair and black roots and Stell had white skin and black features. They both wore glossy lipstick and lilac nail varnish.

'I'm bereaved,' he told them.

'Oh,' said Stell.

'Shame,' Shaz whispered.

Bereaved. He'd never used the word before. It came out of him and he didn't know it was in there. Maybe every word in the English language was lodged somewhere inside him? All the words he'd heard as a child and read in books and listened to on the radio and the television. Words he didn't know the meaning of and composite words made up of the parts of other words. Nonsense words like ninglethroatynop.

He needed to taste it on his tongue. 'Bereaved.'

'Who was it? Your wife?' Shaz asked.

'Not a kiddie?'

He shook his head. 'Kitty.'

'It's his wife,' Stell said. 'It's your wife, isn't it, darlin'?' She mouthed the words as though she was talking to a deaf man. 'Your wife?'

My life, he wanted to say but it was too much to share. Ruben felt as though there was something inhabiting him, some alien presence. Could there be a part of himself that he had never noticed before, never suspected?

'Awful,' Stell said. 'You need to see somebody. When did it happen?'

He left them standing at the gate. Got back behind the wheel and dropped off the last of his milk. He unloaded the empties at the depot while the gateman asked him over and over again what had happened to him.

He drove home and changed his clothes and walked down to the doctor's surgery. The receptionist told him he was wasting his time and that Doctor couldn't possibly see him without an appointment, but Ruben waited anyway and around 6.30 the doctor called him into her wood-panelled room.

Ruben told her what had happened. He told her about the milk-round and the two women taking him into the house and giving him tea with sugar and brandy. He told her about being inhabited and about meaning being meaningless and reason being unreasonable.

'Has something changed in your life?' the doctor asked. 'Anything traumatic?'

'Kitty was killed,' he told her. 'Murdered.'

'And who was Kitty?'

'My lover,' he said. Another new word. Popped out of him clean as a daisy.

'It sounds like depression,' the doctor said.

'Not madness?'

'No. Not that.'

'I'm inhabited by depression?'

'You could say that, yes.'

'I'm older than I was a week ago.'

The doctor looked at him. He could see in her face that she'd thought of a joke, but decided not to tell it.

'You sound like a poet,' she told him. 'You're mentally exhausted.' She touched her forehead, above her right eye. She had long manicured finger-nails. 'I think it was Conrad Aiken who suggested that T. S. Eliot's nervous breakdown might have been caused by the severe strain of being an Englishman.' She smiled.

It was the kind of thing Kitty would have said. Then Ruben would have asked her who they were, this Conrad Aiken and T. S. Eliot, and they would have talked through the night. He wondered if Kitty's spirit, if that was the right word, was trying to contact him through other people. If Kitty was inhabiting the doctor just as the depression was inhabiting him.

'Can you give me something for it?' he asked.

'We have our own counsellor here,' the doctor said. 'I'd like you to talk to her. How would you feel about that?'

'I don't feel too much today.'

'But if I make an appointment for you, is that all right?'

'Yeah, whatever it takes,' Ruben said. 'I don't wanna be a cracker.'

He came awake in the night with a vision of Sam Turner standing by his bed clutching a short sword. But there was nothing there, just Ruben and the inside of his head. The newspapers and the newscasters were speculating on what had happened to Turner, where he was hiding out. Some said Scotland or France, the south of Italy or Amsterdam. One hack had him in Argentina and another in Norway.

Ruben didn't know where he was. He only knew that when the guy stepped back on to British soil it wouldn't be long before he was buried under it.

23

Merlin and Prospero worked their magic in the realm of time, leaving the mundane spatial expositions to lowly and local conjurors and sorcerers. Diamond Danny worked in time and space. He worked in time for the world of truth and responsibility and, ultimately, for freedom. And he worked in space for his daily bread, to pay the rent and to buy himself as much time as he needed to re-enact the time that had been taken from him, his birthright.

Time. The time of his life which was now and always and the times of his life which were the moments he held in memory and could retrieve at will. There were the times before fortune was twisted out of shape and the times after. The times before grew on fertile soil and proliferated in his memory like green shoots in spring. The times after were an ocean of sand.

As a boy his parents had taken him, every year, to stay with his great-uncle Matthew in Whitby. The small cottage in Nathan's Yard by the harbour had two tiny bedrooms, one of which was used by his parents and the other shared by little Danny and his great-uncle. Even now Danny would hesitate at Nathan's Yard and look at the house whenever he was in Whitby. It had been sold when Great-uncle Matthew died, shortly after the time when fortune was twisted out of shape, and since then it had been resold many times. Now it was combined with the house next door and used as a B&B. It had bright yellow paintwork and a front door with a glass sun in the upper panel. It was barely recognizable.

Back then, Danny didn't remember paint at all. He remembered that the cottage was dark. There was electricity but the only bulbs were screwed into ceiling fittings and must have been of low wattage, one to each room. The windows were small and encrusted with dirt and salt from the sea. Great-uncle Matthew didn't have a wife to clean them and being a simple fisherman he could not afford the luxury of a cleaning woman.

Danny's mother suspected that Great-uncle Matthew preferred the windows to restrict the light. 'He's on the open sea all day,' she'd say. 'When he comes home he wants the comfort of confinement.'

Like Prospero's cell. But Danny only made that connection many years later, when the old man was dead and gone.

What he remembered more than anything else were the nights. Great-uncle Matthew was a silent man. He spoke few words, none at all to Danny. To Danny's parents he would come out with the occasional word or phrase, or he would answer a question. But it would never amount to more than a series of grunts, and always in that strange East coast dialect which was composed entirely of diagonal vowels.

Danny would go up first. He would squeeze between the two beds and look out of the window into Nathan's Yard below. He would climb on to the soft feathery mattress and snuggle into one of its hollows, pulling the sheets and eiderdown up to his chin. It was always cold at first, no matter what the weather, but would warm up and on some nights become so hot that he would push back the sheets and sleep with his arms and shoulders bare.

Usually he would be asleep when Great-uncle Matthew

came up the stairs and entered the bedroom. But if he was awake he would listen as the old man dragged his deformed shape up the rickety staircase and stood by his bed to undress. First his dark knitted jerkin, which he wore in all weathers, then his boots and workpants, releasing a rare and exotic body odour into the dark chamber. Great-uncle Matthew slept in his vest and long johns, and within a few minutes of laboured breathing the gentle rumble of his snores would fill the room.

But whether he heard Great-uncle Matthew come to bed or not, Danny would always wake when it was time for the old man to fill the chamber pot. This activity took place in the dark and was therefore unseen, an audible experience with more than a hint of pong. Sometimes so strong that it made the boy's eyes water.

His great-uncle's bed would heave and creak as the man shifted his weight from the hollow of the centre to the edge of the mattress. Danny would listen as the two bare feet slapped on the boards and the scrabbling for the pot took place. The stream of piss would hit the bottom of the pot and continue splashing into itself for what seemed an eternity. Danny thought it would never stop, that Great-uncle Matthew would turn himself into a waterfall, a pissfall, and that the pot would overflow and the room fill up until the beds were rafts, afloat in the stinking effluent of the old man's bladder.

But that never happened. Great-uncle Matthew would splash his stuff into the pot until the pot was full and then he would stop. He would put the pot on the floor and back-heel it gently under the bed. In the morning, when Great-uncle Matthew had gone to his cobble, Danny would inspect the pot. It held a quart of cloudy orange piss which obscured the bottom. But the wonder of it was that it was full, always, to within half an inch of the rim. It was impossible to lift. If you tried you were sure to spill it on the boards and then mother or Great-uncle Matthew would know you'd been messing with it again.

Danny didn't try. But he made sure he was on hand when his mother or Great-uncle Matthew carried it to the outside loo to dump it and rinse it out later in the morning. They had to be careful. If they made one tiny mistake and got the body of liquid slopping about inside its container there would be nothing to stop it coming over the rim. More than once Danny had seen both of them stop dead halfway down the stairs, under the picture of Napoleon at Waterloo, holding their breath until the foaming piss settled back into the pot before they could carry on.

'Deadly cargo,' Danny's father called it with more than a hint of irony in his voice. But Danny never saw him attempt to move the pot himself. 'Oh, oh,' he'd say, passing his wife on the stairs, 'the chamber pot from Hell.'

What Danny had learned from Great-uncle Matthew was invisibility. Great-uncle Matthew was not a teacher, he was a misshapen beast. He had no learning, no culture. He was like Caliban. And, like Caliban, he could be persuaded of a reality that existed only in his own mind. He could be captivated, beguiled.

When he was doing the business with the pot in the middle of the dark night, Danny had only to move slightly, as if turning over in his sleep, and Great-uncle Matthew's stream would falter and terminate. You could imagine its stillness in the pot in the moonlight, a slight swirling motion and the haze of rising steam. There would be an intake of breath and then one, two, perhaps three drops more would splash into the pot. Danny would regulate his breathing, he would lie still and quiet, and eventually Great-uncle Matthew would continue to empty his bladder.

Because Great-uncle Matthew could not piss into the pot when there was someone else in the room. Or at least he could not piss into the chamber pot when someone else was conscious in the room. Not when there was a chance of him being observed. He could only do it when he felt he was alone, when he didn't have to worry about prying eyes or ears.

So Danny practised invisibility when he was around. It meant being quiet and still inside yourself so that the old man forgot you were there. And Danny found he could be invisible, or nearly so, whenever he wished. Not only with Great-uncle Matthew, but with his mother and his father, with his teachers and his friends, with anyone at all.

And it's a great asset for a magician, almost a prerequisite, to be seen when you need to be seen and then to slip away without moving from the spot.

For two days now he'd patrolled Calmeyers gate, watching the entrance to the flat of Holly Andersen, waiting for Turner to show himself. But there'd been no sighting of the man. Danny was beginning to think that Sam Turner might also be blessed with invisibility.

He fantasized that the two of them passed each other in the street, neither aware of the other's existence. Two ghosts dancing around the living corpse of this woman. He conceded that he may have underestimated Sam Turner. The man, after all, was trained and experienced in surveillance techniques. Not exactly magic in itself, but it would be necessary for him to understand the principles of concealment. He would know how to make himself small and anonymous.

For his own part, Danny had left nothing to chance. He wore not one stitch of clothing that he had brought with him from York. His coat, trousers, boots, shirt, sweater and fur cap were all purchased in the streets around the Scandinavian Hotel in Kongensgate. He was a Norwegian citizen right down to his thermal underwear and woollen gloves.

What it was about Prospero, he mused, as with Merlin and all the great magicians, was the consciousness of the cycle of confinement and release. When Prospero was released from his responsibilities in Milan he was immediately confined by the tempest to the small island which in turn would become his responsibility. In Milan he was free but confined by his responsibilities; on the island he was physically confined but free to practise his magic. He used his magic to confine the native population and the spirits of the island and consequently found that he was confined once more by his responsibilities towards them.

At the end of the play he has the strength of character and the courage to renounce his magic and as a result he is given back his rightful freedom in the city of Milan.

Danny would renounce his own magic after the final illusion. There would be no Milan for him, with which to replace it, but that didn't matter. There would be redemption of a kind. He would be free. He understood that in a strange way Sam Turner was his own version of Prospero's island. The life of Sam Turner was the cell in which Diamond Danny Mann was imprisoned and it was only by bringing Sam Turner down that Danny would demolish the walls that confined him.

Through the long days and nights in Oslo Danny made lists in his head. He listed the things he missed: his own bed and Jody, the smell of his sheets freshly returned from the laundry. Television commercials. Why? For God's sake, why? His slippers, which he could have and should have brought with him if he'd known he was going to be here so long. The photographs of his mother; the portraits of her alone and of the two of them together. The one taken in Blackpool on the front after he'd wheeled a toy horse out of a department store. The other of her face, the background a blur, which he had taken as a timed exposure the day he left school. His mother's hard-earned furniture. The Chesterfield. The Ercol chair with the broken back in the kitchen (must get that repaired as soon as he got home). The water. The privacy and familiarity of his own house. His mirror and trolley in the bathroom. The silence. The temperature. Minster FM in the background. The English language spoken without an accent. His books. Sunday morning. Fish and chips. Real ale. All-Bran.

The lists got longer and longer. He would spring awake in his hotel room and add one more item to the list – Evensong at the Minster – though he had only been once, years ago with his mother. But it didn't matter, he missed it now, terribly, achingly, while he was confined to the foreignness of another land. And once awake he would search around for other things to add to the list, anything would do, even if it was available in Norway it didn't matter. Brown sliced bread, raspberry jam, his car with the faulty seatbelt. He wanted the list to grow so that it formed a bridge between Oslo and York, a physical walkway that would lead him back home.

Danny observed himself at times like this. His obsessiveness was something he had inherited from his mother. Her father, his grandfather, had apparently been the same. It was a family trait. Obsession and will, together they got things done. They were movers and shakers. There was a cluster of genes which defined them as separate from other people, made of them a natural elite. This in turn meant that they didn't fit in and were subject to misunderstandings. But that was the price you paid. There was no point in grumbling. To become a master magician you had to fork out a bag of gold and your heart and your soul.

Obsessive. But that wasn't the only thing. What Danny had also inherited from his mother and her ancestors was courage, real courage which involved a large slice of imagination.

That was what had enabled her to go on after fortune was twisted out of shape, and what had enabled Danny to become a magician and rise above the herd of humanity. Courage and imagination.

He had watched the street, Calmeyers gate, for two days and seen not a sign of Sam Turner. But there had been a boy there, a young man, early-twenties. He'd been there all day today, off and on, watching and waiting. Danny had been watching and waiting at one end of the street and the young man had been watching and waiting at the other end. Not even in the street, really, but way down over the intersection at Henrik Ibsen's gate, so far away he could have been watching another street.

Which was exactly how they worked, policemen and detectives. They didn't show themselves, they used others to do the legwork. So although he hadn't seen Sam Turner in person, Danny was convinced that he had seen someone who was working on Sam Turner's behalf.

When he'd been nursing the idea for the Sam Turner illusion Danny had not realized that Turner was a magician as well. But he was beginning to see it now. They were worthy opponents. Diamond Danny Mann had earned his reputation by studying the masters and practising their craft. Sam Turner belonged to a different fraternity and was a past wizard in the black art of surveillance.

Danny was sure that the young man hadn't seen him. He had been careful to leave Calmeyers gate three times to change clothes and to alter his posture and body language. Nothing special, nothing that would stand out. He'd walked the length of the street in a black donkey-jacket and a woollen cap. He'd returned an hour later with the shuffle of a bespectacled elderly gentleman, complete with black cane and leather gloves. And towards the end of the afternoon, when the shadows were long on the ground, he'd managed an impersonation of a Norwegian businessman complete with white shirt and camel overcoat.

He'd noticed the boy, Sam Turner's assistant, taking an interest in a Norwegian sailor wearing a T-shirt and waterproof jacket, a peaked cap with a badge. The sailor was gripping the pavement with his toes to stop himself rolling overboard, and Danny had clutched his buttocks together and gritted his teeth and passed so close to the young man that he could have reached out and touched him. But he still didn't merit a second glance. The boy's eyes were full of the sailor.

Later there had been another man with a limp and the furtive sidelong glances of an alcoholic or a drug addict, and the boy had been similarly fascinated by him. Danny's magic had kept him concealed. Danny's magic and his subtlety. Sam Turner and his crony were easy, like playing with children.

Sitting alone in the Scandinavian Hotel writing lists of the things he missed in his confinement, Diamond Danny Mann decided to give it a few more hours. Turner might be prepared to play cat and mouse but the magician certainly was not. If he saw Sam Turner the next day he would go ahead and dispose of the third girlfriend, Holly Andersen. And if he didn't see Sam Turner the next day he would do exactly the same.

That would be courageous and imaginative. To take the woman's life without sighting Sam Turner at all.

Because the man was here, in Oslo, he had to be. The alternative was unthinkable. The illusion depended on his presence.

Danny smiled to himself. He added one more item to the list. An Americano on the terrace of the City Screen café, overlooking the river in summertime. He switched off the bedside light. The woman's fate was sealed. There was nothing anyone could do about it. The magician turned on to his side and within a few minutes he was asleep, snoring gently, slipping into dreams of earlier, less troubled days.

24

Sam and Geordie had been in Akers-Mic in Kongensgate, browsing through one of the largest collections of CDs in Europe. Sam had bought a couple of Jo Ann Kelly recordings, songs he'd only heard rumours about. He'd found an early collection by Shirley Horn and a few of her friends. Songs recorded in her living room which every record shop in England had told him were deleted. He'd found nearly two dozen CDs he thought he couldn't live without but whittled them down to three so he'd stay within his own estimation of who he was.

'Some kind of frugal early-twenty-first-century romantic private eye,' Geordie said. Soon as he said it he thought he'd gone over the top. On the other hand he wanted to keep the mood frivolous and relaxed. Didn't want Sam disappearing inside himself.

Sam took it on the chin. 'Frugal? Maybe,' he said. 'Cash always has a way of getting away. I used to suspect the rich guys had a magnet, so it didn't matter how you tried to hang on to it, they always got it back.'

'It's the Protestant work ethic,' Geordie said. 'Makes it impossible for you to enjoy anything unless you've got into a sweat earning it.'

'That's true, too,' Sam said. 'There was a time I hated that. Being trapped inside some concept from the Middle Ages. I'd go spend all my money, then I'd go around spending everybody else's, trying to break free.'

'But it didn't work?'

'Made me a few enemies,' Sam said. 'Bought me some

debts. Didn't feel any freer at the end of it. More of a prat, though. That's when I realized that the old Laingian thing was true.'

'Laing?'

'Yeah, old guru type from the sixties. Dead now. Said something like, "the me that I'm trying to be is the me that's trying to be it". Maybe he was quoting someone else, I don't know. Made sense to me suddenly. Put me in touch with my own slave and my own free man. They were always at war but these days they live together. Still have the odd scrap, but they know they're dependent.'

'You could've bought all those CDs,' Geordie said. 'Put them on a credit card, pay for them later. That's what every other guy would've done.'

'Trouble with that, Geordie, I'd be paying twice as much. Making The Man even richer than he is now.'

'But you'd have them,' Geordie told him. 'And right now they're still in the shop, sitting on the shelf, and you can't take them home and listen to them. You've held them in your hand, you know you'd really enjoy every one of them, and you know you'll never get hold of them in England.'

'That's all right,' Sam said. 'I can live with it. This is not gonna stop me sleeping nights.'

'And the debt would?'

'Yeah. I'd be wild-eyed. Start drinking again. Sell my music collection and pour it down my throat. This's the kind of guy I am.'

They were in the Coco Chalet in Prinsens gate, drinking dark Italian roast and waiting for the Andersens, Holly and her partner, Inge Berit. Sam had taken JD's glasses off and apart from the beard he looked more or less normal.

There were candles on the tables, and white paper tablecloths. In one corner was an old His Master's Voice record player with a brass horn sitting on a carved mahogany dresser. The coffee was hot and as black as night and tasted smooth and bitter in the flickering light. The café had mirrored walls and the wooden seats were arranged in small booths and before Sam had finished his first cup of coffee he called the waitress over and ordered another one.

'I woke up this morning with a plook on my neck,' Geordie said.

Sam looked over his coffee cup. 'There're times,' he said, 'you dangle a conversation under my nose and I don't know what to say. It's happened before, with other people, when I've been drinking, out of my skull. Or sometimes on a case when I've come across a psycho, say, or someone who believes the world is a mirage.'

'What're you saying, exactly?'

'Well, plooks,' Sam said. 'You woke up this morning with a plook on your neck. What'm I supposed to say about that? Seems like the most mundane subject in the universe. Somebody's plook on somebody's neck. I've got other things on my mind.'

'That's because it's not your plook on your neck,' Geordie said. 'If Sam Turner woke up with a plook on his neck it'd be a perfectly valid subject for discussion. We'd've got started on it over breakfast and we'd still be talking about it now. Wouldn't be long before we were enquiring where the emergency room was, get the fucker lanced.'

'I don't wake up with plooks,' Sam told him. 'Last time I had a plook, Margaret Thatcher was in charge. Since she's been gone my blood's purer.'

'It's this attitude you have,' Geordie said. 'Like some things are good for conversation and some aren't. And you're not consistent about it. Another time you'd've thought plooks was a great subject.'

'Never.'

'You would've, Sam. I know you.'

'Never in my wildest dreams would I have anything to say about plooks. I can't think of anything less interesting. God only invented plooks to bore people to death. It's one of His ways of making life harder for people who can't see past the end of their nose. And it keeps all His mates in the cosmetics industry sailing round the Caribbean. Wherever they go, I don't know. Mustique?'

Geordie smiled. He had this smile that involved his eyes, something between a smile and a frown, and it conveyed a knowing irony. Janet couldn't stand it and told him not to do it, but Sam had never said anything about it. Geordie spoke through it. 'See what I mean? You're talking metaphysics already. *God only invented plooks to bore people to death.* You start off telling me plooks aren't interesting and a couple of breaths later you're considering their place in the order of the universe.'

Sam sipped from his cup. 'Great coffee,' he said. 'Say what you like about Norwegians, but they know how to make coffee.'

'Is that the end of the plook conversation?'

'Yeah. Tell me something interesting.'

'How about sex?'

'What kind?'

'When I was young,' Geordie said, 'I dunno, maybe I was seventeen . . .'

'Couple of years back?' Sam said.

'Funny. D'you wanna hear this?'

'So far my tongue's not hanging out,' Sam said. 'I'm at the stage I'm suspending my disbelief, waiting, hoping, the story will be a good one. But teenage sex? Y'know, it doesn't hold a lot of dramatic possibilities. Not much chance of a slow build and an unexpected, even enlightening, resolution. But I'm listening.'

'It's not a story, it's an anecdote. Something I remember from being sixteen, seventeen, when my whole body was tuned to sex. My brain, too. I'd wake up in the morning and I'd be thinking about sex, and I'd go to bed at night and the last thing I thought about, that'd be sex, too. And in between, all day long, there'd be sex everywhere: in my mind, in my fingers, my eyes, my ears. I could be turned on by the sun shining on my arms, or if there was no sun, then just by the thought of sun on my arms. You know what I mean?'

'Where are you going with this?'

'Nowhere special. I'd look at girls on the street and I'd imagine having them in bed or having them right there on the street. It was safe because I wasn't gonna do it, but inside my head I could watch this girl, any girl really, walk along the street and within a couple of seconds I'd have her clothes off and we'd be going at it, back door, front door, you name it, she'd have me in her mouth and I'd have her in my mouth and there'd be juices and sweat everywhere. It was a whole orgy. And then the girl would've walked around the corner and I'd look up and here comes another one. I couldn't stop it, it was like that for months, seemed like years, I couldn't think of anything else.'

'Sounds more or less normal,' Sam said. 'That's why people hate teenagers, because they're like that.'

'And then I'd get the guilts,' Geordie said. 'Like I'd wonder if they could see what I was thinking, the girls I was having these fantasies about. Because I'd know that it was written all over my face. Staring eyes, tongue hanging out, bits of drool on my chin. And I'd think if they could see my brain working away on them, they'd call the police and have me arrested. I was always surprised I got away with it.'

The outer door opened and two middle-aged women came into the room. They looked around, from table to table. Sam got to his feet and took a step forward. 'Holly,' he said. 'Hi.' He was smiling, happy to see her.

Holly Andersen smiled back, not quite as broadly as Sam. They stood in front of each other and stared. Geordie could see they hadn't finished with each other. They'd given up and gone in different directions, made separate lives for themselves. But they hadn't finished with each other, there was still something living there between them, something neither of them had been able to kill. It was important to note it, Geordie thought, to know it was possible. He didn't think either of them would want to restart their relationship, and if they did restart it there would be no guarantee that it would work. But there was something there nevertheless. It was obvious that both of them knew it. And Geordie picked it up in the space of a few seconds, tangible as the cups on the table and perhaps just as fragile.

Sam held out his hand and she took it and for a moment they came together in a dry embrace. Their lips grazed each other's cheeks. When they stood back Sam said, 'Twenty years?'

'Nearly,' Holly said. 'Nineteen. You've grown a beard.'

'You haven't changed,' he said.

But she laughed him away. '*You've* stayed young, Sam, while I've grown old.'

He shook his head but Geordie could see she was right. Her face was on the point of collapse. The crow's feet around her eyes had trampled the flesh, giving her a tight, skull-like appearance. You could see she had been beautiful a long time ago but the years had eaten their fill of her.

'This is Inge Berit,' Holly said, indicating her friend, a woman the same age as herself. Small and blonde with a tummy like a football.

'Yes.' Sam gave his hand to the other woman. 'We met before, briefly.'

'Pleased to meet you again,' Inge Berit said with her Norwegian accent.

'And Geordie you've met,' Sam said.

'Yes, hello again,' Holly said. Inge Berit smiled at him and offered her hand. Geordie took it and gave it a shake.

'Come and sit down,' Sam said. 'D'you want coffee?'

When they were settled Holly said, 'Geordie told us you think someone wants to kill me.' She said it lightly, in the same tone of voice she might have used to pass the time of day.

'That's right,' Sam said. 'Two people, women, two of the women who lived with me before I met you, have been killed.'

Inge Berit said, 'We thought you were making a joke.'

'Nicole?' Holly said. 'Nicole's dead?'

Sam nodded. 'In Leeds, last week. Someone broke into her house in the middle of the night. Stabbed her and her husband.'

Holly drew in her breath. 'My God. And who else? The other one, what was she called?'

'Katherine.'

'Yes, Katherine. I can't believe this.'

'It's true,' Sam said. 'Katherine was in Nottingham. It was the same scenario, the same guy. The only thing that connects them is me.'

They fell silent. Inge Berit put her arm around Holly's shoulder and pulled her close. Holly reached up and held her friend's hand. 'Do you know who he is? Anything about him?'

Sam shook his head. 'We're getting closer. There's

some indistinct video footage back in England, and Geordie thinks he may have spotted the guy here yesterday.'

'In Oslo?'

'Calmeyers gate.'

'Jesus, Sam, you're frightening me.'

'You should be frightened,' he said. 'Both of you. I'd like you to be frightened enough to go away.'

'Where to?'

'Wherever,' he said. 'Get out of town, out of the country. Go to Paris or Rome, anywhere but Oslo for as long as it takes to get this guy off the street.'

The two women looked at each other.

'We could go to the Politi,' Inge Berit said. 'They'd give us protection.'

'That's an option for you,' Sam said. 'But the first thing they'd do is arrest me and send me back to England. The English police think I killed the others.'

'And how do we know you didn't?' Inge Berit said.

Holly put a hand on her friend's thigh and squeezed gently. 'I know,' she said. 'Sam's capable of a lot of things, but he wouldn't do that.'

'Cheers,' he said.

Inge Berit looked at her friend, then turned her attention back to Sam. 'Could you be wrong about this?' she said.

'I don't think so. There's a chance, but do you want to take it?'

Holly's friend shook her head. 'No, we'll leave tomorrow. I don't know where, but we'll go somewhere.'

Holly said, 'What does he look like, just in case.'

'Sometimes wears a trilby,' Sam said. 'Might have braid on his trousers, like a waiter.'

'He's one metre seventy-eight and sixty-eight kilos,'

Geordie said. 'He's clever, obviously. But he thinks he's cleverer still, so he'll probably give himself away.'

'What makes you think that?' Holly said.

'I was watching the street yesterday,' Geordie told her. 'This's my speciality, surveillance. I get the surveillance jobs because I've got the patience. And because I've done a lot of it, I know how it works.' Geordie looked at Sam and the two women, to make sure he had their attention.

'When you're watching somebody,' he said, 'the most important thing is they don't see you. Soon as they see you the game's over. So you've got to make yourself as small and quiet and invisible as possible. And you do that by not being in the same street as the guy you're watching. Best possible way is to have a flat in the street you can use and if that's not possible you need to be in another street, wherever, but so far away that you can't be seen as part of the terrain. Then you use glasses, binoculars, which I always have with me. To the other guy you're just a speck on the landscape, but because you're using binoculars you can bring him up as close as you like.

'All right, so that's the principle. You still with me? Good. The next thing is, if you don't want to be seen you don't do anything that's gonna draw attention to you. Like in movies they have guys on surveillance wearing shades. They're wearing shades in hotel foyers or outside in the middle of winter. Nobody does that in real life. You're on surveillance you wanna fade into the back-ground. And that's how I spotted him the first time, because the guy came down the street with a limp. I don't know what he's supposed to be, maybe a druggie, something like that, and he's dragging his left leg after him, really pronounced limp. I mean, how many times do you see that, a guy with a limp? Sometimes you see somebody on crutches, but not that often, and you might see some old guy with a stick. But somebody limping really sticks out. So I check his height and weight and you can bet the guy's a dead ringer for the one we're after.'

Geordie laughed. 'Limping down the street. I ask you? Who does the guy think I am? He might as well be dressed in a clown's costume.'

'I don't understand how you can be so sure,' Inge Berit said. 'Some people do have a limp. The height and weight could be a coincidence.'

'You're right,' Sam said. 'But we work with statistics. In this situation if we see somebody with a limp and the right height and weight, we can be fairly sure he's our guy. It's circumstantial evidence, but we're sure he's watching Holly, waiting to see if I make contact. If there was another guy with the right height and weight, we'd put him on the list as well.'

'And there was,' Geordie said. 'Somebody dressed like a sailor. But when he came up close he was the same guy. The limping guy without the limp and a different hat.'

'Then why didn't you stop him?' Holly asked.

'On what grounds?' said Geordie. 'Pretending to limp? What we have to do is find where he's based, then we can watch his every move. And we can stay one step ahead of him.'

'We'll take him tomorrow,' Sam said. 'Once we know you two're out of the way, doing some shopping on the Champs Elysées, I'll take a walk along your street, maybe even go into your flat. You'll have to leave us a key. Then, when our man makes his move, we'll be waiting for him.'

'Be careful, Sam,' Holly said.

He shrugged. 'I can look after myself. Once we know you two are out of the country everything'll go like clockwork.'

'I hope so,' Inge Berit said.

'Relax,' Geordie told them. 'We're professionals. We know what we're doing.'

'You OK?' Sam asked.

They'd stopped for a sandwich in a small café overlooking the harbour. Geordie had put away a baguette full of shrimps and mayonnaise without a word. He'd demolished a slice of cake covered in marzipan and was dropping irregularly shaped sugar lumps into his second cup of coffee.

'Fine,' he said.

'Liar.'

'I'm fine. I'm working, earning money. I'm eating and I'm sleeping. I've got good health and I'm young and I'm away from home in a foreign country which I haven't been to before, and it's great. I'm grateful to the master of the universe for giving me these privileges.'

'But?'

'But nothing. I'm having the time of my life.'

'You're missing Janet and Echo and you're depressed.'

'What about you?' Geordie asked. 'I suppose you aren't missing Angeles.'

'Yeah, I'm missing her, Geordie. But I'm admitting it.'

'OK, I'm missing them. I'm not sleeping too good, thinking about them, worrying.' He laughed. 'A game of football would be good. You know what I mean? That's what I usually do at home, works every time. All that aggression and sweat, the one thing in the universe makes you forget who you are.'

Sam was quiet. He traced his finger through a spill of cold coffee on the wooden table. 'I could use some of that,' he said. 'This guy is ravaging my past, picking out the good bits, the parts worth remembering, and laying them to waste.'

He looked out over the water, fixing his eyes on the

horizon. 'I could hardly bear to look at Holly this morning. I kept seeing this spectre over her shoulder. Death as a dark shadow, a ravenous spirit searching her blood and her body for somewhere to be.'

'Jesus, Sam. She'll be out of the country tomorrow. We've done everything we can.'

'Yeah, I know. I just hope it's enough. With a guy like this, someone who believes passionately, you can never be sure how they're gonna react. To kill these women just to set me up takes a really weird mindset. He'll have everything stacked in his favour: God, morality, justice, truth. Because of something I did to him, or something he imagines I did to him.'

'You should know who he is, Sam. Someone you've hurt so bad that he's prepared to kill innocent people to get back at you.'

'Yeah, there's that as well,' he said. 'I think I should know who it is, too. I can't come up with an answer, though. One thing I keep thinking is the guy must be nursing something from his childhood. It must've been traumatic. Something a young mind couldn't cope with.'

'Some kid you've wronged?'

'I dunno, Geordie. And if it is that, some kid with a twisted mind because of me, then I don't want to know. But I have to, because if I don't he'll go on working his way through everyone in my life.'

25

Quarry House, the building which houses the Department of Social Security HQ in Leeds, is like something out of the Third Reich. Designed and built in the dying days of the Thatcher era, it imposes itself on the city's skyline with the authority of a jackboot.

Coming in from York and travelling the Leeds urban motorway towards the centre of the city, Marie passed under the shadow of the building with mixed feelings of disgust and fascination. 'You'd need a really good reason to go inside,' she said to Celia, sitting next to her in the passenger seat. With its heavy rectangular design and the mystic symbolism of its central, star-like, rooftop emblem it could have been a fitting monument to Albert Speer.

Celia glanced back at the edifice. 'I can't believe someone has designed a Social Security building in such a way that it puts people off going inside. It seems so perverse. Surely it would be better to abandon the concept of Social Security altogether?'

'Buildings like that come out of the gap between reality and dreams,' Marie said, 'out of that space between what people believe they want and what they really want. The man who designed it probably sees himself as a liberal humanitarian.'

'You don't think it could have been a woman?'

'No way,' Marie said. 'The bricks are held together with testosterone. If you half-close your eyes you can picture Mussolini or Hitler standing in the doorway.'

She pulled into a parking space opposite the Grand Arcade and switched off the engine.

Celia opened the car door and stepped on to the pavement. 'Will you pick me up from here?'

'Yes.' Marie glanced at her watch. 'Five o'clock OK?'

'That'll give me three hours,' Celia said. 'Plenty of time to buy a few old clothes.'

Marie left her spinning round on the pavement. She caught her in the rear-view mirror crossing towards the Grand Arcade, an ancient figure on her spindly legs, black beret pulled down over one eye, Marlene Dietrich-style.

She drove out to North Lane in Headingley, parked the car and went into the Taps. The landlord was a burly man with a clipped white beard and moustache and a smile that continued past his face and reached deep down into the depths of his brown eyes.

Marie told him a long, complicated lie about how she was writing a book around the Rolf and Nicole Day killing and that she'd like to meet some of their neighbours and friends.

'I didn't know her,' he said. 'Nicole Day. Wouldn't have recognized her. She was in here once or twice according to a couple of the locals, but I don't remember her. Him I did know, Rolf. Called in from time to time. He'd prop the bar up and make a pint last forty minutes. Thin wrists, like a woman. Glasses. Not much hair. Guys in here called him the Professor.'

'Is there anyone else I could talk to?' Marie asked. 'Someone who knew them both?'

The landlord looked around the bar. 'Not at the moment,' he said. 'But Steve'll be in soon. He lives at number thirty-seven, actually talked to Sam Turner before he killed the woman, or maybe it was just after. I'll introduce you.'

Marie got herself a large glass of cold red wine and

tried to warm it between her hands while she watched the regulars at the Taps. There'd been no doubt in the landlord's mind that it was Sam who did the killings. The police and the press had done a real job on him. He'd been tried and found guilty. The hangman was checking his rope, oiling the hinges on his trapdoor. Sam had always been a survivor but his future was looking increasingly bleak in the face of the evidence in this case.

Maybe that was how it would end? A long and charmed life, forever lived on the edge and brought to a sudden ironic end by a series of events in which he was implicated but never actually involved. Sam would recognize the scenario. She could see him grinning as he said, 'Just remember . . . if the world didn't suck, we'd all fall off.'

The outer door of the pub opened and Marie watched a pink and golden youth carrying the best part of fifty years walk up to the bar. He ordered a drink and exchanged a few words with the landlord. He glanced over his right shoulder at her while his host was pulling the pint. Attempted a long-distance smile.

He paid for the drink and supped the top off. He hitched up his tracksuit trousers and ambled over to Marie's table. 'They tell me you're writing a book,' he said.

'You're Steve?'

'The same. The man who met the murderer.'

Marie knew women who would consider him good-looking but she couldn't understand why. She felt waves of antipathy coursing through her body. There must be a relationship between the chemical reactions that stimulated sexual responses and the muscles that created the cringe.

'Who was that?' she asked. 'The murderer?'

'Good question,' he said, pulling out a chair and settling

himself opposite her. 'The guy I met was called Sam Turner, a private investigator from York. And he's the guy the police are looking for. But it might not be him.'

'What makes you think that?'

'I didn't think this up myself. My sister-in-law works for the Coroner's Office, so it's her theory. The woman, Nicole Day, she was killed around the time that I was talking to Sam Turner at my house. He was looking for somebody called Bonner, and this was nine o'clock in the morning. I'd come back from my morning run. I was listening to the news headlines.

'He had a scrap of paper with the name and address on it. But the address was my house, number thirty-seven, and I'm not Bonner, no one called Bonner lives there, I didn't need to be a detective to know that.' Steve smiled knowingly, as though he'd made a joke.

'Anyway, the guy accepted that he'd got the wrong house and I watched out of the window. He went up the street to number seventy-three, tried there but there was nobody home. I'm still watching him through the curtains. He comes back down the street and he stops this black woman, lives at number twenty, bit tasty, just divorced her husband. And I see her shaking her head so he's asking her the same question: where does Mr Bonner live? But there's nobody called Bonner in the street, the police checked everybody. Used to be an Alison Bonner who lived at fifty-four but apparently she died five years back. A widow. Her daughter sold the house to a speculator.

'After that the guy, the detective, he got back in his car and drove away. And nobody's seen him since. Me, I've gone over it time and time again. This was a guy looking for somebody called Bonner. The police come along and tell me he was the murderer but I can't put the two things together. First I can't believe he'd just killed the woman with a knife because he'd be covered in blood or at least be rattled. But he was calm. He was pissed off when he couldn't find this Bonner guy, but he wasn't someone who had just killed somebody in her bed.

'Second I couldn't buy the other theory, that he was looking for the woman, for where she lived, so he could kill her. That he was knocking on house doors in the street, waiting for her to open the door. That the Bonner thing was just an excuse for him to go knocking on all the doors. If the guy was that stupid he'd never've got away with it. He'd be locked up by now. So that whole idea is a no-no.'

'You don't believe he did it?' Marie asked.

'What I thought for a while, I thought he might've gone mad. You know, deranged. He'd killed the woman or he was gonna kill her in a few minutes and the balance of his mind had gone. So he was wandering around with this Bonner thing in his head, and maybe Bonner was just somebody he'd made up or somebody out of his childhood. You know, like a school teacher or something.

'But I gave up on that theory as well because the guy has been so good at avoiding the police. They don't have no idea where he is. Which means he's bright, right? Which means he's not mad or deranged or doolally but he's thinking and keeping himself free.'

'So who did it?' Marie asked.

Steve put his foot on a stool and tied the lace of his trainer. 'I don't know,' he said. 'That's the short answer.'

'What were you saying about your sister-in-law and the Coroner's Office?'

He took another two inches off the top of his pint and glanced back towards the bar. He leaned forward conspiratorially. 'They're not convinced the detective did it either. He was in the street round about the time the woman was killed, but her husband, Rolf Day, he was killed at least eight hours earlier.

'What the police thought, what everybody thought, was that Sam Turner came sailing into the street in the morning, killed both of them and then drove back to York. But because Rolf was killed eight hours earlier than Nicole that theory doesn't fit.

'The police are now saying that Turner was there all night, but that doesn't fit either because I saw him arrive and park his car in the morning. Could be that he killed the guy the evening before, went home and slept through the night in his own bed then came back in the morning to top the woman. But why would he do that?

'Top and bottom of it is that the police need to nail him because if he didn't do it they don't have a clue where to look for the killer. But people at the Coroner's Office aren't too sure, and the forensic people, they can't find a sign that he was in the house.'

'Do they have any evidence at all?'

Steve shook his head. 'Nothing much. Nicole was the kind of woman, she'd Hoover the house every day, disinfect the toilets, wipe down the work-surfaces in the kitchen. You never saw her without a duster in her hand. There's some threads, look like they might be from a black overcoat, they found them snagged on a spell inside the back door. And they found a single pubic hair, blonde, female variety. Nicole was brunette.'

'Female?'

'Yeah. Vaginal hair, the stem with some kind of plastic coating.'

'Not a real hair?'

'Yes, a real female vaginal hair, blonde, but the stem of it had some kind of plastic residue as though it had been stuck in something.'

'Plastic surgery?'

Steve shrugged his shoulders. 'They don't know what to make of it. Might've been some kind of model, a teaching aid. They have things like that at the hospital, also the university. And Rolf was connected to the university.'

'They don't think it was connected to the killer?'

'No. It doesn't fit.'

'Where was it found, in Rolf's bedroom?'

'No. The sitting room. On the carpet in the bay window. Could've been there for weeks.'

It was after ten and Marie was alone in the office in York. She composed an e-mail to Sam's Hotmail account, told him about her day. It was dark in the town, no moon, only a few tourists and residents watching the flood waters licking their way towards the centre of the city.

Marie stopped and listened, thinking she'd heard a footfall on the stairs. But no one would come to the office at this time of night. Perhaps one of the other tenants leaving after a spot of overtime?

She finished the e-mail and hit the *Send* button. She switched off the computer and fastened the top button of her coat, feeling a chill go through her body. She checked the keys to the outside door were in her pocket and was about to leave when she heard another movement on the stairs.

Scraping sound. Not the kind of noise you'd make if you were on legitimate business, on your way home after a long day at a desk.

Marie opened the office door softly and moved through the vestibule to the top of the staircase. It was unlit but the upper steps were dimly illuminated by the reflected light from Marie's desk lamp.

She peered down into the gloom, feeling tension tightening her stomach. Those tiny hairs rising on the back of her neck. She strained her ears, listening for a movement or the sound of breathing.

'Is someone there?' she asked, keeping her voice steady. Appearances can be critical at a time like this. If there's someone there and he detects fear in your voice he's liable to be more confident. And that's the last thing you want, a guy who is sure of himself. If there's a guy there at all, you want him to be a wimp, someone who thought he might be able to follow through but has already got doubts.

When there was no reply she backed away and returned to the office. She stood with her hand on the telephone, wondering if she should ring the police. Wondering if she could take their derision when they found no one in the building but a hysterical female private eye.

She controlled her breathing. Shook her head and gave herself a sharp talking-to. Working on a murder case was never pleasant but it could get to you when it was close up. And Sam being away, out of the country, didn't help. At least when he was around he'd manage to put things in perspective. It's no wonder you're in a state, she told herself. Your house is flooded, your boss is on the run, Celia sounds as though she might be terminally ill and there's a madman running around killing off Sam's ex-lady-friends. Last week everything was running along in semi-boring mode, there was order surrounding most of the things in life. Now there's nothing but chaos and it looks as though it'll get worse before it gets better.

She lifted her hand from the telephone handset and decided to go home. Celia would be waiting for her. She wouldn't think about the stairs to the street door. She'd just waltz down them and get outside the way other super-heroes do. Heroines, too.

So resolved, loins girded, Marie strode out of the office and was halfway across the vestibule before she stopped dead. The man standing at the top of the stairs was precisely the kind she'd worried about when her imagination had taken off a few minutes earlier. No, longer than that; his archetype had hovered on the fringes of her perception since she was a small girl. Whenever she'd had the willies or the heebie-jeebies they were inevitably connected with a picture of this kind of primitive.

The first thing was the beer on his breath, though he was still several feet away from her. He was big, broad as well as tall, and he wore tight black jeans with a leather belt and a brown suede jacket. On his feet he had black slip-ons with ornamental chains across the top and between the black of the shoes and the black of the jeans there was a flash of sky-blue socks.

It was only when he stepped towards her and she backed into the office that Marie noticed the growth of hair on the back of his hands. She moved towards the phone but he was watching every move and came quickly across the room to cut her off. He took the phone and ripped it from its socket on the wall. There was a moment when he was going to throw it across the room but he thought again and placed it on the desk.

'Don't try anything like that,' he said. He spoke quietly, a note of weariness in his words. His tone gave the lie to his appearance. Marie had expected him to be loud, overbearing, bullying, but he was none of these things. On the other hand his jaded control was in itself unnerving, giving the man's suppressed violence a sharper and perhaps more jagged edge. Marie suspected a cocktail of alcohol and steroids running through his bloodstream. This was a situation which could go very badly wrong.

'What do you want?' she asked. 'There's no money here.'

'Turner. The detective.'

'Sam's gone away. He's out of the country. We don't know where.'

The man shook his head slowly. He came towards her and took her by the wrist. He walked around the office, taking Marie with him. His hand was so large that his fingers wrapped almost twice around her wrist. He peered into Celia's small cubby-hole and opened the broom cupboard to make sure Sam wasn't hiding in there.

He brought her back to the computer desk and sat her down on the chair. He stood in front of her. 'Listen,' he said, 'I'm not the kind of guy who hits women. But I'm not good at the moment. The other day I hurt a guy for no reason at all. Dragged him out of his bed and opened up the back of his skull.

'Where I am at the moment, I don't have no plans to hurt you. But if I don't get the right answers I could lose it. You hearing what I'm saying?'

Marie could hear him clearly. No problem at all. She began shaking. Her teeth were chattering in her head and she lost the natural rhythm of her breathing. Small breaths caught at her vocal cords, forcing her to come out with tiny cries that seemed to unsettle the man and add to her own distraction. But she couldn't regain control of herself. The man was saying he wasn't going to hurt her but he was also saying that he might crack her head open.

He was so volatile, so out of it, that he didn't know himself what was going to happen next. As he grappled with the competing emotions within him small flecks of spittle gathered at the corners of his mouth.

'First, I'm gonna ask you again,' the man said, 'where's Turner? And don't tell me you don't know.'

Marie couldn't speak. Her mouth and throat had dried up and she was convinced that this man was going to turn on her. She only hoped that he wouldn't inflict as much damage as he was capable of.

'You gonna answer me?' he said. He used the back of his hand to wipe his mouth.

Marie moved her lips. She tried to speak but the words wouldn't come. She shook her head, clenched her fists. There was no way of defending herself against him. He was huge, twice her weight, and that element of intelligence which allows us to obey the rules of civilization seemed to have abandoned him. She'd fight if she had to, go for his eyes and his balls, she'd *try*, but there was no way she'd be able to beat him.

His hands encircled both her wrists and he stretched her arms apart as if he were crucifying her in the air. She came out of the chair and watched as he brought his large face up against hers. His broad forehead set itself against hers.

'Talk,' he said. Marie thought her arms would come out of their sockets and she realized that she was still making those small cries. She fought to regain some control over her voice.

'You're hurting me,' she said. 'I don't know anything.'

The man released her arms and pulled a chair over from Geordie's desk and stamped on it. The legs broke away and splintered like kindling. He kicked it and the remains scattered around the office, the solid circular seat banging against a small table and sending that rolling over against the far wall.

'Oslo,' Marie said. She hadn't meant to say it or thought of saying it. The two syllables had somehow come together inside her brain and been catapulted out of her mouth.

'Now you're talking. Where's that?'

'Norway. We don't have an address.'

He picked up one of the chair legs and held it in both hands like a baseball bat.

She closed her eyes and waited for him to shatter her

skull. In the space of a few seconds her throat dried up and she fully expected to die. 'You can threaten all you like,' she said with her eyes closed, but finding and riding her courage, 'I don't know where he is in Oslo.'

Marie opened her eyes and they stared at each other, neither of them blinking. The man was the one who finally cut the eye contact. He looked away and flung the chair leg on the floor. 'You work for the guy, right?' he said.

'Yes.'

'You should get a different job. This guy Turner, he's a slimeball. You should do a proper job for somebody who's a genuine employer.'

He walked to the door. When he stopped and turned around Marie thought he was coming back for her. Her heart began racing again. 'I'm sorry if I frightened you,' he said. 'It's important to me. And I'm sorry about the chair. There was no need for it. You're not the one. It's the detective I want.'

Marie listened to his footsteps receding down the stairs. She heard the street door slam and she listened to the silence. She reached in her coat pocket and took out her mobile. But she didn't ring the police. The guy had gone now and the thought of staying up half the night giving statements to the boys in blue was more than she could face.

She booted the computer again and sent another note to Sam, told him he'd need to buy a new chair for the office.

She walked down the stairs and locked the outer door, turned in the direction of Celia's house and a warm bed. The job had its good moments too, she told herself, as well as the bad. And anyway, you can't have everything, where would you put it?

26

Geordie had gone back to the surveillance of Holly and Inge Berit's flat in Calmeyers gate and Sam was sitting in the window of his own flat in Osterhaus gate. He'd stopped by the Internet café in Storgata to pick up his messages. One long one from JD, cogitating on the nature of capital punishment, and two shorter notes from Marie about a pubic hair and a guy who'd muscled his way into the office late at night.

People who want the death penalty are often idealists, JD said in his e-mail. They envision and imagine a world cleansed and purified of crime and evil. They want a moral and ordered world in which everything ugly, everything unseemly, is banished. The ritual of the state killing a criminal by hanging or electrification or lethal injection is not envisioned as ugly or even violent; it is seen as a cleansing act, it is seen as considerate. Justice. An eye was taken and now an eye is being taken in return.

Another problem with capital punishment is that when they have it, the people who believe in it want it not only for the murderers of policemen, but for the murderer of anyone; they want it for rapists and child molesters; and they want it for burglars and car thieves, especially when it is their own house that has been robbed or their own car that has been trashed.

Sam didn't know what he would do when he finally came face to face with the man who had taken the life of Katherine and Nicole and was now looking to take out Holly. He could imagine killing him, taking him by the throat and squeezing until all sensible life had fled from his body. And Sam Turner didn't think that would be an inappropriate response. It would be a personal answer and there would be revenge and something like honour involved. There would be no question about whether the death of the murderer would act as a deterrent to other would-be madmen. There would be no question about whether the murderer deserved to live or deserved to die. It would not be a reasonable act because there would be no thought behind it. Sam was enraged by the senseless deaths of these women whose only crime was to have spent a part of their lives with him.

And his rage was cold as ice. He didn't shout or scream, he didn't throw things around or make idle threats. He didn't call for justice. He didn't need or wish for the help of the state. He pared his finger-nails. He waited to get his hands on the guy.

Sam Turner wasn't a violent man. He'd fight to defend his patch. While no one would describe him as a pacifist, he didn't believe in the death penalty, and in abstract terms he would argue for a more rational and less political attitude towards criminality. But what he was faced with now was not an abstract problem but a human one. Others were suffering and dying because of their association with him. His past relationships and memories were being negated. The people and experiences which had helped to form him were being obliterated. It was as if a mean flood tide had crashed over the aft deck of his life and washed everything away. The tide had receded now, was regrouping, waiting to launch itself at him again. It was a battle for survival.

He had no argument with the content of JD's e-mail. The barbarity of state-sponsored execution for whatever reason would not lead to a reduction in crime and Sam would never align himself with those who argued for its reintroduction. But in personal terms whenever he thought about the man with the trilby hat and the braid on his trousers, the man who might have left behind a vaginal pubic hair on Nicole's carpet, then he would begin to shake and his blood would boil. Something ancient and coiled within him would lift its dark head and run a slithery tongue over fangs dripping in venom.

He tried to focus on Angeles back home in York, take his mind off the killer. But Angeles and he might be drifting apart as well. They lived in different worlds. It seemed to Sam that he'd been in this position before. Like there was always another woman on her way out of his life.

And was Angeles safe back in York? With the guy Marie had described hanging around, were any of the people in Sam's life safe? He sounded like the same guy who had taken Sam's photograph that day, ended up kneeing him in the balls and leaving him on the pavement. But the guy had raised the stakes since then, coming looking for him in the office late at night, smashing furniture and frightening Marie.

What was that all about? Were there two of them involved in the killings? Was Sam supposed to be in two places at the same time? If he were to take care of all his friends he'd have to be.

He held the picture of Angeles in his mind. Kept it there before him for as long as he could. Dark curls lightly gelled. Tanned skin with a hint of a Southern American ancestor. A greed for life and experience which activated her features and her mind and her wit and kept everyone around her thinking that their time on earth was a long cosmic party.

But the vision wouldn't hold, the fine features of Angeles kept slipping away into the skeletal characteristics of Nicole. Sam had always been haunted by the way

Nicole had shed weight while they were together. When they'd met she'd been an unresisting, bright and healthy woman, her eyes set firmly and innocently on the future. Eyes you'd never forget, dark perforations that reflected so deep inside you you'd begin to shiver. She gave everything to Sam, her body, her money, her energy, her innocence and her health. For however long it took he accepted her lifeblood and watched her fade away, first her expectations and her hope and then her physical health. He gave grief in return. And he blamed her for the warm soup of guilt and self-loathing that became his everyday habitat.

When she left, after she took off down the hallway towards the street to meet her phenomenologist lover, Rolf Day, Sam turned up the volume on Dylan's 'St Augustine' and poured alcohol down his throat until a million pus-encrusted devils came for him straight out of Hell. When he came back to consciousness the following day he was lying in a flood of his own piss and vomit. He staggered to his feet and made for the door to the bathroom, but he couldn't manage it. The door wouldn't keep still and the mechanics of balance had shifted; the only way he could keep upright was if his head was on the carpet. When he crashed into the frame around the bathroom door he was already spinning back into oblivion, just had a moment to remind himself of Nicole's plum-coloured silk blouse and that she had managed to get away in the nick of time.

Nicole had had a thing about hygiene, hated dust and dirt with a passion. Sam trashed the house, took an obscene pleasure in tramping the garden through the living room, watching the bright kitchen as it dissolved into an ocean of stale grease.

And then there was Holly. She appeared like magic a few days before the bailiffs arrived to reclaim what was left of the house. Took him away from all that. For a time.

Another good woman with a mission. Save Sam Turner, show him he's not alone. All she'd need was love.

She had a thing about hygiene. Nicole. She was back there in the frame, her skeletal features as if freshly resurrected from the grave. *She had a thing about hygiene.* Of course, the pubic hair couldn't have lain on Nicole's carpet for more than twenty-four hours. Nicole got withdrawal symptoms if she didn't get her hands on the Hoover once a day. That pubic hair, that blonde vaginal hair, had definitely been left behind by Nicole's killer.

Sam tried to think it through. There was a clue here, in this hair with a plastic residue around the root. Someone had taken a single hair and tried to embed it in a plastic substance. But there was no sense in that, unless it was one of many. As in the reproduction of a vaginal bush. But Marie had already checked with the teaching hospitals and the local universities and there was no department that had such a thing or could think of the need for one.

Some product of the porn industry, then? A love doll? There was a market in life-size dolls, usually cheaply made inflatables. But at the upper end of the market there were companies offering dolls with real hair, life-like breasts and up to three multi-speed vibrating orifices. You bought the kit, a lube smelling of taramasalata and a couple of AA batteries.

Sam was doubtful. He hadn't thought they were dealing with a sex freak. Neither Katherine nor Nicole had been raped or sexually abused. Maybe because the guy's doll kept him satisfied? But was it possible that he took a love doll with him when he was out on a killing spree? And if so, why? Was he trying to impress her?

Preoccupied with a single pubic hair and where it

might lead, Sam was slow and dulled when Geordie came around the corner from Calmeyers gate. He registered the figure, that it was a young male, but it took time to see that it was Geordie and that he was looking up at Sam in the window of the flat.

The kid seemed to be drunk, swaying from side to side on the narrow pavement, at one time stepping off the curb and reeling into the street, his arms flailing around to keep his balance. Sam had no time for drunks, having been one himself for half his life. But Geordie wouldn't get drunk on the job, not in the middle of the day. He watched as his friend struggled back on to the pavement. Geordie put his back against the stone wall and let himself sink to the ground. His eyes were locked on Sam's face. Sam didn't come alive and move for the stairs until he saw the trickle of blood ooze from Geordie's sleeve and run in a crimson line towards the gutter.

He carried Geordie up the stairs, two at a time, and laid him on the kitchen floor. Geordie was mumbling incoherently, his pupils floating upwards as if he was trying to peer under his own forehead. His face and lips were pale and his skin cold and clammy. He was gasping for air.

'What happened?' Sam said. 'Geordie, try to hold it together. I don't want you dying on me.' As he spoke he pulled off Geordie's coat and sweater. His shirt was soaked with blood and there was a deep slash in the kid's shoulder. Sam couldn't tell if an artery had been severed, but he applied pressure to the wound and dragged Geordie over to the telephone so he could tend to him with one hand while he phoned an ambulance with the other. He pressed each side of the wound gently but firmly together.

During the fifteen minutes it took for the ambulance

to arrive Geordie regained consciousness twice. The first time he complained of cold, asked where his coat was. Sam reached for the coat and covered him with it, at the same time maintaining pressure on the gash of his shoulder. The second time he came around he wanted to vomit.

'What happened, Geordie? Did you meet the guy?'

Geordie looked as though he was going to answer but his eyes disappeared into the top of his head. Then he opened them again and said, 'He was in her flat, Sam. He was waiting for her . . .

'I went after him down the street and spun him around. He said something. He brought the axe up and I saw he's gonna open my head with it . . . I ducked, Sam. I saw it coming and I ducked and tried to roll away over the pavement.'

Geordie closed his eyes and held his breath for some moments. 'I was too slow,' he said. 'I got my head out of the way but took it in the shoulder. Sounded like a log splitting. I dunno what happened to him. Next time I looked he'd gone. Then I remembered the flat and somehow got back to you.'

Tears ran down Geordie's face and Sam wiped them away with the flat of his hand. 'You're OK,' he said. 'What was it he said when you spun him round?'

'A word, sounded like *Katha*. Does it mean something?'

'*Katha*. I think it's a meditation. Something to do with the *Upanishad*.'

'Hinduism?'

Sam shook his head. 'It's older than that, connected with Vedic culture. Ancient stuff, mystery religion. You sure that's what he said?'

'*Katha*, yes, that's what he said.'

'We might be looking for a priest. Some kind of holy man.'

'There wasn't much holy about him, Sam, not with that chopper in his hand.' Geordie winced with the pain in his shoulder. 'He took my binoculars.' The kid closed his eyes and lapsed into oblivion.

He was still unconscious when the paramedics arrived and strapped him into a stretcher. Sam held his hand while they carried him down to the ambulance.

'Did you see what happened?' the paramedic asked, one of those ambling men who segue through life without apology or explanation.

Sam shook his head. 'I found him in the street. Is he gonna be OK?'

'He's lost much blood. Are you coming with us?'

'I'll follow you,' Sam told him. 'Where we going?'

'Ullevål Hospital.'

'Look after him.'

'That's my job, sir.'

Sam watched as the ambulance turned into Storgata. Then he legged it along Calmeyers gate to the flat where Holly and Inge Berit lived. The street door had a digital lock with an intercom and he leaned on all the buttons until someone buzzed him in.

There was a brass and chromium lift but Sam took the winding stone staircase with its mosaic of tiny tiles covering the walls. One of the first-floor flats had a pram outside and the strains of a children's song came from behind the door, something about a train and a station. Sam followed the stairs to the next landing.

Vague feeling of *déjà vu*, not enough to stop him in his tracks but enough to make him falter. Flat five had a small framed Russian icon, the *Kazan Virgin and Child*, pinned to the wall beside the door, which was slightly ajar. There was the sound of running water.

Sam knocked, expecting no reply. He pulled the door open and she was there at his feet, her quilted jacket on the floor a few feet away in the entrance to the kitchen. Her Lapp hat with the ear-flaps was between her feet. She wore the high boots she had worn in the Coco Chalet; the same full-length skirt, though it was now raised to display one of her thighs.

Holly's head was cloven apart. Something had come down with tremendous force across the hairline, splitting the skin and bone almost to the bridge of her nose. Her eyes were like bottle tops, staring in opposite directions. Apart from that one ugly gash there were no other marks. The single blow had done the job.

You've stayed young, Sam, while I've grown old. He had spoken to her a couple of hours earlier. Held her in his arms. She would never grow old now. Someone had made sure of that.

One of her hands was caught in her hair, the fingers entangled there, as if caught in a spider's web. But the other hand was clenched into a tight fist, down by her side, close to her body. Sam went down on his knees, reached for the fist and held it for a moment, surprised at its warmth.

He prised open the fingers of the fist, one at a time, hoping that within he would find a Hitchcockian clue. A gold medallion with the killer's name and address, some irrefutable proof that would lead him directly and instantly to the man who was responsible for this mutilated and broken body.

Zilch.

The fist was simply a fist, a reaction to the sight of the killer bearing down on her. There was nothing clutched within Holly's poor dead fingers, no tell-tale locket screaming identity. Only her hand and her fingers and her mother's ring, which she had worn since her eighteenth birthday.

Sam didn't know if there was life after death. He doubted it. The universe was complex and he was prepared to be wrong. But even if people somehow came back again and again in a succession of reincarnations it wasn't possible to reclaim the past. Holly's past would never live again, and neither would Sam Turner's. There were fewer and fewer witnesses to the fact that he'd had one.

It was not the sound of a footstep behind him, nothing audible, that made him turn his head. Inge Berit was standing at the top of the stairs. She wore the same black cape she had worn at the Coco Chalet, the long boots with the heels. Her bag was slung over her shoulder and one of her gloves had fallen to the tiled floor. Sam thought her mouth was wide open, but that was before he took in the size of her eyes.

As he turned and got to his feet, exposing Holly's prostrate body, Inge Berit took a step backwards down the stairs. She lost her footing and for a moment Sam thought she would go over and crack her head on the steps. But she grabbed for the handrail and saved herself, pulling herself back on to the landing.

Later, he couldn't remember when she had started screaming. It could have been at that point, when she pulled herself back, but it could have been a long time before. She may already have been screaming when he turned and saw her for the first time.

He took a step towards her but she grabbed the straps of her bag and wielded it like a weapon. 'Keep away,' she said. She screamed for help in Norwegian: '*Hjelp meg, hjelp meg. Mord. Morder.*' Her voice cracking with rage and frustration. 'Holly . . . ahhh.'

The door to the flat opposite opened and a barefoot

teenage boy looked out. Sam ran before it was too late. He brushed past Inge Berit and ducked as she swung her bag at his head. Must've been a bottle in there because it cracked against the wall. He hesitated at the turn and looked back, desperate to explain, to comfort and quieten her. But her face was a mask of outrage and hatred. Behind her Holly's body was prostrate in the doorway to the flat, a lake of water spreading from the bathroom and flooding the hall where she lay.

Sam took the steps fast, Inge Berit's accusations darting after him like the tail of a kite.

He stopped at the flat in Osterhaus gate to collect his coat and rucksack. He was checking that the wad of twenties he'd brought from England was safe in the side pocket when he heard a car come rapidly along the street. He glanced out of the window as the police left the car blocking the road and headed for the entrance to the flat.

Sam locked the door and went out to the rear balcony as footsteps thundered on the stairs.

'Politi. Open up,' a voice shouted through the door. Sam looked down at the cobblestones in the courtyard, tried to convince himself he could take the fall, land on his feet and live to tell the tale. But he rarely believed his own stories.

The roof was an easier option.

'Politi. Open the door,' the cops shouted. They hammered on the wood with their fists.

Sam stood on the balustrade and hoisted himself on to an area of coping around the perimeter of the roof. A magpie trying to grab forty winks tottered off along the tiles sideways before taking to the skies.

Sam let himself fall into the gap between the coping and the roof tiles as the noise from the flat door rose to a climax. The cops must have smashed it off its hinges and he could hear them running around in there, inspecting the loo to see if he'd got out that way. A couple of them came on to the balcony and spoke to a third who was down in the courtyard. Sam's grasp of the language wasn't perfect but good enough to work out that they thought he'd be far away by now. 'Down by the docks,' the cop in the courtyard was saying. 'We should be watching the ships.'

He could hear them ransacking the flat, collecting the things he'd left behind, one of his shirts and a couple of books that Geordie had left by his bed. A photograph of Janet and Echo.

Two of them carried the loot down the stairs to their car, while one of the others shouted a racist joke after them that was not made funnier by the change of language. But the fourth one came back to the balcony. He lit a cigarette and Sam watched the tiny clouds of smoke rise above the level of the roof. The man's shoes scuffed on the floor as he paced back and forth.

When he was joined by his friend the first man said something that Sam couldn't understand. There was a period of quiet which was unnerving. Sam wanted to lift his head and look over the coping, see what the two of them were up to. But he didn't move. He held his breath and kept low.

There was a scraping sound followed by a release of breath which was far too close and as Sam watched a man's face came over the coping like a rising moon. It was less than a metre away. A large square face with a square jaw. Brown eyes and even teeth. He had the dark blue jowls of a man who shaved more than once a day. He looked at Sam and smiled and then turned back to his friend on the balcony. 'Bjorn,' he said. 'I think we've earned ourselves some promotion.'

Sam scrambled to his feet and moved away along the rooftop as the cop heaved his considerable bulk over the coping. Sam moved on to the tiles, slowly ascending towards the peak of the pitch. It was slow going until he learned to use the edge of his shoes to stop himself slipping back. The cop behind him was gaining ground, all the time talking in a low guttural mutter, something like a shepherd might use on a frightened animal. It was a reassuring sound, intended to slow the heartbeat, keep panic at bay. Sam shut it out.

He concentrated on picking his way, testing the reliability of each tile before transferring his weight. He knew that back on the balcony the other cops would be radioing for reinforcements, making sure they had the building surrounded. The time he had available to make his escape was strictly limited.

As he continued to ascend the pitch Sam could see the outline of a metal cage on the end of the roof, way over to his left. Looked like an exterior fire-escape and represented his only chance of evading capture. He glanced back at his pursuer, who was still too low on the pitch to see Sam's escape route, though the guy was now little more than a metre below him, still gaining ground.

Sam changed direction, picking his way crab-like over towards the left. The cop did the same, though not entirely abandoning the incline, so that he remained underneath Sam on the pitch but continued to come closer to his feet.

They travelled another ten or fifteen feet in this way before the cop felt able to make a grab for Sam's shoe. He kicked out, but at the same time he lost his grip on the tiles and felt himself begin to slide down the pitch of the roof. The cop let out a yell as one of Sam's feet collided with his neck and the two of them clattered down the pitch, bringing several of the tiles with them.

The cop went over the coping and disappeared and Sam banged his head and felt himself trapped in the area between the coping and the beginning of the pitch. He was nauseous and couldn't work out if it was because of the blow to his head or the fact that he'd just watched a man fall to his certain death.

He got to his knees and peered over the coping. The cop was still there, hanging in space. He was clinging to the guttering with both hands, the toes of his shoes bearing some of his weight by digging into the mortar between two bricks. And underneath him there was nothing for three storeys until the hard cobblestones of the courtyard.

Sam looked down at the man and did some unconscious calculations. He could lean over the coping and reach the cop's hand, somehow try to convince the man that he could let go of the guttering and make a wrist-to-wrist link with Sam.

But then what?

The cop was too heavy to lift back on to the roof. After a while Sam would have to let him go or the two of them would be dragged over. He looked down and engaged the man's eyes. He shook his head and the cop looked away. Sam didn't have to spell it out.

Down in the courtyard there were two other cops who were shouting for their comrade to hang on. Someone was getting a ladder.

Sam wanted to stay and watch, see if they made it in time or if the cop hanging on to the guttering would fall before they came with the ladder. But there wasn't time for that.

As the light began to fade he inched his way over the rooftop, making his way to the end of the building. He caught a glimpse of something flashing in the late sunshine over by Calmeyers gate and stopped momentarily to focus on it. There was a single figure, obviously male but too far away to make out any facial features. He was holding a pair of binoculars to his eyes, training them on Sam as he made his way along the rooftop. As he watched the man lowered the binoculars and turned away. Sam couldn't tell if there was a movement of the man's arm, a salute of recognition. The man walked away and was soon obscured by the rooftops.

Sam didn't know how he knew that the figure with the binoculars was the man who had murdered Holly and the others, but he knew all the same. And he knew that the man had outclassed him again. This was someone who could make Sam do exactly what he wanted and when he wanted.

And Sam's own malleability, his seeming inability to refuse the murderer's wishes and aspirations, had led to another death. There was no doubt that this shadowy figure was a brutal and conscienceless killer, but by the same rule Sam Turner himself was complicit in the deaths of the women whose only sin had been to give themselves to him.

Sam got back to earth via the service ladder attached to the outer wall, all the time expecting the cry to go up and a fresh influx of police to come pouring in and drag him off to the cells. He found himself in a small alley off the cobbled courtyard and, keeping his back to the wall, snatched a moment to watch the police with a ladder, trying to position it below the cop who was still dangling from the guttering.

While they were occupied with that Sam had time to move into the overhang which led to the back entrance of the flats. He tried the first door and found it locked. The second door was the same. The third was unlocked and gave easily. Sam stepped inside. He held his breath and listened.

In another room a dance band was playing and a

singer, in a voice filled with emotion, was accentuating the lyrics:

> *No tiene pretensión,*
> *no quiere ser procaz*
> *se llama tango y nada más.*

Made you think of the house where you were born. All the things and people you'd ever known and lost.

He was in a kitchenette. There was cold fish soup in a pan on the cooker. Over in the corner was an antique Norsk cupboard painted with red roses on an ultramarine background, chipped gold-leaf frame defining the limits of each door. Sam took a dishcloth from the sink and wiped the roof-dirt from his hands. He gave his trousers and shoes a rub. If he made it to the street he wanted to look halfway decent.

The kitchen door led him into a hall where the music became louder. In the room to his right a couple were dancing the tango. The man was black and wearing cord trousers with braces and a light blue shirt, two-tone dancing shoes. His woman wore high-heels and a skirt with a hemline cut on the cross, bare breasts and spectacles. Their eyes were locked together.

Any other time, any other circumstances, Sam would've stayed to watch.

But he stepped past the opening to the room, took a gabardine raincoat and peaked cap from a hook by the door, and let himself out of the flat, finding himself by an exit a hundred metres further along Osterhaus gate.

The police car was still there but only manned by a solitary cop. The others must still be struggling with the ladder in the courtyard.

Sam had wanted to go to the hospital to see Geordie, find out how the kid was doing, make sure he wasn't going to die. But he would be mad to go there. The police would be swarming all over the place. The best he could do was to return to the Internet café and get word through to Janet. She would be the best tonic for Geordie. A word from her would get him back on his feet quicker than anything else in the world.

Clinging to the shadows, he slowly moved out of the area and a few minutes later hit the anonymity of Henrik Ibsen's gate, walked past a chrome and glass fashionable café and allowed the silent tentacles of the international city to wind their way around him.

27

You had to speak through an intercom because everyone else had gone home and there was only the counsellor in the building. Ruben checked his watch – 7.35 – and hit the intercom button with the index finger of his right hand.

There was a grating sound from the grille. It sounded like a steam train pulling into a station. And her voice, when it came, was distorted. The register was wrong for a human being, too high. It would've been all right as special effects, one of those films that have human beings flying over treetops, women who are hybrids, crosses between people and animals.

He pushed his face close to the grille. 'What did you say?'

The hybrid again. 'What's your name?'

'Ruben Parkins. I've got an appointment.'

The grating sound made him pull away. 'Push the door and come upstairs.'

Weird, seeing the place like this. Every time Ruben had been to the surgery previously the place was buzzing. There were the receptionists in their white coats, old-age pensioners and mothers with babies. One time he'd been here and a guy had a heart attack in the waiting room, clutching his chest and rolling around on the floor. Some of the kids thought it was a circus. Doctors came out of their rooms, running down the stairs to get the receptionists to help. In the end it was one of the single mums who'd called an ambulance on her mobile. Didn't stop the guy from dying but the paramedics said it could've done if she'd rung a minute earlier.

The place was deserted, eerily silent. Ruben walked the length of the hallway and started up the winding staircase. Plush pile carpet, ebony handrail polished as bright as a saint's foot.

When he got to the upper floor he didn't know if he should sit in the waiting room or go into the doctor's surgery. But the counsellor's voice sang out, saying, 'Come straight in, Mr Parkins.' Nothing like it had sounded over the intercom. Fairly good voice, middle-class, like Katherine's, you could tell she'd been studying somewhere. A woman who understood you had to sound the vowels and the consonants. But there was no edge to it, she didn't need to put you down.

She was sitting behind the doctor's desk. Slim woman, stylish, short brown hair, thirty-five, forty, silver choker round her neck, black round-necked top with long sleeves. A smile on her face, but not too wide.

'Come in,' she said. 'Have a seat.'

There was no choice about seats. There was the one she had which was obviously taken, and then there was the one this side of the desk. Wooden job with arms, no padding. Ruben sat on the edge of it. He waited.

'My name's Sarah Murphy,' she said. 'I'm not a doctor. The doctors in the practice retain me to talk to some of their patients. I don't have access to medical records.' She paused to make sure she had his attention. Held his eyes without blinking.

'Sometimes people come to the doctor with a problem that isn't strictly medical. Maybe it falls somewhere between a medical definition and what we call a life problem. When the doctor thinks that is the case she suggests the patient comes to see me, and she thought that in your case which is why we are meeting here now.

'We can meet six times, and usually the client feels better about things after that time. If it's necessary we can then arrange a further six meetings. If there has been no change in the client's condition then the doctor could prescribe medication, or she might want to get a second opinion.

'Do you want to ask me any questions?'

'She thought I was inhabited by depression,' Ruben said.

'And what do you think?'

'If the police had found the guy, I wouldn't be here.'

'The police?'

Ruben took a deep breath. 'Kitty was my girlfriend. She was killed in her own bed. Somebody came in and knifed her. I found her the next morning and the police think it was her ex-husband. He's on the run.'

'Is this the same case I've been reading about in the newspapers? The private detective?'

'Yeah. He killed another woman in Leeds. Now he's gone missing. But the police had him when he killed Kitty and they let him go.'

'You're telling me that you're depressed because the police let the murderer go.'

'Yeah. They shoulda kept him. Banged him up. Then the other woman would still be alive.'

'You knew the other woman, the one in Leeds?'

'No, I was just saying.'

'Because it seems to me that the main reason you're depressed is because of your girlfriend's death. Would you agree with that? It could be that facing up to that is too painful, so you're transferring your feelings of pain on to the murderer, looking for revenge.'

'Yeah.'

'Do you understand what I mean, Mr Parkins?'

'I wanna kill the guy.'

'That's a normal response. In the same circumstances almost everyone would react in the same way.'

Ruben didn't reply. He knew what she meant but she didn't know what he meant. She thought that was something to say, that he wanted to kill the guy. But Ruben didn't care whether he said it or not, he wanted to kill the guy, and if he got half a chance he would do it. He didn't care if they banged him away for life. They could do what they wanted, it wouldn't make any difference. He didn't have a life, anyway, so how could they take it away from him?

'What happens,' he told her, 'I go to sleep. I was delivering milk but it didn't get delivered. I loaded up the van and sat behind the wheel for two hours, never moved. Today I thought I'd go for a walk, keep myself fit. But I got to the corner of my street and stood there for fifty minutes. I couldn't go for the walk and I couldn't turn round and go back home. It was like I was paralysed.'

'Those are classic symptoms of depression.'

'And I'm crying all the time. Sometimes I'm wiping my eyes because I can't see properly. Maybe I'm watching a match on the telly, whatever, I can't see it and it's like I've got something in my eye. But there's nothing there. It's tears. I'm sitting there crying my eyes out and I don't even know I'm doing it. This's me, I don't cry. Supposed to be a man.'

'I think we should talk about Kitty if you feel up to it. How you feel about losing her.'

Ruben closed his eyes. 'Kitty was the best friend I ever lost. All she wanted was good things for everybody, especially me. I'm confused. My heart hurts. Every time I take a drink I know it's gonna end up as tears. I think about the last moments. What she was thinking of. Did she call out my name? I'm not sure she's not still alive and every day of my life is some terrible joke. Someone's fooling me. I want to kill the man who stole away our future.

'I can remember the feel of her, her kiss, the scent of her. I can't believe it when I wake up and find it's a dream. She's got me in the palm of her hand. I don't know what it is, but I'm not all here. Somebody's put out the light in me. It's like I've been swallowed by a snake. I'm still alive but there's no point to it.'

'What about nights?' she asked. 'Do you sleep?'

'I want to sleep all the time,' Ruben told her. 'When I'm sleeping it's like it never happened. Kitty's still here and everything's normal. I go to bed at night and I can't sleep. So I slug back a few beers and then it gets easier. Makes me feel like shit in the morning, though.

'Sometimes I sleep in the day. I'll be watching the box in the afternoon and there's nothing on you wanna watch. There's these women with the freak-shows, Oprah, Ricki Lake, guys who sleep with their girlfriends' mothers. I don't wanna see that so I snooze through it. One minute I'm awake, the next I'm asleep. Then I'm awake again. Like that, maybe a couple of hours I'm floating around. If it wasn't for the guy, Sam Turner, I'd be thinking seriously about topping myself. Only I can't afford to leave it to chance he'll get away with it. I'm keeping myself going so I can take him out.'

She maintained eye contact. She looked as though she didn't know where to go next, but she pulled something out. 'OK, let's look at that for a minute. This is hypothetical but I'd like you to respond if you can. If this man, this detective, is arrested by the police and brought to court and found guilty . . . if he's punished by the state, sent to prison . . . how would you feel about that?'

'It's not gonna happen?'

'I'm not suggesting that it will happen, but if it did? The police are looking for him.'

Ruben thought about it. 'If it all came out,' he said eventually. 'If he admitted it and said why he did it. If they banged him away for the rest of his life. Maybe that would be enough. I don't really know. It wouldn't bring Kitty back. She'd still be dead and I'd be walking round wishing she wasn't.'

'Have you considered that the detective might not be guilty?'

'Yeah, I have. And it seems to me he fits the bill. I've been in prison myself. That's not something you do without learning lessons. One of the things I learned was that just because a guy's in prison it doesn't mean he committed a crime – it means a judge sent him to prison, that's all. Sometimes the guy did the crime and sometimes he didn't. The system isn't infallible, it's crap. I want the right guy, the guy who did for Kitty. I'm not looking for a scapegoat. But everything points to Sam Turner.'

'You see, Mr Parkins, what I believe will happen is that the police will capture this man. And if he's guilty he'll go to prison for a long time, maybe for the rest of his life. What I'm trying to discover is how you'll cope when that happens. I'd like to think that you'll accept that, that you'll remember the good times you had with Kitty and be thankful for them. And that you'll find a way of carrying on with your life. I know that doesn't seem like a possibility for you right now, but I'd like to think that it will gradually seem more possible as time goes on.'

Ruben shook his head.

'I don't expect you to achieve that by yourself, Mr Parkins. I'm here to give you all the help and support I can. And there are other agencies that can help in different ways. Let's say that that is our goal. Now, it's usual to meet weekly but I think we ought to try to see each other twice in the next seven days. How does that sound?'

'Sounds fine,' Ruben said. 'I like you. It's good to talk. But you haven't heard what I'm saying, not entirely. You heard some of it, but there's other parts you don't want to hear.'

'I've been trying to listen,' she said. She had a genuine smile on her face. 'This is the first time we've met. Maybe next time you can tell me what it is you think I haven't heard.'

'I'll tell you now,' Ruben said. 'I wanna strangle the bastard who killed Kitty. I wanna do it with my own hands. That seems like the only thing that makes sense to me.'

Around the Lace Market Ruben knocked on the door of another B&B. 'Can you spare me a moment?' he asked the man who answered. He showed him the photograph of Sam Turner. 'We're trying to trace this man and have reason to believe he stayed in this area recently. Have you seen him before?'

The man took the photograph into his bony hands. Thin fingers, long, like twigs. 'What's he done?'

'We don't know that he's done anything, sir. We need to talk to him because we think he can help with our enquiries into a couple of rather serious incidents.'

'I don't know him,' the man said. 'Never seen him before.'

Ruben wasn't convinced about his own impersonation of a policeman. He'd known cops all his life, talked to dozens of them and listened to dozens more while he was waiting for them to decide what to do with him. But his impersonation wasn't true. It was a cliché. That was because he couldn't believe in himself as a copper. To be a good impersonator or a good liar you have to believe it yourself, or as near as possible.

Still, it was good enough to get by. One hotelier this afternoon had asked to see his ID and he'd had to admit he wasn't a cop. He'd told the truth: that Kitty had been killed and he was checking out if the guy had been in Nottingham that day. The man had softened immediately, introduced him to the receptionist and showed her the photograph. But she didn't recognize the detective.

Ruben used the cop impersonation because it saved explaining everything. When he told people his girlfriend had been murdered, they took a step back. It was as if Kitty's death marked him out as someone with a curse. People recoiled from him because he'd been visited by tragedy and, like a disease, he might still be carrying it and pass it on to them.

He liked the counsellor, Sarah Murphy, with her silver choker and her middle-class way of explaining everything in words of one syllable, desperate to be understood. Or maybe the desperation was to avoid being misunderstood? She had something of Kitty in her. Not a lot, but it was there. She knew things out of books and from courses she'd attended. But she'd never been on the street and was attracted by and frightened of men like Ruben.

What it was, he recognized her professional manner and the propriety with which she conducted their interview as a veil to hide her own insecurities. And she knew he did. Ruben had managed to tell her so without saying a word.

He smiled as he approached the next B&B. It was more democratic that way. If he hadn't found some weakness in her he wouldn't have continued the counselling. Because she'd have had all the power and he'd have been a geek. There would have been no point in seeing her. She would have patronized him and he would have resented her for it. And then he'd have been stuck with the depression.

Ruben hadn't read any textbooks. In the joint he'd read novels. Cowboys. Cops and robbers. And he hadn't been on any courses. Unless you counted the small business start-up course. But he knew the difference between grief and depression. Grief was something he had to cope with by himself. It was grief that made him cover his head with the duvet and scream at the top of his voice for an hour at a time. It was grief that made him want to explode.

But depression was something else. He couldn't manage that on his own. They were related, these two, grief and depression, but they weren't the same thing. Grief was somewhere he had to dwell for a time before he came back to the idea of getting on with his life. Depression wasn't like that. It was a prison cell.

Which makes her into some kind of key, he thought. Sarah Murphy, the counsellor, working away to open him up.

28

Danny's internal slave-driver had been hard at it since the unfortunate incident in Calmeyers gate. He didn't know if he'd killed the young man or not. He'd seen the ambulance take him away and he'd watched Sam Turner make his escape from the police. There hadn't been time to hang around. He'd stopped the kid, that was certain. He'd felt the blade of the axe cut into the flesh and, for a moment, he'd seen the shock in the young man's eyes as the blood drained from his face.

Danny hadn't slept through the night and as he put his bag on the conveyor belt at Gardermoen he reflected that it didn't really matter if the young man was still alive. It didn't matter if he had seen Danny's face and could identify him. Who would believe him? The police in two countries would now be looking for Sam Turner. The illusion was coming to its conclusion. The authorities would be under pressure to find the detective and bring him to justice.

The plane taxied along the runway and waited in the queue for takeoff. The pilot apologized for the delay, assured all the passengers that they would be airborne within a few minutes. The magician eased his safety belt, rolled his left hip where it had pinched him. He turned and smiled reassuringly at the Asian woman in the window seat next to him.

He had accomplished what he had come to do. The Oslo section of the illusion had been completed success-fully, or nearly so.

Until the incident with the boy it had been a doddle. The doors to the flat had opened easily enough, causing Danny no trouble at all. Once inside he had put on two pairs of latex gloves and removed his clothes as usual. It was a pity he couldn't use the bayonet, but he'd never have been able to take it on the plane. Aesthetically it troubled him that he'd had to purchase the hatchet, though when he thought about it it was a more practical weapon.

Intellectually Danny agreed with Nietzsche: 'You only need to start thinking of culture as something useful and all too soon you'll be confusing what is useful with culture.' Still, needs must. In the same situation, Danny consoled himself, the *Übermensch* would have considered a hatchet beyond good and evil.

He had expected both of the women to return together. He would wait for them to remove their outdoor clothes and act quickly. He had already unplugged the phones, drawn the curtains to the street.

But Holly Andersen arrived alone. Through a chink in the kitchen door he watched her close the outer door behind her and remove her Lapp hat and quilted jacket. She was humming something from a show, an old tune. As she moved to hang up her clothes Danny came for her. She didn't reach the peg. Her jacket and hat fell to the floor as he brought the hatchet down on her head. She didn't say anything. No sound came from her lips. She stood on one leg for a moment, her long skirt somehow entangled in her arm, and then she went over heavily.

Danny watched for a minute as her body went through the shaking and shuddering. There was no real life there, only a mess of nerves and tissue in convulsion over the loss of central command. When she was still he dropped the latch on the door and went to the bathroom. There were splatters of blood on his forearms and another on his forehead and his right thigh. He washed himself clean and got back into his clothes. He placed the Norwegian cap on his head and pushed it forward from the back. Reminded him of Bogey in *The African Queen*, one of his mother's favourites.

He washed the hatchet and placed it in the inside pocket of his overcoat.

He put the plugs in the bath and the wash-basin, blocked the overflows and turned on the taps. He turned on the shower as an after-thought.

He stepped over Holly Andersen's body on his way out and took the steps down to the street. He was sure it was all over. He would go back to the hotel and make arrangements to check out. Go back to England and normality. Back to Jody.

When Sam Turner's lackey had attacked him, flinging him back against the wall of a building, Danny had acted instinctively. There was no time for premeditation. He had reached for the hatchet and used it. He'd seen the young man rolling over on the pavement and grabbed his binoculars and made his getaway as quickly as possible.

Couldn't resist returning later, though, in time to catch the detective scrambling over the rooftops like the insect he was.

The plane taxied forward, hesitated as though gathering enough will-power and courage before flinging itself down the runway like a charging rhino. Danny closed his eyes. He loved planes. Had always been fascinated by flying. The trip to Thailand had been one of the high spots of his life. He had relished flying there and back almost as much as he had delighted in his experiences in Bangkok and the Chao Phraya River basin. Danny couldn't understand people who were frightened of flying. He had been amazed to discover that there were psychologists who specialized in aerophobia and acrophobia, actually made a living out of it. In reality the sky was a safer place to be than the roads or the high seas. If he wasn't a man he would choose to be a bird, an eagle or an albatross with all the power and soaring majesty of wingspan and speed. A solitary predator with the ability to spot a trembling whisker from a mile in the sky and the dexterity and velocity to take it with talon and beak before the creature could sigh.

There was a young man towards the front of the cabin who had tried to drink himself senseless and failed. He was big, broad-shouldered and bearded, and was wearing an orange shirt and baggy trousers. His voice, when he spoke to himself or one of the stewardesses, was a few decibels above the acceptable and his sentences were liberally laced with expletives.

The other passengers were quieter than normal, each of them wondering if the man was going to cause real trouble, perhaps degenerate into air-rage.

'Gimme a drink,' he said to the stewardess.

'In a moment, sir.' She went forward, through first-class.

'Bitch!' he shouted after her. 'Give a man a drink.' He got to his feet and twisted around, looking towards the rear of the plane. 'Fucking drink, here,' he said, before collapsing back into his seat.

Mancunian accent, Danny decided. And the man was older than he'd first thought. Thirty-five, thirty-six, with a liver maybe fifteen years older.

The stewardess returned and the man was on his feet again. He lurched over his fellow passenger to grab her but she leaped out of reach. 'Where's my drink?' he said.

'If you wait a minute the Captain will come and talk to you,' she told him.

'Don't wanna Capt'n, need a fucking drink.' He extricated himself from the man he had fallen over and followed the stewardess towards the rear of the plane. She stood her ground a couple of seats in front of Danny.

'I think it would be better if you returned to your seat, sir,' she said. 'You're disturbing the other passengers.'

'To hell with them – Southern slapheads. Open the door, let 'em all get sucked out.' He made another grab for her but she took a couple of steps back.

'I really can't serve you anything at all if you're not in your seat, sir.'

'Lying bitch! I was in my seat to start with.' He appealed to Danny and the Asian woman sitting next to him. 'Did I get a drink when I was in my seat?'

The Asian woman said he should do what the stewardess told him and go back to his seat.

'Jesus,' he said. 'I only want a drink. 'S'not unreasonable.' Then he stood with his legs apart and screamed at the top of his voice, 'GET ME A FUCKING DRINK.'

The stewardess lost it at that point. She turned and ran for the rear of the plane. The man in the orange shirt went after her. Some woman screamed and a couple of men got out of their seats. As the big man went past Danny the magician stuck out his foot and tripped him, bringing him crashing down in the aisle. He stayed on his face for a couple of seconds and then raised himself on to his knees.

Danny waited no longer. He unfastened his safety belt and got to his feet. He stepped into the aisle behind the drunk and pushed him down on to his face. Then he stood on the man's back and shouted for the stewardess to help him.

She came down the aisle with a couple of towels and another stewardess followed with more linen. Together, while Danny kept the man down, the two women managed to tie his hands behind his back. Every time he protested the second stewardess gave his hair a yank and banged his head on the floor. 'Sorry,' she said each time. 'Oops, sorry again.'

They tied a towel around his ankles and another

around his knees. When they'd finished, the first steward-ess told Danny he could return to his seat. 'We'll sit on him until we get to Newcastle.' She gave Danny a big smile. 'Thank you very much for your help,' she said. 'We wouldn't have managed without you.'

Admiring glances from the other passengers, especially the women. The Asian woman sitting next to him melted in her seat. She had each of her tiny hands on the edge of the armrests and sank back into the upholstery with her eyes closed and her lips parted. From time to time she would turn to him and stare until she got his attention. 'Thank you,' she'd say. 'Thank you very much.'

The plane approached Newcastle International Airport, the River Tyne and Hadrian's Wall both visible in twisted outline as the airliner dropped below the level of the clouds. Danny waited for the touch of landing, that bounce as the great metal bird fought against its compulsory grounding and then the rapid deceleration, pushing him forward into his straining seatbelt.

'Can I ask passengers to remain seated for a few minutes?' the Captain's voice said over the intercom. 'The local police will be removing the individual who attacked one of our flight attendants.'

Two police officers entered the plane from the rear and two more from the front of the plane. They unceremoni-ously bundled the drunk along the center aisle and out on to the tarmac where they had a dog and a van waiting.

'The Captain wants a word with you,' the flight attendant said to Danny. 'If you don't mind waiting?'

He stayed in his seat, nodding at the passengers who left the plane as they smiled at him and thanked him again for his bravery. When they'd all left the plane the Captain came along the aisle with hand outstretched. 'You are a very brave man,' he said. 'I wanted to let you know how much my crew and I appreciate your actions back there. Without you the whole situation could have got very ugly.'

'Really,' Danny said, 'I only did what anyone . . .'

'No, that's not true. No one else intervened. I want you to know that my report will strongly recommend your bravery is officially recognized.'

'I'm sure there's no need for that,' Danny told him. 'I only did what I had to do.'

'And thank God you did, sir,' the Captain told him.

'I really don't want any fuss,' Danny said. 'I lead a quiet life and I like it that way.'

They left the plane together and walked towards the waiting bus, through the ranks of passengers who applauded as Danny passed them by. At the entrance to the bus the first stewardess, the one who had been harassed by the man in the orange shirt, took a step forward and kissed the magician on the cheek. The Asian woman who had been sitting next to him on the plane also came forward with a kiss of her own. A news photographer caught Danny receiving the kiss, the light from the flash causing him to blink. And they all waited until Danny was on the bus before following him aboard.

The handshakes and the kisses continued inside the airport terminal. And after Danny had been interviewed by the police and got rid of the reporters from the *Guardian*, the *Sun*, the *Daily Mail* and Channel 4 News, there were still a few of the passengers waiting to add their thanks.

Danny was flattered. He was worried about the attention of the press but he was flattered nonetheless. He hadn't thought of himself as brave when it was happening but the weight of public opinion was beginning to get to him. Surely these people couldn't all be wrong.

29

Alice Richardson had married Sam Turner shortly after he split from Holly Andersen. She was looking for a father substitute, though at the time she would have denied it. She loved the fact that he was so much older than her, that he had seen life and acquired what she liked to think of as wisdom. And she believed the silly things he said because they seemed to have more authority than the silly things that occurred inside her own head.

She folded the *Guardian* and put it on the piano stool. She couldn't believe that he had murdered those women, or that he was capable of murdering anyone. Alex, her partner for the last fifteen years, had pointed out that people change, and that you never really know another person. We all manage to hide behind the person we imagine ourselves to be.

But what did Alex know? Not a lot, unfortunately. The main problem with him was that you didn't have to be bright to know him very well after a few minutes in his company. A man by whom Alice would be severely embarrassed if she ever accepted responsibility for him. He was the centre of his own universe, had analysed himself and was anxious to pass on to the rest of the world the fruit of his discoveries about human nature. 'I'm a lucky guy,' he'd tell complete strangers. 'I can't help it, I'm just lucky.' Almost every sentence that left his lips began with the word 'I'.

She shook her head. Alice didn't want to think about

Alex. It was thinking about Sam that had brought him into her mind. Contrasts. You defined each person in terms of the others you met. You constructed an invisible and unconscious table in your mind, with the best ones at the top and the worst ones at the bottom, and as you went through your life you added and subtracted different characters, pushing some of the earlier ones towards the bottom or the top, only occasionally completely replacing the top one or two with new names.

Alice's list, when she tried to access it, had only a few constant characters, and Sam Turner was one of them. Before they had married, when she was twenty-two, he had been way up at the top of the list. But a week after the ceremony he had begun dropping rapidly. Within two to three months he was at the bottom, and for a year or two after they separated he remained as the anchor-man. She didn't think she'd ever meet anyone as disappointing as him. She didn't want to. One was enough.

And then, imperceptibly at first, he'd begun to make a comeback. She'd only really noticed when she found him at the halfway mark, and for the last six or seven years he'd got back in there with the leaders. Not number one, but probably in the first four.

And yet there was a truth in what her partner, Alex, said about never really being able to know another human being. She didn't know Sam, not really. What she had responded to in him all those years ago was not something known, something concrete in his character. If she had known him at all it had been in the sense of his potential. She had recognized something in him that was as yet undeveloped, and might never develop. And she had been young enough and naïve enough to believe that she could provide the impetus for that spark of potential to develop into a substantial reality.

She had been unable to face the fact that the Sam Turner she had married was a man in flight from hope. That he recognized no potential in himself or in anyone else. That Sam thought of the whole of humanity, including himself, as food for worms. He was interested only in an all-out escape from his daily reality. He was never so happy as when he was drunk or unconscious. Alice couldn't understand how she had thought that that was so attractive before the wedding. It was years later that she realized it was because she was also in flight. From adulthood, from responsibility, from the person she feared she might be or was on the way to becoming.

In the past four or five years she'd seen more of Sam. They weren't close friends any more but she'd see him on the street and they'd stop and talk. He hadn't aged much – some thickening around the waist, the beginnings of jowls amid his creased face. He'd never been particularly pretty. Always interesting, though; you could look at his face for hours. It was like a story book. And then he'd asked if she had some time, could they go for coffee? Coffee was his staple. Alice couldn't think about coffee without thinking about Sam.

She'd taken him up on it a few times, hesitantly at first, not wanting to find herself spiralling back into the mistakes of her youth. But he wasn't a predator and he didn't come on to her. He talked about himself, about his relationships with women and his work, and he enquired after her as well, wanting to know more about Alex and her children and about her job as an administrator at the university. He was interested in her, Alice realized, not as a potential sexual partner but as someone who had been a part of his life. And if you'd been part of Sam's life you would always be part of it. He would never give up on you, not totally.

For the last couple of years Alice had found herself

disappointed, somehow let down if she met Sam in town and he didn't offer her coffee. He'd occasionally be busy with his blessed detective business, on the way from one job to another or to relieve one of his operatives, and he'd be full of regret about it but there were people dependent on him. Alice remembered the times she had been dependent on him. The hours, sometimes days, she'd sat waiting for him, knowing that he was head down in a gutter somewhere or in the arms of some floozy who'd promised him a drink.

But it had changed now. He didn't drink any longer. That spark of potential she had recognized all those years before had kicked in and filled out the man. He wouldn't harm her. Never. There were many people in her life who might be tempted to injure her, even Alex when he was in one of his moods or if she managed to rouse his temper, but she couldn't imagine Sam doing anything like that.

Though it was true that you never really knew another person. She was absolutely sure she wasn't wrong, not about Sam Turner, but her doubt wouldn't be stifled. It simply was a fact of life, you could never be absolutely sure.

She put on her coat and wound a long lamb's wool scarf around her neck. At the street door she stepped into a pair of new green wellington boots and strode over the sandbags on her front step. The garden and the street were a lake. There was a break in the weather and the sun was reflected in the smooth surface of the water.

Alice paddled through it. It was shallow on the garden path but by the time she got to the public footpath it was already near the top of her boots. Black river water, almost half of it silt, and giving off a stench of decaying organisms. The river was still rising, almost five metres above normal now. If it continued for another couple of days it would be in the house. They'd already taken up the carpets on the ground floor and had been living upstairs for the last ten days.

There were army trucks at the corner of the street and soldiers were laying sandbags, trying to keep the properties safe. For people lower down, closer to Terry Avenue, it was already too late. Their houses were awash and many of them were abandoned to the rising waters. Soldiers ... dear God, most of them looked little older than Dominic. Sixteen, seventeen years old. Alice didn't know how old you had to be to join the army, but looking at some of these kids she thought the entry age should be raised. What if there was a war, she wanted to ask their commanding officer, are you going to give them guns?

Hannah and Conn were waiting for her at the school gate, seemingly unconscious of the waders that reached to the top of their thighs. Hannah, ten years old now, was chatting to one of her friends, completely oblivious of her brother. Conn, the baby of the family, just past his seventh birthday, was gazing up at the sky as if expecting rain. They were as different as toast and marmalade, these two. Hannah was her father's daughter, somewhat self-obsessed but in possession of a modicum of empathy for others which seemed to have bypassed Alex, the sperm-donor. Conn, named after Alice's father was, like his grandfather, enquiring his way through life. He was forever inquisitive, a silent boy with big eyes and a degree of warmth far beyond anything Alice had discovered in herself. He certainly hadn't inherited that from Alex or his line and it was either a throwback to one of Alice's forgotten Irish ancestors or some kind of blessing. A gift from the angels.

Alice smiled. She had let her religion lapse and now only the terminology remained. That and the guilt. Especially the guilt. But she kept it close to herself, hidden in case it should somehow leak out and taint her children. Conn meant sense, reason and intelligence, and Hannah meant gracious, and these were the qualities that she wanted them to embrace. She didn't want them to be bound by the strictures of organized religion, slaves to medieval ideas and sensibilities.

God was a wonderful idea, she thought. But He was never there when you needed Him. He had spread himself too thin – trying to be everywhere at once. And a God that let Himself get into a state like that really wasn't worth bothering about.

'Have you seen Dominic?' she asked.

'He's by that green car,' Conn said. 'With his friends.'

Dominic was with two boys from his class and a girl who looked like a boy with eye-shadow and a pierced lip. A swagger of fifteen-year-olds, Alice said to herself, pleased with the invention of the collective noun.

'They're going to Lauren's house to smoke dope,' Conn said.

'I don't think so,' Alice told him. 'Dominic doesn't smoke.'

'That's all you know,' Conn told her.

'It's true, Mum,' Hannah said. 'They smoke dope and then they do an orgy.'

'Really? And do they tell tales on their brothers and sisters?'

'Probably do,' Conn said. 'That's what happens in families. Everybody is fighting for the attention of their parents.'

Alice pulled him close. Seven years old and he already knew too much. There was something dreadfully wrong with the education system. It wanted them all to conform at the same level of cynicism and neo-maturity, producing a generation of political luvvies who thought it was clever to work overtime without getting paid. You could step out of the footprints of the church but you couldn't avoid what came in its place.

Dominic waved as they went past his group on the other side of the road. 'You coming home for tea?' Alice called.

He shook his head. 'I'll be back by ten,' he said. 'I'm eating at Rafiq's.'

Rafiq gave her the thumbs-up with both hands, the pale sunlight glinting on the lenses of his National Health spectacles. Vegetable curry and chapatti again, seemed to be the only thing Dominic ate these days. Said that meat made him sick; too much fat, too much protein, human beings weren't designed for it.

Hannah and Conn were both like Alex in a way, their natural father. But Dominic was different. And it wasn't because she or Alex treated him differently from the other kids. It was a simple genetic thing, and it showed.

Alice had told Dominic that his natural father was someone she'd lost contact with. A man she'd been fond of, but who in the end had not proved reliable enough to marry. And the story was essentially true. The only part of it that was not true was the part about losing contact.

TOLS, she called it in her mind, indulging her generation's preference for acronyms. That One Last Shag with Sam long after their relationship had died, after she'd moved out of the house and come back to collect the last of her belongings. A suit she never wore, a Van Morrison album she never listened to and a collection of copper-bottomed pans she'd inherited from her mother. TOLS on the couch in the sitting room.

She was fully dressed apart from her knickers and he was in his boxer-shorts and T-shirt, his breath stale with whisky fumes. TOLS with no love or passion. She acting out of guilt and compassion and he following the unconscious urgings of his genes, spreading seed.

297

When they'd finished she struggled out of the house with two cardboard boxes of belongings. In the tiny flat she'd found for herself she played the Van Morrison album while lying in the bath and envisioning a future. And all the time one of those sperms was struggling up the moist lining of her uterus, through into the fallopian tubes and penetrating the cell membrane of her egg, beginning the process that would eventually result in Dominic.

And maybe that's what it was about, this long-term relationship with Sam Turner? Being the bearer of a secret. Because apart from her there was no one in the world who knew the real identity of Dominic's father. Dominic himself seemed entirely uninterested. He had come out with a few questions but had seemed to accept his mother's vague answers. Alex had also been inquisitive during the first weeks and months of their relationship, but during the last ten years he had never breached those areas again.

And Sam? Sam was so out of it in those days he wouldn't have remembered that they'd done it. He'd assumed that Dominic was the result of an encounter after Alice had left him, which was true. And at the same time it wasn't true at all.

She couldn't have told Sam at the time. He wouldn't have been interested. He would have been incapable of processing the information. If it didn't lead to a drink in those days he wouldn't bother taking it on board. But the real reason that Alice didn't tell Sam was because it might have forced them back together. It had been bad enough living with the guy by herself, she couldn't imagine taking a baby into the situation.

And so she'd become the bearer of the secret. The only one to know of the connection between this now almost respectable man and her lanky teenage son feeling his way to maturity and adulthood. She fantasized that she would tell them both one day, introduce them casually to each other. *Dominic, this is Sam, your father; and Sam, this is Dominic, your son.* One day, when they'd both grown up, when she was sure they could handle it. The biology, the connection, the length of time that they'd been kept from the truth. She'd dreamed it a hundred times. Half the time the dream turned into a nightmare. The other half it felt good, warm, like being part of a second family.

And now Sam was in trouble again. Maybe the worst trouble he'd ever seen. The women he'd left behind or who had left him in the past were turning up dead. It must seem to him almost as though they had never happened. And the people who didn't know Sam Turner, the police and the media, the authorities generally, who had always been his enemies, seemed intent on laying the blame at his door.

Now, they seemed to think he was in Oslo when Holly Andersen died. There was a witness who found him with the body, and one of his staff was hospitalized in Oslo. It seemed like someone's outlandish plot. And Sam, in his bungling way, was playing into their hands.

Because she would never believe he was a murderer. Not Sam Turner, the father of her eldest son. Not in a million years.

But you can never be entirely sure, she heard Alex saying inside her head. *Sometimes people go over the top. They crack, turn into somebody else. Something that you, they, nobody ever expected.*

30

When he left the flat Sam made his way to the Internet café and sent a message to Janet, copies to Celia and Marie and Angeles, make sure she had some support. He told them Geordie was in the Ullevål Hospital and that he was injured but that he wasn't going to die. He told Angeles in a separate note to expect a call from him.

Sam took a tram up to Holmenkollen and looked out over the Oslo fjord from under the shadow of the ski jump. He didn't have time to climb to the top of the jump. He'd never been much of a tourist anyway and he wasn't in Holmenkollen for the view or as a visitor to the ski museum. It was part of his route back to England.

Before leaving the town he'd got together some kit and he was wearing a pair of new Norwegian boots in soft brown leather, a dark blue Finnish suit, neat little hat – kind of cross between pork-pie and Borsalino – and a Burberry coat which he left unbuttoned so it flapped in the wind. He still had JD's glasses perched on his nose but he'd had his hair cut so short you couldn't tell if he had any until he took the hat off.

As the moon rose he found a silver Volvo V70 estate with Swedish plates sitting outside a timbered villa. With all the skill of a seasoned car-thief and working only with a pen-knife and a multi-purpose screw-driver set which he kept in a pouch in his rucksack, he had the thing unlocked and rolling down the hill within thirty minutes.

He needed a few hours and the signs were favourable that he'd get them. Through the windows of the villa it seemed as though the car's owners were settled for the night. Their hostess was serving up a large pink trout on a silver platter. The centrepiece was accompanied by small copper dishes of melted butter, marinaded cucumber and white potatoes that had been graded for size. The red wine was flowing into crystal glasses as big as melons. There was a log fire blazing in the grate and the women's décolletage was emphasized by the soft glow of beeswax candles. The men were middle-aged, secreting success and excess through every pore. They wore smiles as wide as the table. Neither of them looked as though they'd miss a silver Volvo estate. They were driving towards oblivion, way past the point of no return.

Sam drove carefully, getting the feel of the right-hand drive and exploring the subtle potency of the five-cylinder engine and power-assisted steering. There was a hands-free GSM telephone, which might come in useful, and a small pop-up menu-driven screen on the dash-board which he could alternate between a map with highlights or as a system of large arrows. Either way it showed him where he was on the map, which route to take and the remaining distance and travel time to his destination. When he stopped to check out the air-conditioning the pop-up screen turned into a television and if he'd had the time and the inclination he could have sat back and watched another showing of *Atlantic City*.

Sam had always been something of a Luddite and he was pleased with himself that he could manage the V70's technology. Took a little time to get to grips with the audio system but he sussed it in the end and listened to a Jacques Brel collection. The only other thing he could bear to play was Villa-Lobos but he decided to keep that for later, when he got out of the city. The remainder of the tapes were all by Neil Diamond – twenty-three of them.

He made his way down the hill, through Slemdal and Vinderen. He got lost briefly in Majorstuen, passed the Bislet Stadium and the Munch Museum and eventually left Oslo behind. He tucked in behind another Volvo and stayed within the speed limit on the E6, heading for the border with Sweden. Saabs and BMWs overtook from time to time, leather-clad bikers in groups of four or five, the occasional classic Cadillac pulsing with rockabilly music. Seemed like there were no old cars in this country that weren't classics. Jacques Brel was ecstatic on the audio system, Mathilde had come back to him again. Sam shrugged and gritted his teeth; some people had all the luck.

He rang Geordie on the hands-free system. Geordie's voice was tiny but already sounding better than it had when Sam had found him in the street.

'I've got the mobile on vibrate,' he explained. 'I'm not supposed to use it in here. I've already spoken to Janet.'

Sam imagined him propped up in bed with the smallest whitest face in Scandinavia.

'How you doing?'

'Good. I'm still alive.' His voice was far off, little more than a whisper. 'Holly?'

Sam shook his head. 'She didn't make it.'

'Fuck, Sam.'

'What happened back there?'

'I was standing on Calmeyers gate, outside that Christian junk shop, a little further down, near the Vietnamesisk Café. It was quiet, no one in the street. I'd been there, what? Ten minutes? Not longer. I saw Holly coming down the street on her own. She went into a shop, then she came out with bread, a baguette or a sandwich. She walked to their flat and went inside.

'I was wide awake, expecting to see the guy. Could be he was following her. So I'm weaving along the street, crossing from side to side, making out like I'm interested in mung beans, sweet potatoes, all that stuff, haricots. But I'm the only one there. There's a couple of Asian women, and there's a guy with a van trying to get a table through somebody's front door.

'So I turn round and make my way back. I'm maybe fifty metres past the flat when I hear the door slam and there he is, on the street. I have to do a double-take because I can't believe he's coming *out* of Holly's flat. I never saw him go in there. He must've gone in before I was on the street. He's been inside waiting for her.

'He's walking fast down the street now, past that Greek taverna, and I'm standing with my mouth open, catching flies. So I leg it after him. I spin him round on the pavement, his back against the wall. He's got an axe in his hand, a hatchet. It's one of those with a blade, like an ordinary axe, but opposite the blade it's a small pick-axe. You know what I mean?'

'I know.'

'He swings at me and gets me in the shoulder. The rest you know.'

'You're gonna be OK,' Sam told him, relief in his voice. 'You're still alive, which is more than can be said for other people he's gone for.'

'I know. I was lucky. They wanted to give me a blood transfusion but I don't believe in it.'

'Bit of blood's not gonna hurt you, Geordie. You looked like you could use some.'

'I've cleared it with the doctor. It means I've gotta stay here a bit longer, that's all.'

'But don't you wanna see Janet, get back home to your family?'

'No need, Sam. They're coming here. I talked to Janet on the phone.'

Sam didn't ask who was paying for Janet and Echo's flight, he assumed it would be him.

He didn't tell Geordie that he was going to find it hard working this case on his own. He made his face grin, hoped it would transmit down the line like that.

'I'm on the road,' he said. 'The police are after me. I have to get out of the country.'

'How, Sam? Where'll you go?'

'I'll find a way. See you back in York.'

'Is that where the next one is?'

Sam nodded. 'Yeah.'

'What's her name?'

'Alice. Calls herself Alice Richardson now, her maiden name. But for about four months she was called Alice Turner.'

'Another marriage made in heaven?'

'Dunno where it was made. She laughed at everything I said. I thought she loved me, but it was because she had good teeth.'

Geordie sighed.

'She seemed to think two and two'd come to make five, if she cried and bothered about it enough.'

'But with you it only came to three?'

'She decided to let me go after a while. I wasn't ready for a relationship.'

Geordie breathed down the phone.

Sam shrugged his shoulders. 'These things happen,' he said.

He rang home and Angeles picked up the phone. 'Don't ask me no questions about where I am,' he said. 'I'm on my way from where I've been, heading for where this lunatic's gonna strike next.'

'I've been worried.'

'You and me both. You being hassled?'

'Some. The day you left the police had me in the station all day.'

'But you didn't say nothing.'

'I didn't know anything, Sam. I still don't.'

'They'll have a tap on the phone, be listening in to this.'

'And my other calls?'

'You can bet on it.'

'I miss you, Sam.'

He whistled through his teeth. Watched another Saab go past at speed, young Swede at the wheel with blond hair in spikes as though he was plugged into the car's electrical system. 'Yeah. I miss you in the mornings.'

She laughed down the line. 'What about the rest of the time?'

'I can take most of it,' he said. 'Evening's bad and during the day, that's bad too. But mornings are the worst. Waking up there's a surge of optimism because it's a new day, you know, just before you open your eyes. Then it all comes back. Bang. Another shit day. I'm still chasing a guy I don't know who he is. I know what he's done and what he's doing. I know where he's heading. But I don't know *who* he is. And you're not here, and whatever happens during the day you're still not gonna be here tonight.'

'I'm not going anywhere else,' she told him. 'I'm waiting for you.'

He let the words hang there, trying to imagine her with the phone cradled against her ear. Dark curls and her skin with its hint of Buenos Aires, a genetic inheritance from her Argentine father. And close by there would be the long white cane, a substitute for her eyes.

'I'm signing off,' he said.

'When will I see you?'

He shook his head. Reached to switch off the phone.

'I love you, Sam,' she managed to say before he broke the connection.

He mouthed the words back to her though she was gone. They wouldn't convey what he felt anyway. His life had been littered with small loves but Angeles was different. And yet each of those small loves had seemed possible at the time. Sam had a genius for wrapping potential in glitzy paper and convincing himself it was reality. He'd taken many a girl off the street under the illusion she was a princess.

He should be there with her, not tearing from country to country in pursuit of some madman. All the women in his life were in danger. How long would it be before this guy, whoever he was, was turning his attention to Angeles, or to Marie or Celia, the women who were part of Sam's life now? According to the pattern, the sequence, the next one would be Alice, but what happened after that?

Sam would have to make sure that he never got to Alice. He didn't know how, he just knew that he had to do it.

He crossed the Svinesund bridge and felt the hairline prickle at the back of his neck as the Norwegian/Swedish border came in sight. There were a couple of lights on in the custom buildings and someone in a uniform by a large container lorry. But the road wasn't manned and the stream of traffic continued on into Sweden without interruption.

Sam changed the tape, pushed the play button on the audio system and listened to the opening strains of the first of the Five Preludes by a Brazilian guitarist who had known Villa-Lobos and who had had his brow touched by the hand of God.

He settled back in the well-upholstered seat of the V70 and aimed it towards Gothenburg. He drove into the night thinking about women who had accompanied him on shorter or longer journeys and who had shared his past. He thought about Geordie stuck back in Oslo and he thought about Angeles in York. And as the kilometres passed he began to focus on Alice Richardson, tried to imagine her in her house in Clementhorpe with her husband and her children. He knew that he wasn't the only one thinking about her, that the man who had already murdered three of Sam's previous partners also had her on his mind.

'But I'll beat you this time,' Sam said out loud. 'Whatever it takes, you're not having Alice as well.'

He parked the V70 on the top deck of a multi-storey car park in the middle of Gothenburg. Bought a ticket for it and stuck it on the windscreen.

He had breakfast in a fast-food joint, baguette with bacon and Brie and two cups of strong black. He pumped the assistant for directions to the docks. He felt good in the new Finnish suit, it took ten years off him, and when he'd handed over the cash it felt like that many years' earnings.

But if that was how much it cost to keep him on the street then it was worth the money. If he was picked up now they'd lock him away and leave him to rot. And there'd be no hope at all for Alice.

The *Stena Germanica* was at her berth but wasn't due to leave for Kiel until 7.30 that evening. He bought a single ticket and sat in the waiting room with a coffee machine and a German tourist with a limp for four hours. They both attempted to breach the language barrier and failed almost completely. Sam discovered that the German liked his new suit but was unable to discover which part of Germany he came from. They settled on sign language eventually and were able to express joint disgust over the warm sludge which the machine served up if they fed it enough Swedish Kroner.

When they got on board Sam went to his cabin and locked the door. He showered and lay down on his bunk, pulling the single white duvet around him. He listened to the chugging of the huge engines and felt the rolling of the ship as it left the shelter of Gothenburg behind. With his eyes closed he allowed his mind to gnaw at the bone of facts and suppositions about the killer. The guy was almost there, still emerging from a welter of leads and clues and random inklings. Sam was looking for a miracle, something that would collect the disparate facts together and deliver an exact portrait of the killer. His choice of language on the phone when he was gloating over the death of Nicole. *When your ex-partner was transformed*, he'd said. That single word, *transformed*. It had to be significant. And in Oslo, when he used the word *Katha* like an incantation, before axing Geordie. *Katha* was not an incantation, it was a meditation or a prayer of some kind.

When he thought of the killer in terms of his language Sam imagined a mystic, a holy man or a latter-day hippie. If that was the case the killings would appear to be sacrificial.

But language wasn't the only thing that was known about the man. The braid on his trousers – that was so odd that it had to be significant. On the other hand he was good at disguising himself. Geordie had recognized him as two, probably three, different characters in Oslo. So the braid could be a blind lead.

And then there was the pubic hair. The distinct possibility that he might have a doll. He could be a ventriloquist, perhaps? Sam shook his head. Ventriloquism brought him back full circle to language again.

It didn't matter how many times he went over the facts the guy refused to come into focus. He was almost there, as if he was tantalizing Sam, standing in the shadows of consciousness. No matter which way Sam came at him he managed to stay out of the light. He was a silhouette, a ghost. He didn't seem to be threatening. Unless your name was on his list.

Sam got out of his bunk and dressed. He went to the ship's buffet restaurant and gorged himself on poached salmon, prawns and tiny squares of herring in mustard sauce. He got himself a clean plate and went back for blue mussels and crayfish, a pile of fresh salad. Ate so much he had no room left for pudding. The profiteroles looked real nice, too good to leave behind, so he put a couple of them in a bag for breakfast.

He ordered coffee and the limping German came over to his table and sat down opposite him. '*Guten abend,*' he said.

'How you doing?'

They smiled at each other for a while. The German pointed at Sam's cup and said, '*Gemein kaffeesatz.*'

Sam took a sip, letting the aroma fill his nostrils. 'After the stuff we drank from that machine,' he said, 'this is bloody marvellous.'

The German laughed. 'Bloody marvellous,' he echoed. '*Komisch.*'

Sam laughed along with him. He didn't get the joke but he knew what people meant about travel broadening the mind. Here he was on the tip of Scandinavia learning the German language without even trying. *Wunderbar.*

There must've been every woman he had ever known in his life in the dream. He couldn't remember which ones were dead and which alive. He looked at them and thought about it real hard, trying to tell the difference, but he couldn't get it. He thought it should be important but in the dream there was a different value system. Death was a thin line on the ground, a chalk line that you stepped over if you felt like it or were pushed, it really didn't matter. Whichever side of the line you were on you could cross back to the other side. There were no absolutes. Life and death were a continuum. Nothing mattered.

The ship's address system woke him and he pulled on his new clothes and went up on deck and watched Kiel approaching through a mist. It was a setting from a horror story, the grey sea and sky, the hazy images and ship's horn moaning at the silent morning. Other passengers on deck were like zombies hanging over the rails in search of a lost mortality. Perhaps the grim reaper had boarded them in the night, slipping from cabin to cabin, leaving behind him a trail of broken promises.

Huge cranes appeared on the dockside, derricks and warehouses and other ships much bigger than the Gothenburg ferry. As the morning mist lifted, the extent of the Baltic harbour was revealed. Gulls soared. The tang of salt was everywhere.

Sam walked through passport control and stayed on the main road. Heavy lorries shipped their loads from and towards the docks. The bulk of them were German but there were Swedish, Norwegian and Finnish trucks and others from Eastern Europe and the UK.

On the outer edge of the dock area Sam found a truckstop. He stood in line with a tray and scored some rye bread with cheese and Spanish chorizo; a large mug of coffee which tasted greasy, as though it had been fried. He sat at a table by the window so he could see the trucks pulling in to the car park. Didn't move for two hours, until he saw a huge Scania V8 with a British registration loaded with a high-sided container. He watched as the driver shifted off the road and circled the café to pull neatly into a space only thirty metres from where Sam was sitting.

The driver was young and athletic. He jumped down from his cab and his knees flexed easily to take the strain. He had a mop of black hair and a ring in each ear. Around his neck was a knotted silk scarf and when he entered the café his face and arms were slick with sweat. He scanned the room without acknowledging anyone and turned to the counter where he bought a can of Coke and a concoction of hard-boiled eggs and herbs swimming in yoghurt and sour cream.

When the driver was settled at a table Sam went back for another mug of coffee and sat down opposite the guy. Sharp blue eyes flashed up at him. Sam smiled. 'You going back home?' he asked.

The driver took a forkful of the egg mixture. 'Who's asking?'

'Call me Sam.'

'And what can I do you for?'

'I'm looking for a lift.'

'You got a passport?'

'Yeah, but I'd rather get through without it.'

The driver smiled with everything except his eyes. 'More than my job's worth, mate.' He looked around the room. 'Let's walk outside.'

He left his meal half-finished and led the way to his truck. The mop of black hair wasn't as thick as Sam had first imagined. You could see right through to the scalp. He climbed up behind the steering wheel. Sam got into the passenger seat, inhaling an aroma of engine oil and stale sweat. The cab was wedge-shaped and behind the seats was a full-length bunk and beyond that a control centre and what looked like a wardrobe. Couple of pinups on the door, photographs of teenage girls with pumped-up breasts, one of them reaching down between her legs to hold her labia apart.

'The going rate's a grand. That's non-negotiable.'

Sam looked over at him but the guy's eyes were fixed on some spot the other side of the windscreen. 'You've got the cash?'

'I've got it, yeah.'

'A mile along the road there's a lay-by. I'll be there shortly after dark. You'll need drinking water and something to eat. A torch with a spare battery. There's a couple of other passengers, and you'll be together in the container. It's not comfortable and you could be inside for up to forty-eight hours. If you don't have the cash, don't bother showing. I'm not a charity.'

'When do we sail?' Sam asked.

'Tonight, just after ten. Croatian rust-bucket called *Ivan Mazuranic.* ETA Immingham Tuesday morning.'

Sam walked into Kiel and found a supermarket. He bought two-litre bottles of Evian water and a selection of German sausage and cheese, a loaf of bread, oranges and pears, and a couple of bars of Swiss chocolate. At a hardware store he bought himself a Maglite flashlight and some spare long-life batteries; a Walther Solace knife with a three-and-a-half-inch blade and a lanyard so he could hang it around his neck under his shirt. Picked up a small plastic cutting board in the same shop, imagining it would double as a platter from which he could eat his food. And at the chemist next door he got a roll of Elastoplast and a bottle of Olbas oil.

At a confectioner's he had coffee and apple-cake and used the lavish gentlemen's room to sort through his purchases. He put one thousand pounds in twenties into an envelope and stuck it in the side pocket of his rucksack. The rest of the cash he'd brought with him and the two passports he taped to the side of his body with the Elastoplast.

When he'd finished he walked back to the harbour and looked for the *Ivan Mazuranic*, to make sure the ship existed. When he found her he wished he hadn't bothered looking. She was so neglected that rust-bucket was a term of endearment. The *Ivan Mazuranic* was an unloved and unlovely vessel coated in a thick film of grease and dirt. Black as fuck. Her sides were crusted with red rust and she appeared to be abandoned. There were no sailors on her decks and no sounds emanated from her apart from the wavelets of the harbour lapping gently against her bows.

While Sam was wondering if she'd make it across the North Sea a taxi arrived and pulled up to her gangplank. The two men who fell out of its doors were blind with drink. The taxi driver left his cab and came around to them. He took a wallet from the back pocket of one of the men and extracted a wad of notes from it. Then he counted off his fare and stuck the wallet and the change back into the guy's jacket.

When the taxi had left the two of them crawled up the gangplank. They're probably the captain and the chief engineer, Sam told himself. He knew from first-hand experience what alcohol was about. In excess it allows you to fail. And failure can be gratifying, even liberating; it relieves you of the need to aspire. Sam had seen it all, done it all, and he couldn't remember half of it.

There was still time for them to sober up before the ship set sail. Sailors drank, everyone knew that. They wouldn't be sailors at all if they didn't manage the odd bottle of rum. Didn't mean they were going to send the *Ivan Mazuranic* to the bottom of the sea.

Though it would be ironic if Sam met his end because

of someone else's drunken behaviour. To get himself off the drink and to stay more or less dry for all these years only to find himself on the bottom of the ocean with a couple of Bosnian soaks. On the other hand, he consoled himself, I started out with nothing, and I still have most of it.

On his way back to the lay-by where he would meet up with the trucker Sam forgot about the ship. He'd be in the container anyway, locked away from the *Ivan Mazuranic* and its filth, its rats and its paralytic officers. Claustrophobia wasn't one of Sam's problems and he hoped that it wouldn't affect his fellow passengers.

The moon was a gold coin on the horizon and the lay-by was void of people or vehicles. The hum of Kiel was audible in the still night air and off to his left the unnatural light of the city gave the illusion of warmth.

The Scania V8 came along the road with dipped headlights and pulled up alongside Sam. The trucker leaned over and unlocked the passenger door, allowing Sam to climb up beside him.

'Fares, please,' the trucker said, a smile on his lips. If anything his hair had got thinner during the afternoon. His forehead was on its way to meet the back of his head.

Sam dug the envelope from his rucksack and handed it over. The guy ripped it open and took out the wad of notes. He flipped through them without counting. He took two twenties from the centre of the wedge and held one in each hand, working them with his thumb and forefinger. He held them up to the light above his door and wrinkled his eyes and his nose for a while until he decided to accept that they were real money.

'There's a lot of cops about,' he said. 'Down by the docks area. They could be after you.'

'I'm not hot,' Sam told him. 'Nobody's looking for me.'

'I should charge you a supplement.'

'They don't care about blokes like me,' Sam said. 'They'll be looking for an escaped prisoner. Somebody important.'

The trucker gave him a long look. 'I'll show you to your room, sir,' he said. He kept that same grin on his face, never varied it. It was an all-weather, multi-tasking, guess-if-I'm-happy facial expression that was designed to hide rather than expose the little boy that crouched behind it.

Sam followed him to the rear of the truck and waited while he manipulated the rods and handles that released the locks on the end of the container. The trucker pulled down an aluminium ladder and Sam climbed up into the darkness above him. 'See you in Immingham,' the guy said as he closed the door behind him. The locking mechanisms clanged and echoed around Sam as he went down on one knee, feeling around in his rucksack for the torch.

Two young men, sallow-skinned, hollow-eyed, were sitting on the base of the container with their legs outstretched. 'How you doing?' Sam asked.

'I am Omed,' one of them said, stretching out a hand. 'This is my friend, Rachid. We are coming from Iraq.'

'I'm Sam. Coming from Oslo, on my way to York.'

'You are English?'

'Afraid so.'

'I love England,' Omed said. 'I am a scientist. I can work. I would like England to be my home, where the government will not try to kill me. I can marry English girl and my children will be English.'

'Just take it one step at a time,' Sam told him.

Rachid, the friend, leaned forward. 'You have food?'

'Some,' Sam said. 'You hungry?'

'Very hungry,' Rachid said. 'Very, very hungry.'

'Tell me when it gets bad,' Sam said.

He moved on along the container, between boxes and packing crates. In a small clearing were a family group: a father with a grey moustache and his wife with staring eyes. When Sam appeared she gathered her three children around her, seeming to bury them in her skirts. 'What's your story?' Sam asked the father.

'We are from Bolivia,' he said. 'We have been in Switzerland but they were going to send us back. My wife's brother is an informer against the robbers. You understand robbers?'

'Yeah,' Sam said. 'I understand robbers.'

'The police, they look after the brother, they keep him safe. But the robbers kill my father-in-law and my mother-in-law, they kill my wife's two brothers and her sister and their children. If we go back to Bolivia they kill us as well. So we have to go to England. We will be safe there.'

'Jesus,' Sam said, getting ready to move on, shining the beam of his torch to the far wall of the container.

'You are English?' the father asked.

'For my sins.'

'You have a house we can live?'

'I'll think about it,' Sam told him.

He shifted a box to one side, carving out a nook about two metres long and one metre wide. He rolled out his sleeping bag and stretched out on it, using his rucksack as a pillow. He listened and tried to interpret the sounds around him. The truck seemed to be in a queue, probably at the docks, moving forward occasionally, then stopping again.

The fearful voices of the Bolivian children and the anxiety in the voice of their mother as she tried to bolster their courage. The braggadocio of the two Iraqis as they tried their best to sound as if they were on a seaside

316

outing. The trickle of liquid as the Bolivian father pissed into a plastic bucket.

This was a trip he could survive, Sam decided. He didn't know about the others. He'd probably have to share his food and water, but that was OK. He'd ration it out, something every six hours, make it last the voyage. At the other end he reckoned he'd stand a better chance of avoiding the authorities than the rest of his fellow travellers.

At least he hoped so.

31

'That's the great thing about detective work,' Marie said. 'There's always something else. I mean it's ninety per cent routine, can bore the pants off you. But at the point where you start writhing in apathy something'll happen to make you sit up and take notice.'

'Ah,' JD said. 'The town's on the brink of imminent flooding. Thousands of people are in danger of losing their homes and you've found something that interests you.'

'Don't talk to me about flooding,' she said. 'I can only get to my house by boat. Yesterday I got in through the bedroom window and I still needed wellies.'

'But you don't find it exciting?'

'Hell, no,' Marie said. 'It was exciting when it *might* happen, but once it's happened it's inconvenient. It's tragic, maybe. You could call it a nuisance or a disaster. But it's not exciting, it's boring. Boring as hell. It means you can't go home. You have to live with other people, and when the water's gone back to normal you've got to clean out the mud and silt and you can't move back in for six months or more, until the place has dried out.

'What's exciting about that? Or the fact that you can't find anyone to insure you? Add to that that the thing you live in is no longer a *des res*, estate agents laugh when you walk through their door. The mortgage you're paying is twice the value of the house.' She handed him a look as hard as prison time. 'No, I don't find that exciting.'

'I used the wrong word,' JD said. 'I'm sorry.'

'You shouldn't use wrong words. You're supposed to be a writer.'

'Yeah, I write books, but I'm not God. I make mistakes.'

'You can say that again.'

'I make mistakes.'

They were on the steps of All Saints church in North Street watching soldiers placing another layer of sandbags on the flood defences. The river was roaring past within the limits that the army had allowed it, content for the moment to display its naked power. But it was like a mob, a fury that could turn at any moment, flip the sandbags aside and engulf the town.

'What was your point?' JD asked.

'Sam asked me to research dolls and doll-makers.'

'Sex dolls?'

'Yes. It's amazing. I knew there were these sad things, blow-up girls that guys take to bed with them . . .'

'Some guys.'

'Yeah, some guys. Don't be predictable, JD, this isn't about you.

'I could never work out how they kept them clean,' she said. 'I knew there was a vagina, something like that down there, but I imagined the thing just filled up with jism.' She laughed. 'You know, as time went on, the girl got heavier and heavier and smellier and smellier.'

'But it doesn't? *She* doesn't?'

'Yeah, I think some of them do. The cheap ones. But you can get all kinds. There's balloons at one end of the market and at the other end there's dolls with a self-lubricating vibrating vagina and anus. You can get them with locks on so the guy you share your room with can't get his end away while you're out at work.'

'Ah, nice touch,' JD said. 'Fidelity among dolls. What if I wanted a nurse?'

'You can have anything you like: nurses, policewomen, French maids, an Asian princess, all the stereotypes.'

'Black policewoman?'

'I expect so. You can order anything you like. Mix and match. You want something fitted to size, no problem. Same with animals. You want a pig or a sheep, you can buy them over the counter. How about a black ewe with a throbbing, erotically noduled mouth?'

'There was a moment earlier when you were turning me on, now it's going the other way.'

'How about this then, big boy? I can get a six-foot-four guy doll with a moustache and chest hair and a penetrating rotating and vibrating tongue and a powered, veined dong all running off four AA batteries.'

'You can get screwed by a machine?'

'Where've you been, JD? All it is, it's a vibrator built into a doll. Nobody gets screwed. These things, they're aids to masturbation. The logical extension of you whacking yourself off in the boys' bogs at school over a photograph of whoever it was.'

'Madonna, probably. Though we had a thing about Katharine Ross at the time. Could've been her.'

'The one in *The Stepford Wives*?'

'Yeah, before my time that, but ... oh, yeah, they turned her into a robot.'

'A doll.'

'But that was an examination of the Frankenstein theme, Marie. Different from sex dolls. What you've got with sex dolls are people who can't hold down normal relations.'

'Or people who don't want to. Guys who find a relationship with a woman too complicated, who want their lives to be simple. Someone who doesn't answer back. That would drive me crazy, someone who never answered back. Living with a doll, can you imagine that?'

'Think about a single person who has a job. He's friendly with his workmates, and most of his relational needs are met by them and some guys he meets in a pub in the evening. But he has a problem meeting women, he can't pull. This is the kind of guy who might end up with one of your dolls. As he gets older his pulling power diminishes but he still has sexual needs. Are you going to deny him a doll? You think he's causing any harm? It could be that the doll stops him thinking about attacking some kid on her way home from night-school. It might have a positive effect for the guy and for the rest of society.'

'I don't wanna ban dolls, JD. What you say could be true. But that doesn't stop it being sick. It leads us to accept second-class citizens. Some of us are worthy of real human beings of the opposite sex. We can have mates and families and live rounded lives. While there are others, living next door maybe, who get something they have to blow up with a foot-pump. If we accept that kind of thing we're not a real community. It means we're not caring enough, we're losing our sense of compassion. We don't want to live together any more. We want to live alongside each other, but not together. Do you see the difference?'

'I hear what you're saying. But I don't have the answers.'

Marie watched a young female soldier humping another sandbag on to the city defences. 'Just one thing you mentioned might help,' she said. 'I hadn't thought about it before, but this guy, the one with the doll with real pubic hair, he's got to live alone. It's like you said, he's someone who doesn't make relationships with women.'

'And why is that significant?'

'It's another link, JD. All the things we know about

321

him, they add up. In itself it might not be significant, but when we come to fit the pieces together it could be very important.'

'You want to do something tonight?' he asked. 'I've got a practice with the band 'til about nine, then we could have a drink, watch the river rising.'

Marie hesitated. Usually when JD asked her out she didn't think at all. She just told him no.

'I'll take that as a yes then, shall I?' he asked.

'No funny business,' Marie said. 'I'll come for a drink with you, but that's it. I'm not looking for an affair. I've got a boyfriend. I don't want to end up like we were before. You're not a sexual object for me.'

'I don't know how I got to be so irresistible,' he said. 'I used to be ugly.'

'You're not ugly,' Marie told him. 'You're a friend with all the limitations that come with it. I don't sleep with my friends.'

'What about hairy Steiner-school teacher?'

'He's not a friend, he's a lover. And he's away. If he was here you'd be drinking by yourself tonight.'

'As I suspected,' JD said. 'I'm a substitute.' He shook his head. 'Still, I'll do my best. Make sure I've got fresh batteries in.'

Marie drove to Harrogate and found the workshop on an industrial estate south of the town on the A61. A long, low black building with no windows, could have been a factory farm or an outpost of the MoD intercepting and analysing suspect e-mails. Anything with the word Allah in the subject line, or America, or oil. But things are seldom as they seem and inside the unit, once she'd got beyond the deeply unfashionable floral-pattern blouse of the bespectacled receptionist, Marie found only production lines of dolls and parts of dolls.

Deborah Innes, the managing director of Dreambabe, was a young thirty. Could have passed for twenty-seven, nineteen with a bag on her head. She had perfected a breathless way of speaking which made her sound constantly astounded, as though her three decades on the earth had yielded no accessible bank of experience.

'We started small,' she said, 'but we double the turnover every few months. The market seems to have no limit.'

And the costs are minimal, Marie thought, looking at the young Asian and East European women who made up the workforce. The operation was simple, trestle tables for benches with the workers standing around them. There were a few sewing machines and staple guns, adhesives and crimping and heat-welding equipment. At one end of the workshop the heads were connected to the torsos, and these were then moved on to the next bench where arms were added. Legs came next and then the additions and alterations to the Dreambabes became subtler. It was possible to walk through the workshop and see the whole process right through to the grinning peroxide tart in crimson suspenders just before she was packed into a cardboard container marked, *Dreambabe No. 5 – Margarita the Mucky Slut.*

'It's a new line,' Deborah Innes said breathlessly. 'Most of the girls are putting in a twelve-hour day and we're still a month behind with deliveries. I've taken on ten more people and it hasn't touched the waiting list.'

'Why?' Marie asked. 'I don't understand where the customers come from. Who are they? Do you have a target profile?'

'Not really,' the managing director said. 'I can glean a few things from the spreadsheet but we haven't done in-depth market research. We advertise in the right places,

I'm sure of that, the sex magazines and the Internet. But we're not attracting new customers.'

'You just said . . .'

'I know, we can't keep up with demand. But it's not because of a massive influx of new accounts. Most of it's repeat orders. From established customers. They keep coming back for more.'

'More? What does that mean? Do they use up the doll . . .'

'Dreambabe.'

'Do they use up the Dreambabe they've got at home and want a replacement or do they order different models?'

'Both,' Deborah said with a twinkle. 'Each time we introduce a new model almost everyone on our books puts in an order. And we get reorders for the same model about once a year.'

'Is that how long they last?'

'Under normal use, yes. We have some punters who are heavier users than others. Some of them will reorder four or five times in a year. We call them the sadists. Not to their faces, of course, just among the staff.'

'Of course,' Marie said without a hint of a twinkle.

They were at the workbench where the mucky slut's hair was being stuck to her bare scalp. Marie reached over the shoulder of an anorexic Pakistani girl and picked up one of the hairpieces that had not yet been smeared with glue. It was synthetic, bearing as much resemblance to real hair as a politician does to honesty.

She watched as another worker stuck two small patches of smooth white hair around the hole between the slut's legs. There was little attempt at realism, the pubic hair was reminiscent of the pelt of a baby seal.

'Do you ever use real hair?' Marie asked. The anorexic girl laughed self-consciously.

'No,' Deborah said. 'We tried it once with a Marilyn-babe but it put too much on the price and our customers didn't appreciate it.'

'Pubic hair?'

'Goodness, no, we've never done that. I meant head hair. I think we sold about two hundred units and went back to synthetics.'

'Do you know if there are companies who use real pubic hair?'

'Not to my knowledge,' Deborah said, turning up her lip in distaste. 'What would be the point? And where would you get it?'

Good question, Marie thought as she drove away from the workshop and headed south towards Huddersfield and the address of an upmarket doll manufacturer called Lady Friendz. But British capitalists had never been put off by a limited supply of raw materials. If there was a demand for pubic hair there'd be no shortage of entrepreneurs making the disadvantaged offers they couldn't refuse. Extra beer money for students, more powdered milk for single parents, an additional fix for a squat of wide-eyed junkies. We're not talking exploitation here. It's only pubic hair. It'll grow back.

And then what? Sterilize the stuff in some kind of steamer, dye it if necessary and stick it around the simulated vagina of a life-size doll so some guy can fuck his brains out and pretend he's not alone. Is this what is meant by a mixed economy? Is this what religious mystics mean when they talk about the interconnectedness of all things?

Marie wondered if she should put an ad in the local paper. *Pubic hair for sale. Good condition. Auburn, crinkly and long.* See how much she was offered. Perhaps put a sample in the post. End up with more than one potential customer and have an auction. Sell it by the strand or charge right over the top for the full set. *Muff for sale, will sell separately.*

Not yet. There was still a possibility of tracking them down. But if all else failed she might have to resort to an advert. If you can't find them by conventional detective work you have to flush them out.

Lady Friendz was not a workshop. It was a minimally furnished one-room office in the shadow of the Huddersfield Town Football Stadium. There was a good woollen carpet the colour of an old blood stain. There were pastel-coloured walls with a reproduction – surely it wasn't original? – Hundertwasser and a spotlight to show it off. And there was the small round gentleman seated at the flat-screen computer monitor with a wide commercial smile on his face.

'Good afternoon,' he said, managing to cram a salacious edge into each of the four syllables. 'Ms Marie Dickens, I presume. Private detective.'

He made the *Ms* sound like a swear-word. There was an ebony rack on his desk with his name inset in what was supposed to be ivory but was probably white plastic. Joshua Whone.

'Yes, I rang you,' Marie said, bringing to heel her instinct to strangle him.

'Indeed you did, Marie.'

I'm not going to get my knickers in a schnoz over this guy, Marie promised herself. He'd climbed the social ladder, sawing the rungs off after him as he went. She glanced at the painting on the wall. When she looked back he was still there, one in countless columns of grey men on the march towards sterility and self-destruction. He was one of Hundertwasser's hated straight lines. The tyranny, the forbidden fruit.

'I'm trying to track down someone who makes

bespoke dolls,' she told him. 'Might be a company, I don't know. Could be an individual.'

'And by bespoke, you mean?'

'Dolls with real hair. Specifically, real pubic hair.'

'Ah.' His eyes opened wider. 'And you being a private detective, Marie, I take it that your enquiries are for a third party rather than for yourself?'

'Does that matter?'

'I'm a businessman, Marie. I'm trying to establish if a sale is on the horizon or if this is one of those occasions that I'm expected to perform my civic duty.'

Marie winced when he used her name. 'I'm not looking to purchase a doll,' she said.

'Because Lady Friendz does have a number of lady customers, if you follow my drift, Marie. Ladies who are looking for Lady Friendz.'

'Do any of your products contain pubic hair, Mr Whone?'

He shook his head. 'We use synthetics, Marie. But of a very high quality. It would take an expert to see that the pubic hair on any of the Lady Friendz dolls was not the genuine article. Lady Friendz are a superior product in every way. We have no real competitors in the market place. None at all.'

'And do you know of other manufacturers or importers who do use real pubic hair?'

'We use some of the finest craftsmen in the country. But there are one or two people who remain fiercely independent. There's a woman in Plymouth who uses organic materials. I may have an address for her.' He tapped a couple of keys on the computer keyboard. 'Just take me a moment.'

'Plymouth is further afield than I thought,' Marie said. 'Is there anyone in the North?'

'There's a young man near York making a name for

himself. I haven't seen his work but one of my customers said he was charged four figures for a doll. Exquisite but expensive. We are perhaps leaving behind the realm of craft and entering into the world of art.'

'Four figures. Is that unusual?'

'It certainly is. We provide a superior product here, Marie, but we have always found that the psychological barrier of four figures is more than most of our customers want to contemplate. For four figures, after all, one could purchase the company of several warm-blooded partners.' He smiled. 'Good-time girls. Escorts. Ladies of the night.'

'The woman in Plymouth and the young man in York, do you have their contact details?'

He took a business card from a neat stack on the corner of his desk and scribbled on the back of it. 'That's the Plymouth address,' he said, gliding the card across the polished surface of the desk. 'I don't have an address for the York chappie, but he's probably in the book. Goes by the name of Nott. Couple of initials which I also can't remember. But you being a private detective, Marie, I'm sure you'll be able to track him down.'

It had been muggy in Joshua's office, not too easy to breathe, but when she closed the door on him the air cleared immediately.

32

Ellen Eccles lit up a Benson & Hedges while standing on the corner of the street. She could see the bay windows of the magician's house and was intent on walking over there and ringing the bell. All she needed was the courage. A couple of tots of the amber nectar would've done the trick, but it was too late for that. She should've thought of it earlier, cracked open a bottle before leaving the house.

If she'd done this with the other men that Marilyn had set her sights on she might've saved herself and them and Marilyn a lot of pain and anguish. Jeremy Paxman would've been left alone to perfect his acerbic journalistic style, the footballer would have topped the goal-scoring table, and Ellen herself would've been able to spend more time in the wild places above Aberdeen. She didn't want to be doing battle with the Sassenachs at this time of her life.

She was still rooted to the spot, getting down towards the filter of the cigarette, when the car came around the corner. It was one of those inexplicable moments of certainty. She didn't know what kind of car he drove, or the colour of it, and the vehicle was already past her before she could see the driver, but she knew it was him. She watched as he manoeuvred the tight left into his drive. Mr Mann left the car and went around to the passenger door. He fiddled with the seatbelt for a long time. From where she was standing Ellen couldn't see if it was somebody or something in the passenger seat. What was obvious was that the magician was having a real job trying to extricate it from the seatbelt. There must be something faulty with the release mechanism. Not the kind of problem one usually associated with a magician.

Eventually Mr Mann got it open and backed out of the car. He had a kitbag under his arm. Ellen couldn't be sure but when he turned towards the house, pulling the garage door down with his free hand, she thought she saw a pair of feet poking out of the kitbag. By the time she'd blinked and taken another look he was already at his door and the bag was on her blind side.

Magicians. What did Ellen know? Yes, it could be a body, ha, ha, ha. But it was obviously not. Perhaps it was a bag full of feet? Some aid to one of his tricks. She'd heard somewhere that you needed an extra pair of feet to do that sawing a woman in half trick. The woman was folded up at the top end of the container with her head sticking out of a hole and what you thought were her feet were actually a pair of model feet.

It began raining again as she flicked the dog-end of her B&H into the gutter. The sky was grey overhead and away to the north it was black. The local news was all about the flooding and how much worse it was going to get. If the river broke its banks in the centre of town there could be another 20,000 people affected. It was already fourteen feet higher than normal. Visitors were being told they should only come to the city if their journey was essential. The police and emergency services didn't want to waste time on traffic problems. The flood was the most important thing, they needed to concentrate all their manpower on that.

Ellen pulled up her collar and moved along the street. She walked up his path to the red front door and punched the bell. She looked at the net curtains but could see nothing beyond them.

Almost a minute passed before she heard him coming to the door. She had been wondering whether she should ring again, or perhaps try a knock, even though she had heard the bell ringing inside the house. Migraine had been hovering over her all day long. Not a pain so much as a dull ache behind her eyes, but always threatening to get worse. Too much television, too many late nights and early mornings. Too much to think about. Too much life with Marilyn.

He was in his shirt-sleeves and looked at her enquiringly, not an unattractive man in spite of his prominent nose. The small patches of premature silver hair at his temples helped enormously. Ellen wasn't sure if she should be pleased or worried that her daughter's taste in men mirrored her own. Ellen would have been quite happy on the arm of this man, or of Jeremy Paxman and many of the others. She wasn't quite so sure about the footballer. A little too rough and ready with his overt machismo and sexuality. The kind who wouldn't take long to get around to suggesting a threesome and who would want to take a bottle of whisky to bed.

'Can I help?' the magician said.

'Sorry to bother you,' Ellen told him. 'I'm Marilyn's mother. Marilyn Eccles?'

Danny Mann shook his head. 'I'm sorry I don't . . .'

'Marilyn, she followed you to Newcastle.'

'Oh, my goodness. That one. Sorry, I mean, Marilyn, yes. Your daughter?'

'Can I come in?'

'I don't know,' the magician said, looking up and down the street. 'Do we have anything to discuss?'

'My daughter is a little odd, Mr Mann. I'd like to see if we can work together to stop her bothering you.' She gave him a smile. 'You don't have to worry about me. I'm completely normal.'

He stood aside and let her walk past him into the house. The living room was a woman's room but there was no sense of a woman in the house. There was a shelf of books and the walls were covered with rather old-fashioned wallpaper. The three-piece suite had covers with a faded floral pattern. On the wall was a velvet picture of a wizard with a black cloak. On the couch the kitbag was now empty.

'Do you live alone?' Ellen asked.

He didn't hesitate. 'Since my mother passed away, yes. Does it show?'

'Oh, no, I didn't mean . . .'

'Please, sit down,' he said. He scooped up the kitbag and made space for her on the couch. 'Can I offer you something? Tea, coffee?'

'No, thank you. I don't want to take up your time.'

He sat opposite her. He sat on the edge of a chair, his knees together, rather prim for a man. He waited, eyes fixed on Ellen.

'Marilyn told me what happened,' she said. 'How she followed you to Newcastle, approached you on the train.'

He nodded but he didn't speak.

'She's a strange girl,' Ellen added. 'She's formed an attachment to you, a kind of obsession. Oh, it's nothing you've done. This kind of thing, it's happened before, with other men. Prominent men, celebrities. It's an illness. She's being treated. On medication.'

'I was rather frightened on the train,' Danny said. 'I didn't know if she was dangerous.'

'She wouldn't hurt you,' Ellen said. 'She might hurt herself. But there'd be no question of violence towards you.'

'If she thought I was rejecting her?' the magician said. 'Those feelings sometimes lead to violence, do they not?'

'She's ill, Mr Mann. She suffers from a condition

known as erotomania. She's preoccupied with sexual passion and morbid infatuation.'

'Jealousy?'

'Yes, intense jealousy. But the medication keeps everything in check.'

'So I take it that she's not using her medication at the moment?'

'She wasn't. When she followed you she wasn't. But she is now. I don't think she'll bother you again.'

'Why have you come to tell me this, Mrs Eccles?'

'I wanted to apologize. I didn't want you to get the wrong idea about Marilyn, or to ring the police. And I wanted to ask you to contact me if you have more trouble from her. If she stops taking the medication again or if she needs it reassessing I can take her back to the doctor. But I wouldn't necessarily know she was bothering you unless you told me.'

The magician got to his feet. 'I'll help in any way I can,' he said.

Ellen no longer found him attractive. She couldn't think what it was about him that had attracted her a few minutes earlier. He was effeminate, almost fey, but with a fierce intelligence. He was co-operating and that was all she had wanted or expected. She offered him her hand and he took it and shook it gently.

But why be so hard on him? she thought as he showed her to the door. Like most people he couldn't see beyond the limits of his own conflict. But that was no reason to damn the man.

33

Ruben went up the stairs and into the doctor's office where Sarah Murphy, the counsellor, was waiting for him. He wasn't disappointed. She looked just as good as he remembered her. Nice smile on her face. Wearing a suit this time, grey for business, but she still had the silver choker on. Little make-up round the eyes. No lipstick.

She looked at his crimson strides for a while, as if she couldn't believe that a guy like him had so much dress sense. And there was a tiny movement around her nose as she caught a whiff of his Brut.

'How've you been?' she asked.

He liked the way her shoulders sloped away from her neck, and how she kept her hands still in front of her on the desk. She'd been an object of fantasy for the last couple of days, since their first meeting, and he'd been hoping for the fantasy in the flesh. But she was subtly different.

Before he'd gone to prison Ruben knew women who could *be* the fantasy. They had the knack of seeing what you wanted and giving you it almost exactly. But Kitty hadn't been like that and that was one of the reasons he'd been so in love with her. And now there was Sarah Murphy and she was the same. He couldn't tell if she sensed what he wanted her to be but he was sure that whether she sensed it or not she wasn't going to compromise herself. She was going to be who she was and nothing more or less.

And the beauty of it was that she still came across real

good. She'd definitely had lipstick on in the fantasy and the fact that she didn't wear any now didn't diminish the memory for a second. If anything it enhanced it. He couldn't think why. He just knew that he wasn't disappointed.

'I've been good,' he said. 'I haven't been paralysed. I've done what I need to do. The grief's still there, but I understand that. I know grief, how it's good for you. Like a natural process, something I have to go through. And I've been sad, a *leetle* bit depressed. But before it was incapacitating me, I couldn't work. Now it's more like sadness. I think I'm over the hump.'

Her smile got wider. 'It's good to hear,' she said. 'But sometimes these things get better before they get worse. There might be a reaction.'

'I don't think so.'

'Maybe not. But it's as well to be aware that it could happen.'

'What I thought,' he told her, 'because I'm so much better and because mostly it's to do with you and the talk we had, I wondered if we should shut up shop here and go for a drink?'

She took her hands off the desk and put them under it, maybe on her lap, he couldn't see where they went. She was lost for words for a moment or two. The smile disappeared but she kept the eye contact. Seemed to be drilling right through him, like nobody had ever asked her to have a drink before. But he couldn't believe that. She was a good-looking woman.

'Somewhere in the town,' he said. 'You choose the place. We don't have to talk about me. We can talk about you. Be more democratic. Get to know each other.'

'That would be rather unprofessional of me, Mr Parkins.'

'Come on, call me Ruben.'

'When someone has been through a traumatic event, like you, with losing Kitty, there are a number of possible reactions. One of the best known is what we call transference. The subject becomes fixated on the therapist or the counsellor. It might feel like affection or love or a strong attraction but in reality it's gratitude. I can only help you, Mr Parkins, if I remain at a distance, retain some objectivity. It wouldn't be helpful for our relationship to go further than the bounds of professional decorum.'

'That's OK,' Ruben told her. 'You don't have to give me an answer now. Think about it for a couple of days. I don't want the professional stuff anyway. I want to get to know you. I've got a feeling about it. I think we could be good. Sometimes I'm wrong and if I'm wrong about it I won't keep you on a string. I'll walk away from it. Kitty taught me that. She taught me how to live better and just because she's dead I'm not gonna go back to the old ways.

'This is not transference or whatever you called it. I'm just asking you to have a drink with me, swap a few stories, see where it leads. That's a normal thing to do. I'm a guy and I like the look of you and you're a woman and you're interested in me.'

'I'm what? Now I know you're deluded.'

Ruben opened his eyes wider. 'Hey, I think we're getting somewhere.'

Sarah Murphy smiled and shook her head. 'You're very direct.'

Ruben gave her a grin. 'I don't hear you denying it. The chemistry.'

'And you don't hear me confirming it either.'

'No?' Ruben said. 'Not with your voice.'

He left her there, sitting behind her desk with a

bemused smile on her face, his mobile number, scribbled on a slip of the doctor's stationery, clutched in her hand.

On the stairs he passed her next customer, a young man as sleek as a wet seal.

It was one of those lucky days. Ruben had known it before he got out of bed. Maybe it was in the stars, if you believed in stuff like that, horoscopes, astrology. What Ruben believed and what he used to tell Kitty was that you made your own luck. If he'd been out trying to make his own luck when he was younger, instead of wanting to fight everybody, rob everybody he saw walking down the street, maybe he'd never've ended up in prison. If there was something in the astrology stuff then all the guys born on the same day as him would've ended up stashed away in Long Lartin. They'd've had their own wing.

As he walked back towards the car park where he'd left the Skoda he looked at the people on the pavement and realized that it never crossed his mind to rob them. Guy there with the business suit, probably had notes stuffed in every pocket, but he wasn't a mark. Just somebody on the street. And it wasn't Ruben's prison sentence, the time he'd spent in Long Lartin that had brought about the change. It was Kitty. And it wasn't the threat of going back in there, spending another chunk of his life behind bars that kept him out. It was the thought of Sarah Murphy with her short brown hair and the scent of her and the feeling that before too long he'd be getting together with her and they'd be swapping stories and lending each other books and be living like normal people lived.

Not that he'd forget Kitty. He'd never do that. She'd always be there for him, somewhere close by, and he'd never forget the way she'd died. Though it was true the last couple of nights the images of Kitty had blurred into an image of Sarah. Ruben had fought that for a while, coming awake in his bed and shaking his head, trying to keep them separate. But in the early hours of the morning he'd surrendered to his subconscious, if that's what it was, something older and wiser than his conscious brain. They weren't the same person, he knew that and didn't want to pretend they were. But there was something about each of them that included the other, something beyond manners and class and physical similarities. And Ruben would discover what it was, that evasive quality. It might take him the rest of his life, but he didn't mind. He had time and the subject was fascinating. Must be like that for people who get Nobel prizes; they find a little thing that interests them and they study it for years and years and they don't ever get bored.

It was like a jeweller's shop but a small place, not one of those with big windows where everything glitters. Ruben went in because he thought he might find something for Sarah, when she came round to the inevitability of them being together. He didn't have a real idea, a ring or a bracelet, maybe, something like that.

When he looked around there was nothing that would suit her. He'd imagined something fine, tiny links made in soft metal, something so smooth you'd hardly notice it. But what they had in the shop was chunky stuff, kind of things that biker chicks went for. A bangle with a couple of skulls on it. Ankle chains looked more like leg-irons.

As he was going out of the door he noticed a cabinet with a selection of teeth in it and stopped to look. They wouldn't do for Sarah, there was nothing in the place that would be good enough for her. But there was one long tooth there, shiny white, mounted in a gold cap and dangling from the end of a chain, that Ruben fancied for himself. He called the assistant over, a short youth with wide trousers two inches too long for his legs. 'What's that?' he asked.

'Shark's tooth. The chain's twenty-four-carat gold.' He opened the cabinet with a key and took out the chain with the tooth and handed it to Ruben.

'There's no marks on it,' he said. 'If it's gold it should be stamped.'

'Indian gold,' the assistant said. 'If it was British gold it'd cost an arm and a leg.' Ruben turned his attention to the tooth. 'Shark's tooth?'

'Yeah.'

'From a shark?'

'Yeah, the genuine article. We import them from California. They're from dead sharks. The exporters guarantee that no animals have been hurt or damaged in any way.'

Ruben laughed.

'You think I'm kidding you?' the assistant asked.

'Hell, no,' Ruben told him. 'I knew it wasn't from a *live* shark. I didn't think there was squads of dentists going down there in frogmen's suits looking for sharks to do a quick job on.'

The assistant didn't think it was funny. He must've got out the wrong side of the bed. 'They're supposed to bring you luck,' he said. 'Shark's teeth.'

Ruben looked at the price tag. 'Thirty quid?' he said.

'Used to be twenty-nine pounds ninety-nine pence,' the assistant said. 'But the boss doesn't like pennies.'

'Put it in a bag,' Ruben said, reaching for his wallet.

He walked up the path of the High Willows Guesthouse, obviously though erroneously named after the two stunted willow trees in the garden. A double-bay-windowed house with a recently added wooden porch obscuring the original front door. He rang the bell and listened to the distant chimes emulating 'It's Now Or Never' somewhere towards the rear of the house. Ruben hummed along with it and when the chimes died he carried on. Elvis Presley was already dying before Ruben heard him but the guy had left some great songs behind. He liked that soaring voice, the way it took hold of you. Should've been in the opera like Pavarotti. Probably would've been, too, if he'd been Italian instead of a truck driver.

But if the world was divided into Elvis Presleys and Luciano Pavarottis the woman who came to the door would have been much closer to Tupelo, Mississippi than the little town of Modena in Italy.

Must be a blonde wig, he thought, the kind of hair that Dolly Parton would choose for a Saturday night fling. Carefully powdered breasts like globular light shades, each wrapped in its own half of a cream-coloured frilly blouse with the top three buttons unused. A short frilly apron hid an even shorter skirt and stiletto heels forced the woman's calf muscles to bulge, giving form and definition to her legs but contracting the Achilles tendons.

Before he'd blinked twice Ruben had interpreted the message that the proprietress of the High Willows Guesthouse was sending out into the world, and the adrenalin pumping into his bloodstream reinforced the conviction that he'd be able to run faster than her.

'Can you spare a moment?' Ruben asked. He showed her the photograph of Sam Turner. 'We're trying to trace this man and have reason to believe he stayed in this area recently. Have you seen him before?'

The proprietress didn't look at the photograph. She licked her lips and blinked her false eyelashes to tip Ruben off she was intelligent. She smoothed her hands over her stomach and looking deeply into his eyes, she said: 'You don't want a room, then?'

The voice was perfect for the blonde wig and false eyelashes. There was a million cigarettes behind it, a quantity of gin or vodka and a whole world of small disappointments.

'No, sorry,' Ruben explained. 'I don't want a room. I'm making enquiries about the man in the photograph.' He waved it towards her but she still didn't look.

'You're not the Old Bill, are you,' she said. It wasn't a question. 'Come in, I've got the kettle on.'

He followed her into the house. Wall lights with tartan shades. Pile carpets. Ornaments of dogs. Photographs of a beauty queen from long ago; *Miss Cleethorpes, Miss Lincoln, Miss Barrow-in-Furness*. Real blonde hair probably, tightly fitting swim-suits, looking quaintly old-fashioned, as she still did today.

The kitchen was Formica and steel. A large modern clock on the wall with false eyelashes and a pink ribbon tied in a bow underneath its chin. Magnetic letters stuck on the fridge door spelling out the words *Wil You Stil Love Me Tomoro*. Not so much a sign of illiteracy as a dearth of magnetic consonants.

'That's how you can spot poverty,' Kitty had told him once. 'People who surround themselves with too much of everything.' She didn't mean lack of money, she was talking about poverty of imagination, poverty of spirit.

'Coffee or tea, Mr . . . ?'

'Parkins,' he said. 'Ruben Parkins. Coffee, please.'

'You can call me Eileen,' she told him. 'Eileen Dover.' She cackled long and loud. 'No, it's Eileen Smith, after the bloke I married. I got rid of him but I've hung on to the name.' She pouted and blinked her false eyelashes again in case he'd missed it the first time.

She gave him a mug of coffee and pushed a milk jug

towards him. She took the photograph from his hand and walked over to the window with it. He watched her smile and nod down at it.

'You know him?' Ruben asked.

'I don't know him,' she said. 'We didn't get that far. Not from lack of trying, mind. But he was here, stayed a couple of nights. The front bedroom, all alone.'

'You sure?'

Eileen looked at the photograph again. 'Yeah.' She gazed out of the window and closed her eyes. 'Sam,' she said. 'Sam Turner. Am I right or am I right?'

'That's his name,' Ruben said, thinking that Eileen Smith suddenly looked good. 'Can you remember when he was here? The date? D'you keep a guest book?'

'He'll be in the register,' Eileen said. She went for the register in the hall and brought it back with her. 'But I can tell you now it was the night of the murder. That woman over Clifton way. He was here the night before and the night of the murder. He left the next day.'

'Did you tell the police?' Ruben asked.

Eileen Smith shook her head, thumbing through the register. 'Here it is,' she said, 'Sam Turner.' She handed the book to Ruben and he looked at the detective's signature, memorized the guy's home address.

'Did you know her?' Eileen asked. 'The woman who was killed?'

'Kitty,' Ruben said. 'It was me who found her.'

'Kitty? Katherine something. I remember now. That must've been terrible. But it wasn't Sam Turner did it, he was here all night.'

'How can you be sure?'

'He was out all day but he came back for his evening meal. He was in his room for a while and then he came down and watched a film on the telly. *Prizzi's Honor.* I sat with him for the last hour. When the movie was over we had a drink. Well, I had a drink and he watched me and we talked until after midnight. Then he went to bed and didn't stir until breakfast.'

'He could've gone out after you'd gone to bed,' Ruben said. 'Kitty was killed in the middle of the night.'

'He didn't go out,' Eileen Smith said. 'I lock up at night, and I sleep like a bird. I've had people try to slip out in the middle of the night, get away without paying. I would know if he'd gone out.'

'Tell me this, then,' Ruben said. 'If he was here that night why did he tell the police he wasn't?'

'I don't know, love,' Eileen Smith said. 'People's motives are never simple. And who trusts the police, anyway? Perhaps he didn't want to hand them a rope to hang him with?'

Ruben wasn't convinced that Eileen Smith's version of events was true. Sam Turner was clever. He could've pulled the wool over her eyes. But one thing was clear now. Turner was here, in Nottingham, on the night that Kitty was killed. He was on the spot. Ruben hadn't heard the police or the media speculate that it was someone else who took Kitty's life. There was only him. No one else could have done it.

34

Danny Mann came out of his front door and stepped along the path to the street. He looked one way and then the other. There was no sign of Marilyn Eccles. Thank God. She'd rung his bell once this morning, twice last night. He had been firm. 'Go away,' he told her. 'Take your medication. I'm not who you think I am.'

'It's no good,' she'd said this morning. 'I can't deal with rejection.' Standing there in her leather jacket and metal chains, dangly earrings. Why would she think he found that kind of thing attractive? The truth was quite the opposite. Danny didn't like loud women, that's why he'd gone to the expense of Jody, considered the Orientals. The universe lived in the tension between the active and the passive and the magician was active and therefore attracted to the passive.

The last thing he needed was a leather-and-steel-clad erotomaniac. Earlier, when he'd pulled back the curtains and seen her on the step, his scrotum had shrivelled to the size of a walnut.

But she wasn't around. It seemed that even nymphomaniac stalkers had to go home and eat occasionally, take a shower and change their clothes.

The clouds had disappeared and the wind dropped to a gentle breeze. There was extensive flooding in the area and a danger of the Ouse breaking its banks in the town centre, putting thousands of homes at risk. People were kayaking and windsurfing on the racecourse. Armageddon was around the corner.

The media had nothing to say about anything but the floods. It didn't matter if it rained here or not because the water was coming down from the hills and the town would be swamped because of weather conditions forty or fifty miles to the north. This was God's sleight of hand, Danny thought. Give the place a few days of bright sunshine and not a hint of rain while up in the hills, out of sight, you pour so much water into the river channels that the banks are washed away.

Danny left his car behind. So many roads were impassable and the police or the army were liable to direct you in the opposite direction to your destination. Drivers were being told not to come to the city. The police had enough on their hands without traffic problems. He still hadn't got that damned seatbelt fixed.

He walked towards the centre and crossed Skeldergate Bridge. People were lining both sides of it, leaning over to watch the volume of black water thundering past. On the banks teams of squaddies were humping sandbags, lining them up precisely under the watchful eyes of their officers. There had been nothing like this in living memory. A strange and unwanted visitor had come to town and the people had left their houses to come and gape.

When he was a young boy people had gaped at Danny and his mother.

When she'd been bewitched by Sam Turner, pulled out of her marriage and her sanity by the illusion of the man's easy-going nature. Sam Turner had been young Danny's first introduction to magic. The overwhelming power of an art that could collect an entire and harmonious family into its arms and scatter it to the winds. And this from a man like Sam Turner, a naïve practitioner without the aid of study or practice, with no knowledge or experience of the culture from which he was working. A wild man of the woods with a talismanic charm of a smile and a roving eye and the gall to use it to his own advantage whatever the cost.

He was the reason that Danny's mother and father argued into the night, why his father shouted and bawled with such urgency that the boy thought the walls of the house would crumble and fall.

A few days after Danny's father walked out Great-uncle Matthew had gone to bed in the small cottage in Nathan's Yard by the harbour in Whitby and never woken from his sleep. Danny went with his mother to arrange the funeral. They stood in a howling wind of angry spirits in the graveyard at the top of the cliffs and delivered Great-uncle Matthew into the bitter pains of eternal death. It blew so hard the coffin bearers had to stop every step or so to regain their balance and the black sky was jammed with witches and harpies and the souls of the damned whipped from the centre of Hell.

The cottage in Nathan's Yard was sold to a small man with bulging eyes, red trousers and a fistful of notes because they needed the money now. He'd get rid of the furniture for them, the man said, might come in for firewood.

And when they got back to York she was on the telephone to *him* before she'd got her coat off, the man who had brought it all down on them, Sam Turner.

It didn't last long. She saw him once or twice during the day when Danny was at school, but then it was over. She came home with her black eye and neither she nor Danny mentioned it. She cried through the night for what seemed like months. She became obsessive and Danny also developed small compulsions. For a year or more he washed his hands so many times each day that they became sore and chapped. But Turner had gone.

He'd found somebody who could keep him in whisky and spent his time with her instead.

And Danny was glad. He had grown and he took up magic and plotted his revenge.

Terry Avenue was blocked. There were soldiers in a boat with a couple of old folks clutching photograph albums and blankets. Since his mother had died the magician had looked twice at old men when he saw them in the street, hoping against hope that he would find his father. But he didn't really believe that it would happen. He imagined his father was dead now, that he had no parents left at all, that he was an orphan.

Orphan Danny. If he played with the concept late at night he could work up a crack in his voice, bring himself to the verge of tears at the way the world had treated him. But he wouldn't allow himself to cry. He had to be strong. His mission was not tied to personal vengeance. He was Diamond Danny Mann and the honour of his family was at stake.

He walked along Bishopthorpe Road and cut into the street where Alice Richardson lived with her husband Alex and their three children, Conn, Hannah and Dominic. There were sandbags at the doorways and the lower end of the street, where the Richardsons lived, was flooded.

Danny stood at the edge of the water and counted down the odd numbers to the house with the green door. He looked at it for twenty minutes but nothing stirred. No one came out and no one arrived to visit.

He went around the back and looked up at the bedroom windows. It would be simple enough to open the back door and creep inside at the dead of night. But did he really want to take the chance of waking five people? Three of them were children, but the eldest boy was almost fully grown. He and the parents would be enough to overpower the magician. And the smaller children couldn't be discounted. What if one of them got out of the front door and raised the alarm?

This one was going to take more thought. He couldn't simply go inside and kill the woman. He would have to find a way of luring her out of the house. And he knew how to do it. If you want to trap a woman who is a mother, you get to her through her children. He wanted Alice Richardson alone. Just her and him and his German bayonet.

35

In a sealed container off the North Sea coast of England Sam Turner sat amidst a flood of seven asylum seekers and thought about his world. The asylum seekers would, of course, give rise to a flood of propaganda from the British government and their media hacks. But no one would mention the flood of armament sales that the same British government sanctioned to the dictators and gang leaders who ruled over much of the third world.

We live under a system that exports Hell to most people on the earth and when a few of them escape and come looking for sanctuary we do our utmost to send them back. Oh, yes, and we send them aid as well, to mask our real intentions. Food parcels and cluster bombs, dropped together and painted the same colour. Foreign aid projects and landmines so a host of juvenile amputees don't die of thirst.

So long as the profits keep flooding in we must be doing it right. After all, what other system of values have we developed in our two thousand years of civilization?

Sam pulled his rucksack closer and switched his torch over to candle-mode. He took a swig of Evian water and held it in his mouth briefly to wet his lips. He took out the cutting board and hacked off a slice of bread with his new knife. He cut a hunk of sausage and another of cheese and began to eat, chewing slowly and thoughtfully, glad he'd given up all ideas of vegetarianism and macrobiotics well before they'd had time to take root. As a background the other occupants of the container snored and shuffled; from time to time one or the other of them would speak in some strange tongue, a seemingly random selection of vowels and consonants. There were no sounds at all from outside the container. There was the movement of the sea as the *Ivan Mazuranic* lurched fore and aft, but no sound of the waves or of the engines that powered the ship.

Sam kept his frustration at bay by sticking to a routine, eating and drinking at regular intervals. He didn't want to be where he was. There was a madman out there stalking the women in his life, taking them one by one while Sam was incarcerated in a sealed container. He kept it all inside himself, it would help nobody for him to let it out, start pounding the walls of his temporary prison.

Something flashed and moved over one of the cartons in front of Sam and he picked up the torch and flicked on the beam. It was the eldest of the Bolivian children, a boy of around ten years, black hair, a round face and protruding eyes fixed on the bread in Sam's hand.

Sam switched the torch back to candle-mode. He took the knife and cut another hunk of bread and cheese. He placed it on the edge of the cutting board and continued to eat his own bread. He chewed until it became liquid in his mouth. After a couple of bites a small hand appeared out of the darkness and took the hunk of bread and cheese. A moment later the food reappeared on the board with one bite taken out of it, small teeth marks clearly visible on the cheese.

Sam shifted the candle, pushed it away from him and illuminated the boy sitting cross-legged opposite him, his cheeks bulging and a wide grin on his face. 'D'you speak English?' Sam asked.

'No,' the boy replied. '*Inglaterra restaurante?*'

Sam smiled. He thought the boy might have made a

joke. 'Your brother and sister,' he said. 'You want to give them something to eat?'

'*Alé, Michael Owen.*'

'Liverpool,' Sam said. 'Is that your team?'

The boy nodded. He reached for the bread again and took another bite. He smiled. '*Favorito*,' he said around the food in his mouth.

There was a footfall and Rachid the Iraqi sat on the edge of one of the cartons. 'It's got bad now,' he said. 'The hunger.'

Sam cut him some bread and sausage and cheese. Rachid took the bread and refused the sausage and cheese. He pointed at a pear and Sam handed it over and offered an orange.

'My friend Omed has been sick,' Rachid said. 'But now he needs to eat and drink. I will take this for him and return for my own hunger? I can take the bottle?'

Sam gave him the opened bottle. 'Bring it back,' he said. 'These kids are gonna need some as well.'

The Bolivian boy's brother and sister came eventually, and later still his mother and father. Between them they cleaned Sam out of everything, a latter-day Jesus feeding the faithful with metaphoric loaves and fishes.

They landed in Immingham, stiff from lack of exercise and anxious they would be discovered and taken away by the police. When the truck began to move and then again waited in line the occupants of the container held their breath. Sam had turned his torch off but he had a mental image of his fellow travellers sitting to attention, their ears cocked for any telltale sounds, the children covering their mouths with their hands in case unintentional utterance escaped them.

The truck stopped and started again several times but eventually it hit open road. Must have been running alongside the river for a while before crossing the Humber bridge and taking off in a north-easterly direction. Half an hour later it slowed and took a turning, twisting route for another fifteen minutes.

They came to a stop and listened to the sound of the driver's door reverberating through the container. Then there was silence. The bastard's gone into a truck stop, Sam thought. He imagined the guy tucking into a bacon sandwich, animal fat mixing with the motor oil and sweat on his face.

But the rod mechanisms that locked the rear entrance to the container began to move. The back door was slowly lifted and daylight flooded in. The children and some of the adults cried out as the light hit their eyes. Sam kept his closed.

The trucker pulled down the aluminium ladder and banged one of the rungs with a large wrench. 'Come on,' he said, 'we haven't got all day. Everybody out.'

The people inside got to their feet, putting their belongings together, but they weren't fast enough for him. He shinned up the ladder and grabbed hold of the arms of Rachid and Omed. 'Move it. Let's go.' He pushed them towards the entrance and turned his attention to the Bolivian children. The youngest one screamed as he lifted her off her feet, arched her back and shouted for her mother in Spanish.

Sam was on his feet and pulling the guy by the shoulder. 'Put the kid down,' he said.

'I want you all out now,' the trucker said, striding towards the entrance with the child under his arm.

Sam grabbed him by what was left of his hair. 'Put the kid down,' he said.

The guy dropped the small girl and turned towards Sam. He swung the large metal wrench at Sam's head. He saw it coming from the moment the idea occurred to the guy and easily blocked it. He took the man's wrist and twisted until the wrench fell to the floor. Rachid, who had come back to help, picked up the wrench and slammed it into the trucker's spine. The trucker went down on his knees and closed his eyes, looked like he was praying for help but there was no one around who loved him enough to get involved.

The occupants of the container slowly filed past the man and climbed down the ladder. They looked around them at England's green and pleasant land, a view distorted by a fine rain and a sky the colour and texture of purple mould. Sam searched for his chariot of fire but it must've been parked somewhere else.

They were in a passing place on high ground with no obvious landmarks. A twisting B-road with chalky fields and a ditch to either side, a couple of crows, a high tree and a biting wind that sent the rain into a forty-five-degree angle.

Omed had climbed into the trucker's cab and was now jumping back down again. 'I have our money,' he said, a wide smile on his face. 'Which we paid him.' The Bolivian man took back the money he had paid the trucker.

Sam wondered about the ethics of taking the money. He turned himself inside out anguishing about it for a long, long second or two. But he was obviously in a minority so he went with the vote and pocketed the grand. 'Things I do for democracy,' he said under his breath.

They dithered and parleyed for a few minutes and finally decided to go back the way they had come, a downhill route. They were a colourful procession for a tiny rural road in Yorkshire, turbans and woven bags, small mirrors sewn into the cloth of the children's dresses, quilted and felted jackets and smiles of relief that their journey was over. Sam taught the children single English words as they followed the road. 'Hedge,' he said, pointing. 'Tarmac, rain, hills.' He said, 'When you're rich and famous, don't forget who taught you the language.'

After a couple of miles they came to a crossroads. To the right was a sign to Market Weighton and York and to the left a sign to Howden and Goole. 'Where you all heading?' Sam asked.

'We have an uncle in Doncaster,' Omed said.

'Manchester,' the Bolivian father said and repeated it, enunciating all three syllables, 'Manchester.'

'You've got a long walk,' Sam told them.

'No, we're going to Manchester.'

They took the left fork and Sam stood and watched them trooping off down the lane. The Bolivian kids waved until they disappeared around a bend. Sam turned and looked down on the Vale of York. The rain stopped falling and he could see the Minster in the distance. Between it and him the rivers had swollen and swept away their banks so the landscape was pitted with fields of glistening water, like tiny mirrors planted on the land.

Angeles would be waiting for him, there in York. The killer as well. There was more violence and bloodshed in store. That was something you could always count on. But Angeles was something else. With her in his world Sam thought he could manage the violence and blood-shed. He didn't know how he'd managed to land her, even less how he'd managed to hang on to her for so long. He couldn't begin to think of a world without her.

As he stepped out and down the steep hill towards Market Weighton a village bobby came by on a bicycle.

'Morning.'

'Morning,' Sam said. And he smiled to himself as he thought what would happen when the cop caught up with the group of asylum-seekers.

36

The house was old but in good condition. The gables were freshly pointed and the lacquered tiles on the roof glistened in the sunshine. Marie had missed it on the first pass and drove to within a mile of Selby before turning around and finding it behind its hedge of conifers.

The building had no name but a small plaque on the wall declared it to be the abode of J. C. Nott. Marie lifted the heavy brass knocker and let it fall on to the oak door. The place sounded hollow and evoked images from countless horror films. There would be nothing within apart from the odd cobweb and a door creaking in the draught from a broken window. There would be the barely audible creepy music to the beat of a pounding heart and the presence of something with enough attitude to make your hair stand on end.

Marie shook the thought out of her head, smoothed down her hair and listened to the distant footfalls in the house, smiling briefly at her own conjectures as the sounds inside the building drew closer.

He was young and down at heel, like a raggle-taggle gypsy or a moth-eaten angel. A slight man with tortoise-shell spectacles and spectacular hair-loss. It was as if an imaginary line had been drawn across his head from ear to ear and all hair-growth forward of that line had been banned while behind the line it was a free-for-all. Surprisingly, this didn't make him unattractive. It added humour to his countenance but once you were over that, which in Marie's case was soon, you had to come to terms with fine features, piercing blue eyes and a masculine jaw-line pitted with a day's growth of blue beard.

She waited long enough for him to be assaulted by another bout of uncertainty.

'Mr Nott?'

'Yes.'

'My name is Marie Dickens. I want to talk to you about your work. Can I come in?'

J. C. Nott shrugged and moved aside to let Marie pass. 'First room on your right,' he said.

It was a high-ceilinged room with a desk and a battered grey-metal filing cabinet. There were modernist paintings on each wall and a stand-alone art-nouveau lamp. On the desk was the head of a woman cast in some form of plastic. The head had no eyes and a hair-style reminiscent of Princess Anne.

'Are you a journalist?' the man asked.

'No, I'm a private detective.' Marie indicated a chair. 'May I?'

'Please.' He watched her sit then perched himself on the edge of his desk. 'I'm not sure how I can help you.'

'What is it you do, Mr Nott? How do you make your living?'

'I'm an artist,' he said. 'I make models.'

'And your customers?'

'Pardon?'

'Your customers. Who are they?'

He shrugged. 'A cross-section. I have customers all over the country, many overseas.'

'Would you describe them as collectors?'

'Some of them are collectors, yes. What's this about?'

Marie glanced at the head on the desk again. It wasn't comparable to the other models she'd seen. In spite of the lack of eyes there was something compelling about it and this compulsion wasn't connected with any lifelike quality. The head was elongated, reminiscent of sculptures by Modigliani and Brancusi with their linear features borrowed from African and Oceanic tribal masks. It was undoubtedly modern and yet encompassed medieval carving and classical sculpture. She took in J. C. Nott's long fingers and wondered if it was possible to combine art with the production processes she'd seen in Harrogate and Huddersfield.

'If I wanted a model, Mr Nott, something that I could take to bed with me at night, would you be interested in the commission?'

He barely hesitated. 'I might, if I found it interesting. But you're being hypothetical, aren't you? You don't want to commission my work, you want me to answer your questions.'

'Suppose I wanted a model which had real hair, would that be possible?'

'I can buy it by the hank.'

'And pubic hair, can you buy that, too?'

The man smiled, one of those dawning smiles of recognition. He had good teeth, Marie noted, and reflexively drew her tongue over her own teeth. There was a moment in the space of his smile when she thought she knew him. This was a man who made dolls for other men to take to their beds, but he had no need of a doll for himself. There was a quiet confidence about him. He knew the power in his hands, in his long fingers, and that was enough for him. Everything else would follow in its course.

'We're talking blonde pubic hair, aren't we?' he said.

'Yes, that's what I was coming to. Was it so obvious?'

'I made a model for a local customer,' he said. 'The stipulation was for blonde pubic hair from an organic source.'

'And you found it?'

'Eventually, yes. There's a couple of salons which collect pubic hair for merkins. I was able to buy the raw product.'

'Merkins?'

That smile again. 'A merkin is a pubic hair wig. Some people don't have pubic hair for one reason or another, they don't grow it, or they lose it and they're embarrassed. So they wear a merkin. Used to be popular in the Middle Ages when there were plenty of lice around. The ladies would shave their hair off to get rid of the infestation, then they'd need a merkin for those special occasions. Nowadays it's more of a fetish.'

'And your customer's name?'

'Is a trade secret, Ms Dickens. If I gave out information like that I wouldn't have any customers at all.'

Marie crossed her legs. She leaned forward and said, 'A blonde pubic hair with some kind of plastic residue on the stem was found at the scene of a murder.'

He tried to do the smile again but this time it wouldn't come. 'That doesn't make it the same hair I used,' he said. 'It could have come from anywhere.'

Marie didn't reply. She watched him.

'Oh, come on,' he said. 'My customer wouldn't be involved in anything like that. I know him. He was here last week.'

'I'm not here to hang anyone,' Marie said. 'If the guy's innocent I'll look elsewhere. But I've got to check it out, you can understand that?'

'There's the Data Protection Act,' J. C. Nott said. 'I'm not allowed to give out personal information. It's against the law.'

'I'll have to go to the police, then.' Marie got to her feet.

'The police?'

'Yes, we're talking about a murder here.'

The man stood, then he sat again and played with a ring on his middle finger. He thought about the police.

'Give me a break,' Marie said quietly. 'Just a clue. He'll never know the info came from you.'

J. C. Nott closed his eyes and took a deep breath. 'Diamond Danny Mann,' he said. 'But he's not a murderer, he's a magician.'

Back at Celia's house on Lord Mayor's Walk, Marie sat in the window of the spare room and watched the students from St John's College spilling on to the pavement. The telephone was ringing downstairs but she didn't answer it.

Working a case was often like this, you gathered together small scraps of information, none of them seemingly important. Time moved slowly and it felt like you were wading about in treacle, getting nowhere. But once it started to crack all the pieces fell into place. One single pubic hair had changed the whole course of the investigation. And because of that seemingly insignificant item the veil which had hidden the culprit was now lifted.

The braid on the man's trousers, which Katherine Turner's neighbour had seen, suddenly made sense. Full evening wear was a uniform to a professional magician. She made a note to check where Danny Mann had been working on the night of Katherine's death.

The telephone rang again. Marie tried to ignore it, wanting no interruption to her thoughts. But the caller was insistent, not willing to give up. She left the spare room and walked along the top landing. On the wall of the staircase was an antique picture of Jesus talking to some children. Marie went down the stairs and picked up the telephone.

'Hello.'

'Marie? It's Janet, in Oslo.'

'Hi, Janet. How are you? And how's the patient?'

'We're fine. Me and Echo're fine, and Geordie's on the mend. We're coming home tomorrow.'

'So soon? Is Geordie OK to travel?'

'They're sending a nurse with us. He'll be all right. But he wants to know about the boss, have you heard anything?'

Marie shook her head. 'Nothing. I don't know where he is. But the case is beginning to crack. Tell Geordie not to worry.'

When Marie put the phone down it rang again before she had a chance to let go of it.

'Marie? Celia?' It was Sam's voice.

'It's me,' she said. 'Where are you?'

'Market Weighton. I can't get through because of the floods. No buses.'

'I'll pick you up,' she said. 'I'm on my way.'

'What about Geordie? You heard anything?'

'He's doing fine. Coming home tomorrow.'

'Good. And the case? You know who it is who's setting me up?'

'I've got a good lead,' she told him. 'You know anyone called Danny Mann? A magician?'

Sam was silent for a moment. 'Danny Mann?' he said. 'Rings a distant bell, but that's all. It's not a name I can put a face to.'

'Keep thinking,' Marie told him. 'I'll be with you in half an hour.'

37

Marilyn was feeling good at the wheel of the magician's car. There was the more or less constant thumping sound from the boot but she tried to filter that out as she headed for Whitby on the North Yorkshire coast.

This was all she had wanted, to be involved with the man. To be a part of his life. The other men, the ones who had decided to live their lives without her, they were the losers. She wished her mother had been at home when Danny called, that Ellen could have been there when she met him, and now, while she was driving Danny's car, Marilyn smiled. Ellen's face would be a picture when she heard about this. There'd be no more talk of medication.

There'd be no need for medication. Because what Marilyn's medication was about, it was about the lack of love in her life. Her medication was a substitute for a real and proper partner, someone who wanted to share his life with her.

'I need you,' Danny had said on the phone.

He needed her because she was his other half. He needed her because he couldn't function as a single entity without the love of his natural partner. Perhaps he'd been a little slow in recognizing the fact, in coming around to the realization of his limitations. But he'd got there in the end. He was a man, after all, not a gender best known for self-insight.

'I need you to help me with something,' he'd said. 'Can we meet?'

It wouldn't have mattered to Marilyn what it was he needed help with. It was enough that he needed her. As a woman you have to be prepared to do whatever your man desires. Marilyn wasn't stupid, she wasn't looking for an easy life. She fully understood that a relationship with Diamond Danny Mann or with any powerful man would mean a certain sacrifice on her part. How could it not?

He was the man. He was the magician. She was the hand-maiden. He performed the miracles, and he was capable of performing the miracles because she was there to do his bidding. This was the way of the world, it had always been like that and it always would be. The man got the glory, the adulation, because that was what he needed, his life blood. But the woman knew that his strength, what others saw in him, was the result of her input. There was a power behind the throne, and behind the throne of the magician there was Marilyn Eccles.

And what did it cost, this abasement? This unselfish acceptance of her role? Not a lot, really. In this instance it cost her a day at home with her mother. It meant that she had to drive Danny's car to Whitby and wait there until the evening when they would meet back at his house in York.

That's all. Nothing else. The occasional knocking from the boot, or not so occasional as it was now, constant thumping in fact, she had to ignore.

Marilyn couldn't ignore it, though she wasn't going to open the boot to see what was in there. Are you kidding? She remembered the fairy stories about people who opened the forbidden box. In one the box was filled with deadly diseases that immediately flew out and attacked her and the rest of the world. In another, when the girl opened the box, she became old and died and fell to dust because it had been three hundred years since her love had given her the box.

So, no, she would not open the boot of the car whatever happened. But that didn't stop her wondering what was in there. It was something alive, an animal perhaps, or even a human being. Or maybe it wasn't alive but something mechanical, a robot or an engine. But if it was something as obvious as that why had Danny warned her against taking a look? What could be the harm in seeing a robot, or a cat?

She fixed her eyes on the road and tried to put the sound of the thumping out of her mind. Marilyn knew how psychology could lead you astray. As soon as you start to think of what it might be in the boot, you have a desire to open it. She knew that she was capable of talking herself into opening the boot, she would convince herself that Danny actually wanted her to open the boot and that the injunction not to open it was a perverse way of telling her she had to.

The mind isn't always on our side.

It can lead us home and it can lead us astray.

It wasn't an engine, nothing mechanical. If it had been something inanimate like that there would have been a pattern to the thumping, a rhythm. But there was no pattern. First there was a kind of frantic kicking sound, then silence. A little later there would be a loud bang, then a series of smaller ones. From time to time there would appear to be a pattern, a solid and regular beat like the drums behind a rock song or the insistent tapping of a code, but just when Marilyn had convinced herself of the regularity it would fall quiet again or the banging would increase in tempo dramatically, turning into a scuffling sound.

Marilyn made up a story. In the story she was travelling from York to Whitby in Diamond Danny

Mann's car and there was a constant racket coming from the boot which Danny had told her to ignore. She wasn't, under any circumstances, to open the boot.

But in the story Marilyn stopped the car and pulled off the road at Boggle Hole. She got out of the car and went around the rear. The thumping was wild, it was as if the boot was packed with wild animals struggling for freedom. She grasped the handle and pulled it open.

Inside there was nothing. There was no interior flooring, no spare-wheel. Nothing. And there was complete silence. She looked up at the sky and the moors around her and there was a vast emptiness, not a bird or a cloud, no whistling of the wind or the hum of traffic on the country road.

When she blinked and looked again into the boot there was no car. There was only Marilyn alone in the universe. The sound in the boot would never return, the car would not be seen again and Diamond Danny Mann would have disappeared into the fastness of space.

There would be no past and no future, no pain and no joy. There would be Marilyn Eccles and an endless empty landscape.

But it was only a story.

As she approached Boggle Hole Marilyn wondered if she would be able to stop herself making the story come true. She played with the idea that because she had invented the story then she would be captured by it, forced to play it out within the parameters she had allowed it.

And the thing, whatever it was in the back of the car, it was as if it knew the story too, and as Boggle Hole loomed into view the banging and thumping in the rear of the vehicle rose to a tumult of sound. Not just impact sounds now, there was breath in there as well, small cries like the whimpering of a child.

38

Alice Richardson looked at her daughter. Hannah was at the school gate with her skirt hitched up, chewing gum and practising flashing her black eyes. She's a tart already and only ten years old, said a voice in Alice's head. It was the voice of Hannah's Irish grandmother, Alice's mother, dead now for five years but still as garrulous as ever. Alice would never be able to shut her up. The gates of Heaven weren't thick enough to keep out all that gossip, composed as it was of magic, gassy, blathering prose.

Dominic was over by the tennis courts head to head with Rafiq and Lauren, all of them laughing uproariously at the latest dirty joke.

'Where's Conn?' Alice asked.

'Dunno,' said Hannah. 'Haven't seen him since this morning.'

'You don't keep an eye on him, then? Your little brother?'

'Oh, Mam,' Hannah said, glancing round to check if anyone had heard. It seemed to Alice that her children could be severely embarrassed by the fact that she drew breath. Hannah had reached the stage where she wouldn't go out with the family unless there was no alternative. Never to the cinema or the theatre and only to a restaurant if there was a wedding or a wake in the family. Unless it was McDonald's, of course, but it never was because Alice refused to eat in a place where they threw the plates away after every customer.

Alice spoke to a couple of the other mothers about the

floods while Hannah continued to preen herself and show off her pre-pubescent body to the world. When Hannah had been growing in her womb Alice had spent the whole nine months bonding with her. Since then she had spent another ten years perfecting the bond. So nearly eleven years, all in all, and here she was watching someone who was a stranger. During the same period, Alex, Alice's husband and Hannah's father, had spent his time bonding with himself and a few cronies down at the pub and his relationship with Hannah was really no worse than Alice's. Alice sometimes felt that everything going on around her might have meaning. It was simply a matter of cracking the code.

'You seen Conn?' she asked Dominic and Rafiq as they passed by on the road, Lauren in a sandwich between them.

'I saw him this morning,' Dominic said.

'I haven't seen him, no, Mrs Richardson,' Rafiq said.

Lauren smiled through her eye-shadow and sucked her lip ring.

When everyone else had gone Alice marched over to the school office, only to find it closed. 'He must've gone home by himself,' Hannah said. 'We can't stand here all day. I'm cold.'

They walked back towards the river. Hannah trudging along in her wellingtons, unable to pick her feet up in spite of her mother's nagging.

In the streets sloping down to the river the hexagonal STOP signs were almost totally submerged by river water. It was as if they were floating there instead of being fixed on the top of three-metre posts.

I'm not going to worry about this, Alice told herself. Hannah was right. Conn had walked home alone. He knew Alice would worry when he wasn't there, at the school gate, but knowing that had not stopped him. *Well, I'm not going to give him the satisfaction*, Alice told herself crossly.

Nevertheless, she found herself walking faster than usual and by the time she entered their street Hannah was fifteen or twenty paces behind her. She waded through the flood waters and stepped over the sandbags at the front door. Alex was standing halfway up the stairs.

'Is Conn here?' she asked.

'No. I thought you were picking them up.'

'Conn wasn't there. I thought he'd be here.'

'Don't worry. He'll be on his way.'

'I am worried,' Alice said. 'He *always* waits for me.'

Hannah came through the front door. She walked up the stairs without speaking, squeezing past her father.

Alice followed her and Alex came last. 'What happened this morning?' Alice asked her husband. 'You left them both at the school gate as normal?'

Hannah and Alex exchanged a glance.

'You did, didn't you?'

'Not exactly at the gate, no. I haven't done that for a while now.'

'Not exactly at the gate,' Alice said, hearing her voice grow shrill, unable to keep it down. 'Then where exactly is it you leave my children in the morning?'

'I leave them at the bus stop,' Alex said. 'They're not babies. There's loads of kids there at that time. He'd be straight to the school with Hannah.'

Alice turned to her daughter. 'You went straight to school?'

'Yes.'

'And Conn?'

'He follows behind,' Hannah said. 'I was talking to Rachel and Sarah. But he was tagging along.'

'You saw him go into school?'

Hannah played with a wisp of her hair.

'You saw him go into school, Hannah?'

Hannah opened her mouth and closed it again. She shook her head from side to side.

Alice sat down heavily on the arm of the couch. Alex reached for his coat. 'I'll go and find him,' he said. 'He can't be far away.' She listened to his footsteps on the stairs. She heard the door close as he pulled it to behind him. Hannah turned away and went to her room.

Alice let herself fall from the arm of the couch on to the cushion. She splayed her legs in front of her and searched the cracks on the ceiling. This was the place she'd never let her imagination visit. From time to time with each of her children she'd come to the brink of this place and always managed to pull back, knowing that if she gave it space in her head there might be a corresponding space in the world.

This was one of those times that happened to other people. Unfortunate people. People quite unlike Alice and her family. It was a statistically untenable event. The chance of its happening to her was so remote that it was impossible. If someone somewhere in England was going to snatch a child today, the odds against it being her own child were enormous. Astronomical. It couldn't happen.

And it hadn't happened; Alice tried to bully her own mind into submission. *It hasn't happened,* she told herself. There are alternative explanations. Alex will be back in a few minutes and Conn will be with him.

But she watched those few minutes click past on the digital display on the front of the VCR and not one of them brought a grain of hope. Everything was thrown into immediate relief. The beating of her heart slowed like a clock which was winding down. The blood pumping through her veins was as if poisoned by cholesterol, it clogged rather than flowed, threatening to form curds of thrombi which would burst the vessels in her heart and head.

Alice looked at the room in which she lived through a darkening tunnel as her eyes glazed over and her mind fought the unacceptable reality which had swooped down from a relatively cloudless sky.

She thought she was dying. She believed that her vital systems were closing down, even in some way that she was complicit in this act of suicide. That the prospect of living the rest of her life without her youngest child was too much to bear. It was as if the organization of her being was split asunder, her soul and spirit flying off in fear and dread and her abandoned physical body falling into an inspiration of torpor and decay.

The alarm bell rang for a long time before she heard it. At first it was intermittent like the bell at the start and end of a round of boxing. It triggered hazy, colourless images of bruised and glistening flesh as two heavyweights in silk shorts swung at each other's heads. The bell transformed itself into a continuous cacophony and the image in her head repeated the same few frames over and over again. A lightning fist from the shoulder connecting with and splitting an area of flesh above an eye, blood and pus spraying out in an arc like a crimson rainbow.

For an instant the bell was a single, modulated scream, tearing the vocal cords of Conn as fear and incomprehension ripped through the tenderness of his form. Alice felt her own body tilt towards spasm as she imagined the abandoned shrieking of her son.

'Mum,' Hannah said, handing her the telephone. 'Are you deaf? It's been ringing for ages.'

Alice took the phone and put it to her ear. Her hand was shaking. She didn't want news. If it was the worst news she didn't know how she would cope with it. Rather, she knew that she wouldn't cope at all. She didn't want Hannah to see her mother implode, to see her disintegrate while listening to a voice on the telephone.

'Hello,' she said. Her own voice seemed as though it came from elsewhere in the room. It was as if her various body parts and organs were distributed in the spaces around her. There was little cohesion to the Alice she'd thought herself to be. Her skin no longer seemed to contain her.

'Mrs Richardson?'

'Yes.'

'My name's Bonner. I'm an associate of Sam Turner.'

'Sam,' Alice said. 'Is he there? Can I speak to him?'

'No, he's not here at the moment,' the voice said. Croaky, hesitant. 'It's about your son.'

'Yes?' Alice's voice was a whisper, her eyes wide open.

'Sam wants you to go to his house. You know where that is?' The man said something else but his voice faded as an obstruction in the airways gobbled up his words.

'What?' Alice said. 'What did you say?'

'Do you know where Sam lives?'

'Yes, I heard that. I know where he lives, but you said something else.'

'There's nothing to worry about.'

'Is Conn all right?'

'I'm sure he is, but Sam will explain. You're to go there right away.'

There was a click as the party at the other end switched off his mobile. 'Wait,' Alice said. 'Is Conn there? Is he with Sam? What is this all about?'

The dialling tone in her ear. She looked at the phone and put it back in its cradle. She got her coat and slipped her boots on and walked towards the stairs. She turned back for an instant to talk to her daughter. 'I'm going out.'

'Where?' Hannah said. 'What'll I tell Dad?'

'I'll be at Sam's house.'

'Sam's house?'

'Sam Turner. Conn's all right. He's with Sam.'

39

The only positive thing you could say about the house was that it was clean and tidy. The magician didn't think much of the area. Densely populated by socio-economic class IV and V whites, net curtains everywhere, young, very young women with babies. Everyone in the street wearing trainers. There were a group of youths standing outside a video shop when Danny arrived and it had been as if someone had tapped each of them on the shoulder simultaneously. A silence fell and they turned as one to watch his approach. Danny kept going, didn't flinch. He could see the idea of a mugging forming in one or two of their brains but his charisma kept him safe.

Sam Turner's terraced house was at the quiet end of the street. It had a fresh coat of paint and the magician let himself in through the front door. He shook his head at the simplicity of it. His opponent was a private detective who had, apparently, never heard of a three-lever lock.

Apart from a small kitchen area the ground floor contained a table and three chairs, off in one corner was a desk with the other chair from the dining set, and a couple of easy chairs in front of a small wood-burning stove. One wall was shelved with books and videos and CDs, and a small CD player was standing at the back of the desk. The telephone was hanging on the wall next to a black and white portrait of a laughing young woman. Probably the man's latest partner.

There were some papers on the desk but the magician collected all of these together and placed them in a drawer. He put his bag on the chair by the desk. He took out a length of green nylon rope and his shining bayonet. He removed a new face-cloth and a roll of masking tape and placed all of these articles on the desk.

He hyperventilated for a while, squatting on the floor and taking short shallow breaths, then, leaving the bayonet where it was, he took the rope, the face-cloth and the masking tape upstairs and placed them neatly on Sam Turner's bedside table next to a paperback novel by Henning Mankell. The bed was unmade and on the floor were a discarded T-shirt and a pair of boxer shorts. The magician curled his upper lip in distaste.

Shortly after he rang the woman called Alice Richardson there was a knock on the door. Danny stood behind the curtain and looked out of the window. There was a big man standing on the pavement. Flamboyant. Black leather trousers and shoes and in the gap between the two a pair of sky-blue socks. When the man turned to look up and down the street Danny could see that he was wearing a black silk shirt. He had a shark's tooth set in a gold cap on a chain around his neck. Over the shirt he wore a brown suede jacket with a belt.

The magician froze. He watched the man while he knocked again. The shark's tooth was a talisman of some kind. Danny didn't know what its exact significance was. The man might not know himself, he looked like a yob, but you never could tell. No one knew better than Danny Mann that things were not always what they seemed.

The man came over to the window and Danny stepped back behind the curtain. He watched the man shade his eyes and push his face close up to the glass, squinting to see through to the interior of the house. He could be a friend of Sam Turner's, Danny thought, or someone he worked with. But there was something about the man's body language, his sense of purpose, which gave Danny the impression that he was as much of a stranger to Sam Turner's house as Danny was himself.

A debt collector, maybe? That seemed closer to the mark, some heavy sent over by a loan-shark to collect on Sam Turner's debts. The magician smiled in spite of himself; the correspondence between a loan-shark and the shark's tooth that was dangling around the man's neck seemed momentarily ludicrous. But the world was filled with weird correspondences. Acts of magic were performed on a daily basis by people who had no knowledge whatsoever. A shark's tooth, whatever talismanic properties it possessed, would work as well for a loan-shark as for an initiated wizard. A schoolboy who purposefully wore odd socks to bring himself good luck and to protect himself from evil was putting himself into contact with the spiritual world in exactly the same way that a shaman or a priest does. Professionals did it with a degree of consciousness and wisdom, but the world of magic was open to all-comers. Anyone who sought esoteric or occult secrets would not be ignored by the beings who inhabited those worlds.

Under other circumstances, Danny thought, he would answer the door to this man, talk to him about the significance of his shark's tooth, get engaged with another practitioner. Because it didn't matter that the man dressed the way he did, that he was obviously from a different class of people. He was another magician, perhaps not a professional like Danny, but he'd heard the music, no doubt about that.

Danny Mann remained frozen until the man moved away from the window. There was another knock on the door, but it had no heart in it and a few moments later Danny heard the man's footsteps receding along the street. The magician breathed a sigh of relief.

His heart was racing and he pulled one of the chairs

away from the table and sat on it. He increased the tempo of his breathing, letting the 'hoo-haa' sounds come from his throat as he hyperventilated, keeping the image of what he had to do clearly before him in his mind's eye. He squatted on the floor and continued the rapid breathing until a thin film of sweat spread over his forehead.

There was another knock on the door and Danny saw from the window that it was the woman. He took a few moments to compose himself and went to the door and pulled it open. She was pale. She had on her green wellingtons and a black duffel-coat, a long lamb's wool scarf wrapped around her neck. She was smaller than Danny remembered. She looked vulnerable standing there on the street.

She took a step back. 'Have I got the right house?' she said.

Danny gave her his professional smile. 'Are you Alice? Come in. Sam's upstairs.'

She stepped over the threshold and removed her boots. She picked them up in one hand and placed them against the wall. 'Will they be all right there?'

'No one's going to run off with them,' Danny said. He chuckled. 'Do you want to go up?'

The woman hesitated as some intimation of danger crossed her mind. She was already trapped and in a fleeting moment became conscious of the fact.

The magician spoke quietly and clearly. 'He's with Conn. I think the boy will be all right.'

Magic words.

Danny watched them work on her. All thought of danger instantly vanished. 'Conn?' she said. 'He's with Sam?' She brought one hand to her mouth. She walked to the stairs and began the ascent. 'Sam?' she called. 'It's Alice. I'm on my way up.'

The magician took his bayonet from the desk and followed her up the stairs.

For a moment the backs of her knees whisked him away into childhood. He was a boy again following his mother up the stairs. He could smell the scent of her clothes in their ancient wardrobe, the warm dampness that constantly pervaded the upper rooms of their house.

Danny's mother would nap during the weekends and school holidays. Danny thought she napped every day, when he was at school, but he didn't always tell her what he thought. *I'm going to take an hour*, she'd say, and she'd go to the stairs. He would follow behind and go to his own room or sometimes stay with her in her big bedroom. He would watch her undress and he would sit on the edge of her bed while she slept. He remembered sitting there with Robert-Houdin's book, *King of the Conjurors*, the words on the page invading his mind with a French accent while his mother muttered and whimpered in her sleep. In his fancy the sleeping woman was a link back to the dead French magician. When he touched her bare arm on the counterpane it was as if he was sitting next to a nineteenth-century legend.

When she reached the top of the stairs Alice glanced back at him, wondering which of the three rooms she should enter. Her eyes took in the shape and form of the bayonet and in a moment her countenance was endowed with the knowledge of good and evil. She hesitated long enough for Danny to throw her through the door of the bedroom. She tripped as she went over the threshold and twisted her body around to break her fall. The magician was on top of her immediately. He dropped the bayonet and pulled on both ends of the scarf watching her eyes bulge as she struggled for a breath of oxygen to soothe the fire in her lungs.

Danny choked the woman until he felt her body sag.

Her eyes flickered and her lips faded to blue. Her head fell over to the right. He unwound the scarf from her neck and lifted her on to the bed. He unfastened the toggles on her duffel-coat and with the heel of his hand applied measured pressure towards the bottom of her ribcage. Her breathing was shallow but regular.

The magician passed the rope over her body and under the bed several times. He tied it tightly. He had intended to gag her but didn't bother. She was semi-conscious and he couldn't imagine her shouting for help after the punishment he had given her vocal cords.

Her eyes focused on him and he smiled. 'Let me introduce myself,' he said. 'Diamond Danny Mann.' He bowed, stooping low so that his fingertips brushed the carpet. 'Welcome to the *last act* of an illusion, my dear.' He reached for the bayonet and ran his finger along its sharpened edge. She wasn't quite the last act. There was still Turner and the blind woman. 'There is nothing you or anyone else can do to alter the shape of this day. The spell has been cast. We are all of us ciphers in the closing stages of a tale of woe.'

When he first trod the boards as a teenager, Danny had perfected a fiendish laugh based on Vincent Price's portrayal of Don Nicholas Medina in *The Pit and the Pendulum*. He hadn't done it for years, but he had a stab at it now, while the woman on the bed was watching him. It rose from his chest like a flight of bats and as he threw his head back and gave it throat, the echoes tumbled around the room like dry bones.

40

Marilyn couldn't work it out. When she'd finally opened the boot of Danny's car on the outskirts of Whitby there'd been a child in there. A boy, couldn't have been more than about seven or eight years old.

He'd moved quickly and was out of the boot and legging it along the tree-lined street before Marilyn could take in the fact that he was there in the first place. Such a small boy, and when he'd disappeared around the corner the boot was empty apart from a length of knotted rope and a wadded face-cloth. What it looked like, it was as if the child had been tied up in the boot, that he'd been gagged and somehow wriggled free while she was on the road from York.

But that didn't make sense.

Marilyn got back behind the wheel of Danny's car and gazed out of the windscreen. She couldn't arrive at an explanation that did make sense.

She took an hour. She found a parking place for Danny's car and wandered around the harbour area looking for the boy. It was a cold day and a thin sun cast pale shadows over the pavements. From the harbour a salty breeze forced the sightseers to hunch their shoulders. There were a few children but most of them were supervised by their parents or elder siblings. The ones who were alone were older than the boy in the boot, in their early-teens, and they seemed to be locals.

Marilyn didn't know what to do next. If she had found the boy she would have asked him what he was doing in the boot of Danny's car. How he had got there, and why he was tied and gagged. Surely Danny didn't know anything about it? A child bound and stuffed into the boot of his car. No, that was unthinkable. Marilyn had a child of her own. A dead child, but still, no one should be cruel to them.

Unless it was a magic trick. Could it be that Danny had bound the child as part of an illusion? Was there an audience somewhere waiting for the child to reappear in the theatre? Why couldn't she find the child in Whitby? Was it because he wasn't there? Was it because he had never been there, and that she had not seen him in the boot of the car at all, ever?

When you deal with a master magician you can never be sure even of your own senses, your own instincts.

There may have been no child, no banging or whimpering coming from the boot. Even now there was probably no rope or face-cloth in the boot of Danny's car. Perhaps the whole thing was an illusion?

And if that was the case there was only one person in the world who would have the answers to her questions.

The magician. Her phantom lover. The man she was prepared, if necessary, to die for. She hurried back to the parking space and got behind the wheel of the car. She headed out of Whitby, back along the coast road, later turning inland and nosing her way to York and Diamond Danny Mann.

Marilyn wondered once or twice during the journey if she was losing her mind. She played with the idea of going back home and taking her medication. But she had a technique for dealing with crisis situations like this. What she would do was simply not think about anything that happened. She would watch and record like in that film where the man thinks he's a camera.

Don't judge anything. Observe it and store it away.

Don't make associations. Standing water on the fields and in the streets as she drove into the city. Don't make the association with rain or flood. Leave it as it is. Standing water in the streets. That's all.

Not easy to do, but the doing kept you calm, left your head cool.

When she got to Danny's street he had left the house and was walking away. Marilyn didn't call after him. She put the car in first gear and followed.

He walked swiftly, a bag gripped in his right hand. He travelled across the edge of town and along Gillygate. Marilyn was stopped at the traffic lights outside the art gallery and thought she might lose him, but as soon as she turned the corner there he was, his purposeful stride marking him out from the other people on the street.

He crossed over to Clarence Street and took a right into a street lined with terrace houses. He fumbled with the lock on one of the front doors for a moment and then he disappeared inside the house.

Don't think about it, Marilyn told herself. Just watch. She reversed into a parking space between two other cars and peered out at the street. It was reasonably quiet. At the top end there was a group of youths outside a corner shop, probably planning burglaries and arson and muggings. A woman with a baby in a pram walked past, and a little later an old-age pensioner with arthritis and a walking stick.

Marilyn kept her eye on the house where Danny was but there were no movements at the windows. Briefly she thought an upper curtain shifted but when she looked at it long and hard there was no sign of life. Marilyn wanted to ask herself what Danny was doing in there. She wanted to know whose house it was and why he was visiting. But she pushed the questions to the back of her mind. Just watch, she told herself. When he comes out you can ask him yourself.

She watched the big man come down the street. He was wearing black-leather trousers and shoes with sky-blue socks and a black silk shirt. Over the shirt he wore a brown suede jacket with a belt. He had a shark's tooth on a chain around his neck.

He stopped outside the same house that Danny was visiting and knocked on the door. Marilyn craned forward, hoping to catch a glimpse of Danny when he opened the door. But no one answered the man's knock.

He knocked again, louder, and then he left the door and looked through the window. Maybe he knocked on the window as well, Marilyn couldn't be sure. He seemed certain that someone was inside the house, ignoring him. And he was right, of course, because Danny was inside the house. Marilyn had watched him go in only a few minutes earlier. More questions building up inside her head. Soon there would be more questions than space.

The big man gave up and walked back along the street the way he had come. Marilyn was tempted to go after him, ask him what he wanted, why he was knocking on the door of the house. She could ask him who lived there, at least he would know the answer to that. But she stayed put. She didn't want to get distracted. While she was doing something else Danny might come out of the house and disappear.

A few moments after the big man turned the corner into Clarence Street another figure approached the house. A woman.

Green wellingtons and a black duffel-coat, a long scarf wrapped around her neck. A small woman, white-faced, one of those who look vulnerable but it's a designer look. Marilyn reckoned she was strong underneath it all, someone who got whatever she wanted.

Danny answered her knock almost immediately. He had his charming magician's smile on his face and held the door open for her while she ducked under his arm. Marilyn reached for the handle of the car door, her impulse to go to the house and confront the two of them. But she held her breath and counted to ten. There could be another explanation. She didn't immediately have to let her jealousy dictate her next move. She'd never suspected Danny of having an affair with another woman. When she thought about it, she'd never seen him with another woman.

On the other hand he was a man.

But today was a day of strange events. Since Danny had called her this morning there had been one thing after another. Now it was late-afternoon and she was no closer to a reasonable explanation for anything. The world became curiouser and curiouser.

41

When Marie collected him from Market Weighton that morning they talked about Diamond Danny Mann. When she told him where the magician lived the rusty old cogs that made up Sam's mind went into action. They began to grind out an image.

First there was a woman. It was a long time ago, during that period when it seemed to Sam that everything was shrouded in mist. He couldn't give her a name. He remembered hair parted in the middle and drawn to each side in a Madonna braid. He knew she was married and that she might be good for a drink if he was nice to her. But the woman wanted more than nice. She wanted out of a marriage that had turned her to stone. A lady on the lookout for a knight in shining armour, or any other kind of illusion.

But what did this woman have to do with obliterating his past partners? She was so far back in time that his memory could not give him a reliable image. What had he done to her to release this avalanche of violence?

The road into York was passable but on either side of it the fields were deep in water. It was like travelling along an endless jetty, a surreal landscape after being holed up in a container for thirty-six hours. The surface of the standing water reflected the sun and captured the sky and the clouds like a giant mirror. The treetops and the roofs of farm buildings were still and silent in their sodden surroundings, as if in fear of their own engulfment. Or perhaps they were mourning the loss of all around them, everything they had regarded as fixtures in their lives?

'Nottingham's a problem,' Sam said.

'Say again.'

'I understand how he got me to Leeds and to Oslo,' Sam said. 'And I can see how he's got me back to York. But how did he get me to Nottingham?'

'You were working on a case there?' Marie asked.

'Yes, I was following a woman. But it's possible she wasn't connected with the client. Can you check it out? The records are in the office.'

'Could be,' Marie said. 'I mean, if this guy has been watching you, it could be that he waited for you to turn up somewhere he needed you to be. Only *after* Nottingham did he begin manipulating you.'

Sam shrugged. 'Whatever,' he said. 'I want to check all the possibilities.'

Marie took him to the Mount Royale Hotel where Angeles was waiting for him. She had booked one of the rooms that overlooked the garden and was standing by the window, staring out as though she could see the wheelbarrow and the late-flowering roses.

She turned when he entered the room. 'Sam.'

'How you doing?'

She took a step towards him but he moved faster and had his arms around her before the door had closed behind him. Her slim white stick fell to the carpet as she searched his body with her hands, reaching under his jacket and into the small of his back.

They stood together for a few moments, each of them maximizing the area of contact. He could smell her hair and feel the dark curls tickling his face and neck. He was aware of the heat of her thighs against his own, the way her fingers kneaded the discs of his spinal column. She was slim but she was fit and her body was strong and muscular. Her blindness gave her an outer appearance of vulnerability but she was fiercely independent and ever willing to take on whatever the world threw at her.

He held her at arm's length and looked at her. She reached out her hand and touched his face, tracing the line of his nose and lips with the tip of one finger.

'You look good,' he said.

'So do you. I've missed you.'

She wore a black satin suit from Paul Smith, a thin cashmere top under the jacket. He wanted to breathe her in, her voice, her mind and body, the dusky tinge to her skin.

'There's coffee,' she said. 'By the bed. And I've brought some clean clothes. I put them in the bathroom.'

He kissed her on the mouth and she put her hand behind his head and returned the kiss forcefully as if afraid it might be the last.

Sam poured the coffee and splashed cream into Angeles' cup. He handed it to her. His own he drank black. She asked him about Oslo and what happened to Geordie and he answered all her questions. He watched her constantly, fascinated by the nuances of movement and facial expressions that had attracted him to her when they first met but that he had forgotten about until he started missing her over the last few days. He told her about finding the body of Holly Andersen in the flat at Calmeyers gate and the characters he'd sailed back to England with in the container aboard the *Ivan Mazuranic*.

Angeles listened. From time to time as he spoke she reached out and touched his hand, and using that uncanny ability she referred to as facial vision, she always knew exactly where it was.

After the coffee Sam went into the bathroom and stripped off his clothes while the tub filled with hot water.

He trimmed his beard, which had a tendency to grow quicker on the right side, and lowered himself into the water, feeling it close around him until he was immersed up to his chin.

He closed his eyes and listened to Angeles moving around in the next room; that sharp tapping of her stick as she negotiated unfamiliar territory. She opened the bathroom door and stepped inside, hovering there for a moment as if measuring the room, gauging the spaces that were available to her.

She came over to the bath and found the chair on which Sam had placed his clothes. She gathered them in her arms and took them through to the bedroom. Through the doorway Sam saw her place them on a low table at the foot of the bed. She removed her jacket and rolled up the sleeves of her sweater. When she returned to the bathroom she sat on the chair and reached for the soap.

'What you up to?' he asked.

'Sit up,' she said. 'I want to scrub your back.'

Sam struggled into a sitting position and let her go at it. 'You like?' she asked.

'Mmmm, magic.'

She lathered him again, kneading the muscles on his back with the knuckles of both hands. 'It's good to have you back,' she said.

Sam tried to think of something to match it but the words wouldn't flow. He reached up and touched her face. When she left him he finished washing and cleared the condensation from the mirror to check there was something left. He knew what it was about the beard, made him look like a social worker. He towelled himself down and walked through to the bedroom. Angeles was in the bed, her clothes lying on the carpet where she had dropped them.

He got in and put his arm around her. He couldn't stop thinking of it as an interval, that when it was over he'd have to go out again and grapple with reality. He began to talk and Angeles listened and they turned out their minds for each other without realizing what they were doing.

When they'd been quiet for a while Angeles said, 'Do you believe in magic?'

'There's so much we can't explain. I believe in sleight of hand and I believe in miracles. I know there are rhetoricians who can talk up a storm and moments and places that are charmed.'

'And this man, Sam, this magician, do you think you can take him down?'

'I never had any doubts about that,' Sam said. 'I only needed to know who he was.'

'And do you know now?'

'Not exactly,' he said. 'But I'm beginning to get a picture.'

Angeles sighed. She said. 'Have you ever read Stephen Crane?'

'*Red Badge of Courage.* I read that.'

'He said that people were not nouns, but adverbs modifying a series of events.'

Sam kissed her on the lips and slid down in the bed. He felt the tension in her arms around his back and couldn't think of any place on earth he'd rather be. Couldn't seem to concentrate on the adverb thing.

Later, as they lay sleeping in a tangle of cotton sheets, the boy came back to Sam in a dream.

And, yes, he had been called Danny. Sam couldn't remember the woman's name, even in the dream. Apart from the Madonna braids he couldn't see what she looked like, either. But he could see the boy. The boy was clearly defined against a white background. He was hysterical, screaming and crying, and all of his anger was centred on Sam.

The woman kept grabbing at the boy, trying to get him upstairs to his room, but he wasn't having any. He was a tornado, howling, spitting and leaping around the room to evade her reach. Sam couldn't hear the words but he could see and feel the single-minded vehemence as it crackled out of the child.

Sam came awake and turned towards Angeles. She was sleeping with one arm covering her face, her breath coming and going with the softness of a feather. Sam turned away from her and looked back at the dream. Fifteen, twenty years had gone past since that time. He was aware of two different Sam Turners; the one he knew now, who viewed the image of the boy with a degree of compassion, and the one from the past who saw the boy as an irritation.

That the dream corresponded to an actual event, he had no doubt, though his recollection of it was at best shaky. He couldn't remember his conscious mind referring to it on one single occasion since it had happened. It was something he'd put aside, another one of those things he'd decided not to deal with.

And there was another scene from around the same time but buried even deeper. Sam remembered Marie asking him if he'd ever hit a woman. He'd avoided the answer even though it was twenty years since the act. But he'd punched the woman with the Madonna braid in an argument about a bottle. Laid into her with both fists, blackened her eye and cut her lip, and this was part of who he was. The details were blurred, the memory only really kicked in at the point when his attack on her came to an end. He saw himself standing with his legs apart, looking down at his fists. The woman was huddled in a corner, her hands covering her face. Sam had been lost for a hundred years and he had suddenly found himself in a body and a mind-set he didn't recognize.

He didn't know why he had beaten the woman and he didn't know why he had stopped beating her. What had prevented him going on to kill her? Some residue of conscience? Some isolated, civilized remnant in his soul?

He'd walked away. Found another bar to prop him up. And the woman with the Madonna braid and the broken face had gone home to her son.

And all the while, as he grew into manhood, the boy had kept it as fresh as the day it happened, perhaps built upon it, elaborated its magnitude, until it had driven him to a frenzy of killings.

But what had it meant to the child? Was it simple jealousy over the body of his mother? Or had he somehow contrived to see Sam Turner as the root of all his troubles? Was Sam the scapegoat for the loss of his father, the disappointment of his mother, or had the boy's damaged mind invented something worse?

Thinking on it all for the first time stimulated Sam's memory. He recalled seeing the boy again. Some time later, after that first screaming fit, but this recollection was even dimmer than the first. The boy had not been screaming and yelling this time, he had been quiet and watchful. And he had not been in that house with his mother. He had been alone. Sam was with another woman, a blonde bimbo, they were on a park bench, drinking, planning how to score another bottle. And as he looked out over the freshly cut lawn Sam had come into eye-contact with the boy. *I'm being stalked,* he'd thought. And he told the blonde woman about it and she looked for the boy but he'd already disappeared, like magic.

And after that Sam Turner had put it aside, left it alone, preferring not to engage with anything that took him away from his own boozy calling. But now it looked as though he might have been right. Young Danny Mann had been stalking him. For years and years and years. All his life. And now he'd stopped the stalking and moved into a different phase.

Sam Turner eased himself out of the bed and dressed in the fresh clothes Angeles had brought for him. When he was ready he leaned over the bed and kissed her on the cheek. He left the hotel room and closed the door quietly behind him. It was time to put a stop to it. Enough people had died. He couldn't afford to lose anyone else.

He arrived at Alice's house shortly after four o'clock that afternoon. Alex Richardson came to the door with a can of Caffrey's in his hand. He smiled nervously when he realized it was Sam standing there behind the beard.

He said, 'Can I help you?' He didn't mean it.

'Is Alice here?' Sam asked.

Richardson did something weird with his shoulders, pushing them forward at the same time as pulling his head back. He frowned, craning forward to look along the street.

'I'm alone,' Sam said. 'Is Alice here?'

Richardson took a gulp from his can. 'She went to meet you,' he said. 'Pick Conn up.'

'Meet me where?'

'What I heard, you phoned and asked her to come to your place. You've got Conn, right?'

'No,' Sam said. 'I only got back here around midday. I haven't seen Conn and I didn't make any phone call.'

Alex Richardson let that sink in while he poked a finger up his nostril. 'That can't be right,' he said. 'Hannah said . . .'

'Is *she* here?' Sam said.

'No, she went round to your place.'

'Both of them? They went together?'

Richardson shook his head. He opened his eyes wide and closed them for a moment. He could be patient. He was used to dealing with idiots. He took another drink from the can. 'No, they didn't both go. Alice went round there to pick up Conn, but Hannah is still here in her room. That's how I know Alice went round to your place, 'cause Hannah passed on the message.'

'Get her down here,' Sam said.

'Now just a minute, this is my house and . . .'

'Just get her down here,' Sam said. He stepped over the sandbags, pushed past Richardson and went to the foot of the stairs. 'Hannah,' he shouted, and then again: 'Hannah.'

Richardson said, 'Jeez, c'mon, you've spilt my beer.'

A door opened and a small girl in a mini-skirt came to the top of the stairs. 'D'you want me?'

'Jesus,' Richardson said. 'Whose house is this?'

'Shadup,' Sam said. He looked up the stairs at Hannah. He spoke quietly and clearly. 'What was the message from your mother? Where is she and who phoned her?'

'You don't have to answer him,' Richardson shouted, his voice cracking. 'He doesn't live here.'

Hannah paid her father no heed. She looked at Sam for a moment. 'There was a man rang. Mother didn't hear it so I picked up and he asked to speak to her. I didn't listen to them. When they'd finished talking Mother got dressed and went out. She said she was going to your house. She said Conn was there.'

'Thanks,' Sam said. The last remnants of youth drained from his face. He turned and pushed past Richardson in the hallway, spilling more of the guy's beer.

He jumped over the sandbags and splashed along the street. Alex Richardson followed him, rubbing at a wet patch on the front of his trousers. 'I pay the bloody mortgage, here,' he shouted. 'I'm the man. I'm the *owner.*'

Sam didn't look back. He had never been able to work out whether Alex Richardson was kidding him or if he really was like that.

When Sam got to Bishopthorpe Road he flagged down a taxi and gave the driver his address. He asked to be dropped off before they reached the street where he lived. Sam knew the routine by now. Danny Mann would be waiting and watching. He wouldn't kill Alice until Sam entered the street, to make sure that the time of death coincided with Sam's presence.

It was as if he was being conjured into existence in this place at this time. The magician didn't give him an option. If Sam arrived at the site of the murder then the spell had worked. But if Sam didn't arrive on site, like in Oslo, if he kept out of the way, then the victim would die anyway and Sam would still, somehow, be implicated.

This wasn't something he could handle alone. He knew very well that the magician could see the entire street from the windows of his house.

Standing out of view he hit Menu on his mobile: Phonebook, Select, J. He thumbed through the first couple of Js until JD's number showed in the display panel. He held the phone to his ear and listened to the speed-dialling, dimly aware that he was being approached by someone who had been leaning against a shop window.

The bleating of the engaged tone allowed him to look up in time to see the guy. The one who had taken his photograph that day, the guy who'd knee him in the balls. Sam had time to sidestep as the big man raised his fist and came at him hard and fast. What was it with this guy? Black shirt and leather trousers today, something swinging round his neck ... a shark's tooth? Sam couldn't remember what he was wearing last time, something just as showy. Was he connected to the magician? And if so, how?

Sam slipped his mobile into his inside pocket and concentrated. The guy had put him down last time, but Sam had been sloppy then. This time around he had his wits about him. But don't be complacent, he told himself. The guy's packing a lot of weight. If he landed a good right Sam would spend the rest of the day sleeping.

Best to finish it quickly.

The big man turned. There was real hatred in his eyes. He came again, pushing his chin forward, wrapping the fingers of his right hand into a tight ball of bone and gristle. Apart from the time with the camera Sam had never seen him before. If it had been the magician he could have understood it. He wouldn't have liked it any better, but he would've had some idea where the guy was coming from. As it was Sam couldn't fathom why this guy hated him so much.

But it wasn't question time. Sam stood his ground as long as possible. He balled up his own fist, made it look as though he was going to trade punches, which was what the big guy would have loved. He saw the punch coming from way back but waited until the guy was totally committed, saw that extra twist of the shoulder as the man anticipated Sam's nose transformed into a spray of gore and cartilage.

Sam ducked, he went down low and heard the fist whistling past his ear as it careered onward into oblivion. At the same time he sprang forward, aiming his head into the fast-approaching solar plexus of his attacker, keeping his knees bent to absorb the impact.

He heard the guy groan as the air was knocked out of him. But the velocity kept the man moving. As Sam came up the big guy's legs left the ground and he went into an involuntary somersault, coming down on his back, somehow contriving to break the fall with the palms of both hands. Sam spun around, adrenalin shooting through his body, and before his opponent could think of getting back to his feet Sam took a well-aimed kick at one of his shins. The man didn't have enough air left to scream with the pain, but it registered on his face and the reaction of his leg quivering on the pavement left Sam feeling almost sorry for him.

A small group of women had come out of the shop and were standing around the doorway giving all their sympathy to the loser and looking at Sam as if he'd crawled out of an old cheeseburger.

He reached for his mobile again and hit redial. But JD was still engaged.

He looked down at the man on the pavement. 'What's your problem?' he asked. 'You wanna tell me about it?'

The big man rolled on to his side and propped himself on an elbow. His lungs still didn't function like he expected. 'You killed Kitty,' he gasped.

Sam shook his head. He remembered the police telling him Katherine had a boyfriend in Nottingham. And that was the accent, that Black Country inflection which was still in the man's speech when everything else had been knocked out of him.

'I didn't kill her,' Sam said.

'You were there,' the big man said. 'I found the place you stayed. The landlady remembered your face.'

'That's why you took my photograph?' Sam said. 'Yes, I was there, but I didn't kill her. I didn't kill anyone. I was set up.'

The man on the pavement tried to laugh but his lungs wouldn't go further than a cough. 'You killed her,' he said. 'There isn't anyone else.'

Sam walked away from him. He rang JD again and this

time he didn't get the engaged tone. He left the big man on the pavement and leaned back on the shop window with the phone pressed to his ear. The women took some steps away. The phone carried on ringing. Sam watched the big man struggle to his knees as JD's message service kicked in.

Sam switched off in case he had to listen to it again. He went back to the guy who was on his feet, but limping.

'The man who killed Katherine,' he said. 'He's in my house.'

The big guy shook his head. 'I've just come from there. There's nobody answering the door.'

'He's waiting for me to show,' Sam told him. 'He's got a woman with him and when he sees me coming down the street she'll get the same treatment as Katherine.'

'A woman went in there,' the big man said. 'Duffel-coat and a long scarf.'

'That's Alice,' Sam told him.

'Why're you telling me this? It was you killed Katherine. You lied to the police.'

'I didn't kill her,' Sam said. 'If I'd told the police I was in Nottingham that night, what d'you think would've happened?'

'They'd've banged you away,' the big man said. 'And fucking whoopee.'

'I need help,' Sam said. 'And I need it now, or another woman is gonna die.'

'You've done for my leg. Even if I believed you I wouldn't be no use.'

'You could hold the guy's attention at the front while I go round the back.'

'Why should I believe you?'

'If I'd killed Katherine,' Sam told him, 'I wouldn't be standing here. I'd walk away and disappear. I don't have anything to gain by asking you to hammer on the front door of my house.'

The big man thought about it. Eventually he said, 'If you're shitting me, I'll strangle you.' Then he said, 'One other thing.'

'Yeah?'

'This guy in the house, the one you say did for Katherine . . . I want him.'

Sam shook his head. 'No way.'

The big man didn't move. 'No deal then.'

Sam shrugged. 'You can have him for two minutes, max.'

'I'm not going to shake your hand,' the big man said. 'Because even if you didn't kill her you gave her a shit time.'

'Have it your own way.'

'But you can call me Ruben. And if it turns out you're taking me for some kind of ride, every time you hear that name it'll be me getting closer to you.' He took a couple of steps and almost fell over. 'Why'd you do that?' he said. 'Kick me in the shin. Jesus, I was already on my back.'

'Sorry,' Sam said. 'I was motoring. It seemed like the right thing to do.'

Ruben shook his head. 'You never hear of Queensbury Rules? How'm I gonna deliver milk on one leg?'

'This isn't our immediate problem,' Sam told him.

'Not for you it isn't. But it's gonna be my problem tomorrow morning. Plus there's the depression, and I was just getting on top of that. Something like this could bring it all back.'

Sam held up his hand. 'You wanna do this thing? Get the guy?'

'Sure,' Ruben said. 'How we gonna work it?'

42

The magician put tape over Alice Richardson's eyes. It was something to do with the way she looked at him. The others had looked at him and he hadn't minded too much, but with this one it was unnerving. He wondered if it was because she was a mother. He wondered how his own mother would have looked at him if it had been her tied to the bed instead of Alice Richardson and he thought she would have had the same look.

These were not the kind of thoughts to be having. He had to be professional about it. It was a performance, like any other, and it was coming round to the finale. If it worked right he would kill the woman as Sam Turner came into the house. The detective would come up the stairs and Danny would give him time to see that she was dead. Then he would plunge the bayonet into Turner's stomach.

He would watch Turner die. He would wipe the handle of the bayonet and place Turner's hands around it, so that his prints were all over it. And then he would take the life of the blind woman, the detective's last love.

The police would see that Turner had killed again and committed suicide. Danny's mother would be avenged. The case would be closed. The illusion would remain.

The magician stripped in readiness. He folded his clothes neatly and placed them on a chair by the window. He stood far enough back so that he couldn't be seen from the street but could still watch the length of it. Magic is like an iceberg, most of it is not visible,

back bedroom door opened and Sam Turner came at him along the landing. Danny lifted the bayonet, realizing that this wasn't how it had been planned. The woman was supposed to die first. Turner came at him with a double-footed drop-kick, something the magician had never witnessed in real life and never imagined would be used against him. He recognized it only from watching wrestling on the television with Jody on a Saturday afternoon.

He slashed at Turner's legs with the bayonet and caught a glimpse of blood before Sam Turner's booted feet connected with his bare chest. He tottered there for a moment, at the head of the stairs, but he always knew that he was going down.

He grabbed for the banister, missed and dived head-first down the staircase. The magician had never been particularly physical but he had dived twice before, when he was a teenager, in the public baths. The first dive had been a belly-flop and it had hurt; the second dive had been perfect, the instructor said the water parted without a sign of a splash. The present dive would be a combination of the two; there wasn't going to be a splash this time either, and it was certainly going to hurt.

But Danny managed to break his fall with his forearms and elbows. He slithered the rest of the way down the stairs and got to his feet. When he looked up Turner was standing at the top of the stairs with the bayonet and a face like a thunder-storm.

In his professional career the magician had never abandoned a trick. There was always something you could do to save the day. But when he saw Sam Turner take a step towards him, the German bayonet clutched in his hand, Diamond Danny Mann decided to make a run for it.

He got to the door and saw Alice Richardson's

wellington boots. There was a coat that must belong to Turner hanging on the back of the door. Danny didn't want to go into the street naked but he knew he didn't have enough time. The boots would be too small for him and as Sam Turner's footsteps clattered down the stairs he decided to ignore the coat also. He turned the Yale and ripped open the door.

He tried to run around the big man and when that didn't work he tried to run through him. Same result.

'Let me get past,' he said. 'I'm not who you want, he's behind me.'

The big man grabbed his arm as he tried to wriggle around to the street.

'Let me go!' Danny yelled, pulling away with all his might. He slipped the man's grasp for a moment and found himself free and able to run. But before he could turn his freedom to his advantage he realized that the man had him by the arm again and was swinging him round.

He saw the big man's fist coming at him and closed his eyes. It was as though if he didn't see it it wouldn't hurt so much or do so much damage.

Wrong again.

43

Marilyn started the car when Danny appeared on the doorstep. She manoeuvred it out of the parking space and hit the horn, wondering with one half of her mind why Danny was naked. But the rest of her consciousness was concentrated on getting him out of there. It was obvious that the big man was going to lay into him.

Before she could get to them the big man hit Danny. Marilyn was inside the car when it happened and the engine was revving and the windows were closed but she heard the bones go. The big man howled and cradled his fist in his other arm as if he'd smashed his knuckles or some other bones in his hand. But he'd broken Danny's jaw. Danny went over in the street, not a stitch of clothing on and his chin and jaw seemed detached, hovering over his left shoulder.

Marilyn drove the car on to the pavement, blocking the entrance to the house and forcing the big man to jump out of the way, so the car was between him and Danny. She leaned over and opened the passenger door and yelled for Danny to get in. He struggled to his feet and fell into the seat. He was saying something but his broken jaw distorted the words so it was impossible to make sense of it.

As she reversed back into the street another man came out of the house clutching a long and bloody bayonet in his hand. He ran for the car and tried to hang on, slashing at the windows and the paintwork with his weapon. But when Marilyn hit the accelerator he lost his grip and rolled into the gutter. She didn't look back; as Danny fastened his safety belt she screeched around the corner and headed towards the town.

She felt a rush of euphoria go through her body as she realized what she'd done. She'd snatched Danny from almost certain death. The first man, the huge one, wouldn't have stopped at smashing Danny's jaw if she hadn't driven the car between them. And the second one, the one with the bayonet, was obviously looking for blood.

Still driving at speed she glanced over at the magician. There was something childlike about him in his nakedness and he was going through some trauma with the injury to his jaw. He held it in position, wincing with pain, and obviously found it difficult to close his mouth. A thin trickle of drool coursed its way down his chin.

'Look at you,' she said as she went through a red light at the end of Clarence Street. She was compassionate. She didn't know why but she was filled with warmth. 'Look at the state of you.'

He said something in reply but she couldn't make out what it was. Marilyn didn't think where she was going, she wanted to put as much distance as possible between them and the two men who were trying to kill Danny. Gillygate was congested so she turned into Lord Mayor's Walk and sailed through another red light at the end and over into oncoming traffic on the one-way section of Foss Islands Road, the heel of her hand on the horn. The oncoming traffic peeled off to let her through, irate drivers hitting their own horns in reply, mouthing obscenities through their windscreens.

When she glanced over at him, Danny had his eyes closed and appeared to be smiling. He felt her gaze and opened his eyes. 'Thank you,' he said. He spoke each syllable slowly, with difficulty.

She reached over and laid the palm of her hand on his thigh. 'It was nothing,' she said. 'I'd do anything for you, Danny.'

They left the one-way system behind and hit the comparative calm of Paragon Street.

She eased up on her speed. Danny moaned softly and shook his head. He was covering his penis with his free hand, an attempt at modesty. He spoke again, 'I thought they were going to kill me.'

'So did I,' Marilyn said. 'Does it hurt?'

'Only when I speak.' He creased up briefly, wincing hard. 'And when I laugh.'

She turned into Fishergate and then impulsively into Blue Bridge Lane, intending to park there and think what to do next. But the river had claimed most of the lane and was gradually climbing up to occupy the rest. Marilyn pressed the brake pedal and the car came to a stop with its front wheels in the water.

'We should do something about your jaw,' she said. 'Shall I drive to the hospital?'

'You could take me home,' he said. 'I'll ask the doctor to come round.'

She looked at him, shaking her head from side to side. 'Where are your clothes?'

'I didn't have time to get them,' he said. 'I had to leave fast.'

Marilyn pursed her lips. 'You're going to have to explain this. I'm not a mind reader. What's going on, Danny?'

'It was an illusion,' he told her. 'My masterpiece.'

She turned to him. 'Who were those men? And whose house was it? I don't understand what you were doing there. Who was that woman?'

Danny pointed at his broken jaw and made an incoherent sound. He appealed to her with his eyes. The sound he made could have been the word 'home', and Marilyn was quite happy to take him there if he would put her mind at rest.

'Were you having an affair?' she said. And then, as an afterthought, 'Who was the boy in the boot?'

'Not an affair,' Danny said. 'I told you, it was an illusion. The boy was necessary.'

'There was a woman in that house, Danny. I saw her go in. And you came out naked. That wasn't an illusion.'

Marilyn waited but Danny didn't reply.

'When she came to the door you were dressed and a few minutes later you were naked. That can only mean one thing.'

'You don't understand,' he said. 'It wasn't what you think.'

'So enlighten me.' Marilyn hit the steering wheel with the flat of her hand, then she hit it again. When Danny didn't reply she settled into a rhythmic thumping, her eyes fixed on the naked man next to her.

'Stop it,' Danny said. 'Will you take me home now? I need to see a doctor.'

Marilyn continued her thumping of the steering wheel. Her lips and eyes were set and she wasn't going anywhere until Danny came up with a suitable answer.

'Stop that,' the magician said, reaching over and grabbing her wrist.

She shook herself free and struck out at him, her hand glancing off his shoulder. Danny struck back, trying to keep his jaw out of the struggle. 'All right,' he shouted, 'I'll tell you. I'll tell you everything. But not here. I'll tell you at home.'

'It better be good,' Marilyn told him.

'It's not what you think.'

Marilyn composed herself and released the hand brake.

She turned the key in the ignition and the starter motor turned over and died. She turned the key again.

Danny groaned and pointed out of the windscreen. Marilyn followed his gaze and saw that the car was slipping forward into the water. She had her foot on the brake pedal and she pulled back on the hand brake but it didn't stop the vehicle from sliding down the greasy slope into the overflowing river. She tried the ignition again but it didn't fire.

'Oh, God,' she said. 'Get out! Just get out of the car.'

She opened the door and slipped into the filthy, freezing water, feeling it grasping at her thighs like a hungry lover. She lost her footing for a few moments and hung on to the car door to regain her balance. The vehicle continued to move down the slope but hit something and came to a halt just before it was fully submerged. The roof was still clear of the water.

'Are you all right?' she asked, looking around for Danny, her anger now completely evaporated.

'Danny?' Then she shouted loudly, 'Danny!'

But he wasn't there. Marilyn splashed her way around to the passenger side and wrenched open the door.

Diamond Danny Mann was underwater, fumbling weakly at the catch on his seatbelt. Marilyn brushed his hands aside and tried to unlock it herself. There was something wrong with the mechanism and try as she might, she couldn't get it to open. As she tried again, submerged by the black water, she heard Danny's last breath escape from his lungs, expressing itself as a series of bubbles heading for the surface.

Marilyn came up for air and dived again to have another go at the seatbelt, but it refused to move. Danny's eyes were open, as was his mouth, and one of his arms was beginning to float in the water.

She came to the surface and shouted for help, climbing

on to the roof of the car. A young cyclist came wading into the water and Marilyn watched him through the sunroof of the car as he finally managed to unlock the faulty seatbelt and drag Danny's naked body to the roadside.

She climbed back into the water and went to him. His eyes were open and staring in disbelief and specks of detritus from the river were stuck to the cornea. Water was trickling from the corner of his mouth. The young cyclist was sitting on the pavement next to Danny's body. He was a blond boy, dripping wet, and he was shaking his head from side to side and looking as though he was going to cry. Marilyn went down on her knees and, cradling Danny's broken head in her arms, she began rocking backward and forward and humming a lullaby that her mother used to sing to her when she was a child.

Marilyn had never seen anyone quite so dead before, not without the ceremonial mask that an undertaker fashions. She wished her mother was here to see how brave she was, how well she was coping with it.

44

Geordie was out of bed, sitting on a chair next to the table. 'The stitches are out,' he said, feeling his shoulder. 'It's still stiff but they say it'll clear up. There'll be a scar but I don't care about that.'

'You like scars,' Janet told him from the entrance to the kitchen. She had Echo on her hip and was looking even more savvy than usual. Sam was standing behind Angeles by the window, both of his arms around her, taking them all in. Ruben, his right hand in a cast, was eating half a pork pie that Janet had brought on a tray with some triangular sandwiches. Sam and Ruben had been released by the police after nearly eighteen hours in custody.

On the couch JD was sandwiched between Celia and Marie, and Barney was gnawing at his shoe.

'What happened to your moustache?' Sam asked.

'Gone,' Geordie told him. 'Janet shaved it off.'

'It was awful,' Celia said. 'You look much better without it.'

Geordie was worried about Celia; the medics had put her on some tablets to try to stop the thing growing in her head. But it was exciting having the boss back on the street. 'So,' he said to Sam, 'tell us the story.'

Sam looked over at Ruben but the big guy shook his head, reached for another half pork pie with his left hand.

'Ruben smashed two of his knuckles,' he said. 'And he was hopping up and down in the street because I'd already done for one of his legs, and now he'd broken his hand as well. All the neighbours were out, keeping well clear but not wanting to miss anything, and that's how we were when the police arrived. Me in the gutter clutching a bloody bayonet. They took us in the van, dropped Ruben at the hospital and put me in the slammer.'

'Why was the murderer naked?' Celia asked. 'Was he a pervert?'

Sam shrugged. 'He didn't want to get blood on his clothes. After he'd killed the others he had a shower. Maybe he thought he'd leave less evidence.'

'So why'd they let you go?' Geordie asked. 'It was your word against his and he was dead.'

'They had the woman who drove the car, and then Conn turned up, Alice's youngest. Apparently he was stuffed in the boot of Danny Mann's car and she'd been driving round the Yorkshire Moors with him all day. Let him out in Whitby and the kid'd had the nous to get a taxi home. The woman with Danny was out of it, crazy.

'And after that they had to check on the things I was saying. What clinched it, the guy was ID'd by a planeload of people flying from Oslo to Newcastle. He tackled some drunk on the plane. There's a couple of air hostesses swear they'll never forget his face.'

'Don't forget the pubic hair,' Marie said. 'It was a lot of work tracking that down.'

'Don't go into that again,' Celia said. 'I can't bear the thought of men with dolls. So undignified.'

'And it's all over?' JD said. 'You're out of the woods?'

'Yeah,' Sam said. 'Apart from the shouting, the media circus, Danny Mann's finished. Gone.'

'He was an illusionist,' JD said. 'That's what I do. Every novel is an illusion.'

'And Ruben?' Marie said. 'You gonna join the firm?'

He shook his head and wiped his lips with a paper

serviette. 'Going back to Nottingham,' he said. 'I've got milk to deliver, soon as this hand is better. Plus there's a woman interested in me. Therapist. We'd make a good match. She's exactly what I need.'

The doorbell rang and Janet answered it. She ushered Alice Richardson into the room with her son. Sam went over and embraced her, asked how she was. He introduced everyone.

'The river level's falling,' she said. 'We took up the sandbags this morning.' There was a tremor in her voice and she was pale.

'Never mind the river,' Geordie said. 'How are you coping? You must've thought the guy was gonna kill you. Shock and trauma like that can make a mess of a person.'

'I'm going to be all right,' she said. 'I slept last night, and I've got a supportive family.' She smiled. 'It wasn't the best experience I've had.'

'And this must be Conn?' Janet said. 'You had a pretty bad experience yourself.'

'No,' Alice Richardson said. 'Conn's fine, but we left him at home today with his sister. This is Dominic.' She looked over at Sam. 'I wanted you two to meet,' she said. 'You've got a lot in common.'

Sam and Dominic looked at each other. All the eyes in the room moved from Dominic to Sam, and then back again, searching their faces.

It was Geordie who eventually let out his breath and whispered a single word.

'Jesus.'

ACKNOWLEDGEMENTS

For their valuable and helpful criticism, comments and insights I would like to thank Anne Baker; Donna Moore; my agent Mic Cheetham and my editor at Orion, Jon Wood. Any inaccuracies or offended sensibilities are the responsibility of the writer alone.